Praise for

'A gorgeous book about
from the darkness and ba
with love and overflowi
Milly Johnson

'An emotional story about loss, grief,
and the beautiful dawn of a second chance at love,
life and happiness. Bittersweet but full of hope'
Judy Finnigan

'Beautifully told and full of hope, this love
story will touch your heart'
Helen Rolfe

'An uplifting read about loss, love and learning to
put yourself back together again after
facing the unimaginable'
Sophie Cousens

'A beautifully written story of love, loss and hope. I adored it'
Emma Cooper

'A poignant but hopeful journey through grief and the
struggle to let go of those we have loved and lost'
Sunday Post

'A beautiful story'
Bella

'Full of heart and tenderness, Anna and Brody
carried me with them every step of their journey
– a truly outstanding book to lift you up'
Jane Linfoot

'A beautiful story about learning to live and
love again. Took me from heartache to
hope, and left me smiling through my tears'
Zara Stoneley

Fiona Lucas is an award-winning author of contemporary women's fiction. She has written heart-warming love stories and feel-good women's fiction as Fiona Harper for more than a decade. During her career, she's won numerous awards, including a Romantic Novel Award in 2018, and chalked up a number one Kindle bestseller. Fiona lives in London with her husband and two daughters.

Writing as Fiona Lucas:

The Last Goodbye
Never Forget You
The Memory Collector

Writing as Fiona Harper:

The Other Us
The Summer We Danced
The Doris Day Vintage Film Club
The Little Shop of Hopes and Dreams
Make My Wish Come True
Kiss Me Under the Mistletoe

Always and Only You

FIONA LUCAS

ONE PLACE. MANY STORIES

HQ
An imprint of HarperCollins*Publishers* Ltd
1 London Bridge Street
London SE1 9GF

www.harpercollins.co.uk

HarperCollins*Publishers*
Macken House, 39/40 Mayor Street Upper,
Dublin 1, D01 C9W8, Ireland

This edition 2024

1
First published in Great Britain by
HQ, an imprint of HarperCollins*Publishers* Ltd 2024

Copyright © Fiona Lucas 2024

Fiona Lucas asserts the moral right to be
identified as the author of this work.
A catalogue record for this book is
available from the British Library.

ISBN: 9780008629045

This book contains FSC™ certified paper and other controlled
sources to ensure responsible forest management.

For more information visit: www.harpercollins.co.uk/green

This book is set in 11.2/15.5 pt. Bembo by Type-it AS, Norway

Printed and Bound in the UK using 100% Renewable Electricity at
CPI Group (UK) Ltd, Croydon, CR0 4YY

For BookTok — the wonderful, entertaining and relatable community of readers and writers that inspire me every day. You like an enemies-to-lovers story? Here you go!

CHAPTER ONE

A sudden jab of pain causes me to pull my hand sharply away from my bouquet of white tea roses mixed with ferns and eucalyptus. A tiny red bead bulges on the pad of my index finger before a drop of blood falls onto the skirt of my wedding dress.

There aren't supposed to be any thorns, I think as I jam my fingertip against the ribbon bound tightly around the stems. I glance at the crimson teardrop on the off-white taffeta and swear.

My father, who is staring straight ahead at the closed church doors, turns to look at me. 'Everything okay?'

I want to let my lip wobble. *No, everything is not okay. I've dreamed of this day for so long and I want everything to be perfect.*

I peel my finger off my bouquet and inspect it. The dark speck of a puncture wound is the only evidence on my body, but the pristine white ribbon is now a smeary red mess.

'Everything's fine,' I say out loud. Because if I say it, it will make it so. And everything *is* fine. I'm getting married to Simon today. It's day one of our perfect life together. That's all that matters.

As we wait for the church doors to swing open and the strains of Pachelbel's *Canon in D* to begin, I can't help being aware of the almost unnoticeable stain on my skirt. I imagine it spreading, seeping through the weave of the fabric until, by the time I reach the altar, my dress has transformed into one of deep red velvet.

Behind me, my best friend, Anjali, fusses with the half train of my dress, fanning it out into a perfect semicircle. At least she's got that right. I'm ashamed to say, in my less charitable moments, I mentally refer to her as my 'maid of horror'. I love her to bits, I really do, but in the two months running up to the wedding, her flat has flooded, she got herself embroiled in a sticky situation at work and almost got fired, and the sleazebag ex she can't seem to get over took out a non-molestation order against her. Not because she was actually stalking him; it was just a series of mishaps and misdialled numbers.

The upshot of all of that is, bit by bit, I've taken on almost all of her wedding-related tasks, and now her only jobs are to a) get my train looking good and b) make sure the pageboy and flower girl got dressed this morning and don't run riot through the ceremony. After that, it's their parents' job to wrangle them.

I grip my bouquet harder, aware that my eyes feel scratchy. I thought I'd feel as light and joyous as a spring breeze waiting outside the church on my wedding day, but after weeks of planning and organizing, it feels as if I've been running a marathon and I've just hit the wall. I can hardly wait until Simon and I can flop out like stranded jellyfish on sunloungers, sunning ourselves on a perfect white beach in …

No. I blink to reset my mental slideshow.

Stay here, Erin. Stay now. Because this moment will never come again, and it's the one you've been waiting for practically all your life.

Not that I've been husband-hunting since I left primary school. Far from it. It's just that I've always had a picture in my head, a dream I suppose, of what it would be like as I walked down the aisle towards my forever person.

I've always imagined standing at the church doors, the most perfect version of myself, and when I step inside, the first thing I'll see is the back of my groom's head as he stands and waits beside his best man. He'll be fidgeting a little, and when the music starts, he'll straighten. I'll be able to tell he's stopped breathing, just for a heartbeat, and then I will walk, eyes trained on him, waiting for the moment he turns and looks.

Halfway down the aisle is when it'll happen. Slowly, he'll turn his head and our eyes will connect. It'll be everything, because while he sees the elegant yet subtly sexy gown, the perfectly pinned hair and the flawless make-up, I'll also know that he sees *through* it, to me – Erin. It's all I've ever wanted, just for one person to do that. No facades, no filters.

In the present, the doors open fully, revealing a church full of fresh silence. After a few seconds of quiet, the sweet notes of a violin pierce through it. I glance at my father, slide my arm through his, and we take our first step together.

As I walk, I make sure to take in every detail – the floral arrangements on the ends of each pew, the sunlight streaming through the stained-glass window, the guests who have turned to look and smile or dab their eyes. And then there's a flash of colour in my peripheral vision. My eyes are drawn to the deep red and blue of the pageboy's Spider-Man mask …

Wait.

What?

I blink but yes, there's no doubting it – Simon's nephew is in full superhero headgear on top of the cute little suit I bought him and he's currently pretending to shoot webs out of his wrists at

3

unsuspecting aunties and uncles as he follows his sister down the aisle. I must admit, I'd been too nervous to pay much attention to the little ones outside the church, but how did I miss this?

I shoot a fierce look at Anjali over my shoulder. *You had ONE job …* the look says.

Of course, she seems blissfully unaware anything is wrong. She grins back. *Isn't this fun?* her sparkling eyes say. *It's your wedding day. Yay!*

I want to strangle her.

However, unless I want to break away from my father and sprint down the aisle, there is *nothing* I can do about tiny Spider-Man right now. I set my face towards the altar and keep walking. Thankfully, an eagle-eyed auntie at the end of a pew spots him and swiftly whips the mask from his head then tucks it into her handbag. I shoot her a look, communicating my eternal gratitude as I pass.

My eyes have adjusted enough to the darkness of the chapel that I can see two figures at the end of the aisle, and even though the groom's hair is a dirty blond compared to the best man's dark brown, in the shadowy interior of the church, they look almost identical. From behind, one might think they were brothers instead of best friends. Both stand with hands clasped in front of them, staring straight ahead, their shoulders rigid with tension. Nerves, I expect. At least on Simon's part. Gil is a whole 'nother story.

Turn, I whisper silently. *Turn and look. It's the perfect moment.*

But then I catch sight of the pageboy again, and my demure smile starts to slide. How did that happen, anyway? Someone other than me *had* to have noticed. Why didn't they say something? I'm so caught up trying to figure it out that I only realize

4

I've arrived at my destination because my father's arm pulls against mine as he comes to a halt. I tear my eyes away from the children as they peel off and their parents scoop them up.

Let it go, Erin.

The moment you've been waiting for is here. It's time to set eyes on your groom.

I take a small calming breath, then turn my head to meet his gaze, and he turns too. It almost seems to happen in slow motion. My pulse skips a little faster. I focus first on his ear and then his cheek and then his …

Wait. What …?

No.

CHAPTER TWO

Thirty-four hours earlier

I wake up gasping for breath, my palm pressed against my chest to still my hammering heart. Oh, no. Not again. I've had the same nightmare, every night, for the last two weeks. I sit up and shudder, the sheet twisted around my legs.

In my dream, each time I reach the end of the aisle, Simon doesn't have a face. No nose. No mouth. Definitely no eyes. Somehow, this is more terrifying than if he were grotesque or injured. The unnatural smoothness of the skin where his features ought to be makes me think of a giant fleshy egg. Ugh.

Simon reaches out, and his fingers brush my thigh. He pats me twice before his hand loses all tension and a gentle snuffle escapes his lips. I take a moment to breathe in the cool night air, then glance at my fiancé. He has a nose, thank goodness. And a mouth. A beautiful mouth.

I exhale. Everything is as it should be.

The dreams are just down to wedding jitters, my mum says. That explains everything – the knots in my shoulders, the headaches, the feeling that I could run to the top of a mountain and scream so loudly I might create an avalanche single-handedly. All perfectly normal, according to every former bride I talk to.

Simon stirs again and throws his arm above his head. I want to curl up against him and feel his warmth, draw some sense of security from him to dispel the lingering spectre of the nightmare, but he's a light sleeper and there's no reason both of us should be bleary-eyed and yawning the day before our wedding. Instead of moving towards him, I edge myself off the mattress, plant my feet on the rug and take one last look at Si before I grab my robe and leave the bedroom of our hotel suite.

After softly closing the door between the bedroom and living room, I make my way to the coffee machine and choose a coloured metal pod. I don't really care what it is as long as it's pumped full of caffeine. I drop it in the hole in the machine and press the button.

When my coffee is ready, I walk to the large doors that lead onto the balcony overlooking the River Dart. If it was July, I'd open them up and step outside, but it's February, so I stay on the sensible side of the glass. I can just about make out the houses clinging to the hillside on the opposite side of the river, in Kingswear. Later, when the sun rises, each row will be a variety of pastel ice-cream colours, but now they are all bleached a uniform bluish-grey by the moon.

In the marina below the hotel, the breeze ruffles the water and the boats bob like seabirds on their moorings. Even though the double glazing almost eliminates all outside noise, I can almost hear their metal halyards slapping against the masts.

It's a sound that makes me feel at home. I've spent much of my working life on boats. Superyachts, to be exact. But having grown up in south-east London, it wasn't something

I planned. My dream, after completing a hospitality degree, was to work at a top city centre hotel, but jobs turned out to be thin on the ground after I graduated, and I ended up taking a position as a stewardess on a motor yacht. The rest, as they say, is history. I worked in the Med and the Caribbean for almost six years, quickly rising to the position of chief 'stew', but then I got engaged to Simon and decided I needed a job on dry land.

If I let myself think about it, I miss it. Not the long hours, the demanding charter guests or the flaming arguments with every narcissistic chef I've ever worked with, but the water. There's something about being near water that's very soothing.

Before my coffee is even half drunk, I retreat from the window to the sofa and pull a thick binder onto the coffee table. A multitude of colour-coded tabs cover the pages inside, and I flick it open at the large red one near the front. As much as I'd like to enjoy the serenity of my surroundings, it's T-minus thirty-four hours until I say 'I do' and I've got a wedding to finish planning.

As I flip through the pages of my main task list, I get an immense endorphin rush from seeing all the filled tick boxes. A chief stew needs to be creative, resourceful and, above all, organized. I can plan just about any kind of event without breaking a sweat. An Eighties disco night on deck, along with wigs, glitter balls and neon leg warmers? No problem. Want a casino party at one hour's notice when the weather is too rough to leave the harbour, the guests are bored and there are twelve hours to fill before dinner? No problem, I can organize it. Piece of cake. And for my boss, Kalinda, I've handled everything from arranging intimate dinner parties with Michelin-starred chefs to coordinating a wild *Great Gatsby* pool party where guests were still passed out on the lawn well after the sun came up.

The thought of planning my wedding didn't bother me at all, but now, with only one day remaining, I realize I may have been a little complacent. I didn't factor in how much more stressful it is when you're the one doing all the planning, but also the one everything is being planned for. Of course, I knew there'd be last-minute snags. There always are. I just didn't realize there would be so many.

My stepbrother wasn't able to come at first, but now he's managed to get an earlier flight, and he's bringing his fiancé with him. Thankfully, we've had a couple of cancellations, but now I need to rejig the seating plan so Adam and Sanjay don't end up sitting with Great Aunt Nadine. It's a long story. I won't go into it.

We're having a gathering of friends and family tonight who've travelled down to Devon for the wedding, but I've spotted the email invite says it's in the River Room and we're actually going to be in the Terrace Room, so now there needs to be a follow-up email to make sure nobody accidentally crashes the ruby wedding anniversary party going on across the hall instead.

I'm about to assign the task to my maid of honour, but then I jot my own name down instead. It was Anjali who made the typo last time around, so it's probably safer if I do it myself.

As I pick up my phone, I have an unexpected dream flashback of the smooth, anonymous face of my nightmare groom, and instead of choosing 'Messages', I choose the photo app instead. When it opens, I click on a folder labelled 'Simon' and scroll back to the top row of images, screenshots of messages he sent me the first season I was back on the yacht after we got together.

I bet every bride-to-be has her wobbles, wonders if she's doing the right thing, but I have proof I've chosen well. These messages are tangible reminders of why I shouldn't let these horrible dreams get to me, no matter how often my wayward subconscious throws them my way.

And it isn't just the past, either. Simon proves he adores me every time he brings home an outrageously expensive arrangement of flowers or when he books surprise trips away to dream destinations just because he knows I miss travelling. No one has ever shown such thoughtfulness, attention, and love to me before.

I know I'm marrying the right man.

CHAPTER THREE

Five years ago

She opens the door to a tiny cabin tucked into the bowels of the gleaming white superyacht and drags her suitcase inside. Unpacking can wait until tomorrow. All she needs now is sleep.

After climbing onto the top bunk, she pulls her phone from her pocket. Outside, the sky is just about dark and the lights of a marina about half an hour's drive from Nassau blink outside the porthole. Tomorrow, she'll familiarize herself with the boat, meet the crew, and they'll prepare for the first set of charter guests. However, before she turns out the light, she has only one thing on her mind.

Hey you, she types into her phone. **Finally got a signal! Made it to the Bahamas.**

When the reply comes, it's just a handful of random letters.

What???!! she fires back. **Is that code for something?**

A minute ticks by, and then a second message arrives:

Sorry. Asleep. Fingers woke up before brain.

Asleep? At this time of the – Her hand flies to her mouth, and she stares at the screen in horror for a moment before hurriedly sending the next message.

OMG! I'm so jet-lagged I forgot about the time difference! I'm sooooo sorry.

Her phone is ominously silent for a while. She holds her breath. Is he cross with her? Has she blown it? She hopes not. She really likes him, the kind of 'like' that could bloom into something more.

I'll shut up now she adds, frantically backpedalling. But then she makes herself a liar by adding, **I'll message in the morning.** And then her phone pings. She almost drops it.

It IS morning here, Erin. Very early morning.

She selects the facepalm emoji, wincing as she presses send, and then follows it up with the blowing-a-kiss one. If there's one thing she knows about Simon, it's that he likes his beauty sleep.

He sends back a sleepy face and then a laughing one. Phew. She's forgiven. She smiles, feeling connected to him even though they're thousands of miles apart, but little by little, her facial muscles relax and then droop.

I can't believe I'm not going to see you for months.

I know.

I'm going to miss you.

Me too.

She pauses, wondering if she should ask the next question or save it for later, but she reasons that he's more likely to give her an honest answer if he's sleepy, hasn't had time to prepare himself a brightly worded script.

Are you going to be okay on your own?

He's had a tough time recently. They all have. But it's been especially hard on Simon. And while what happened was awful, it had the unexpected silver lining of bonding them together, friends seeking comfort that evolved into something deeper.

His next words are a punch in the chest.

Without you? Never.

Her stomach goes cold. She has a sensation of falling. As much as his words thrill her because they reveal how much she means to him, she knew she shouldn't have taken this opportunity to work abroad. She should have stayed in London. Simon needs her.

Only kidding he adds after a short while. **I'm going to be fine. Stop worrying about me.**

Are you sure? she types, her brows scrunched and tight.

Is he just saying what he thinks she wants to hear? Simon has a tendency to do that sometimes, she's discovered. He'd much rather avoid confrontation than get into any messy emotional stuff. But she really, really wants to know if he's okay. Honesty is all she requires from him in this moment.

I'm sure. Enjoy yourself in the Caribbean.

She sighs. I'll try.

You'd better! I'm certainly going to make sure I enjoy myself here.

CHAPTER FOUR

Present Day

I pull my coat closer around my neck and edge nearer to the patio heater next to my table. This is my favourite place to have breakfast in Dartmouth. The inside portion of the café is the ground floor of a four-storey building tucked into the steep hillside, and the spacious covered courtyard is popular come rain or shine, thanks to the amazing fare made from locally sourced produce.

I check my phone. How on earth can Anjali be … thirty-three minutes late? When we met up in the hotel foyer, she told me she just had to nip back to her room because she'd left her phone charging on the bedside table, but that she'd be right behind me. I would have waited for her, but it's first come first served here, so I said I'd run ahead to get a table.

To be honest, I'm a bit annoyed that the one time in my life it really should be all about me, I'm in danger of being late for my nail appointment because she can't get here on time.

I take a sip of my coffee when it arrives and ponder that last thought. *Should* it be all about me? I'm getting married, not being crowned queen of the fricking universe. Oh, God. Am I turning into a total bridezilla? I am, aren't I?

But then I remember how much I'm there for Anjali. Always. No questions asked. Like last month, when her dog was sick because she'd accidentally allowed it to eat something it shouldn't, and she'd been so distressed while it was being treated at the vet that all she'd been able to do was sit on the sofa and cry, and I was the one who'd mopped up all the vomit and diarrhoea and made her cups of tea.

When she finally pushes her way through the queue outside the entrance and collapses into the chair opposite me, I cross my arms. 'What took you so long?'

She stares back at me, her eyes huge, and then her face crumples. Without saying a word, she rests her elbows on the table, places her face in her hands, and sobs loudly.

The little headache that's been pulsing in my left temple for the last week and a half drums more insistently. But then I see how hard she's shuddering, and I get up and crouch beside her. 'Hey …' I say, rubbing her thigh gently. 'It's just a wedding. People do it every day. I shouldn't make such a big deal. I'm sorry if I got salty with you.'

'It … isn't … that,' Anjali manages between sniffles.

'Then what is it?'

'It's Vincenzo. He's … he's … got a new girlfriend!' And the crying shifts up a gear. Enough to make some people at the surrounding tables turn around and look quizzically in our direction.

I should have known it must have had something to do with Anjali's scummy ex. I make soothing noises as she vents her heartbreak. And I order two huge bacon sandwiches for consolation. There's not much that a good bacon sarnie can't make you feel better about, I reckon. Once Anjali is on the way to being properly watered and fed, I try to help her regain her sense of perspective.

'We had that bonfire,' I remind her. 'Deliberately added everything you had of his or everything he'd given you to the flames. There was a reason for that. And you broke up months ago.'

She nods sadly and takes another huge bite out of her sandwich. A little blob of ketchup drips down her chin, and I hand her a napkin so she can dab it away.

We sit in silence for a few minutes, and then I remember something that might cheer her up. 'Actually, and don't hate me for this, Anji, I *may* have done a little matchmaking on your behalf with one of Simon's ushers.'

I'm pleased to see a promising glint in her eye as she washes down a bite of sandwich with a glug of hot tea. 'The best man?' she replies hopefully.

I wilt inside. Does the woman never learn anything? That would be out of the frying pan and into the fire. And there is no way I'm going on double dates with her and that man. Not until hell freezes over.

'No, not Gil,' I say firmly. 'I was thinking of Lars. He's one of Simon's work friends. Norwegian. Tall. Very hot.' And a total sweetie too. He writes poetry and cooks like a dream. All I need to do now is cure Anjali of her bad-boy addiction so she can see how perfect he is for her.

A flicker of a smile curves her lips. 'Sounds promising. But why not Gil? What have you got against him?'

Ugh. Where do I start? 'He's moody.'

The glint in Anjali's eye intensifies. 'Brooding,' she counters, 'aka "hot".'

The next word is on the tip of my tongue before my brain registers it. 'He's rude.'

'How do you mean?'

I shrug. 'He just stands around glaring at people, hardly saying a thing.' At least, that's how Gil behaves every time I see him. He's consistent. I'll give him that.

'Strong and silent type,' Anjali says, 'aka—'

'Don't!'

'Just sayin' ...' she says with a wink.

'You have rocks in your head,' I tell her, resurrecting a phrase I'd heard recently in a black-and-white movie. Anjali and I love a girls' film night in with wine and pizza. Anything from the 1940s to the 1960s will do, but Doris Day and the Hepburns are my favourite. Those women were just so neat and stylish. They had it all together.

'He's a dreamboat,' Anjali counters, catching on.

'Nuh-uh. He gives me the heebie-jeebies.'

'I wouldn't mind playing a little backseat bingo with him.'

'He's a fink!'

'What, Erin? Are you seriously telling me he doesn't razz your berries?'

I almost spit my tea out when she says that, and then we both get a fit of the giggles, drawing some curious looks from surrounding tables.

This is why I can never be mad at Anjali for too long. She's just so much darn fun.

When we calm down again, I let out a long sigh. It's not that I can't see *some* of what my maid of honour is saying about Gil, but it's not the entire picture. I know things about him she doesn't. Things that would make even Anjali 'I love 'em when they treat me mean' Perrine run the other way. But I can't tell her that. All I can do is gently steer her in another direction and hope she takes the bait.

'Listen … Gil never seems to have long-term relationships and he's never in one place for long, and ever since you broke up with Vincenzo, you've been saying you want someone who'll stick around. Someone who'll adore you and be in your corner, no matter what.' I look her in the eyes, so she knows I'm saying this straight from my heart. 'I don't want to see you get hurt again.'

Anjali's smile is sappy. 'I know you don't … Besides, I was only yanking your chain to help you forget how late I am. Go on, then … Tell me about this Lars.'

CHAPTER FIVE

Present Day

I'm trying to thread a stud earring into my ear as I walk through the doors of the Royal Marina Hotel's function room. Where is the stupid hole? I can't seem to find it. I've mentally labelled this our 'wedding eve' gathering. Almost thirty family members and close friends have travelled some distance for the wedding and are staying at the hotel, so we thought we'd host an informal get-together this evening, a chance to catch up before the whirlwind of the big day.

The plan was to arrive early to check everything had been set up to my satisfaction, and to have a few minutes of peace and calm before the rest of the guests arrived. But then the local hairdresser I'd booked to do my hair tomorrow called, crying apologetically because one of her kids needed to have an emergency appendectomy and so she's going to be at Torbay hospital until early next week. I had enough to do today as it was, and it took every spare second to find someone who can do bridal hair at short notice. I just hope she got what I meant about not going too mad with the curling iron. I don't know why, but ringlets make me look as if I'm about five years old, instead of the almost thirty-something sophisticated woman I'm desperately aspiring to be.

As a result, instead of arriving at the gathering looking elegant and unflustered, I only had fifteen minutes to throw my dress on and do my face. My armpits feel like furnaces and, without checking in the mirror, I can tell my face is flushed and blotchy.

'Here's the blushing bride!'

I glance over to see Simon's Uncle Terry raising a pint glass to me as he props up the bar.

Yup. Flushed and blotchy.

I smile brightly back, still stabbing relentlessly at my earlobe. Finally, the post slides through, and I click the butterfly on the back. It's supposed to be a low-key gathering, but given the rowdy shouts from a group of men in one corner and screeching and giggling from a gaggle of women in another, it seems as if some of the crowd are already in party mode.

My mother strides up to me, with my stepdad in tow. They've only been together a few years, but it's nice to see her happy. Settled. He joined the board of trustees of a charity she founded for parents who had lost children because of sudden infant death syndrome. They bonded over their shared experience of losing a baby, but more than that, I think he's good for her.

'Erin!' Mum opens her arms and I walk into one of her all-encompassing hugs. I used to live for these hugs when I was a child; when Mum came back from wherever she'd been campaigning, pouring her heart into helping other people, and suddenly all that passion and focus was trained on me, it felt like being bathed in sunshine. But they hadn't happened nearly often enough.

She holds my shoulders and straightens her arms so she can look at me. 'How are you doing?'

I give a little shrug and say what I'm supposed to. 'I'm happy.' But then I throw a bit of honesty into the mix. 'And maybe a little exhausted and overwhelmed. It's a lot to—'

'I know, baby,' she says, releasing me. 'We're all feeling it.' She glances up at her lanky husband. 'Aren't we, Emir?'

He looks down at her with his soulful brown eyes and nods.

I frown. I don't see how she can feel overwhelmed at planning a wedding when she hasn't really been that involved. Next week sees the launch of the charity's latest big awareness campaign, and so she couldn't even come down a day early to help.

I greet Emir, kissing him on the cheek. 'It's hard when we all know someone is missing from the room, someone who should be here but isn't,' he says.

Oh. That's what they're talking about.

They think I'm sad about Alex. My younger brother. And I am, I suppose, when I have more than half a second to stop running around like a headless chicken. I was only two when he died, so I don't remember him. But I do have an image I've built of him that sometimes fills that shadowy space – a brother who has my fair hair and brown eyes, who's a little bit taller and a little bit skinnier, who has my father's nose while I sport my mother's.

'Now, where's that gorgeous man of yours?' she asks, scanning the room.

I give her another shrug, a little embarrassed I can't answer. I expected to find Simon showering in the suite when I burst in, late myself, but the place was empty, so I hurried downstairs, thinking he might have got here before me, but ran into Mum and Emir before I could check. 'I'll see if I can find him.'

I do a sweep of the function room, and the spacious terrace

outside, dotted with tables and patio heaters, but there's no sign of him.

He's been out on his brother's boat all day with a group of his friends. They'd planned to head out of the Dart estuary to Start Point and back, a manly hurrah to celebrate their friend's last day of so-called freedom. Simon already had his stag do, of course, but Gil lives abroad now and hadn't been able to return to the UK for that, so Simon's other friends had thought it a great excuse to have a do-over. Of sorts. I just hope too much booze hasn't been involved. If I learned anything from my time on yachts, it's that alcohol and large bodies of water aren't the best of companions.

They were supposed to be back an hour and a half ago. I look around, hoping to spot one of Simon's ushers in the crowd. If I had my colour-coded binder with the contact details, I could call around, find out where they are, but it's tucked away safely in the suite upstairs. I'm just about to spin around and head for the lifts when I bump into Simon's sister, Rachel.

'Oh, God! Thank goodness I've found you!' she says, her eyes a little wild. If Simon is a bit extra at times, Rachel takes it to the next level. 'I've got a dire emergency!'

Of course she has.

Because that's just what I need right now – another emergency.

Even so, I'm looking forward to being her sister-in-law. Simon's the youngest of five. Being effectively an only child, I've always envied him his large, sprawling family, even if they hurl insults at one other as often as they hug. This is the reason I pause my hunt for her brother and ask her what the matter is.

'It's a disaster! The hotel has booked us the wrong rooms.'

'You haven't got the balcony overlooking the river, away from the marina?'

She waves a dismissive hand. 'No, no ... We've got that.'

Good. Because I had to wrangle hard with the hotel to meet my soon-to-be sister-in-law's exacting specifications.

'But there's no door!'

I blink. 'No door?' How can that be? A hotel room has to have a door, doesn't it?

'Yes. No door between the rooms.'

'An interconnecting door?'

She nods. 'I can't leave Poppy and Rufus on their own in a room, can I?'

Nope. She's right about that. Even a single gal like me knows it's probably wrong to leave a four-year-old and a two-year-old unattended overnight. But Rachel didn't mention needing an interconnecting door until now, and it didn't occur to me. I feel awful. With my background, it's the sort of thing I *should* have thought of.

'So that means Leo and I will have to split up and share with a kiddo each rather than leave the door open at night, which is hardly ideal.' She grabs hold of my hands. 'Will you help me sort it out, Erin? I've tried myself, but the flaky boy behind reception just started crying.'

I glance towards the doors that lead out to the hotel's reception area, but I don't need to see the receptionist to tell what sort of state he might be in. Rachel can be pretty forceful in full flow. It's probably something to do with being the only daughter among four sons. 'Uh ...' I begin. I want to help her, but I've also only just arrived at my party and I haven't found my fiancé yet.

'Oh, thank you so much! I knew I could count on you. I'm thrilled you're going to be part of our family. Us girls will have to stick together!' With that, she plants an emphatic kiss on the side of my head and chases down a waiter with a tray of flute glasses.

I turn and begin walking towards reception, but before I reach the doors, there's a metallic click and thump, like a PA system being turned on, and Simon's voice comes out loud and clear. 'Where's my bride-to-be?'

CHAPTER SIX

Five years ago

She considers stewardess uniforms something to be endured. Oh for a pair of trousers! But no, once again, the basic daytime uniform on this yacht is a skort. When on charter, it's teamed with a white shirt with epaulettes, or a polo shirt when not. At least it has pockets, a secret place where she can stash her phone. Not that she's supposed to check it when on duty, even if the full-on nature of her job would allow her a second to do so, but every time she feels a notification come in, she has to hide a smile. It's another message from him. Each time her pocket buzzes, she feels she's floating a little higher above the deck.

She smiles as she delivers Espresso Martinis to the four guests sunning themselves on the bunny pad on the sun deck, then nips back down the stairs to the main salon, where the bar is, and starts mixing up another batch. These guests are *thirsty*.

Two hours later, when she takes her break, she hurries back to her cabin tucked into the bow on the lower deck, and closes the door behind her. She's left her cabin mate and second stew, Marisol, tending to the guests, so for once she's all alone.

She really should sleep because she's utterly exhausted, but of course she's not going to. She pulls her phone out of her pocket, almost dropping it she's so excited, and wakes it up so she can read the messages. It's been buzzing constantly.

> Hey, gorgeous!
>
> Just wanted to say hi. I'm thinking of you.

And then a couple of minutes later:

> Are you thinking of me too? I hope so.

There's a gap of a few minutes and then another flurry:

> I know you're probably working. I know I should shut up and let you get on with it.

Then there's a kooky emoji and:

> But I can't help myself!
>
> Why do you have to be so far away!!!!
>
> I want to see you right now! Can we FaceTime?

She can't help laughing. This is what she likes about him – he finds it so easy to say what he's feeling, which makes it easier for her to express herself too, even if she still is much more guarded than he is.

That message was over two hours ago. He's probably fast asleep by now, seeing as the UK is five hours ahead of the Bahamas. She would *love* to video call with him, but maybe not when the bags under her eyes would incur excess luggage fees. Instead, she scrolls down and continues to read.

> Are you really not going to be home until April? That's too long!

There's ten minutes between the timestamp of that message and the next, and she gets the feeling he was thinking hard.

> No, I really don't think I can wait that long.
>
> How much are flights to the Bahamas?

She sits up when she reads that one, almost bumping her head on the roof of the cabin. He can't be serious, can he?

> Not much. Well, not if I sell my car.

She can feel her heart pumping as she reads on.

> I'd do it, you know. Just to see you again.
>
> Just to see that smile.
>
> I love that smile.

Her heart feels as if it's inflating like a helium balloon. If he keeps going like this, it just might either pop or fly away.

> You can't! she types back. You'll get fired.

Her phone pings almost immediately, making her jump. He's still up!

Don't care.

It would be worth it.

She holds the phone to her chest. *Simon, Simon, Simon … Do you realize what you're doing to me?* Not even her mum has been to visit her when the yachting season's been underway. She only gets a few days off now and then, and it's a long way, and then who's going to look after the charity while she's gone?

But Simon would do that for her? It's everything.

CHAPTER SEVEN

Present Day

I spin around to find Simon standing on a small podium at the other end of the room, a mic in his hand. I can tell just from the tone of his voice that he's more than a little tipsy. A gaggle of his ushers stand nearby, including *him,* the best man, lurking at the back of the group, noticeable because of his black shirt and black jeans amid the denim and crisp white shirts. He looks like the vulture of doom. And if the groom is late to his own wedding-eve get together, then the best man must have had something to do with it, or – at the very least – should have prevented what did. How did they sneak in here without my noticing anyway?

I shoot Gil a death stare. *You got him drunk?* my look says. *On a boat? The night before his wedding? What kind of idiot are you?*

The vulture of doom meets my gaze and blinks nonchalantly. For a few seconds we play a game of chicken where neither of us wants to admit defeat and look away, but then Simon spots me. His face lights up and I so I unhook my gaze from his best man – what a misnomer that is! – and gratefully turn it towards the *actual* best man in the room, my gorgeous groom. 'There she is! Erin, light of my life, come up here ...'

My face flushes as everyone turns to look at me. There's something about being the centre of attention that makes me feel uncomfortable. I suppose I'm a get-on-with-it-quietly-in-the-background kind of girl, which is probably why the hospitality industry suits me so well. The crowd parts before me, and I dip my head as I walk through it. Moments later, I'm beside my groom. Someone hands me a glass of champagne.

Simon turns to face me. 'Erin ...'

I give him a what-the-heck-are-you-doing smile, but he just beams back at me.

'You know I am the luckiest man alive to be marrying some- one like you ...' A murmur goes through the crowd, mostly from the women. '... and I know I'm going to have the opportunity to say this all again tomorrow, but I just want to take a moment to raise a glass to you, and to thank you for taking this "fixer- upper" on.'

I shake my head, smiling indulgently. *You know that's not true,* I tell him with my eyes.

But he just carries on. 'I wouldn't be the man I am today without you.'

'Aww,' a few of the single ladies say. One even wipes a tear from the corner of her eye with a folded tissue.

'I mean it!' Simon says, brightening further. Goodness knows the man adores an audience. But I love him for that. He's brave where I feel conspicuous and confident while I fake it to make it. But I'm getting there. Simon has just as much of a positive influence on me as I have on him. Maybe more so.

'Erin keeps me grounded, reminds me of what's important in

life.' He turns to me and raises his glass. 'And she always pairs my socks when they come out of the wash.'

That earns him a laugh, which is what it was designed to do, even from me, because it's true – I do always pair his socks, but only because I can't stand to see one blue sock and one black sock propped up on the coffee table when we're watching TV in the evening. All I can think about is going and getting the other of one of the matching pairs and swapping one out. Totally selfish, really. And maybe a little neurotic. So maybe I'm the lucky one that Simon puts up with my slightly rigid personal rules and tidiness?

Simon lifts his glass higher. 'To Erin,' he says and takes a sip. The rest of the guests follow suit, but he can't help adding, 'After tomorrow, there'll be no escape!' He hands the mic to one of his pals and pulls me into a kiss.

I laugh against his lips. 'Idiot,' I whisper.

He pulls back and looks into my eyes. 'Yes, but I'm *your* idiot. Don't forget that!'

People begin talking and drinking again and I step down off the podium, glad to be back on the same level as our guests once again. I love how demonstrative Simon is, how unafraid he is to say how he feels, but I can't seem to love the spotlight the way he does. It's too bright, too glaring. Too revealing of all the little flaws, unticked to-do boxes on my personal growth inventory.

But I'm not going to think about that now. Tomorrow is my wedding day, and if there's one time in my life to let myself feel special, this is it.

I spot Rachel talking to some of my bridesmaids and I nudge Simon in the ribs. 'Your sister needs someone to chat with reception about her hotel room,' I tell him. 'It hasn't got an interconnecting door.'

My groom rolls his eyes, then squeezes me to him and plants a slightly drunken kiss on the side of my head. 'Rachel's a big girl … She's more than capable of sorting hotel room issues out on her own.'

I'm about to argue with him, to point out it's our responsibility as bride and groom to make sure our guests are being looked after, when one of his ushers comes over and high-fives him before half stumbling, half dragging him away towards the rest of his rowdy friends. Rachel must have sensed me looking at her because she gives me a cheesy grin along with a thumbs-up gesture, and I sag.

Shooting a longing look at Simon, who is already holding court, having launched into a funny story about his day on the water while many of our friends look on, I put my glass of champagne down on a tall table and head back towards reception. My motto is, 'If you want something done, you'd better do it yourself', and if planning your own wedding doesn't send you crashing headlong into that uncomfortable truth, I don't know what will.

It takes twenty minutes, but I manage to talk the hotel into swapping Rachel into a suitable room. She won't have her river view, but I'm sure the interconnecting door is more important, and what else does she want me to do? I'm not fricking Superwoman.

When I've finished sorting that out, I spot a waiter heading towards the function room with a tray full of glass flutes. Although I'm wearing heels, I sprint across the lobby and intercept him, shooting him my most winning smile before swiping two glasses. I chug the first one while he's standing there, looking slightly astonished, put the empty glass down, then dash back into my party.

I can't see Simon anywhere. I dart this way and that, slopping champagne on people's toes, but getting away with it because, hey, I'm the bride! I shoot past the buffet, thinking I must grab something to eat shortly, because I realize my stomach has been growling at me for hours, but I've just been ignoring it.

Argh … Where is he?

I feel like I'm in one of those dreams where you're just running, running, running but never getting where you want to go. One more circuit of the room. If I don't find him then, I'm going to find the first chair I can and collapse onto it.

Just as I'm about to give up, I round the corner and see Simon near the doors to the terrace, along with some of our friends. I swear I've searched this spot at least three times before, but they're chatting in relaxed groups, and it looks as if they've been there a while.

I manoeuvre my way past a few of Simon's aunties and uncles and arrive on the fringes of the circle. It's only then that I realize I'm standing next to the vulture of doom.

'Erin,' he says, nodding slightly.

'Gil,' I reply through clenched teeth, although I'm seriously tempted to call him 'Vulture'. Dressing in all black, like he's going to a funeral instead of a wedding? What is he thinking? I'm tempted to tell him the Eighties called and said they wanted their gothic vibes back.

'Erin!' Simon says, beaming at me and spreading his arms wide. He's holding an orange juice, thank God. I don't even have to squeeze between him and his best man, because as soon as Gil sees me coming, he backs away. Maybe it's a good thing he can't seem to stand being within ten feet of me.

I try to join in the fun, but I can't anchor myself firmly in any one conversation. The words keep flowing around me and I drift away on their current without actually hearing them properly. It doesn't help that, as much as I try to ignore it, a Gil-shaped shadow glowers on the fringes of the group.

What *is* his problem? He greets Anjali like a long-lost friend, actually *smiling* at her, leaving me wondering if I knew his face could actually do that, but also wondering why he never shows me even half that warmth. What did I do to him that was so awful? It can't be the … well, the thing we never talk about … because Simon was just as much a part of it as I was, and he's been Simon's ride-or-die since they were at school together. I just don't get it.

And it bothers me. I know I shouldn't let it, but it does. It's not even that I want Gil in particular to like me, more that it gives me hives when I think *anyone* doesn't. The more I chew it over, the angrier I become. Why can't he make an effort, this day of all days? Is that really too much to ask? And, by the way, it should have been *me* enjoying the party and standing next to Simon, sipping my drink, laughing at something funny someone just said, not him.

In one smooth motion, all the frustration, the tiredness, the anxiety and overwhelm I've been feeling all day – even the mild, unspoken and unacknowledged irritation I'm feeling at Simon for being late to the party – gathers into a searing beam of light which focuses on the best man.

If it was up to me, I'd tell him to take a hike. Preferably off a short pontoon and into the river. But I can't do that to Simon, and I don't want to make a scene, so I just stuff all those annoying emotions back down again and sit on them, like an over-packed suitcase bulging as you try to zip it up.

To distract myself, I turn to Anjali. 'Do you have the bridal emergency kit for me?'

'Oh, yes,' Anjali says, nodding.

Well, this is promising. But it is Anjali we're talking about, so I do a bit of extra digging. 'Lipstick, tissues, spare tights?'

She nods. 'All bought and assembled from the list you gave me. I even found this lovely little bag to put it all in. It's just …' She rummages in her handbag and then a look of horror passes over her face. 'I *promise* you I have it! It must be up in my room. I'll just go and—' She jogs towards the lobby, as the rest of us watch her go.

'What's she forgotten now?' Simon says, laughing amiably. 'I hope it's not her dress. We can't have her walking down the aisle in her underwear!'

My gran would have said that Anjali would have forgotten her own head if it wasn't screwed on, but I bristle slightly at Simon's joke. I know she drives me crazy, but I'm fiercely protective of my best friend. And it's not as if his choice of BFF is winning any prizes.

'At least she gives a crap,' I reply, smiling sweetly while casting a sidelong glance at Gil. 'Which is more than I can say for some people.'

The best man turns his stony expression on me. 'What are you trying to say, Erin? That I don't?'

'*Do* you? Because Simon and I went to a lot of effort planning this pre-wedding gathering …' Well, I did, but that's not the point. 'But you're standing there looking as if you're bored to tears.'

Simon claps his best friend on the shoulder. 'Gil's all right. He's just feeling a bit jet-lagged, aren't you, bro?'

Gil says nothing, which only makes me more irritated. I feel that zip on my overstuffed suitcase of emotions straining somewhat.

It's most unlike me to be snarky, but I find I can't help myself. 'We can always find Anjali another dress,' I say, giving Simon a disapproving look. 'Let's just hope your boy's not so jet-lagged he loses the rings.'

Gil, who until that moment had all the expression of one of the statues in the hotel's formal garden, looks taken aback. The dark rain cloud that lives permanently above his head melts into drizzly mist for a few seconds, but then his expression hardens again. Keeping his eyes trained on me, he slowly and deliberately pats his pockets.

Simon notices what he's doing, and the smile slides from his face. 'You *have* got them, haven't you? I thought I told you to keep them on you at all times.'

There isn't even a flinch of shame from Gil as he blinks, looks at Simon and says, 'Whoops. I'll just check my room.' And before Simon – or anyone else – can challenge him, he turns and strides away.

'He's going the wrong way,' I say as he disappears through the large doors that lead onto the terrace. 'He's going the wrong way!'

I look at Simon and wait for him to do something, *say* something, but he just shrugs, so with an irritated sigh, I dive through the open doors, hot in Gil's wake.

CHAPTER EIGHT

Present Day

At five-four, I'm not exactly petite, but Gil has a head start and *really* long legs. When I step outside onto the wide deck of the terrace overlooking the river, I think it's empty, but then I see a flash of movement at the far end, where a yew arch leads into the hotel's neatly manicured gardens. I speed up, even though I'm in heels.

Thankfully, the sky is clear and the moon is out, so after a few seconds, I'm able to spot a dark blur moving swiftly down one of the gravel paths to where a stone balustrade edges the garden, the river lapping at its base.

I could call out, but I don't. I don't want Gil Sampson to think I want anything from him. Even though the night is chilly and I'm only wearing a short-sleeved dress, I don't notice the cold at all. My anger is enough to keep me toasty and warm.

For a moment, an ornamental conifer blocks my view of him, but then I round it and spot him a short distance away, leaning against the barrier. I'm about to ask him what the hell he's playing at, why he isn't scouring his hotel room for our wedding rings, when he pulls a small box from his pocket and flips it open. Two perfect circles of white gold glint in the moonlight, echoing the pale dancing slivers on the dark water beyond. I stop cold in my tracks.

What the …?

The *rings*?

He had them all along? Then why …?

The weariness I've been feeling all day drops from my shoulders like a heavy cloak falling to the floor. Without it weighing me down, all the tension, stress and irritation I've been doing my best to keep a lid on has no choice but to rise free. I take the tangled mess of it, collect it into a ball of searing energy, and hurl it towards the shadowy figure a couple of metres away. 'You bastard!'

Gil startles, causing the jewellery box to jump out of his palm. Thankfully, his reflexes are lightning quick, and his fingers curl around it before it can tumble into the murky river. I'm so furious I don't even care.

'How could you?' I think I scream the words, but when I hear my own voice, it's so low and menacing it sends a shiver down my back. 'You had them in your pocket the whole time!' I shake my head, unable to believe even Gil is capable of this, but the velvet box in his fist proves me wrong. 'How could you be so cruel?'

Doesn't he realize the pain it would have caused me – and Simon – to believe, even for a moment, that those rings were lost?

He stares back at me, his face totally blank, and I have no idea what he's thinking. For a moment, I suspect he's going to defend himself or at least give me an explanation, but then he shrugs. It's the most infuriating gesture in the history of the universe.

'I was going to steal them,' he says, the slanting moonlight picking up the sharp jut of his left cheekbone. 'Pawn them and buy a motorbike, but … *whoops!* Busted.'

'Don't even …'

His mouth becomes a thin line. 'Don't like where I'm going with this? I'm just reading from the script you wrote for me, Erin. I thought you'd be pleased.'

The fact he's making no sense makes me even angrier. I'd push him clear over the top of the balustrade and into the river, but he's still holding the rings. 'What are you talking about?'

'I'm talking about the little story you've got going in your head about me.'

I surprise myself by letting out a snort of harsh laughter. 'Don't flatter yourself. To write a … What did you call it? A *script* about you, I'd have to spend more than a nanosecond thinking about you. Which I don't.'

His eyebrows rise, and the look he gives me back makes my palms itch. I want to smack it from his face so badly, but being carted away in a police car for assault is not how I want to spend the evening before my wedding.

'Oh, yes? Then why "joke" …' he does that annoying air quote thing with his fingers '… about me losing the rings in the first place?'

I don't have an answer to that. I don't know why I said what I did.

'You don't know me well enough for it to be funny but not cutting, Erin. You have to *like* someone for that sort of thing to work. You're a smart woman. You know that.'

He's right. It was a jab, pure and simple.

This is the reason I dislike my fiancé's best friend. He sees the things I hate most about myself, the petty, imperfect things I'm desperately trying to erase. And he never fails to not only spot them, but to hold them up to me like a mirror.

I come back with the only thing I can think of. 'Well, that was a really shitty thing to do. Maybe you don't know *me* well enough to play cruel jokes on me the night before my wedding.'

He looks straight at me, his stare unwavering. It makes my skin crawl. Or tingle. I'm not sure which. 'I know you a lot better than you think.'

I shake my head. 'No … because if you knew me, if you knew how hard the last few weeks have been, you'd never have …' and then – oh Lord – I morph from being all fire and brimstone into a soggy marshmallow. I choke back a sob, unable to continue. Fabulous. Now I'm crying in front of him. The very last thing I wanted to do. It's like his evil superpower is the ability to make me unravel at the most inconvenient moments.

The night has become blurry, but I see movement, sense the heat of a palm only a millimetre away from the skin of my bare arm. I flinch. 'Don't,' I whisper harshly as I swipe at my eyes. I don't want his concern. Or his pity. I shiver, suddenly aware of the cold air puckering the skin of my bare arms into goosebumps.

He steps back abruptly. 'Why? Because I only have nefarious intentions? Because I can't possibly feel bad to see you like this?'

I stare back at him. My answer must be written all over my features, because he eventually wipes a hand over his own face and turns in a slow circle. When he's facing me again, he sighs. 'You know what your problem is?'

Yes, of course. *I'm* the problem. I fold my arms. 'No. What? Please enlighten me.'

He seems more amused than wounded by my sarcasm. 'Okay,

point taken. Maybe it's my problem. Yeah, that's more like it, but… whatever …' He's still making no sense, but I find I'm curious rather than angry and I wait as he gathers his thoughts then turns to look at me. 'You always think the worst of me, Erin. You won't ever give me a chance.'

He's surprised by that?

'You know why that is, Gil.'

The three of us agreed to never speak about it after that summer five years ago, but he has to know why. Whatever Gil might be, he's not stupid either.

'Enlighten me,' he says, echoing my words. His tone reminds me of how it feels to rub velvet the wrong way.

I'm about to break our rule and mention the unmentionable. I'm about to give it to him straight when the light catches off my wedding ring, and I realize he's still holding the box. Instead of answering him, I snatch it out of his hand. I don't have the time or the energy for his games tonight. 'I'm giving these to Simon to look after,' I say, backing away with my prize 'You're right – you can't be trusted.'

He laughs again and shakes his head. 'And you say there's no script.'

I've had enough of his bullshit, so I ignore him. My heels dig into the gravel path as I spin around and head towards the light spilling out of the function room, taking long, even strides back towards the terrace.

CHAPTER NINE

Present Day

I take a deep breath. The moment is finally here. My wedding day. It's a bright and sunny February afternoon and I'm standing beside my father outside of the quaint church in the village of Lower Hadwell and the doors open. I had a mishap with my finger and a rose thorn, but the situation is contained – just about. Other than that, everything is perfect.

Every detail of my walk down the aisle is how I envisioned it, from the flowers to the hankies dabbing at eyes. Okay, there's a minor page-boy wardrobe snafu, but it's quickly rectified by a quick-thinking aunt. I'm so full of happiness I feel as if I'm gliding above the flagstone floor.

Simon doesn't turn and look when I imagined he would, but I don't worry about that either. There are two figures waiting to the side of the altar, just as they should be, and that is enough. Because I need to stop getting fixated on silly little details. I know Simon loves me. I've got a lifetime to see it shining from his eyes.

I feel as if I'm in a strange, hyper-aware bubble when I reach the end of the aisle. Everything appears misty through my veil, and it's with a strange sense of unreality that I turn my head to look at my groom.

And there it is.

The *look*.

Everything I've been waiting for. Everything I've been hoping for.

Warmth, adoration, affection. Desire. He looks past the veil and the perfectly applied make-up, past my skin and bones, even, and deep into the core of who I am. And he loves every part of it. Every part of *me*.

I knew it. I knew Simon was the right choice. I …

My thought comes to a halt as my focus shifts from his eyes to the details of his face. The brows are heavier than I'm expecting to see, the nose a little sharper. And his lips, instead of meeting in a flat line, hold the gently curving arc of a Cupid's bow.

What …?

I'm not staring into Simon's face, but Gil's.

Time stands still. I can't move. I can't even breathe. But then I spot who's standing next to Gil and relief rushes through me. It's Simon. But he's standing where Gil should be and vice versa. I stare at him to catch his attention, and when he turns his head, I mouth, 'Switch places!'

He frowns and shrugs.

Oh for all that is good and holy. We only had the rehearsal yesterday. I've done everything else to plan this wedding. All Simon had to do today was turn up and stand in the right spot, and he wasn't even paying enough attention to get that right!

I'm about to turn to Gil, to see if I can get more joy from him, but I catch the sight of my parents and Emir sitting in the front pew. They don't seem to have spotted the mistake. In fact, as I search the faces of the congregation, I realize no one else is batting an eyelid.

And then the music fades, and a hush falls on the church. Both men standing beside me turn and look as the vicar steps forward. 'Dearly beloved, we are gathered here today to join Gil and Erin in holy matrimony ...'

CHAPTER TEN

Present Day

The vicar's words hit me like a punch in the temple. The joining of *Erin and Gil* in holy matrimony? I don't think so!

I turn around again, twisting my body, desperate to find a face that looks as shocked as mine must be. But Mum is smiling. Anjali gives me a wink and a thumbs up. I shoot a look at Simon and he seems … not happy, but not upset or furious. He looks … ambivalent.

He doesn't care about the vicar's mistake, that he's trying to marry me off to his best friend instead of him?

I make a noise that is partway between a hiccup and a sob. What's happening? This can't be real. It can't …

Warm relief floods through me.

It can't be real.

It's *not* real.

I want to turn to the gathered audience, laugh and say, 'It's just a dream! I'm having another one of those stupid night-mares!' But even in my dreams, too many years of being the 'good girl', of not making waves in the hope it might get me a pat on the head or some gold-plated words of recognition, fuel my actions. Even when the minister asks if someone knows why Gil and I shouldn't be joined in matrimony, I keep my mouth shut.

But I don't need to say anything, do I? I just need to *do* one thing ... I need to wake up.

And it'll happen in a moment. It always does. I rarely get to hear the vicar launch into his spiel, but why *wouldn't* my jangled subconscious go the extra mile the night before my wedding? After tomorrow, the dreams won't have any power over me, so it's making sure this one counts. But I'll have the last laugh because, in a few seconds, I'll startle awake, heart pounding, and all of this will be a fleeting memory.

So when the vicar asks us to turn and look each other in the eye, I do it. I feel like a robot, as if I'm standing outside myself, all the leads to my emotions disconnected and dangling.

When Gil's eyes go soft, even though his jaw is still tight, his manner contained as always, I hear him say he'll take me to be his wife, for better or for worse, for richer or for poorer, but I feel nothing. And when my mouth opens and closes, when I tell him I'll love him and cherish him until death us do part, I don't mean it. They're just words. Sounds. Vehicles to propel me through this moment to the next.

I barely feel the slide of the wedding band onto my finger, even though Gil has trouble getting it over my knuckle, causing the congregation to join as one in indulgent laughter. His ring goes on perfectly. No problems at all, and I stare at it as the minister's words wash over me.

Before this congregation ... Joining of hands ...
Husband and wife.

I dully register a cheer behind me, but I'm still looking down at the band of white gold. I can see myself reflected in it, tiny and distorted, and I can't seem to make myself look away.

And then the next words hit my auditory processing nerves loud and clear: 'You may now kiss the bride.'

CHAPTER ELEVEN

Five years ago

The superyacht *Island Queen* gives one last burst of the aft thrusters as deckhands leap around the stern, throwing lines and tying them off on cleats on the dock. The week-long charter has been full on, lovely guests but they were very high energy and wanted *all* the activities and parties she could cram into those seven days.

Freedom, the chance to rest and relax for the next two days, is within her grasp and she can almost taste it. It's even better than usual because today is her birthday and she'll be able to go out with the rest of the crew and celebrate, rather than handing other people glasses of champagne.

She lines up in her 'whites' with the rest of the crew and bids the guests a sunny farewell, but maybe she's a little more distracted than normal, because she can't help glancing down the dock to see who might walk their way.

It's silly, really. He said he wouldn't be able to get away to visit because of the new job he's started with a well-respected ad agency, but before that, he was *so* insistent he'd make it out to see her sometime soon. Even though he's gone a little bit quiet on the subject, she's secretly hoping it's just a ruse to throw her off the scent. It would be just like him to fly in and make the day magical.

Once they've waved the guests off, she's got plenty to keep her busy. The chief stew likes to get the boat turned around straight away after the guests leave so they can relax properly on their days off, knowing it's all done, so Erin's on 'beds and heads', stripping off sheets and wielding toilet brushes, until the interior looks exactly like the glossy photos in the boat's brochure.

She's just smoothing down the last set of sheets and arranging the pillows 'just so' when a deckhand raps on the door. 'Someone's here for you.'

Her heart almost stops. But then, before the deckhand can say anything else, she's practically shoving past him to race aft, where the passerelle is extended to allow people to walk between dock and boat.

The first thing she sees when she arrives on deck is the most massive bouquet of exotic flowers she's ever seen, so huge that it's completely hiding the man carrying it. She rushes towards him, hardly able to wait until he climbs the short flight of steps leading to the main deck and turns to lay them on the large outdoor dining table.

'Erin Ross?'

Her pulse skips but her stomach nosedives. It's an English accent but is it …?

Oh.

It's not him. Just a delivery guy, who's looking rather perplexed. He's probably not used to seeing recipients of flowers like this looking as if they might burst into tears. And it's not as if they're not stunning. It's just …

'That's me,' she says, smiling as brightly as she is able. 'They're beautiful.'

The guy nods and jogs back down the stairs and she's left to manhandle the massive arrangement through the narrow passages. Where on earth is she going to put it? It can't go in her tiny cabin. Marisol would lose the plot.

In the end, she plonks it on the table in the crew mess – she'll find a permanent spot later – and then takes out the small card tucked within the foliage and opens it. A typed message says *Happy Birthday, Erin! And the surprises aren't over yet. Be ready at 2 p.m. – a car is coming to pick you up. Si x.*

A car! Hope bursts through her like a flamethrower once again as she dashes off to her cabin to find something to wear. It needs to be summery but not too floaty, a little sophisticated without trying too hard. And she's got to find the perfect dress and be ready to go in … she checks her watch. Argh! Thirty-five minutes! And she's got to find the captain first to get permission to go ashore a little earlier than planned.

She just about makes it. At one fifty-eight, she is standing at the marina's reception when a sleek black car arrives and a driver steps out and opens the door for her. She peers inside, hoping someone is already occupying the back seat, but finds it empty, so she slides onto the pale leather and folds her hands in her lap. 'A car' he'd written, and this certainly was a car, but she'd expected a taxi, not something like this.

Half an hour later, the car stops outside a jeweller's in Nassau. The driver opens the door for her and hands her another small white envelope. *I wish I could be there with you, but I wanted to do something special. Inside, the jeweller is waiting with a selection of earrings. Choose whichever pair you like best. Simon x*

Twin emotions tug her in different directions: disappointment that Simon had been telling the truth all along about not being able to get off work, and mushy, fuzzy feelings that he's made her feel so taken care of.

She chooses a delicate pair of studs from the selection, three strands of gold woven into a knot, and presses them into her ears the minute she is in the car back to the marina. No, she decides, as the car leaves the city centre and heads back towards the coast, she doesn't just feel taken care of. Simon's thoughtfulness has made her feel like a princess.

CHAPTER TWELVE

Present Day

Gil is holding my hands. I rip one away and without caring who sees it, pinch the skin on my forearm hard. I have to wake up! There is no way I'm going to …

Oh.

Too late.

Gil's lips meet mine softly, gently. But somehow it feels as if a ten-ton truck has slammed into my body. There aren't fireworks. The world doesn't stop. But there is skin brushing against skin, nerve endings firing frantically to send messages all over my body: raising my pulse, loosening my taut muscles, causing my entire being to get tingly.

I have a sudden flashback to the night I first met Simon and Gil. I was back in London after my second winter yachting season and one of my university friends, Megan, had dragged me along to meet a group of her friends at a bar. We'd arrived at the place, tucked away down a tiny alleyway near Piccadilly, and pushed our way through the crowded space. When we got close to the bar, I'd spotted two rather good-looking guys and my body had flushed with interest as I'd locked eyes on one of them. And it hadn't been Simon.

But that had been *before*. Before the accident. Before I knew what kind of man Gil Sampson was.

That memory is all I need. It's like being doused with a bucket of icy water. All the warm and fuzzy feelings my body is betraying me with evaporate at the exact moment Gil pulls back and smiles at me.

There are cheers and whistles all around us. To me they sound like baying dogs, or the screech of hungry seagulls. My eyes narrow. I won't forget who this is, no matter how good a kisser he is.

I've never really liked Gil, not after that first summer, but now I realize I might actively hate him. Especially as he is rudely invading my dreams the night before my wedding.

It must be that stupid argument we had at the party. Well, he's got his revenge now, hasn't he? Not that he's ever going to know. Because there is *no way* I'll reveal any of this to anyone when I wake up. It will go with me to my grave.

I pinch myself again, but it does nothing other than make a nasty red mark on my skin. I try again, harder, and almost end up crying out, but when I look up, everything is just as it was moments before. Same church. Same vicar. Same groom staring into my eyes. Not in a sappy way, of course, because Gil is far too cool for that.

But then I glimpse the man standing behind him. Simon. And my heart squeezes painfully. The jovial expression he was wearing earlier has given way to something else, something darker … edgier.

Guilt cuts through me like a freshly sharpened knife. I've just kissed another man. *Right in front of him!* No wonder he's not looking happy. And yes, I know it's a dream, and I know in this surreal version of reality we're not together, but clearly my subconscious hasn't been able to let go of the idea of him, because why else would he be standing there beside Gil as his best man looking ... well, jealous?

I want to shove Gil aside and throw myself into Simon's arms, but I'm frozen to the spot. *Wake up, wake up, wake up* I chant inside my head. Because I really need to now. I need to stop the madness, because this dream is *way* too stressful, and I'll be getting married for real in a matter of hours. I need to have a good night's sleep and wake up calm and refreshed and serene.

As the ceremony continues with songs and readings and a short but dull sermon, I do all I can think of to wake myself up. I pinch my arm, my hands, the tips of my fingers ... basically, anywhere I can reach that won't be too obvious to someone watching me. I bite my lip. I do mental gymnastics, trying to get my brain to snap out of slumber and find its way back to consciousness, but none of it works. I begin to fantasize about standing up abruptly, running back down the aisle in a rustle of off-white taffeta, and then down the lane and into the waiting river. The cold water might be enough of a shock to do the trick.

But it seems even in the depths of my subconscious, the programming to always be calm and collected can't be undone. *Now*, I keep telling myself. *Do it now!* But I don't move. And the minutes keep ticking past.

As the vicar drones on, my gaze keeps sliding off my groom onto Simon. He's the one thing that's anchoring me, keeping me sane. That look I saw on his face is the one bit of reality in this whole messed-up scenario.

Maybe that's it. Maybe, just maybe, if I can get to Simon ... talk to him, possibly even touch him, it could short-circuit this weird trip my brain is on and I'll wake up? The more I think about it, the more I realize this has to be the key.

Simon. My love for him. *That's* what's going to bring me home.

I try to catch his eye, but it's as if he's deliberately avoiding looking at me, and before I can work out how to get his attention properly, we're standing again, organ music is playing and I'm walking back down the aisle with Gil, seeing the smiling faces of my friends and family. Traitors.

We turn for the photographer in the vestibule, looking over our shoulders, framed in the arched church door, and then we're out into the February sunshine.

I do as I'm told by the photographer as he puts us through a series of poses. I put my arms and legs in the right places. I pull my cheek muscles tight into something approximating a smile as wedding guests filter out of the church and gather around us.

I search for Simon and eventually spot him hovering on the fringes of the crowd near the back. He trains his eyes on me, his expression serious. Our gazes lock and I swear he knows what I'm thinking, but before I can work out if I can snatch a moment to go over to him before we leave the church for the reception, I'm being ushered towards a waiting vintage Rolls Royce by my groom – the same type of car I'd picked but this one is silver instead of white, and at least four decades older.

As the car pulls away, Gil leans towards me, grateful for the relative privacy of this moment, and I can see in his eyes he's ready to take full advantage of it to kiss his new bride. Extremely thoroughly.

My hands shoot up to his shoulders, halting the progress of

his mouth to mine. 'Don't you *dare* ruin my make-up!' I say with a nervous laugh.

He blinks, and I'm not sure if I just see the message in his eyes or he says the word out loud, but I hear it in my head all the same. *Later* …

I swallow and swivel round to look out of the lozenge-shaped window at the back of the car. Our guests have gathered at the lychgate, all faces turned towards the retreating Rolls. Some are waving.

And at the front of the crowd, a few steps ahead, as if he started running after the car then realized it was useless, is Simon. I press my palm against the glass and stare back at him. Even when the lane twists and my view is filled with dry-stone walls and dead bracken, I don't turn back and face my groom.

CHAPTER THIRTEEN

Present Day

I hardly pay attention to where the bridal car is taking us until we reach the crossroads in the centre of Lower Hadwell. I expect the car to turn right, towards the main road that will take us further down the river to Dartmouth, but when it turns left, I sit up straight and frown. I shoot a look across at Gil and realize he's not perturbed in the slightest, which only makes me irritated.

Where are we going? The reception is supposed to be at the Royal Marina Hotel. But I realize I can't ask questions without getting embroiled in an exhausting conversation about why I don't know where my wedding reception is being held, and even though this is only a dream, I can't be bothered. I feel stressed enough already.

But then my substitute groom glances across at me and I see a playfulness in his eyes. He suppresses a smile. It's as if he knows *exactly* what I'm thinking and he's finding it amusing, which makes me want to whack him on the head with my bouquet.

Great job, Erin! Why this dream? Why this man? Are you trying to make yourself have a breakdown before you get down the aisle for real?

The Rolls slows to navigate both the narrow road and the steep hill leading towards the river. We pass within inches of stone cottages painted in ice-cream colours, and then the road widens and turns near the Ferryboat Inn, coming to a halt by a jetty jutting out over the narrow stony beach and then across the deep green water of the River Dart.

My groom gets out and goes around the back of the car, before opening my door and holding out his hand. From the glimmer in his eyes, I can see that he's waiting for me to ask a question. I don't want to give him the satisfaction, but I'm so confused I can't help myself. 'Where...?' I begin as I mindlessly take his hand, forgetting that usually, I'd rather stroke a slug than touch him. The only possible venue in Lower Hadwell would be the village hall, but there's no way it could hold a hundred and twenty people.

'You always knew this bit was going to be a surprise,' he says as he leads me towards the wooden ramp with rails that connect the road to the pontoon.

I did?

Now I *know* I'm dreaming. There's no way I would let anyone else loose on arrangements for this day. 'I let *you* plan our wedding?'

He stops at the top of the ramp, looking bemused. 'No, you know I didn't.'

'But ... We were supposed to have the reception at—' I shut my mouth. No. That's not right. There is no 'we' for me and Gil. I have to remember that, no matter how real this all seems. And, as if to remind me of that fact, the breeze from the river curls around me, lifting the fine hairs on my bare forearm and I shiver.

I try again. 'I thought the reception was going to be at the Royal Dart Marina …'

A wicked little glint appears in Gil's eyes and I shiver a second time. The two things are not connected. They're not. 'I *may* have let you believe you'd guessed correctly, but actually, that was a tiny red herring I planted. I always told you the reception venue was going to be a surprise, even if you insisted on overseeing how each table would look, down to choosing every last bit of china and cutlery and obsessing over the seating plan.'

I want to say something but my head is empty of words.

Gil gives me a knowing look. 'You had to give me *something* to plan, E. I couldn't let you have the whole thing to yourself as your private control-freak project.'

Coming from Gil, this would usually be fighting talk, and I'm about to pull myself up to my full five-foot-four and let him have it, but then I catch the look in his eyes. There's humour there. Not the biting, caustic kind of humour he usually hurls at me – the way he did in the hotel garden less than a day ago – but a warm, indulgent humour, suggesting he not only sees this side of me but quite enjoys it. I'm not sure what to say in response, so he makes the most of my uncharacteristic silence and leads me down the pontoon.

I know this village well. Simon's parents live in Lower Hadwell, and we've spent many lovely weekends here over the years. It's why we chose to get married here – a no brainer compared to my home patch in south-east London. I'm utterly charmed by the chocolate-box cottages, the steep hills covered with fields and ancient woodlands, the changing moods of the river. But now I stand and stare at the passenger ferry sitting at the end of the pontoon, a vessel I've climbed aboard many times, and I know I've never seen it like this. I'm completely astonished.

The local ferryman runs this service all year round using the same repurposed crabber his father sailed before him. It's a wooden boat, about twenty feet long. Usually, brightly coloured nautical flags are strung between a small mast at the front of the boat and a post at the hull, but today they've been replaced with white bunting. Ribbons and posies of white roses to match my bouquet are fastened at strategic points around the boat.

I turn to Gil, my mouth open. 'We're getting on this?'

He's looking carefully at my face, assessing my reaction. 'We are.'

'But what about the guests? How will they ...?' I trail off, noticing the larger vessel waiting thirty feet away from the jetty, similarly decorated, engine idling. I'm so gobsmacked that all thoughts of Simon and finding some way to get to him leave my head.

Gil climbs aboard the ferry, and then with one foot on the floor of the boat, the other on the bench nearest me, he extends his arm and offers me his hand.

I don't know if it's because of his smart dark suit and waistcoat, or the wind that is ruffling his too-long hair, but he looks like he just stepped out of a period drama. I mutely place my hand in his without argument or resistance. I'm unprepared for the jolt of energy that shoots up my arm – like electricity, but sweeter. Maybe that's why I don't tell him I can manage very well on my own, thank you very much, and allow him to help me into the boat.

The sharp wind whips around us as the boat pulls away, heading across a narrow point at a bend in the river to the centuries-old stone quay on the opposite bank. Before I'm even aware I'm shivering, Gil's jacket is around my shoulders. I don't know why, but that one simple action causes my eyes to fill. I turn and lay my head on his shoulder to hide my tears. I don't want to see the half-smile that's been playing on his lips all day fade, to see his eyes darken with concern.

As we prepare to dock, waiting for fenders to be dropped and ropes to be fastened, my curiosity kicks back in. Where are we going? I take Gil's hand and step from the boat onto the stone jetty and then follow him up the narrow stairs to where yet another car decked out with white ribbon is waiting. I've been so bamboozled by the whole nightmare … dream … whatever it is … that I forgot to think about that. This side of the river is mostly farmland and winding lanes. Where on earth could we be …?

My eyes snap wide open and I freeze. The seconds tick loudly inside my head and then I turn to my groom to find a smile I've seen on his lips a million times before in my waking life; I'd just never been able to interpret it. I'd always thought it was a sneer of some sort, but now I realize it's merely his way of hiding something he doesn't want anyone to know. This smile hides Gil's secrets.

'No …' I begin, trailing off as my eyes scan the wooded hillside, searching for the roof of a whitewashed building that peeks from the trees high above the river, even though I know I can't see it from this spot. 'Not there … You can't have!'

CHAPTER FOURTEEN

Present Day

I'm still stunned as the car comes to the end of a long, winding driveway. The trees hugging the lane become more sparse and then, finally, it's as if they step back out of the way to reveal a sloping green lawn on one side of the drive and an elegant Georgian mansion on the other. Gil didn't confirm or deny my suspicion, but now the secret is out.

I'm clasping his hand tightly, more to anchor myself to something – anything – than because I need to hold on to him. 'How did you manage to book this place?' I whisper.

This is Whitehaven, not just my dream wedding location, but my dream location for just about anything. I didn't even know what it was called or who owned it when I first fell in love with it. I came to South Devon for a holiday once when Mum and Dad were still married, and one day we got the ferry from Dartmouth up the river to Totnes. During the boat ride, I spotted a lonely white house perched on the top of a steep and wooded hillside, its bottom floors obscured by woodland. The house became visible for a few moments, and then it disappeared again behind the trees, as if it had been conjured up from a fairy tale and then swallowed back into the mists.

When I first visited Simon's parents and found out he lived in Lower Hadwell, it felt like fate, and if we went out on his friends' motorboats, I always positioned myself on the starboard bow to glimpse this mysterious mansion.

It was Simon's mum who told me its name and that it had once been owned by a famous actress, Laura Hastings, and that after she'd died, it had fallen into disrepair. The new owner was even more reclusive than the last. After her very public and very messy divorce from a more recent Hollywood A-lister, she'd bought the place and begun restoring it to its former glory.

In the last couple of years, the grounds had been open to the public for one weekend each summer, mostly to raise funds for the charitable foundation the new owner ran and I stood at the gates the very first day, ticket in hand. Just to see the fairy tale up close, to walk in the gardens I had no idea even existed, a closely guarded secret of the surrounding woodland.

I called, of course, when I'd been looking for a venue for my wedding – my *real* wedding, to Simon – hoping that the fact the public were occasionally allowed inside the thick stone walls and tall iron gates might mean they'd be open to holding the reception there, but I received a firm but polite 'no'.

I turn to Gil and wait for his answer.

'A couple of years ago, I did some work for the owners,' he tells me.

'I didn't know that!'

Duh. Well, of course I wouldn't. *This is a dream, Erin. You have to keep reminding yourself of that. In real life, he's probably never even met them.*

But Gil doesn't know he's a figment of my imagination so he answers my question anyway. 'I didn't tell you. I couldn't ... It's not the usual sort of work I do, but Louise Thornton contacted me – I don't know how she found me or who recommended me – and asked if I'd do some cybersecurity work for her. I'd heard you talk about this place so often that it intrigued me and I took the job. The only problem? I was sworn to secrecy. It was that week you wanted to visit that vintage fashion exhibition at the V&A and I couldn't go with you. Do you remember?'

I nod even though I don't.

'She was grateful, said she'd love to return the favour if ever she could, so the day after you said yes to me I called her and, long story short, here we are.'

I smile. I'm impressed with myself. The level of ingenuity and detail in this dream is beyond anything I've ever experienced. Maybe I have an absurdly high IQ and never truly realized it before. For a moment, it makes me feel like a superhero, but then I realize I must have been slacking in my waking life if I haven't tapped into it by now.

I turn to look at the frontage of the mansion, filled with tall, elegant windows. Its stonework had been crumbling the last time I visited, weeds pushing up through the curved steps that led to a drawing room as if the woodland was stubbornly reclaiming the land as its own, but now there's a fresh coat of milk-white paint over the whole house, and cracks and crumbling corners have been seamlessly restored. I can't believe I'm here, even in this wildest of wild dreams.

Warm fingers lace between mine and Gil tugs me away from the drive and down a wide path that curves round the building and then out of sight. I let him pull me, eyes still trained on the house, until we duck through an arched gateway and emerge into a large walled garden. I remember this. When I visited, it was just unkempt grass with gnarled fruit trees clinging to the walls. Today, a sprawling marquee covers most of a clipped, green lawn. My mouth drops open when Gil leads me to a smaller awning that acts as a covered porch to the main tent.

This is … This is …

Perfect.

The photographer's second-in-command is already here, beckoning us to a corner of the garden so he can snap a few shots of us. Before I comply, I take a peek inside.

Is it possible to feel like you're dreaming when you're already dreaming? Because I do. I recognize my style and taste in the table settings, in each piece of silverware and crockery, in the floral arrangements that hang above the tables, trailing tendrils of ivy and fern that reach down towards the pure white linen and crystal. I see my handwriting on the name cards, and I've clearly been practising my calligraphy harder in this version of my life. When I look up, I discover the ceiling of the marquee is a mass of fairy lights, and I instantly know how magical it will look when the sun sets.

My heart cracks a little, because while all of this is perfect, it's a little *too* perfect. I'm sad – no, devastated – that this isn't what my real wedding will be like, and I berate my subconscious for throwing this up the night before it happens for real. It's really quite cruel. I don't want to think of my actual wedding as second best.

That thought is enough to shock me out of my blissful, fairy light bedazzled haze.

You just said it to yourself. It's not real. You can't get caught up in this.

And so I turn and follow the photographer to where he wants to put me, and I do as I am told, my body assuming positions almost on autopilot, my cheek muscles cramping from the rigid smiling. But all the while my mind is whirring, trying to work out how I can slash a hole in the fabric of reality and return to normal sleep, to normal life.

Guests start trailing in through the gate. Some head for the marquee, filled with powerful heaters and waiting staff holding trays of champagne and soft drinks, and some drift towards us, smiling and pulling their phones out to grab a few quick shots. I search for Simon's head amid the throng. I need to find him. I need to get to him.

The photographer lines up my bridesmaids to my left and Gil's ushers to his right. I could possibly lean behind Gil and touch Simon, but I suspect he's just out of reach, so I stare at him as often as I can, trying to send a telepathic message to turn round and catch my eye, but it's almost as if he's steadfastly refusing to look at me. When, finally, all the shots are done, he sets off with the rest of his and Gil's buddies towards the marquee without even a backward glance.

No, I want to yell. *It's not supposed to be like this! It's supposed to be you and me.*

I gather up my skirts and run after him as well as I can in a huge white dress, but just as I'm about to catch up with him, a hand circles my wrist and I'm stopped in my tracks.

It's him. Gil.

Once again snarling up my life and getting in the way of my happiness.

'Hey,' he says, and without asking me what I want to do, he pulls me into the tented porch of the marquee and then through a curtain into a small area that has been sectioned off to be used as a cloakroom.

I pull my wrist from his grip, tugging far too hard, because he was only loosely holding it, and I ending up smacking myself in the face with my hand. Ouch.

Even in this strange dream, it hurts like crazy. I prod my nose, which I am now sure is turning pink and swelling to twice its normal size. And then, because I'm frustrated and angry and fed up with being here in this strange, taunting paradise, my eyes begin to sting and I let out a loud sniff.

'Hey,' Gil says again, and it's even softer this time. His arms come around my shoulders. 'What's up?'

I shake my head. I could let it all out. I could yell out all my frustration, even though it would make no sense to him, but I don't. Too many years of battening down the hatches and keeping it all inside.

His lips press softly to the top of my head. It's such a tender gesture that the tears balancing on my bottom lashes fall. 'We … we ought to be getting in there,' I half whisper, half croak. 'It's time to make our entrance.'

A low chuckle rumbles next to my ear. 'No.'

'But everyone's waiting!'

He pulls back to look at me. 'Let them. What are they doing to do? Start without us?'

This is more like the Gil I know, doing whatever the heck he wants with no thought to anyone else. 'But—'

'No, Erin … I know you've been looking forward to this day for months, if not years, but you've been driving yourself into the ground trying to get ready for it despite my attempts to come alongside you, and we've been on the go all day. You need this. Let's just take this moment to pause, recharge ... And then, I promise, we'll jump back on the merry-go-round.'

Much to my surprise, I realize he's speaking the truth. He described me perfectly, but sometimes I'm so busy diving in and saving the day that I forget I do find large groups tiring and overwhelming. Maybe this is a distress flare from my subconscious telling me to slow down a bit.

'Okay,' I say slowly.

Gil smiles as I look up at him, and then he leans towards me.

I place a hand on his chest and turn my head to look at a bright red coat on a rack beside me, laughing awkwardly. 'Oh, now I see. You almost had me with all that sensitive BS ... I think you have other reasons for wanting to get me on my own.'

He says nothing, and when I flick a glance back up at him, there's humour in his eyes. 'I'm always looking for an excuse to do that.'

The hairs stand up on the back of my neck as I see his eyes drop to my lips. I know I should move, turn my head again as his torso presses hard against the palm I still have flattened on his chest, as his face gets closer. I suck in a breath ...

'Oh, *there* you two are!' Both our heads snap round and I see Anjali holding back the flap of material that makes up the door of this makeshift cloakroom. 'What are you doing in—' She stops herself and shakes her head. 'Forget it. I don't want to know!'

I back away from Gil, realising what might have happened if she hadn't come bursting in. I'd told myself I needed to disengage from this stupid dream, emotionally if not consciously, and here I was getting sucked in to it again. And in the worst possible way! With the actual love of my life probably on the other side of a flimsy canvas curtain. I feel sick.

'Anyway ...' Anjali says, holding back the entrance flap. 'I'm here to ruin your fun, because everybody is ready to welcome the new Mr and Mrs Sampson into their wedding reception.'

I smile weakly, smooth the skirt of my gown, and let her lead the way.

CHAPTER FIFTEEN

Five years ago

It's late. She's in bed and her roommate is asleep in the bunk beneath.

Hey, you … she types.

He didn't reply to her message earlier in the day, but she knows he always goes quiet when something's up, the same way she does.

You okay?

She's on the verge of dozing off, her phone on her chest, when it vibrates and brings her back to full consciousness.

Yeah.

That's it? Her stomach twists.

You sure?

He sends her a smiley face emoji, but it feels like a cop-out.

She senses he's not telling her something, which makes her want to leap out of bed and jump on a plane. She could be in London by lunchtime tomorrow. She's worried he's not coping but putting a brave face on it.

She types **I wish you'd open up to me** then deletes it. She's not sure it would make any difference. She's also not sure their relationship is at the point where she can ask him to bare his soul. It had been all light and breezy … fun … before tragedy had struck. In the aftermath, they'd talked a lot, but time has crept on and Simon seemed to rebuild himself. She thought it was a good thing, thought it showed he was healing. Maybe she should have factored in that building also usually involves walls.

Maybe she's being paranoid, but after all they've gone through she didn't expect to be on one side of that wall while he was on the other. It feels like the thing that brought them together is now slowly pushing them apart.

Her phone buzzes.

Off to the pub. Catch you later?

She stares at the words. He's putting on such a brave face. She nods reluctantly as she replies, even though she knows he can't see her. **Yes** she types, then adds **Have a good time!** And unironically adds a thumbs-up emoji just to show how fine she is too.

CHAPTER SIXTEEN

Present Day

Finally, I know exactly where Simon is. He's only a couple of metres away, sitting four chairs to my right. We're at the top table, finishing our main course of a chicken thing with vegetables (the last thing I'm paying attention to is my food), but between me and the man I'm planning to marry when I wake up is my father, one of my bridesmaids and the man I actually exchanged vows with only a couple of hours ago. This dream couldn't get any more complicated. Or bizarre.

An icy sensation travels down my spine, lifting the fine hairs on my back. It's gone on for so long now that I'm getting worried I'll never wake up. What if this *isn't* a dream? What if I'm at the mercy of the multiverse, and somehow I've slipped into a parallel life, one where I have clearly lost my mind?

As the full horror of that thought sinks in, I freeze, broccoli halfway to my mouth. I drop my fork and it lands on the plate with a clatter. I stare at it for a few seconds, then begin to laugh, a sound that comes deep from my belly and causes my substitute groom to glance sharply at me. I shake my head, unable to stop laughing. No, that's so ridiculous. Of *course* this is a dream. It can't be anything else.

'Are you okay?' Gil asks, his brows pinching together. He does that a lot, I realize. Frown. When he's around me, anyway. And I didn't even know I'd noticed it enough in real life to save and record that detail so my imagination could include it here.

'It's just …' I will myself to stop laughing and crease my mouth into something approximating a straight line, even if it twitches a little. 'Just the joy of this happy day.'

Gil's eyebrows relax, but only a little. He's still looking at me as if I'm being really weird. Which I am, so I can't really object to that.

Simon is looking at me with a strange intensity, as if he's been waiting to catch my eye. It makes me shiver. Partly because it feels like an ice bucket of reality has been dumped over my head and partly because I realize I've missed this look. The run-up to the wedding has been crazy, stressful, and we haven't had as much time together as either of us would like.

Communication passes between us, even though neither of us speaks or even moves. I don't know what was said; I just know it was *something*. And that something is aching deep inside my chest, pulsing like a heartbeat. So when Simon stands up and leaves the top table, heading out between other tables full of chattering guests as they eat their last mouthfuls and fall into easy conversation, I follow him with my eyes. And as he nears the exit, I rise from my seat, ignoring Gil's curious gaze, and head in the same direction.

I take a little longer to cross the room than Simon does. Friends and family members want to congratulate me, say what a lovely day it's been, so when I reach the exit, I can't see him. I step into the deserted bar space where the drinks reception was before the main meal and look around, but it's empty.

I'm about to turn around and go back when Simon appears,

pressing a finger to his lips. He holds a tent flap aside and for the second time that afternoon, I'm hiding out in the cloakroom, but this time with the man I'm actually supposed to marry.

We stand there staring at each other. I feel strangely breathless. 'I've been waiting to get a chance to talk to you all afternoon,' I say. My fingertips twitch as I ready myself to reach out and touch him, to end this nightmare once and for all.

The intensity of his stare deepens. 'I know.'

My heart skips a beat. It feels like he does know. He stands out from everyone else in this dream as being more real. 'Do you know why?'

He nods and my stomach flips. This has been an unusual dream so far – too real, too orderly, despite the alternate casting for significant roles. There have been no teleportation moments when I arrived in a new place with no explanation. My teeth haven't fallen out. No one has started flying, and I've been to the loo – twice! Who does that in dreams? Also, you don't normally know you're dreaming when you're in the middle of one, and you rarely meet someone else who knows it too.

He steps towards me. 'You married the wrong man.'

'I knew it!' I say, lurching forward and grabbing hold of his hands. 'But how does this work? Are you dreaming too and somehow we're sharing the same one? Or have I wandered into one of your dreams or you into mine? And how do we stop it? How do we wake up?'

Simon looks confused.

'From this nightmare,' I add quietly.

He lets out a relieved laugh and pulls me into his arms.

'I knew you'd see it eventually,' I tell him. 'I knew you'd work it out.'

His eyes become sad. 'It took me too long. My life has been a misery since I let you slip through my fingers, Erin. I was stupid to break things off all those years ago, paving the way for Gil to swoop in and have you, and in the last few weeks I've been watching you as the day got nearer and thinking what an idiot I was. I love you. I've always loved you.'

My heart is singing at his words. These are the things I always want him to say, but he hardly ever does. Not because he doesn't feel them, but because they're buried so deep. This is the Simon who swept me off my feet when we were first together. But my brain is sorting through the sounds and syllables and realizing something is off, something doesn't add up.

'But wait … What do you mean, you let me slip through your fingers? We're together. We've always been together.'

Simon takes my hand and presses it to his chest before covering it with his own. 'We are now … That's all that matters.' He leans towards me, his eyelids closing.

No. This is all wrong.

I put my hands up, intending to push against his chest, but I'm a little late. Simon's lips meet mine for a fraction of a second before I back away, and it's at this exact moment that the flap of the cloakroom door moves and I hear Anjali's voice. 'Erin! It's time for the speeches. Seriously, do you think you and Gil can stop sneaking off together so I have to come and find—'

I'm aware this doesn't look good: the bride and best man found in the cloakroom, just a bit too close for it to look totally platonic. Simon and I spring apart.

Anjali's eyes are wide. '*Simon?*'

CHAPTER SEVENTEEN

Present Day

Anjali looks at me and then at Simon and then back at me again and her expression of surprise hardens into a frown. I lunge forward, reaching for her, but she backs away shaking her head, and then runs off out of the cloakroom. I shoot a look at Simon, whose mouth is a grim, straight line and take off after her. Simon tries to pull me back, but I'm too fast for him. I slide out of his grip before his fingers close around my lower arm. 'I'll be back in two secs,' I say as I go through the flap to the main tent. 'I promise.'

I catch up with Anjali as she's about to head outside into the walled garden. She doesn't even wait for me to say anything, but turns to face me as soon as I get near. 'What was that all about?'

'All what?'

She folds her arms. Anjali might be ditzy, but she's very good at reading a vibe, and clearly she picked up *something* going on between me and Simon that's caused her antenna to twitch. 'It looked very much as if you and Simon were about to kiss when I walked in.'

'I … It wasn't … It's not like that!' Technically, yes, our lips met, just for a split second, but I was trying to avoid it. 'There's nothing between Simon and me,' I mumble, looking away. And I'm telling the truth. There isn't. Not in this upside-down version of my life.

'He's your ex, Erin. And it's your wedding day.'

The look she gives me threatens to strip the flesh from my bones.

'I thought I knew you ...' she says, shaking her head, and then she exits the marquee and strides off into the dusk.

I have no idea what to say, so I let her go. I haven't done anything wrong, but nobody here would ever understand. I head back into the cloakroom, where Simon is waiting for me.

'We can't be seen together,' I tell him. 'Just ... just let me get through today and we'll talk ... We'll sort this all out.'

'Get through today? What do you mean?'

'I mean, we should keep our heads down and I'll call you tomorrow.' And, hopefully, tomorrow won't exist, because I'll have woken up, awkward double groom situation completely averted.

Simon's expression becomes thunderous. 'You don't mean ... Erin! You can't leave the reception and have a wedding night with him. Not now we know this whole day was a huge mistake!'

'It's not the right moment for us,' I plead feebly. 'Another time, another place ... *that's* our moment.' I look him deep in the eyes, because this is the truth, even though he doesn't know it. 'Trust me?'

Simon's jaw is tense, but he nods. 'Okay, I trust you.' He glances at the cloakroom door. 'You go first. I'll be out in a couple of minutes.'

I almost slide round the thick white flap of marquee fabric, not wanting to reveal anyone else is inside, and when I turn around I get the shock of my life: Gil is standing there.

'Dessert has been served. We're waiting to do the speeches.'

This is definitely starting to feel like a dream now. All this running around, this repetitive feeling of trying to accomplish something and being interrupted or thwarted at every turn …

I twist my head to look at the cloakroom, praying that Simon does nothing impulsive, like leaping from inside to claim me, and I place my hand in my groom's and I let him lead me back to the top table.

I sit down and see over a hundred smiling faces staring happily and expectantly at me, waiting for me to be the perfect bride I always knew I'd be. Instead of smiling back, I slide down a little in my seat.

One thing I'd been looking forward to on my wedding day was being the centre of attention, even though I'm not usually a 'look at me' type of person, but on your wedding day, you're allowed, aren't you? However, I'm now quietly wishing I was invisible as my father clears his throat and stands up to speak.

Dad teaches engineering at Aberystwyth University and his genuine passion, nay *obsession*, is Formula One. Just don't let him corner you at a party when he's a few beers in and let him talk to you about Grand Prix stats. You'll be stuck there all night. So I ready myself for the barrage of Formula One jokes and references, about how my groom and I have stayed the course and the chequered flag is waving today as we cross the finish line (I heard him practising that one last night when he thought nobody could hear him), but he turns to me and looks down at me with such warmth, such love, that I'm close to being a blubbering wreck within seconds.

'Erin,' he says. 'I'm so proud of you today. You look beautiful, absolutely perfect, but more than that, I'm filled with pride at the amazing woman you've become ...'

That's it. I lose all composure and sob into my dinner napkin as he carries on talking. I hope to God I'm wearing waterproof mascara. Dad isn't usually like this, you see. He talks about facts and figures, empirical data, not emotions. He's never been one for the warm and fuzzy stuff, even though I know it's there, deep down. He just doesn't have the language for it. Part of the reason Mum left him, I think. And he's never been much of one for gushing praise, either. Or crushing criticism, it has to be said, for which I've always been grateful. And, logically, I know he loves me and that he's proud of me; I just never expected to hear him say it out loud.

I hardly hear the end of his speech, or the beginning of Gil's, because I'm too busy trying to hold myself together, but the need to put on a good show, to not be an absolute mess in front of all my family and friends, overtakes me and I suck back my tears. When Gil mentions my name, my head jerks up.

'I know Erin doesn't need anyone to take care of her,' he tells the gathered crowd. 'In fact, I'd like to see anyone try ...'

This garners him a laugh and I look around, wondering if I'm this transparent to everyone I know. I don't like that idea at all.

'But I love her because of this, not in spite of it,' he continues. 'I love her drive, her independence, her intelligence ...' It's okay while he's talking to me in the third person, but then he turns and looks me in the eye. 'Erin ...'

I swallow. My chest feels suddenly tight.

A murmur travels around the room. 'How sweet' I hear from one direction, and 'That's adorable' from another. I want to look away, but I know it will be the wrong thing to do. I know I will just draw more attention to myself and that's the last thing I want.

'Erin, I promise I will always be there for you. I will *always* have your back. And I know that you're accomplished and successful and probably the most together person in this room … Well, marquee …'

I blink back the moisture that's gathered in my eyes. If only he knew.

'But I will love you for the rest of our lives, not because of all the amazing things you do, but for all the amazing things you are.'

I see the truth of it in his eyes and it breaks me. I drop my face into my hands and heave in a jagged breath, struggling to keep the tears from flowing once more. This is the best speech ever, I think, as he continues to wind the rest of the room around his little finger. Simon's better be this fricking good, otherwise I'll …

Simon.

The best man.

The man who almost kissed me in the cloakroom.

As Gil proposes a toast to me and everyone lifts their glasses in my direction, I smile back weakly. I am certainly not the paragon of virtue and womanhood Gil is toasting. I want to slide under the table and crawl away.

And then, of course, it just gets worse, because it's Simon's turn. I hadn't even noticed him return to the top table, probably because I've been staring at the tablecloth more often than not since I've been back in my seat.

The first minute or two of Simon's speech sweeps over me. It's the usual – embarrassing stories and jokes told at the groom's expense. I hear him talking, but I'm not paying any attention to the words. Or at least not until I hear him say my name.

'Of course, everyone knows that Erin and I were an item before she and Gil got together,' Simon says. I see some glazed smiles, a few frowns among the guests, because this is the sort of detail you'd usually gloss over on someone's wedding day, isn't it? 'But what you may not know is that we both saw her that first night we met and I could tell from the way Gil was doing his "death laser" stare thing he was interested. So just for a laugh, I swooped in and started talking to her first. You should have seen his face!' Simon guffaws.

Gil's expression is probably the same one he wore that night, jaw tense, lips tight – much more like the Gil I know rather than the one I've seen today who looks deeply into my eyes and tells me he'll love me forever.

More eyebrows in the audience pinch together. There's a ripple of awkward, too-high laughter, but Simon doesn't seem to notice that the gathered crowd isn't finding this as funny as he is.

'I was just going to string him along for a bit, then hand her over …'

My spine becomes even more rigid. As if I was something to be passed around with no say in the matter! But I can't be cross with Simon, can I? This is my subconscious speaking. Is this really how I view myself, even after all the hard work I've put in to get past my shyness, my insecurities? That's kind of depressing.

'But then I got talking to her and I realized what a great girl she is, and I couldn't seem to bring myself to do it. I mean, I know we're both good-looking fellas, but he's got that dark and mysterious brooding thing going on that girls love. Look at him! He's doing it right now!'

And doing it he is. I've never seen Gil look at Simon this way before; it's usually me he reserves the death stare for. But now I start to wonder why. What did I do to deserve it? Certainly nothing like this.

'But …' Simon says, sighing, 'Erin was working on boats more than half the year … well, those of you who know me know I'm a bit of an out of sight, out of mind kinda guy, and I've never been good at texts and messages and keeping in touch. I'm still rubbish at it!'

And he is. Was. Apart from that first winter I was away from him, he's never really been one for lengthy text discussions. But maybe he didn't need to. Once things get more serious, you're not wondering what the other person's feeling all the time, are you? There are things understood that don't always need to be said.

'But Gil was good at that stuff … He's always been better at words and technology than me. But give me a rugby ball, and I'm your man!'

There's a raucous cheer from a far corner of the room. Simon's rugby buddies.

'I suppose, if you were being uncharitable, you could say that Gil swooped in and stole her away from me …'

I look up to find Simon looking straight at me, his gaze intense. Is he going to say something? Is he going to repeat what he said in the cloakroom? He can't. He won't, will he …? I hold my breath.

'But the truth is, it was all my fault. I let her slip away. Didn't realize what I had until it was too late.'

The atmosphere of awkwardness in the room dissipates, but it does nothing to stop the clenching of my stomach. I stare back at Simon. I don't shake my head, but the warning is there in my eyes and I know he sees it.

He opens his mouth and closes it again. Then he turns a floodlight-strength smile on his audience. 'Which I suppose makes me the best best friend ever!'

There's a ripple of relieved laughter.

'Gil's going to owe me. Big. For a very long time.' He grins at his best friend. Gil gives a tight smile back. He's looking less tense, but I wouldn't call his body language relaxed. Even though I've secretly been fantasizing about getting one over on him for years, I realize I don't want it to happen this way. There's no sense of justice, or of victory, just a deep swirling in my gut making me very uneasy.

Simon catches my eye again, and I know he isn't finished. I close my eyes and look away. I should never have followed him when he left the top table earlier. What have I done?

'But the best man – sorry! – the *right* man got the girl, as they say.' My stomach rolls as Simon lifts his glass and proposes a toast. 'To the happy couple. May every day of your marriage going forward be filled with as much love, honesty and fidelity as today.'

CHAPTER EIGHTEEN

Present Day

In the moonlit shadows cast by three towering beeches, a discreet distance from the main marquee, is a row of portable toilets. I'm hiding in the one on the far end. Doing my best to ignore the smell, I lean my head against the wall and close my eyes. I can't even sit down, because there's no lid and I risk staining my bum blue with the toilet cleaner. (More proof I didn't organize this part of the wedding – I'd have insisted on the Portakabin type.) I know someone's going to come looking for me eventually, but I just need a few moments to myself. The last few hours have been a nightmare. Literally.

There's a loud knocking at the door. My startle reflex is so strong that I almost topple into the toilet bowl of blue goo. 'Erin? Are you in there?'

I swear softly under my breath. It's Gil. I've been avoiding him most of the evening under the pretence that we have to socialize with our guests – and I made sure I had long conversations with as many as I could pin down. I had to. Cutting the cake with Gil, doing a first dance with Gil, my face pressed into the clean cotton of his shirt, was all too weird.

'Erin?' His tone is softer now. He sounds worried.

I clear my throat. 'Yes?'

'Are you okay?' He tries the door handle, but I make sure the lock is firmly engaged. 'I'm fine.' My voice comes out hoarse. Not very convincing.

'Good …' That one word sounds wary, hesitant. I don't think he believes me. But then he'd be right not to, wouldn't he?

'It's just that it's almost eleven. We're supposed to be leaving soon … and we've still got the bouquet toss to do.'

Ugh. The last thing I want to do is come out of my rather stinky sanctuary and lob my wedding bouquet across the marquee at a group of women. I don't like the tradition anyway. Mostly because it's a horrible waste of gorgeous flowers.

'Can we skip that bit?' I ask. 'The bouquet toss, not the leaving bit?' I'd do just about anything to get out of Whitehaven at the moment – something I never expected to feel or think.

'I thought you were going to do it because Anjali had said how much she'd like to catch the bouquet once, but this is your wedding day. And if there's one day in your life where you don't have to put other people first, to let them guilt you into doing things for them, this should be it.'

I frown. I do that, don't I?

Gil tries the handle again. 'So, are you coming out?'

I look at the lock. My fingers stretch towards it, but then curl into a fist. 'In a minute. I've got, you know … *stuff* … to do.' Which is a lie. For some reason, I don't want to see Gil's face right now. I don't want to be alone with him in a darkened garden once again, even though I know there won't be any shouting this time.

'Go ahead. I'll catch up with you.'

CHAPTER NINETEEN

Present Day

I walk onto the dance floor and a cheer goes up. I play the part, smiling, holding the bouquet above my head like a trophy to be won, even though I'm dreading what's coming next.

Gathered in the middle of the dance floor are twenty to thirty women, most eyeing my bouquet up with hunger. Some have a 'what the heck! This'll be a laugh' glimmer in their eyes, and they elbow their friends and pretend to do warm-up exercises. Some are definitely not single and are there under false pretences.

Anjali joins the end of the loose semi-circle. Instinctively, I know she's placed herself there so there won't be too many competing pairs of arms. She catches my eye and gives me a meaningful look.

I turn and grip the bouquet with both hands. After a couple of moments of stillness I breathe in deeply and mentally picture where Anjali is standing.

One … two … I make a little dip to get a better swing and then, *three …* I squeeze my eyes shut and send it flying up and over my head.

I turn round to track its progress and see that there, right beside my maid of honour, is Simon. There's a moment of complete hush where all other eyes in the room are trained on the floral missile, but he locks his on me. I hold my breath as Gil and I watch to see where it lands.

There's no larking around now. Women jostle, rise onto their toes, straining just to get a millimetre closer. One of my tall cousins is right behind Anjali, ready to intercept the bouquet with her long arms, but Taryn grabs for it a split second too late, and another hand shoots out and wraps around the ribbon-bound stems.

Not Anjali's, but Simon's.

She spins around to see who robbed her of her rightful prize, ready to put up a fight, but when she sees who it is, she falters. He does a gallant little bow and hands it to her.

She holds it up triumphantly, beaming at everyone and shooting me a you-almost-blew-it look, then she turns back to Simon to thank him. But Simon isn't looking at her; he's looking at me, and when he sees Gil slide a possessive arm around my waist, his expression hardens and he wraps his arms around Anjali and pulls her into an enthusiastic kiss.

More cheering, even louder than before. Because it's what everyone roots for at a wedding, isn't it? The best man and the maid of honour finding romance. What could be more perfect?

What could be more terrible?

I'm watching my best friend and the man I love making out right in front of my face.

Someone yells 'Get a room!' and everyone laughs.

But I don't laugh. I want to be sick. I want to look away. But I can't seem to make my body follow the instructions my brain is giving it. I'm frozen, and when Simon's hand smooths down Anjali's back to cup her bottom, I feel vomit in the back of my mouth.

I look away and see Gil staring. He's just as astonished as I am.

'You said we were out of here the moment the bouquet toss was done?' I manage to croak out.

He nods.

'Then let's get out of here.'

CHAPTER TWENTY

Five years ago

Hey you …

She waits. This is the third time she's sent out a feeler this week. No scrolling ellipsis. Nothing. She's been away from him for two months now, and while communication has become gradually more patchy as his new job has got more and more demanding, he's never not answered before.

Has something horrible happened?

Again.

Or is it much more predictable than that? Is he ghosting her? Has he found someone else?

She doesn't know.

All she knows is that it feels as if he's turning into a different person.

CHAPTER TWENTY-ONE

Present Day

The dark around the car is almost impenetrable. I could believe we were travelling through a vast nothingness – no road to hold us up, no stars above to wink our way – were it not for the fact that the headlights pick out snatches of our surroundings. Shorn stubs of winter hedgerows greet us at every turn, punctuated by the occasional leafless tree. Twice, a rabbit darts across our path, causing Gil to touch the brakes lightly.

I collapsed into myself as soon as the car door closed, trapping me in a confined space with a man I've always said I hated. I hardly heard the friends and family cheering as we sped away up Whitehaven's drive and joined the winding country lanes.

I have no idea where we're going. Some fancy hotel, I expect, with a honeymoon suite to die for and fluffy white towelling robes. It's the sort of place I would book for a night like this. At that thought, I shiver, even though the temperature is comfortable inside Gil's Audi.

For my wedding with Simon, we'd planned to stay at the same hotel as the wedding reception, the Royal Marina. We were going to …

No. Not *going to*. We are. We will.

I've got to stop thinking about that version of my life as if I've changed tracks, as if I'm travelling away from it and it's never going to happen. It's still waiting there for me as soon as I wake up and open my eyes.

I squeeze the skin of my thigh between thumb and forefinger, trying again for the millionth time to rouse myself to consciousness, even though I know it won't work. But that's me. I don't give up. I survive. I muddle through. It's all I know how to do.

Gil isn't saying much. He's concentrating on the winding lanes, which can dip and turn in most unexpected places. I want to ask where we're going, but I suspect I should know, so it'll only raise questions I'm far too tired to answer. And I already feel small and unsure of myself. I don't want to sound even more like a child. *Are we there yet?*

But all is not lost, because while I've been sitting here in the silence, I've hatched a plan for what I'm going to do when we arrive at the hotel. I'll play along at first — checking in, maybe even taking a quick peek at the room. If there's a bar, I'm going to waste some time there drinking champagne, saying I'm too wired to settle down and go to bed. I'm going to push back bedtime as far as possible, because I want us both to be exhausted.

Too exhausted, if you know what I mean?

The next bit of my plan is a little fuzzy, so I'm going to have to wing it, which is definitely not my skill set, but somehow Gil will end up snoring (and unsatisfied) on his side of the bed and I'll quickly and quietly get dressed in the en suite then slip out of the room and down to reception. Once there, I'll get them to call me a cab and I'll be on my way. Exactly where to, I'm not sure. I'll figure that bit out when I get to it.

I'm steeling myself for a drive of an hour or more in the thick silence, but it's only another five minutes before Gil turns the car down an even narrower track, then brings it to a halt. The headlights are no help, illuminating only a tall evergreen hedge that is as neat and cultivated as the lanes are wild and unruly.

I climb out of the car warily, not waiting for Gil to come round to my side and open the door. Once outside, I see nothing I'm expecting to. There is no floodlit exterior of a former country manor turned into an exclusive couples' hotel. No sound. No light of any sort, apart from the glare of the Audi's full beams.

Where on earth …?

Gil strides round the hedge and seconds later a dull yellow glow illuminates a short path that carves through a small but gorgeous country garden. I follow him along it to an arched porch on a building that seems smaller than a five-star hotel should be. Much smaller.

'Where are we?' I ask quietly as he unlocks a hefty wooden door dotted with wrought-iron studs and gestures that I should go in ahead of him.

It's much bigger on the inside than it looks on the outside. We walk into a small flagstone hallway with a beautiful wooden console table and open guest book, and then into a good-sized vaulted kitchen with exposed beams and a long pine kitchen table. Lights are on in strategic places, creating a warm, cosy glow throughout the ground floor. Someone must have come in and got it ready for us.

'It's part of the Whitehaven estate,' he explains. 'I initially considered the gatehouse, at the end of the main drive, but thought we wouldn't want to be disturbed by hearing our guests leaving, and then Louise mentioned this gamekeeper's cottage.'

As he tells me all this, Gil's eyes are fixed on mine. There's something in his demeanour I don't quite recognize, and then I realize it's because he's nervous and is desperately trying to hide it. He's worried I won't like it.

I take a few steps and peek through a doorway into a cosy living room with two large, squashy sofas. There are woollen throws and plump cushions in dark green and berry colours, baskets of logs and books on the coffee table and at the far end of the room, set into a rough stone wall, is a giant fireplace, complete with softly crackling fire.

On one hand, I'm flummoxed. There's no bar to lose myself in, no reception desk with a phone I can tiptoe down to and use to order a cab. Just me and Gil, and no obvious means to sneak away without him knowing. On the other hand …

'It's gorgeous,' I say, turning to look at him. And I mean it. It isn't what I was expecting, and isn't what I would have chosen for myself, but it's possibly better.

He smiles at me. I mean, *really* smiles. It changes his face completely, lighting it up. It's such a surprise to see such unfettered joy on Gil Sampson's face that I laugh, possibly out of nerves, possibly because it's infecting me too.

He hasn't smiled like this all day, I think, as he picks me up and spins me around. On his wedding day. Why is that? It's not that he's not happy to be marrying me, because he wouldn't be grinning like this now if that were the case. Most puzzling. I always thought Gil was just naturally grumpy, but maybe there's more to it. Maybe he's just more comfortable being one-to-one with someone than amid all those people?

A bit like me, really.

He stops turning and lowers me so my feet touch the floor. His arms are still warm and tight around my back, and he pulls me even closer, his face nuzzling into the curve between my shoulder and neck. And then nuzzling turns to kissing.

'I … I think I'd like to take a shower,' I stutter.

He places another kiss just below my earlobe. I have to resist closing my eyes. But then he lets me go – reluctantly, I can tell. 'Okay. Why don't I grab us a couple of glasses of what's chilling in the fridge and then you can join me down here when you're done?'

I see him glance towards the roaring fire, to the warm throws and pillows that could easily make a cosy nest, and I know exactly where his mind is going. It would be the perfect spot to end a wedding day like this.

If I wasn't me and he wasn't him, of course.

I back towards the hallway, where I presume the stairs to the bedroom and the bathroom must be. 'I'll just …'

But Gil is already on his way back to the kitchen, a man on a mission.

I exhale, turn and run up the stairs two at a time, then tie my hair back out of the way and take the longest shower in the history of womankind, scalding my skin with the warm water, scrubbing every millimetre of myself at least three times over.

I'd imagined fluffy white robes in my wedding-night fantasy and the en suite doesn't disappoint, so I pull one on over my still-damp skin, free my hair from its messy bun, and then crawl under the duvet of the vast four-poster bed that takes up most of the bedroom. The mattress is possibly the softest thing I've ever laid down on and it's only seconds before my eyelids drift closed. I'm just so tired … Maybe this is the answer, I wonder, as my thoughts start to jumble and fade. Maybe if I can fall asleep in this dream, I'll wake up for real.

'Erin?'

I say nothing. I don't move. I'm not sure who I'm trying to kid I'm asleep, him or me. When I don't hear anything more, I crank an eyelid half open.

Crap. How did he move so silently? Gil is standing by the side of the bed looking at me, aware I'm squinting back at him and most definitely not asleep. 'I kinda crashed,' I mumble, hiding my reddened face in the soft white pillow.

I feel his weight dip the mattress and a second later his hand brushes my knee, which is sticking out from the duvet, and then under under the hem of my robe, travelling up my thigh.

I don't even think about it. I reach out and smash my hand down on top of his, stopping it in its tracks.

The mattress dips again as he shifts. I don't know how, but I can tell he's looking at me. 'Erin?'

I lie still for a moment, my breath warm around my face, and then I flip the hair away from one eye and twist my head to look at him.

There's a look of genuine concern on his face, as if what I'm feeling right this second really matters to him. I don't know what to say. For a few seconds, fragments of sentences whirl around my head. I even try to spit one or two of them out, but they emerge hopelessly jumbled.

I get so frustrated at myself, and then at this whole stupid marathon of a day – how it's just been one disaster after another – that the emotions all catch up with me at once and I start to cry.

Fabulous.

He says nothing as I bury my head back in the pillow, too ashamed to look at him. Instead, he turns off the overhead light in favour of a small reading lamp on his side of the bed – he takes the left, because I'm sprawled out all over the right – and then, for a few moments, I hear movement but I'm not sure what sort. I make myself very still, vaguely aware both that I'm trying to help him forget I'm here and also how ridiculous that is.

And then the duvet flips back, and he slides underneath and scoots right up next to me. I hold my breath. Without trying to remove my robe, he pulls me closer, spooning into me firmly but also gently. I'm surprised to find we're a perfect fit, whereas Simon always finds a way to dig an elbow into my back, no matter which way he lies.

Warm skin presses against the backs of my calves and heats the towelling robe at my back. An arm rests heavily on my waist. His hand doesn't move, doesn't peel back the edge of my robe and explore, but it might be about to. I don't know whether to scream or laugh hysterically.

'Gil … I'm …' My throat seems to be filled with gravel. I swallow and try again. 'I'm not … I mean, I don't think I can …'

'Shh.' His hand moves, but only to curl tighter around my waist, and his mouth is near to my ear, his breath tickling the sensitive hairs below and behind it. 'Are you okay?'

I hiccup. Just once. I'm unsure if it's an attempt to stop myself from sobbing or if I'm trying not to laugh. But he's being so … so unlike the Gil I know, so *nice*, that I know I have to answer him somehow. I shake my head, fluffing up my hair up on the pillowcase.

He pulls me closer. 'You've been in a weird mood all day. I thought it was just nerves, but it's not, is it? If it were, you'd be feeling relaxed and happy now.'

This time I nod. I can't lie. Not when he can practically feel my heart beating through my back.

He presses a tender kiss on the back of my head and smoothes my hair down. I close my eyes and a single tear leaks from below my eyelid.

'I don't know what's going on with you tonight, but I know it must be something big.'

I squeeze my face up to quell the sudden rush of tears.

'I can wait,' he says, and I detect absolutely no trace of resentment in his tone, which is a surprise, knowing how selfish this man can be. '*We* can wait. We've got the rest of our lives.'

He stretches away momentarily, and the little reading light goes off, leaving me staring into the dark, and then he curls himself back around me.

Now, I think. *Sleep, come and claim me. Take me back to my real life, to the real world, where everything makes sense and none of my emotions are topsy-turvy.* But sleep weaves an elusive dance over the next few hours. I wait, but she doesn't come.

CHAPTER TWENTY-TWO

Present Day

My mouth is dry, and I swallow. My eyes are closed and I'm surrounded by warm, soft cotton. The mattress is incredibly comfortable. It's almost like lying on a cloud, but I don't feel as if I've slept very well.

I've slept …

My eyelids ping open. I've slept!

That means I am now awake. I press my palm to my chest. Oh, thank God! I'm finally awake.

I roll over and breathe out, chuckling to myself. What a way to almost sabotage your wedding day, Erin! You'd better hope this deep and almost unending beauty sleep means you're going to be the perfect blushing bride.

'Hey …' The voice is warm and rough and near my ear. My heart rate doubles. Firstly, because I'm supposed to be alone on the night before my wedding and secondly, because even if my groom had snuck into our hotel room, defying all warnings of bad luck to see me this morning, it's not the right voice.

Gil reaches across and snaps his reading light on as I simultaneously jump out of my side of the bed, tugging the duvet with me as I clutch it around my neck. It's the wrong move. Because if I pull it away from the bed, I'm also pulling it away from him. And he's not wearing very much. In fact, it doesn't look like he's wearing anything at all.

He grumbles and catches the corner of the duvet just before the crucial moment and everything is revealed. 'Cold …' He tugs the duvet back towards him, causing me to stumble and almost lose hold of it myself. That's when I realize I'm not wearing anything either. Oh my God. How did that happen? I glance down at the floor beside the bed and spot a crumpled towelling robe. I must have got hot in the night and thrown it off. But what am I going to do?

My eyes dart towards the bathroom door. I want to run in there and lock myself in so badly, but how am I going to do that with just one duvet? One way or the other, one of us ends up naked.

Gil rubs his face with his hand and grimaces, yawning widely. He looks at me standing on the opposite side of the bed, the soft white duvet only just covering my dignity, and I see the moment he stops feeling sleepy and starts feeling something else …

How? How am I back here? I didn't even think it was possible to go to sleep inside a dream and then wake up again. Has anyone even done that before?

But whatever the mechanics, the physics or philosophy of dreams are, I don't have time to think about it. I need to get …

Gil doesn't exactly smile, but I can see a glint of naughty humour in his eyes as he gives the duvet another swift tug. It's enough to make me lose my grip, but I dive for the robe on the floor at my feet and a split second later, I'm covered again. 'I'm just … I need to …' I say as I shuffle sideways like a crab, circling the bed, keeping my bare bottom away from his view until I reach the bathroom door and dive inside, locking it behind me.

I use the toilet, because I really need to wee, and then, because I can't think of anything else to do, I take a shower. I spend as long as I can, but then there's a knock on the door. I don't turn the water off so I can hear him better, but I do stop moving.

'Are you okay in there?'

I reach for a towel to cover myself, even though the bolt is firmly drawn on the door. 'Yes!' I squawk.

There's a couple of seconds of silence and then he adds, 'Want company?'

'Um … no!'

I have no idea where he is or what he's doing, whether he's standing there waiting for me to unlock the door, ever hopeful, or whether he's getting dressed somewhere else in the bedroom. I stand motionless until it feels safe to move again, and then I sit down on the closed toilet lid.

What am I going to do? I'm in here and my clothes are on the other side of a locked door. I hear Gil moving around the bedroom and eventually he comes back towards the door and raps on it gently. 'Erin? We've got to go in five minutes, or we'll be late to the airport.'

'The airport?'

'For our flight to St Lucia.'

I look round the walls, but there's no clock in the bathroom. However, the sky beyond the bedroom window is inky black. 'What time do we need to be there?' I ask shakily.

'Ten, and it's a three-hour drive, possibly longer if we get stuck behind a tractor on the A303.'

I cross my arms, tucking my hands into my armpits, and hug

myself. I'd ask whose stupid idea it was to leave for a honeymoon at the crack of dawn, but I think I already know the answer.

'Erin?'

I clear my throat. 'I'll be out in a moment.' I start to panic, but then I realize this could be my salvation. If we've got to leave for the airport in five minutes, there's no time to … you know.

I listen carefully and after a while I can't hear Gil moving in the bedroom any more. I place my fingers on the door bolt and nudge it softly, then turn the handle millimetre by millimetre and crack the door enough to look into the bedroom.

It's empty.

I can hear movement downstairs and then the slam of a car door. I dart out into the bedroom and discover a small case sitting on the bed. I recognize the long soft grey cardigan poking out. It's one of my favourites. I grab for it and find one of my standard travelling outfits underneath: soft cotton jersey trousers and a long-sleeved top, as well as fresh underwear. I grab the lot and scuttle back into the bathroom where I get dressed, glad for the familiar items in the midst of all this chaos.

And then, when I can delay it no longer, I go downstairs and get in the car. I guess I'm off to St Lucia.

CHAPTER TWENTY-THREE

Present Day

I tiptoe past Gil's sleeping form, slide out of the French doors, closing them softly behind me, and emerge onto a terrace with the most amazing view. I've seen Halcyon Cove from the sea before, and watched wistfully as guests were taken away from the yacht on the tender to enjoy a day of beachside luxury at the upmarket resort. I always promised myself I'd visit one day, and even set aside a chunk of my yachting tips in a savings account so the money would be there if ever I got the chance.

The resort is stunning. There are turquoise pools, cabanas, lush gardens, clipped lawns and tall palm trees. Every building is white, but the style is a mix between traditional colonial and ultramodern luxury. Halcyon Cove sits in the shadow of the smaller of the two jutting Piton Mountains that St Lucia is famous for. Near the water, there's a golden curving beach and an endless horizon of blue water, and inland lie sloping hills that lead up into the rainforest. We're reminded of its proximity by the high-pitched, rhythmic calling of frogs wherever we go.

Our cottage perches above the main resort on a steep, wooded hill. It's not the biggest or most expensive villa in the resort, not by a long shot, but it's perfect for a honeymoon couple. Along with a cosy, bright white living room with shutters, a couple of sofas and a desk, there is a bedroom with a four-poster bed and gauzy white curtains and French doors that lead onto a terrace with a small table and chairs and two loungers facing a small private plunge pool.

I sink into the water with a sigh, letting my head rest back against the edge, face the setting sun, and stretch my arms out. I desperately need some downtime to relax.

Being married is exhausting. At least, it is if you're spending every waking moment trying to act the part of the deliriously happy honeymooner without actually having the honeymoon, if you know what I mean?

The only way to cope has been to do what I do best – organize. And I have organized the crap out of this honeymoon. I've impressed even myself with the level of ingenuity and the sheer number of activities I've crammed into the last forty-eight hours.

It was easy enough the first night. I just pulled the old 'I'm too jet-lagged to keep my eyes open' stunt and fell asleep, fully clothed, on the vast sofa in the cottage's living room. I woke in the early hours to find a blanket gently draped over me and Gil sound asleep in the super king-sized bed. It's so huge that it made him look small, all curled on one side with his hand tucked under his cheek. I only know because I crept past him because I was busting for a wee. He looks so harmless when he's asleep. Almost boyish.

Then, since it was 5 a.m., which is mid-morning UK time, I stayed up leafing through the thick folder sitting on the desk in our sitting room. By the time Gil surfaced, I'd booked myself for a spa day, alone – essential pampering after all the stress of the wedding planning – followed by a night for the two of us at the weekly beach barbecue with local entertainment, including limbo dancing, fire eating and a rum tasting session. By the time we got back to the cottage, full of eight different types of rum, neither of us were in any fit state to get all lovey-dovey, so I even risked crashing out on my side of the bed instead of the sofa.

I woke up with Gil spooned around me, so I wriggled myself free and was sitting on our deck when he finally surfaced.

Before he could get any ideas of convincing me to come back to bed, I jumped up, planted a big kiss on his cheek and excitedly told him of the catamaran trip I'd planned for the whole day, including visits to the botanical gardens near Soufrière, bathing in some thermal pools and a tour round an ethically run cocoa plantation. I also checked the excursion was fully booked, so there'd be twenty other people and absolutely no chance of anything inappropriate going on.

Gil had baulked a little when he'd heard my long-ranging plans, but I fixed him with innocent puppy-dog eyes and a soft smile. *St Lucia has always been on my bucket list,* I said. *I've dreamed of visiting each and every one of these destinations.* It was surprising how quickly the usually intractable Gil Sampson crumbled and went along with it all. If I didn't dislike him so much, I'd have thought it was quite sweet.

I also didn't realize I had it in me to be quite so manipulative, but sometimes a girl's gotta do what a girl's gotta do.

Anyway, we got back from the catamaran trip about half an hour ago and Gil crashed out on the bed, face down, and was asleep within minutes. Seems like the sea air really got to him, which is surprising since he lives only a couple of miles away from Simon's parents on the River Dart. All that travelling to big cities to do important, super-secret computer stuff must have turned him soft.

And maybe that's why I'm two days into my honeymoon and Gil has yet to address the fact we haven't, um … consummated our marriage yet. I can see the questions behind his eyes, although he's doing a good job of keeping them hidden. But he hasn't been grouchy, hasn't complained. If anything, he's been horribly understanding. Which only makes it harder to be so mean to him, so I'm a bit cross with him for that.

I'm going to leave him to sleep as long as possible, even though there's a chance we might miss our dinner reservation at the fanciest restaurant in the resort.

I close my eyes and try to relax but it's hard, even though the setting sun is warming my face and the water lapping around me is almost body temperature. But I've never been very good at relaxing, partly because when I manage to slow down and switch off, I often find I get maudlin, and I have no idea what that's about. Other people chill out to feel happy and peaceful. For some reason, it makes me want to cry. I feel the tears like pins and needles in the backs of my eyeballs now … but at least I know why I want to sob.

I've had enough of this, I silently cry to any deity who might be listening. *I want to wake up. I want to go* home!

Yep. Relaxing on my own is definitely a bad idea. Because now I've got time to think about *why* I'm not waking up. And any answers I come up with are not good.

I've considered I might be dead and this is the afterlife. Which means I'm stuck with Gil in hell for eternity, because this certainly can't be heaven.

Or maybe all that quantum physics stuff is right and there are millions upon billions of universes, all with different versions of our lives, and somehow I've fallen through a trapdoor into the wrong one, although how Gil and I could *ever* be a thing, even amid infinite lifetimes, is still beyond me. But at least this answer gives me hope – because if I got into this life, maybe there's a way back. I just have to find it.

I kick my feet idly in the water and roll my memories of the week running up to my wedding in my head, trying to work out when the switch could have happened. Everything was fine the night of the party with all our friends and family. Well, not fine because I had that horrible argument with Gil, but at least it was all *normal*. And then everything seemed fine the in the beginning part of my wedding day, right until I stepped inside the doors of the church.

Somewhere in those fourteen to fifteen hours between leaving the party the night before the wedding to walking down the aisle, something happened to switch everything around. I just need to work out where I was and what I was doing, and then maybe that will give me a clue how to get back.

I let go of the side of the pool and let the water buoy my body up, arms outstretched, eyes closed. It's like being in one of those immersion tanks, I think, apart from the odd tickle of warm breeze across my face and upper torso. I don't fall asleep, but I shift into a different level of consciousness, one where I'm only partly aware of my surroundings, just alert enough to keep my body in the right position to stop it sinking. My thoughts also float free.

I don't know how much later it is, but my equilibrium is disrupted when cool water splashes onto the exposed parts of my skin, then a warm pair of hands circles my waist and pulls me backwards. I end up with my back pressed against Gil's front as he sits on the little ledge at the edge of the pool, his arms tight around me.

I go still. 'What's the time?' I say lightly, although every muscle in my body is taut.

'About half five,' he mumbles against my neck and his voice is still rough with sleep.

'Half five?'

'Uh-huh.'

I push myself away towards the other side of the pool. 'We've got reservations at six.' I try not to look at him as I drag myself out of the water and onto the terrace.

'I thought maybe we could skip it and get room service,' he says as I walk back towards the French doors.

'Don't be silly!' I reply breezily. 'The Lookout is Halcyon Cove's most prestigious restaurant. It's fully booked the rest of the week and the food's supposed to be fabulous. This will be our only chance to do proper fine dining. And, if we're going to make it, I need to start getting ready now.'

CHAPTER TWENTY-FOUR

Present Day

We arrive at The Lookout on the dot of six. The restaurant is on a small hill at the opposite end of the bay to Petit Piton. The exterior looks similar to many of the other hotel build-ings – colonial-style, painted white – but the interior decor is more in keeping with a five-star hotel in any major city. We walk onto a large wooden deck overlooking the bay, filled with elegantly laid tables. The sun hasn't long set, and the sky is orange and yellow, smudged with lavender clouds. I couldn't imagine anything more romantic if I tried. Crap.

As we near the wooden balustrade at the edge of the deck and the waiter pulls a chair out for me, I spot a couple on the next table who are obviously honeymooners, just like we are.

Well, maybe not *just* like we are.

They have their hands interlaced on the tabletop and she pulls one away to feed him a piece of her starter on a slender spoon. They have an aura about them, an energy, but all of it is focused on the other person. It's like the rest of the world doesn't exist.

I look away as I sit down and when I look back up again. I'm staring into Gil's eyes. I know he's seen me watching them, and

I swallow down a lump in my throat. 'I can't wait to see what they've got on the menu, can you?' I say, smiling brightly at him, hoping I am capturing just a little of that buoyant, joyous energy radiating from the table behind him.

'I suppose so.'

'You don't sound very excited. The Lookout isn't just the best restaurant in Halcyon Cove, it's supposed to be one of the best restaurants on the island.'

'Is it? I wouldn't know. You didn't actually let me in on our plans.'

I take the napkin from the table and place it carefully in my lap. 'Is that a problem? I thought it would be a nice surprise.'

Gil makes a sound that is half-grunt, half-laugh. But he doesn't say anything else.

I pick up the menu and peruse the selection of mouth-watering dishes listed. There is steak tartare and caviar, or octopus ceviche with samphire. But I can't choose between the pan-fried scallops and beef carpaccio.

I can feel Gil watching me as I study the menu. What's up with him this evening? And why is he being so touchy that I booked us a nice meal? That I planned something lovely for him? This is who I am. Simon loves the fact that I take charge, that I know what I want, and I go out and get it. He's grateful that I do these little things for him. It just goes to show how unsuited Gil and I are.

We eat our starters in silence. The one downside is that I have a ringside view of the other honeymoon couple, and they're beginning to annoy me. Seriously, it's as if they can't be a molecule apart from each other, even for a single second. I don't know why they didn't just order room service and maul each other back in their cottage or wherever they're staying. Gil turns to see what I'm scowling at, watches them for a few seconds, then turns back. Now he's frowning too.

We both choose the Dover sole as our main course, served with a potato dish I can't even remember the name of and seaweed hollandaise. It's possibly the most delicious thing I've ever eaten. My plate is emptying far too quickly, possibly because conversation isn't slowing us down. At this rate, we'll be in and out of the restaurant in under an hour, which feels like a defeat. However, halfway through his fish, Gil stops, puts his knife and fork down and looks at me.

He's been stewing. I had a feeling he was. He gets a certain expression on his face where you can practically see the cogs in his brain going round, then when he's ready, he spits it all out. I steel myself, expecting the same surly barbs he threw at me in the hotel garden back in Dartmouth the night before the wedding.

'I do like the meal, Erin. And I am pleased you booked the table here, but ...' He sighs. 'Don't take this the wrong way, but marriage is supposed to be a partnership, not one person doing everything, deciding everything for the other. I appreciate the hard work and thought you put into planning this, into everything we've done so far, but you haven't bothered to ask what I would like to do, or where I would like to eat.'

I swallow the morsel of fish I've been chewing and fix him with a blistering stare. 'We've only been married three days and you're saying I'm a bad wife?'

Gil inhales and exhales slowly. I know I am testing his patience. I don't care. He's definitely testing mine. 'No. That's not what I'm saying, Erin. Don't put words into my mouth. It's just …' He closes his eyes briefly, shakes his head, then opens them again. 'I get the feeling you'd be as happy visiting every tourist attraction on St Lucia without me, that it wouldn't matter if I was here or not.'

I stab a bit of samphire with my fork. I'm not going to let him spoil this meal for me. Once I've eaten it, I say, 'Planning is my love language.' If Gil knew anything about me, he would understand that. I know it must be confusing for Gil, but I will not betray Simon just because it would stop Gil feeling bad. I'm sorry, but I won't.

Gil watches the emotions play across my face and his features soften. 'I know that, Erin. But there's something more going on here. Tell me. Tell me what's going on with you.'

He reaches across with his right hand to touch the fingertips of my left and I pull it away so fast that I knock my wineglass over. There's an awkward silence as a waiter rushes over to mop up the liquid, then hurries off to get another glass.

Gil's face is a rigid mask. 'Did you actually just flinch when I touched you?'

'No.' I shake my head, maybe a little too emphatically. We both know I'm lying and that knowledge settles between us like a heavy weight.

'You've been acting weirdly ever since you said "I do".'

'Actually, it's "I will" in England. People always get that wrong—'

Gil pushes himself back from the table slightly, making the silverware clatter. 'You know what, Erin? I really don't care what the wording of the service is. That's not the point.'

'Then what *is* the point?'

He looks at me. I mean, really looks at me. 'The point is,'

he begins smoothly, 'as you rightly say, we're on day three of our honeymoon, but my bride seems to be doing her best to avoid me.' He flicks a glance at the couple behind us, who are lovingly spooning dessert into each other's mouths. 'Not only that, but she can't seem to stand being in the same room as me.'

He says this last bit a little too loudly, which causes the female half of the other couple to stop slurping chocolate mousse off her husband's spoon and turn to give us … well, Gil … a pitying look. I'm suddenly furious with her. And with him.

I roll my eyes. 'Oh, of course … It's about sex. I should have known!'

Gil gives me a withering look. It seems I wasn't quiet with my reply either, as the people at the table on our left all turn their heads. I'd planned on having a nice dinner tonight. I hadn't factored in there'd be a floor show – and that Gil and I might be the headline act.

He catches my gaze and holds it, but this time it's not irritation or frustration I see. He's begging me to understand. 'Of *course* I want to make love with you, Erin. I love you … and it's our honeymoon!'

I swallow and look down at my lap, aware that in most circumstances, this would not be an unrealistic or unreasonable expectation. If I weren't so traumatized by navigating my way through this never-ending nightmare, I might even feel sorry for him. But I can't let myself.

'But it's more than that … isn't it? Something's up. I'm worried about you.'

For some reason, his words bring tears to my eyes. But I don't need him to worry about me. I don't need *anyone* to worry about me. I can take care of myself. I always have. And I don't like him thinking I'm weak. It shores up my resolve to see this thing through. I can't let him win.

'It's just … It's just the aftermath of the wedding, all that stress. I'm fine. We're fine.'

Gil shakes his head slowly. 'No, we're not. You're not. You haven't been right since our wedding day.'

'You've said nothing until now, so it can't have bothered you that much.'

'I've asked you countless times if you're okay.'

I give a one-shouldered shrug, conceding his point.

'I was hoping you'd open up to me. I know the run-up to the wedding was busy and stressful. And I know the day itself wasn't a hundred per cent easy, not with your mum, your brother … And I don't know what's going on with you and Anjali, but I saw her being really cold with you at one point. Have you guys had a fight? Has that got something to do with this?'

My stomach swoops and all the butter my Dover sole was drenched in seems to congeal in my intestines. Gil noticed that? He was paying more attention than I realized. And if he saw that, maybe he also saw …

There's another swoop, stronger this time. What if Gil suspects *everything*?

I look back at him in panic. Is it there? Can I see it in his eyes?

But even if I do, I'm not going to open that can of worms. I can't.

'I'm honestly fine. Me and Anjali … It was … It was a misunderstanding. And you're right – it was *a lot* running up to the wedding.' I laugh, but instead of coming out light and breezy, it sounds as if I've got a fishbone stuck in my throat. 'I'm just … I don't know what I am at the moment. But I'm sure I'll be back to normal again soon.' I smile at Gil, try to replicate what the honeymoon bride behind me has been doing all night with her partner. 'Honestly.'

Gil's jaw hardens. He shakes his head and looks away, and then he raises a hand to catch a waiter's attention and asks for the bill. We haven't even had dessert.

CHAPTER TWENTY-FIVE

Five years ago

It's late when he sees the phone light up with a message notification. Past midnight, in fact. A knot forms in his stomach.

It's her. Again.

He knows he should ignore it, delete it without looking at it. He stares at the screen for a few seconds, his limbs momentarily paralyzed, but eventually he reaches out and picks the phone up from the kitchen counter. His thumbs move and swipe almost without conscious decision, bypassing the heartfelt resolve he is trying to stick to.

Simon? Are you there?

He closes his eyes and inhales deeply. She deserves the truth, but …

The phone dings again.

You haven't replied to any of my messages for almost two weeks. Is something wrong? Are you okay?

And then two more arrive.

I'm not angry.

I'm just worried about you.

Oh, God. He can feel himself weakening. He knows it's the wrong thing to do, but he can't tell her it's all over like this, not through a message. This is a conversation that should be had face to face.

But that isn't possible. She's thousands of miles away.

He presses the phone to his chest, hoping that hiding the bright screen will dampen the twitch in his fingers to reply.

It doesn't work.

He misses her so much. It's like an ache … But he can't tell her that.

Inhaling again, he places the phone face down on the counter and walks to the other side of the kitchen, where he pulls a random mug off the crowded drainer and presses a button on the fancy coffee machine one of his flatmates brought with them to their new shared flat. Who cares about the caffeine? He won't sleep for hours now, anyway.

The phone buzzes. He flinches.

No, he tells himself as he puts his cup down and takes four strides across the kitchen. This is a bad idea.

It doesn't stop him typing, **I'm here.**

He almost hears her sigh of relief as he waits for her reply, which arrives only a second or two later.

Oh, thank God! Are you okay?

He stares at the screen for a moment before replying. He's already in so deep. What's one more lie?

I'm fine.

CHAPTER TWENTY-SIX

Present Day

The resort provides golf buggies to ferry guests up and down the steep hills to the villas and cottages and we ride one back to our love nest in silence. When we pull up, Gil jumps out and strides inside, slamming the door behind him. I smile weakly at the driver, whisper my thanks, and slide from my seat.

I stare at the closed door for a few seconds and then decide to use my key fob to open the side gate and walk around to the deck and pool area at the back. My way is lit by a string of lightbulbs and when I turn the corner, I spot a champagne bucket and two glasses on the table near the railing. Oh, God … Gil must have set this up earlier.

I wince.

Beads of condensation drip down the neck of the champagne. I swallow. After the night I've had, I could really do with a glass. Would it be … would it be bad if I opened it? Or should I wait for Gil?

But if Gil's anything like Simon, he's got to the sulking stage of an argument, which means I won't hear anything more from him until morning. I breathe out in relief. Not the way

I'd planned to ensure my honour stayed intact tonight, but I'll take it. And if Gil is anything like Simon, he'll be ready to gloss over it and move on in the morning, which means we could possibly do the rainforest trip as planned. I was really looking forward to that.

And, yes, I know thinking this way makes me seem like a heartless bitch, but I wouldn't be worrying about riding gondolas through the rain forest if this was my *real* honeymoon. I'd be running inside and doing anything and everything I could to save my marriage. But that's the point, isn't it? This isn't my marriage. It isn't even my real life.

But then I look at how perfect the arrangement is, how romantic, and I weaken. After staring at the bottle for a few seconds, I pull it from the bucket and unwrap the foil. I pop it quietly and pour some into both glasses, then I pick one up and head to the French doors that lead into the bedroom. Gil is sitting on the edge of the bed facing away from me, staring at nothing.

I put the flute down on the console under the window. 'Peace offering,' I say quietly, and he looks up.

I see the moment he remembers the surprise he planned, and I also see the thought behind his eyes. *Idiot,* he tells himself. *What were you thinking?*

I feel a tug of sympathy for him. *Nothing wrong*, I want to answer. Because it wouldn't be, not usually.

I turn and head back to my glass of bubbles, sitting frosty and fizzing on the table outside, slide into one of the chairs and let out a deep sigh. The moonlight carves a broken path on the sea to the horizon and there are almost more stars than sky above me. I'll just sit here, taking it all in, until Gil falls asleep and then I can creep into bed beside him.

I'm almost at the bottom of my glass when I hear a noise. He walks towards me, barefoot, shirt unbuttoned, and places his glass on the table. After topping us both up, he sits down opposite me. He doesn't look as if he's sulking. He doesn't even look pissed off. He just looks … tired. And maybe even a little sad.

There's another tug inside my chest. I do my best to ignore it.

'Sorry,' I say. For what, I'm not exactly sure, but then apologizing for everything and anything when I feel awkward is my MO so it really shouldn't surprise me.

He nods. 'So you're ready to tell me what's going on with you?'

My eyes open wide. No. I certainly am not. But I'm very ready to sweep it all under the carpet. 'I've told you, I'm—'

'I swear, Erin. If you tell me you're fine one more time, I'm going to lose it.'

While he seems calm and still on the outside, I can tell it's because he's holding himself taut, straining to keep everything on the inside. I shiver, even though the night has not yet turned chilly.

Well, he's stolen the only possible response I had. I shake my head and stare into my glass for a long while. When I look up again, Gil is still waiting. It's obvious he's not going to let this drop. I should have known. Gil Sampson is *nothing* like the man I love.

'Don't do this to me,' he says. 'To us.'

'What? What am I doing?'

'This isn't you.'

Well, he's wrong about that. 'Yes, it is. This is me,' I respond. It's everything else in this crazy world that isn't real.

'No,' he says, shaking his head. 'This … this dishonesty.'

I sit up straighter. 'That's a bit strong.'

He blinks slowly, then fixes his eyes on mine. I'm tempted to look away, but I resist the urge. I need to do this; I need to meet him in this moment. 'This isn't how we operate,' he says. 'This isn't how it's been for all these years we've been together, not since Megan …' I'm too distracted by the mention of her name to fully comprehend what he's saying, but then he continues. 'Where's the open, giving Erin who isn't afraid to say what she thinks and feels? The woman who's knows how to be vulnerable, who's not afraid to show every part of herself to me?'

I stare back at him, no words in my mouth, no thoughts in my head. I'd like to know where that woman is, too. In fact, I'd very much like to meet her.

He takes hold of my hand, the way he tried to do at dinner, and there's such intensity in his expression that I don't pull away. It's like I'm held in a tractor beam. 'That's the woman I love. That's the woman I thought I was marrying …'

So *not* me, then. I almost laugh. Somehow, him saying that makes this easier. 'That woman isn't real,' I say softly. 'She's an illusion. A figment of your imagination.' *Just as much as you are of mine,* I add silently. So now we're quits. I feel quite liberated.

He drops my hand, stands up and walks away, running a hand through his hair. He does this a lot when he's stressed, I realize. I've even seen him doing it in real life, on the rare times he's back in the country and the even rarer times he sees Simon and me together rather than just Simon on his own.

Suddenly, he turns and strides towards me. I would get up and back away, but I can't push the chair back from the table fast enough. He crouches down beside my chair and takes my hands. 'Please, Erin. *Please.* Whatever you think you can't tell me, you can. You can trust me.'

I close my eyes and bring my hands up to my temples, digging my fingers into my hairline. My head is swimming. I don't know what to do.

It's the soft touch of the pad of his thumb on the back of my hand that undoes me. I can't tell him everything. He'd never believe me and it would just make him even more upset and angry if he thought I was playing games with him. But maybe I need to be honest about one thing in particular. We clearly can't go on like this.

I open my eyes and look at him. My voice comes out as a scratchy whisper as I nod towards the other chair. 'Sit down.' I can't have him this close.

There's a flash of relief across Gil's face, but then he sobers. I swear he knows I'm about to break his heart.

I take a deep breath and blow it out. My pulse is booming inside my ears. 'You're right. Everything's not fine. Not by a long shot.'

'What is it? Is it—?'

I hold up my hand. 'Please … just let me get this out.' I can hardly make sense of it myself, and I'm never going to manage if Gil interrogates me, picking my story apart. I take a moment to regroup and then I let him have it. 'I think … I think maybe we made a mistake.'

Confusion is written all over his face. 'About …?' He looks around to the trees, to the stars, searching for an answer. 'About our honeymoon? About St Lucia?'

I shake my head. 'About us.'

His lips press together and he frowns. Hard. 'You … You think we made a mistake getting married?'

I nod. I want to cry. I know this isn't real, but in this moment it feels like it. I've never even broken up with someone before – I'm always slavishly loyal until the moment they dump me out of the blue – let alone ended a marriage.

'But we've been together for years. You said this is what you wanted! For months you've done nothing but talk about the wedding and plan, and talk and plan …'

I nod again. I know this must make no sense to him. And there's no way I can rectify that. This whole scenario makes no sense to me either. We're in the same boat.

'And you couldn't have told me this four days ago? Before I stood in the church like an absolute mug waiting for you?'

I look down at the floor. 'No.' It's the truth. I couldn't have.

'Why?' There's a catch in his voice that makes me look up sharply. I've never seen Gil look anything other than unreadable or cocky in real life, but the last few days he's been weirdly nice, acting like a normal human being. Though right now, he looks like I punched a hole in his chest and closed my fist around his heart.

'It's …' I stop to wipe away a tear I feel rolling down my cheek. 'It's complicated.'

I expect that rough, barking, sarcastic laugh of his to erupt out of him, but he just stares at me, completely at a loss. I can't stand to watch him any more, so I push my chair back and walk over to the nearest section of railing overlooking the bay. I don't want him to think I'm walking out on him. I just need some space, some air.

When I glance round a minute later, he's sitting on the chair still, his elbows on his knees, his head in his hands. He must sense me looking, because his head bobs up and he meets my eyes. For a few long heartbeats we just stare at each other and then a change rolls across his features. Realization. Revelation.

My stomach goes cold as his expression hardens.

'It's Simon, isn't it?'

CHAPTER TWENTY-SEVEN

Present Day

'Wh—what makes you say it's got something to do with Simon?' My stomach is properly churning. All those bubbles might not have been such a good idea.

'I saw your face when he kissed Anjali after she caught the bouquet.' Gil's expression is blank now. 'At the time, it didn't sit right with me, but I told myself that maybe you were surprised.'

I nod mutely. It had certainly been a surprise.

'But after what you've just said, I realized there might be another explanation for the complete look of shock and, yes, pain, I saw on your face. I'm right, aren't I?'

My first instinct is to deny it. I hadn't planned to go this far with my revelations. I don't want to hurt Gil like this, even though I've fantasized about crushing his soul a thousand times over. And if it isn't a dream, if I've slipped into this life and this is my future, I can't keep pretending. I need to stop pleasing everybody else and go after what I want. And what I want is Simon. There's no reason we can't be together in this version of my life, too. All I have to do is be brave enough to say what I want and stuff what anyone else thinks.

Easier said than done when you're staring into a pair of eyes that look like dark hollows. My lips have suddenly gone dry and I moisten them before giving my answer. 'Yes,' I say, and it's barely more than a rough whisper. 'You're right.'

Gil's mouth drops open as if he can't really believe what he's hearing, even though he said he knew already, and then I see a pilot light go on inside him, a tiny flame that seems harmless but is only a precursor to a full and raging inferno. My insides begin to quiver. What have I done?

'How long?'

I frown. 'How long what?'

Gil leans forward and practically spits the words at me. 'How long have you been screwing my best friend behind my back?'

Tears roll down my face and I shake my head. 'No … You don't understand! It's not like that …'

He folds his arms. 'Then explain it to me. *Please.*'

This is the Gil I know. Caustic and sarcastic. Able to reduce me to the size of an amoeba just by looking at me. But there's no comfort in this familiarity. I swipe at my face with my hands and sniff back the snot gathering inside my nose. 'I … I can't.'

'Come on, Erin,' he says with faux geniality. 'It's not that hard. Did it start in one of those patches where you were home from yachting, or is it a more recent thing? That's all I need to know.'

I feel like withering away, or dissolving into a puddle and sliding through the gaps in the decking. I close my eyes and try to take a steady breath. I chose this path. I've got to see this through. There's no turning back now.

I open my eyes again. 'You want the truth, Gil?'

He gives a curt nod of his head.

'Well, the truth is that I have *never* betrayed you.'

His eyebrows rise. 'You haven't had sex with him? Not since we've been together.'

'N-no …' I stammer. And it's true. As far as I know, this Erin has never been tempted by Simon since she got together with Gil. 'But I love him.'

There. I've said it. Laid my truth out there. I thought there would be a raw spot left behind where it had been ripped from me, but I feel surprisingly numb, surprisingly light. Maybe that's why more comes pouring out from inside me.

'And I can't lie to you any more, Gil. I thought I could pretend, thought I could make it right, but I can't. And I'm sorry … So sorry.' I bury my face in my hands and sob. When I've got it together enough to speak again, I look up at him. 'And you're right – I shouldn't have gone through with the wedding, no matter how hard it would have been. I should have said something sooner.'

But it appears Gil has no appetite for being right this evening, because he just looks at me as if I'm something he should wipe off the bottom of his shoe and then he turns, walks off the deck and disappears into the night.

CHAPTER TWENTY-EIGHT

Present Day

It's over fourteen hours before I see Gil again. I've practically been wearing a rut in the white painted floorboards of the cottage's living room, pacing backwards and forwards in front of the French doors, waiting for him to return. Just after eleven, I hear the main door slam and I stand up.

Gil is still wearing the same dark trousers and dark shirt he had on last night and he looks as if he got about just as much sleep as I did. None.

I want to ask him where he's been, if he's okay, but I also know the bombshell I dropped last night gives me no right to ask those questions, no right to ask anything of him at all.

He strides past me through the sitting room without looking at me, jams a pod in the machine, and presses a button. When his coffee is ready, he takes it straight outside to the terrace.

Okay. So this is how it's going to be. From enemies to not-quite-lovers to enemies again.

I hover in the doorway. Gil is facing away from me, deliberately, I guess, and I can't blame him. If this were real life and I was in his shoes, I would do the same. No, scratch that. I'm not sure I could be this restrained. If Simon did this to me after our wedding, I think I'd push him over the deck railing.

But Gil has always been like this. One thing that I both admire about him but also irritates me the most is his iron-clad self-control. But I've never really understood it. Where was it that one night when he really needed it? The night of Megan's accident? I've never even seen a chink in his armour since, but maybe that's why. Maybe he feels worse about it than I give him credit for. Maybe he was determined to change, to atone in some way.

The hours tick by. Gil drinks three more cups of coffee, which I want to tell him is probably not good for his nerves, but I daren't open my mouth and he says nothing to me. In fact, he doesn't even look at me. It's excruciating.

Evening closes in, and when it gets to about nine o'clock, my stomach rumbles. I've eaten nothing all day while I've been tiptoeing on eggshells around Gil. The room service menu is on the coffee table, so I pick it up, but it takes me ten minutes to pluck up the courage to venture out onto the deck. Gil is sitting at the little table near the railing, a row of empty miniature glass bottles lined up in front of him. From the order, I'd guess he started off with the whisky and bourbon, went on to tequila, gin and vodka and now has only vermouth left.

I clear my throat. 'Do you … do you want something to eat? I was thinking of ordering room service.' I'm definitely not in the mood to be seen in public, and I doubt he is either.

He turns his head slowly and looks at me for the first time today. 'Fine.'

'What do you want? I was thinking about getting—'

'Whatever. I don't care, Erin. Order whatever you like.'

I flinch at his tone. Usually, I'll rush in if someone is annoyed with me, do or say something to defuse the situation and make things right, but I need to stick to my truth now I've said it, no matter how uncomfortable it is. But that doesn't mean sitting in this fraught atmosphere isn't chipping away at me. I've got to find some way to reach a truce with him, for his sake as well as mine.

'I never wanted to hurt you,' I say with a lump in my throat. 'But I can't help what I feel.'

He shoots me a savage look. 'For Simon.'

I bite my lip and nod.

'I hope the irony's not lost on you – that those are the exact words I said to you the night we got together.'

Of course, I have no memory of this so I just keep quiet.

He shakes his head, his mouth twisting into a harsh smile. 'I can't believe what an idiot I was. Even though you'd been broken up with Simon for months, I held off telling you how I felt out of loyalty to him. Misguided loyalty, as it turns out.'

I look down at the menu in my hands. 'You're not an idiot, Gil.'

'Yes, I am. For believing you were who I thought you were. For trusting you. With all of …' He trails off, unwilling to expose himself that much. 'What I can't understand is why wait until now to say anything? Why not last month or last week or even when you reached the top of the aisle and you saw Simon and me standing there together? Why couldn't you have made your decision then?'

I feel a deep sense of shame. Even though he doesn't know what I know, he's right. I *could* have said something a lot sooner, but I was being typical Erin, going along with what everybody else wants, not making any waves, thinking I could sort it all out on my own. 'I'm sorry,' I mumble again. Because that's all I can say.

'And you know what the real cherry on top is?' Gil unscrews the lid on the vermouth, knocks it back in one go, and grimaces.

'There are no seats on any flights out of here for the next three days, at least.'

I blink. He's leaving?

Well of course he wants to leave. Isn't that what I've wanted all along too? I've just been so focused on waking up that it didn't enter my head that I could have bought a ticket and flown out of this awkward situation. He must be really desperate to see the back of me if he's willing to stump up for a last-minute fare back across the Atlantic.

'No flights at all?'

Gil screws the lid back on the bottle and lines it up with the rest. 'Oh, there are flights, but they are all rammed full. Something to do with a storm or hurricane to the north-east of Guadeloupe yesterday, meaning there's a lot of people wanting to head back to Europe whose flights were cancelled and every available standby seat is spoken for five times over.'

'I had no idea …' I suppose we've been in our honeymoon bubble, even if it hasn't been much of a honeymoon.

'So we're stuck here …'

With each other, I add silently.

He closes his eyes, and I can tell the same images are flashing through his head that are through mine – us cooped up together in this cottage, studiously avoiding each other, trying to be civil when civil is the last thing we feel.

And then I have an idea.

'Look … I understand that you'd be on a plane in the next

forty seconds if you could, that you can't stand the sight of me at the moment. But it's going to be days until we can get out of here and I've got all these activities planned—'

'Are you kidding me, Erin? Seriously?' He stands up, pushing the chair back from the table with a clatter. 'You've just taken a torpedo to our marriage and you want to do couples massages or go walking through the rain forest hand in hand, playing the part of the perfect happy honeymooners?'

He's looking at me as if he'd like to blister my skin with the heat of his stare, and I can't help it. Gil being oh-so-superior and oh-so-right flips all my trigger switches. It always has. Any sympathy I have for him is drowned out by the voices of a thousand old resentments. 'I know this sounds bonkers, but hear me out before you bite my head off!'

He gives me this supercilious look and waves his hand as if he's actually giving me permission. I'm tempted to … to … I don't know what I'm tempted to do, but it's going to involve blood and pain. And possibly a fall from a great height.

I remind myself that I am the bigger person. Always. I will not let him make me lose my cool. I take a moment and centre myself before starting again, even though my jaw muscles are so tight I can hardly move my mouth to speak. 'I'm not saying we do things *together*. I'm suggesting we split the activities. Like, I'll do the massage and you can do the zip lining, for example.'

Gil stops looking quite so smug. 'That's not a bad idea.'

If I weren't so shocked he's given me credit for something, that he's actually agreeing with me, I might feel pleased with myself. I decide to press my advantage, knowing that this plan is the only way either of us is going to survive the rest of our honeymoon with our sanity intact.

'This way, we won't be pacing around in this atmosphere of fire and brimstone for the next few days. And then you can get an early flight out, I'll get the one we booked home, and we never have to see each other again if we don't want to.'

Gil's expression had become thoughtful instead of haughty, but now it hardens again. I've gone too far, I realize. And I was so close to brokering a fragile truce as well. I shouldn't have said that last bit, reminding him of our impending divorce … or annulment … or whatever the heck it'll be.

'What do you think?'

'I agree.'

'About me doing the massage and you doing the zip lining? Because we can switch if you want?'

'To never having to see you again for the rest of my life.' The way he delivers it, so seriously, without any of the evil sarcastic humour he usually employs, is an unexpected stab to my heart. I know Gil and I have always squabbled, but no one has ever despised me this thoroughly. And then he twists the knife once more, echoing my own words back to me. 'If I don't want to.'

'I'm going to bed,' I say, with the most dignity I can muster.

I take long strides towards the bedroom door, but Gil is too quick for me. He gets there first and stands in my way. 'Not so fast …'

He takes a couple of pillows off the bed and throws them at me. 'I'm sleeping in here …' He nods in the direction of the living room. 'Since you're so desperate to get away from me, you can take the sofa.'

CHAPTER TWENTY-NINE

Five years ago

There's a break between charters. Most of her American crew mates have taken the rare opportunity to go home for Thanksgiving, so it's quiet on board, which isn't a bad thing. She's realized she needs time and space to think – about Simon, but also about what happened this past summer.

The dreams are back. The ones where she's running through a house, one that starts off fairly normally but spawns new rooms at an alarming rate, each with a different decor and cast of characters. A party is in full swing, bodies everywhere, and she can't seem to push through them fast enough, or open the right door to find her friend, even though she can hear her screaming.

And then the screaming turns to whimpering, and then the whimpering stops.

That's when she wakes up gasping, her heart a piston in her chest.

There's a knock on her cabin door. The South African deck-hand nudges it open, wanting to know if she wants to go out to a club with them, but she shakes her head, even though it's Saturday night and she should be out there living her life, enjoying herself, seeing new towns and enjoying a different country. That's why she started yachting in the first place, wasn't it?

But that was before the accident. She feels as if she's had too much life since then, even though she's only twenty-three.

She eyes the phone on the shelf beside her bunk that serves as a nightstand. What she really wants to do is talk to Simon. Somehow, he always makes everything seem better. And she suspects he might be struggling too. It's probably why he's been quiet. He might not want to burden her.

She had a patch like that herself over the summer, just before she started the winter season. She felt numb. She'd cried enough, she thought. Talked enough. But now it turns out that maybe she didn't because the nightmares just won't stop.

She picks the phone up and pulls up Simon's number from 'recents'. She just wants to hear his voice, especially since they've been back in contact for the last couple of weeks. His messages have been short and monosyllabic, but she supposes that's better than nothing.

However, the phone rings and rings. She sighs and sinks back down onto the mattress, then taps out a message:

Can we talk? It's important.

Not always the best way to get Simon engaged. Sometimes he shies away from serious things, but she has a gut feeling he needs this as much as she does.

Much to her surprise, a message pings back a few moments later.

Important? How?

How does she say this ...?

> Can I call? It's too complicated to type.

A minute goes by and then he replies.

> Signal not great here – and it's expensive for you. Better to stick to messages.

He has a point here, though at this moment, she is tempted to empty her bank account just to hear his voice. The boat's Wi-Fi can be patchy out at sea, but it's usually okay in port.

> Are you okay?

It takes her by surprise. She's been so busy checking in on him, making sure he's doing okay without her, that being on the receiving end of the question stops her in her tracks. If it was anyone else, she'd put on a good front, bluster it out, but this is him. The very man she might be about to fall in love with.

> Not really.

> Why? Horrible charter guests?

She sighs. The guests are fine. The work is fine, if demanding. Truly. It's the one thing in her life that's going okay. But she doesn't want to waste time and energy typing all of that in, so she gets straight to the point.

> I can't stop thinking about the night of the party.

She waits, her pulse a steady beat in her ears.

Oh.

A breath leaves her body and she deflates along with it. She knows he finds this difficult.

It was different in the early days after Megan's accident. It seemed all they did was talk about it. Simon was a mess, maybe even more so than her and Gil, and she came to realize he was much more sensitive than she'd given him credit for. People loved Simon. He was funny and charming, seemed to have the world at his fingertips, and gave the impression that he had it all together, that he knew what life was about. Secretly, she'd thought he was a bit of a show-off, but then the accident had happened, tearing her faulty first impression of him to shreds.

And it was talking through the night, pulling together in the aftermath of what had happened, that had forged a deep friendship between them, a friendship that had slowly turned into something more. A relationship that *might* have become really serious if she hadn't moved thousands of miles away at the crucial moment.

She stares at his non-committal answer on her phone screen and tries to work out whether she should push it or let him off the hook. A few months after the accident, there was a shift in Simon. It was as if the door to a place inside him that had opened started slowly closing. Pretty soon he batted the subject away if she raised it, a pained look in his eyes. *We need to move on*, he said. And he was right. Of course he was. No matter what happened to Megan, they still had their futures to think of. Time wouldn't stand still, even if it felt unfair that it didn't.

But what if moving forward is becoming more and more impossible? What if you feel you are being dragged back into the past, like seaweed wrapping itself around your legs and dragging you under? You can't ignore it. You have to cut through it to break yourself free.

Stuff it. She decides it's now or never. Her fingers fly over the keyboard.

I keep having dreams about her. Megan.

She dreads another monosyllabic reply but sighs with relief as, after a minute or so, his message lands.

It was a traumatic experience to lose someone like that. It's not surprising your subconscious is trying to process it.

Thank you! That's exactly what it feels like.

She just hasn't been able to find the words to describe it until now. **I feel so guilty** she types.

She closes her eyes. It feels good to admit this rather than run from it, rather than attempting to bury it in new experiences, professional achievements and a shining, fake smile.

We all do. We ALL feel responsible.

She nods, even though he can't see her. It feels nice to not be so alone.

But it doesn't mean we ARE responsible he adds.

I know. But I can't stop wondering. What if I'd done something different? What if I'd gone to search for her earlier, or turned left instead of right when I came out of the front door?

It's not useful to think that way he counters, which is more the response she'd expected when she brought the subject up.

She knows she shouldn't push him too hard, but she can't seem to stop herself. There's something inside clawing at her, desperately trying to find a way out. She's scared it'll tear her to shreds if she doesn't find some way to release it.

But I can't stop it running through my head. Even when I'm asleep.

Three dots keep appearing on his side of the message thread. She knows he's trying to work out what to say, so before he can come up with a good and logical reason, she ploughs on.

I know it sounds counter-intuitive, but I have this feeling that if I could just pick through it all, go over what happened that night bit by bit, I might be able to let it go once and for all.

There's no reply for a while. He stops typing or deleting. Either he's given up and put his phone down or he's paying really careful attention.

My memory is patchy, obviously. Two beers and way too much vodka to thank for that. If I could just fill in the gaps …

She can hear the warning tone in his voice when his reply comes.

Erin ...

Please, Simon. I'm lonely and I'm homesick and I'm grieving in a strange country thousands of miles away from home. Please help me. I need to talk it through with someone who understands, someone who was THERE.

Minutes pass. One, then two. Then ten.

She curls up on her bed in the dark, too sad to cry. She has no idea why this feels so devastating, but it does.

And then, just as her mind starts to drift between consciousness and dreams, her phone buzzes and lights up one last time.

Okay. Maybe you're right. Talk to me.

CHAPTER THIRTY

Present Day

I arrive at the wooden dock approximately ten minutes before the boat is due to leave. It's bigger than I expect. I'd pictured a speedboat, similar to the tenders we had on the yacht that could hold maybe ten people, but this is a sleek fifty-footer with two decks.

It's my turn to go on the excursion today, and I'm really looking forward to snorkelling. It's about time I got to do something with a little exercise attached. In the last two days, Gil has been zip lining and on a hike to the top of the smaller of the two Piton mountains. I ended up doing a tour round a chocolate plantation yesterday, complete with tastings and spiced rum hot chocolate. It seemed like the perfect way to soothe my misery, but I felt queasy afterwards.

And then last night I went on the sunset and champagne cruise. I thought it would be relaxing, but it turned out to be quite depressing. The rest of the boat was filled with canoodling couples and I stood out like a sore thumb. Even though it was already dusk, I jammed my sunglasses on, then spent the entire trip crying behind them. It was something I'd earmarked to do with Simon when we went on our honeymoon. In that moment, I missed him so much it felt as if someone had carved a hole in my chest.

And I scared myself. When I tried to picture him, his face wouldn't come fully into focus, as if he was the dream, not the real person. And then I got back to the cottage where Gil was hogging the living room, watching some obscure movie and chowing down on room service, and I just got incredibly irritated with him for sitting there, invading what should be *my* honeymoon with his angular, unblurred features, and his giant feet up on the coffee table.

A handful of people are already bagging seats on the top deck of the boat, and another fifteen or so are waiting to go across the gangplank onto the swim platform at the back.

Once I'm on board, I breathe out. Just being on the water again soothes my frazzled nerves. I want to take in as much of the scenery as possible, so I head up top. Thankfully, the upper deck has a hard white canopy, which means I won't be getting sunburnt. I'm just squeezing past a few people, heading for the perfect spot, when I stop and do a double take.

Gil?

He spots me glaring at him and stares back at me, mirroring my confusion.

'What are you doing here?' we both stay at the same time, and then in unison we answer, 'Because it's my turn.' There are a couple of heartbeats of silence while we stare at each other. 'Erin …' Gil begins, as I say, 'Stop doing that!'

I feel as if I'm at a disadvantage standing up, so I plonk myself down in the seat opposite. I don't want him to think that I'm going to leave.

'I thought you were going on the shopping trip to Castries,' he says to me, his voice monotone.

I shake my head and sigh. It really is like being married. He hasn't been paying attention to anything I've told him in the last twenty-four hours, which is kind of impressive, seeing as we've only exchanged a handful of sentences. It's not like the details could have got drowned out in the sheer volume of conversation.

'No ... I said I *didn't* want to go on the shopping trip. I said I wanted to do the snorkelling.'

Gil folds his arms and hooks one foot on top of his other knee. 'So did I.'

I make a show of getting myself more comfortable on the hard plastic seat. 'I'm not going anywhere.'

His gaze is almost nonchalant, but I can hear the grit in his tone. 'Fine.'

Here we are then. Stalemate. Yet again.

I mean, I get it. He thinks I'm being a total bitch, and I suppose he has a right to. I dumped him on his honeymoon. But he doesn't understand. I want to get up and shake him by the shoulders, tell him it's not real – *he's* not real – so can he please just get over himself and let me have this?

Gil uncrosses his leg. He's wearing board shorts and a linen shirt, unbuttoned. I'm trying very hard not to look at the toned muscle between where the two edges don't meet. Instead, I tilt my head and stare at him until he looks back at me.

'What?'

'There is a snorkelling trip at this time every day,' I tell him. 'You could come tomorrow if you wanted to.'

He shakes his head. 'Be my guest. This time tomorrow, I'm hoping to be up there ...' His head jerks towards the vast blue sky above us. 'Sitting comfortably in an aeroplane seat and on my way back to the grey and drizzle of London. You go tomorrow, if you want to.'

I start to state my case, I'm interrupted by the rumble of the engine and jolt as the boat pulls away from the jetty. It seems our argument has been settled for us.

And now the boat is so full, that I have no option but to sit opposite Gil for the whole of the forty-minute journey to the first snorkelling spot. I can feel my blood pressure rising with every nautical mile.

In the end, I decide I'd rather stand, so I head to the stern and stare out at the wake created by the boat's propellers. The water settles within a hundred metres and the memory of the boat that tore through it becomes forgotten and untraceable.

The thought makes me shiver, even though the Caribbean sun is warm on my skin. What if that's me? What if I've spent too long in this ... 'in-between' place now? What if, even if I try to go back to my waking life, it's not possible because the link has been severed? Will I just fade away, forgotten, like the churning waves?

My mood isn't helped when I look away towards the front of the boat and see a girl in a string bikini strolling over to Gil. She sits down in my empty seat and begins to chat with him. He doesn't perk up or lean forward, but he does talk back to her.

Urgh. I look away in disgust.

CHAPTER THIRTY-ONE

Present Day

I float face down in the clear blue water. The only sound is my breath rasping in and out of my snorkel. Below me, the ocean floor is maybe five or six metres away. The volcanic rock is covered in coral of all shapes and colours: multi-coloured tubes, delicate black feathery fans, bright orange baubles clustered together in their hundreds.

And the sea life …

Vast shoals of tiny silver fish glitter like shards of sunlight as they dart this way and that, sometimes engulfing me, sometimes shooting away if I move too quickly. I can see round fish – angel fish, I think – with stripes and spots, and silvery snapper with long yellow stripes. Now and then I see a flash of sapphire, which may or may not be a blue tang, but it never stays still long enough for me to work out if it matches the picture on the 'Sea Life in the Caribbean' leaflet that I picked up from the hotel reception.

I push myself through the water with a lazy breaststroke, taking myself further away from the boat but not far enough that I can't see it if I lift my head out of the water and look behind me, which I do every few minutes, just to make sure I can still see it anchored a short distance away.

I stop swimming, allowing myself to float. The water is so close to body temperature that it's almost as if it isn't there, as if I'm suspended weightless above this surreal landscape. Almost as if I'm flying.

This is the first time in days I've felt like myself, that I've felt even remotely relaxed. I wish I could stay here all day. Possibly for the rest of my life.

The gentle waves nudge me along bit by bit. I let them take me where they want. We've got a whole hour here, and last time I checked my activity tracker, we still had twenty minutes left.

I'm just about to turn back towards the boat when I spot a creamy pink shell on a sliver of white sand between two large rock formations. A conch. And it looks as if it might be empty.

It would be wrong to take it home with me, but I'd like to have a closer look. I fill my lungs, then dive. The gap is narrow and as I swim down between the rocks, a surprisingly strong current tugs at me. I know I need to be careful here.

I'm within a body length when I feel a telltale prickling in my lungs. Frustrated, I do a one-eighty in the water and kick back towards the surface, where I gulp in a few mouthfuls of air before diving back down, putting all my effort into reaching the shell this time.

It's no good. I time it wrong and end up fighting the current as it's pushing back against me. I run out of breath even more quickly than the previous attempt and have to return to the surface. I give my body a moment to calm before diving again. This time, I wait at the entrance to the short rocky ravine until the current turns and pulls the other way, allowing it to propel me towards my prize rather than push me away from it.

My fingers touch the shell as I get close to the point of no return, but it's heavy and so smooth that I can't get a grip on it. I glance back at the surface to judge how far away it is, then swim another stroke closer. Both my hands close around the conch. I twist it around to check I'm correct about it being empty, then push back towards the surface, dragging it with me. I'll return it to its resting place shortly.

Once I've blown the air out of my snorkel and grabbed some oxygen, I float, mask submerged, and run my fingertips over the hard, silky surface, delving into the opening, marvelling at the soft pink colour. I'm just about to turn it over to examine the nobbles, spikes and ridges on the exterior when something tugs at my foot.

I scream and drop the shell.

Our snorkelling instructor had said it was unlikely there were sharks in this area, but he hadn't been able to rule it out completely.

Trying not to panic, I pull my face from the water and bring my legs under me to tread water, hoping I'm not about to be up close and personal with a pointy white face with several rows of teeth and two soulless black eyes.

I'm almost right. But only because Gil has just the one row of teeth.

'You made me drop my shell!' I say, but I forget that I have a snorkel in my mouth, and it just comes out as unintelligible babbling. I hook the mouthpiece out with my fingers and try again.

He looks back at me, bemused, then shakes his head, dismissing that piece of information entirely. 'Erin, I—'

'It might not matter to you, but it matters to me!' And without waiting to listen to his muffled shouting, I jam my snorkel back into my mouth and dive back below the waves. Whatever Gil has to say can wait.

I spot the shell on a rocky ledge below me and head for it, but I'm overtaken by another figure shooting past me, streamlined like a seal, and just before I get my hands on the conch shell, he scoops it up, practically snatching it from my grasp, then pushes off the rock with his feet and heads upwards. Hardly able to believe his audacity, I make a flurry of frustrated little bubbles, then follow him back to the surface.

When my head breaks the water, I rip my mouthpiece out and start talking, even as I'm spinning around trying to pinpoint exactly where he is. 'What toxic little game are you playing now?'

He frowns at me. 'You wanted the shell ... so I was getting you the shell.'

'I'm quite capable of doing that myself, thank you very much!'

He shoves it in my direction, and I grab for it, almost dropping it a second time before pulling it to my chest. 'You're welcome,' he adds, with that all-too-familiar sarcastic tone of his.

I glare at him. If he thinks I'm going to thank him, he's got another think coming. It was his fault I dropped it in the first place. I do my best to ignore the little voice in my head telling me that if it had been anyone else who'd done that, I'd be thanking them, not tearing strips off them. But I don't want to listen to it.

'I'm surprised you found the time to come and dive for shells, anyway,' I say. 'I thought you were too caught up with your "little friend".'

Gil looks back at me as if he has no idea what I'm talking about.

'In the bikini,' I remind him sweetly.

Gil's gaze doesn't waver. 'Really?'

'Really *what*?'

He pushes his wet hair out of his eyes. 'You think I'd do that? On our honeymoon? Just to get revenge or something?'

He has a point. Even though I've never particularly liked Gil, now I think about it, I'm not sure he would stoop that low to score a point over me.

'I don't know why I bother,' he says, pushing backwards in the water but still facing me. 'I only came to tell you we're moving on to the next snorkelling spot in a few minutes. You've drifted quite a way from the boat.'

I quickly check the coastline and realize he's right. It's a complete rookie mistake and I should know better. We're floating closer to the rocky headland than we were earlier. I am grateful that he came to find me. If I were him, I probably wouldn't have bothered.

I don't know why I react to him the way I do. I'm like a puffer fish, inflating hard, poking out my spines every time he's close, and especially if I sense any hint of judgement or displeasure in him.

I have no sensible response for him, and if we're going to be leaving this spot soon, I need to put the shell back where it belongs. When I dip my face in the water, I can't see the two rock formations I found it in any longer – we must have drifted while we were arguing – so I pick the nearest patch of suitable sand and deliver it there.

I'm surprised to see Gil's legs treading water as I near the surface on my return. I hadn't expected him to wait for me, but then I see he's cleaning his mask before we swim back to the boat, and realize maybe he didn't.

I look past his head, scanning the waves between us and the beach, and then, frowning harder, I spin in a slow circle, my eyes searching the horizon. When I come face to face with him again, my stomach feels as if someone just dropped a lead weight inside it.

'Gil …' I croak, hardly able to get his name out.

He looks warily at me. 'What?'

'Where's the boat?'

CHAPTER THIRTY-TWO

Present Day

Gil twists to look behind him, then paddles frantically to check the opposite direction. 'What …? Where …?' He turns back to face me, eyes wide. I've never seen Gil scared before, not even on that horrible night, and my heart pounds even harder.

He treads water in a circle. 'It can't have just …'

But I think it has. It's just that neither of us wants to say it. The boat is gone. It's nowhere to be seen.

Gil swears creatively and at length, describing just what kind of idiots the boat captain, the tour organizers and anyone on St Lucia involved in the planning and execution of this snorkelling adventure are. And then he turns to look at me.

'You just couldn't help yourself, could you?'

My arms stop moving while my legs kick underneath me. 'What?'

He fixes me with one of his intense and uncomfortable stares. 'Super-independent Erin … Can't possibly stay with the group and snorkel. You have to go off on your own …'

'You are *not* turning this around on me! I could still see the boat. I kept checking regularly, and even if you're right, they should have done a head count before they left. Standard procedure. It's not my fault the boat left without us.'

Gil says nothing, but the fire leaves his eyes. I suspect he knows I'm right.

But then I have another thought … I pause as a larger wave rolls past us and close my mouth so it doesn't end up full of salt water before carrying on. 'Someone has to realize we're missing, don't they? Even if it's your friend in the white bikini!'

'I told you … She's not—'

'Okay. Whatever. The *girl* in the white bikini. Better?'

Gil gives a grudging nod and then we both turn and look in the direction the boat came from to deposit us at this location, even though neither of us is sure that's the way it departed.

'So we just need to stay here,' I say, a tiny bubble of hope inflating inside my chest. 'We need to stay by the reef so they'll know where to find us.'

Gil glances towards the shore, which is visible but quite some distance away. 'I'd guess it's about a mile back to the beach. And we have no way of knowing if the tide is working with us or against us, or if there are currents that will tire us out before we get there.'

Oh. So while I've been trying to think positive thoughts to stop myself from panicking, Gil has calmly been calculating how likely our deaths are. How on brand of him. I feel a surge of whatever feisty flight or fight reaction he's been having, which is quickly followed by a barrage of thoughts, all containing pieces of information I now wish I didn't know from my yachting days – like the biggest part of us someone on a boat will be able to see is our heads, which are roughly the size of a cabbage, and surprisingly difficult to pinpoint amid the undulation of even relatively calm seas.

We tread water an arm's length away from each other in silence for what seems like an hour, but what my waterproof fitness tracker actually confirms is ten minutes. And then we do it for another ten. And then another. The tiny balloon of hope in my chest begins to leak air.

'They'll have to do another head count when they leave the next snorkelling spot,' I shout at Gil over the waves. 'They could catch their mistake then!'

'Maybe,' Gil yells back, and I can tell he's thinking what I'm thinking – the likelihood of them making the same mistake twice is high.

My balloon of hope deflates completely and it makes my limbs feel heavy. I'm tired … and while I'm not a bad swimmer, I know we're going to need the endurance of Channel swimmers to give ourselves a chance. I've seen movies where this happens to people and those films never, ever have a happy ending.

The message to panic finally works its way from my brain to my extremities and I suddenly lose all coordination. Instead of bobbing in the water beside Gil, my head disappears under the waves. The shock of the water on my face causes me to scrabble my way back to the surface, and I arrive coughing and spluttering, spitting out seawater. I grab for Gil and pull myself to him, not caring if I'm pulling him under in an attempt to anchor myself onto something warm and solid. And floating.

He manages to avoid a complete dunking, but he swallows almost as much salt water as I have. 'Erin!' he says in a loud, firm voice, after spitting it out.

It's no good. I hear my name, but the word makes no sense

to me. It doesn't stop me clawing at him like he's a life raft, or one of those inflatable crocodiles that seem to be for sale at every beach shop the world over.

'Erin!' He's shouting now and using his superior strength to prise my hands from him and clasps my wrists together in his hands. 'Get yourself under control or we're both going to drown!'

The word 'drown' slices through my panic like a knife, cutting me off from it momentarily. I process what he's said and realize he's right. I've got to pull myself together.

He lets go of me, and even though all I want to do is cling on to him, I manage to keep my hands to myself. I stare at him, teeth chattering, even though the surrounding water is pleasant enough to qualify as a lukewarm bath. 'What ... what are we going to do?'

Gil nudges himself towards me, and this time his hands slide around my waist. 'Do you want me to be honest?'

I'm not sure I do, but I know I need him to be, so I nod.

He looks at me for a few seconds. 'I don't know what to do, Erin. I don't know how to get out of this by ourselves, but I know one thing ...'

He must see my eyes dart all over the place as I take in the distant mountains, the uncompromising horizon, the billions upon millions of gallons of water we're floating in. My pulse, which has only just slowed down, begins to skip again.

Gil moves his hands to my face, cupping my jaw to make me look at him. My hands come to rest on his shoulders, gripping him for support but calmly this time. Our legs kick in unison.

'I will do anything and everything to make sure you get through this.'

You. He said 'you'. Not 'we'. And I suddenly realize what he means and just how far he will go to make good on that promise, because a promise it was.

Once upon a time, I'd have remembered his history, I'd have remembered what happened five years ago, and I'd have scoffed at his words, flung them back at him with sarcasm probably, but I don't do that now. Because I believe him. With every fibre of my being, I believe Gil would die here on this reef to make sure I survive.

CHAPTER THIRTY-THREE

Five years ago

It's been a few days since he said he'd talk through the night of the accident with her, but neither of them has brought the subject up since. She thought she'd dive right in when she got the go-ahead, but every time she picks up her phone she has a wobble and puts it down again.

Stop being such a coward, Erin. This is what you wanted, remember?

She grabs her phone, types and presses send before she can second-guess herself.

What's the first thing you remember about that night, about getting to the party?

It's not a hard question, but it takes Simon a heck of a long time to answer. They'd exchanged a few inane 'how are you doing?' messages about twenty minutes ago. Maybe he's got busy since then?

How you looked amazing in that dress.

She blushes and smiles. She hadn't known Simon that long when the accident had happened. She'd been home from the Caribbean, considering whether she should just fly down to the Med and see if she could get some work there, when Megan had suggested she stay with her for a couple of weeks so that they could catch up and have some fun. Megan hadn't been her closest friend at uni, but Erin had liked her 'take no prisoners' attitude. She'd been as shy as Meg was outgoing, so when her friend had dragged her along to social events on campus, she'd been secretly pleased. She'd made new friends, met new people that she wouldn't have otherwise. And last summer it had seemed Megan was still making sure her friend lived life to the fullest.

That's when she'd met Simon and Gil. Meg's brother knew Gil from work or something, and Meg had been floating on the edges of their friendship group for a couple of months. After that first meeting in the bar, she and Meg had hung around with them a few times over the space of a fortnight. And then someone Simon had a tentative connection with through his rugby team had invited him to a house party and he'd suggested they all go along as a foursome.

I think I was already quite tipsy when I got there she replies.

She and Megan had done a little pre-drinking before they'd arrived at the three-storey house in Fulham. The host's parents were away in the Seychelles, and he'd decided to make the most of it.

I wish I remembered what I thought when I first saw you that night.

Truthfully, she hadn't really thought that much about Simon before that night. He'd just been that good-looking, rather too-charming-for-his-own-good mate of Meg's. How things had changed by the end of the night.

What did we do first? she types.

The beginning of the party was always a bit of a blur to her. Later, they'd all sobered up pretty fast. Some of those crystal-clear memories were the ones haunting her sleep.

It's a bit of a blur to me too he admits. **I remember roaming from room to room, talking to different groups, laughing, listening to music. No single conversation stands out to me.**

The words stop for a few moments, and she senses he is wracking his memory for useful details.

I remember you telling me to not let you drink too much, because you had to go to Sunday lunch with your mum the next day.

She smiles. **You laughed at me.**

Did I? I don't remember doing

He doesn't finish his sentence, and the dots that indicate he's typing disappear. She worries someone's interrupted him, that he's been called away and they won't get to finish their conversation.

But then he's back.

Oh, yes. I suppose I did. I told you it was a bit late for that. You also ordered us to keep an eye on how much Megan drank, because she was what you called a 'runner'.

A chill goes through her. She doesn't remember saying that, but it proved to be scarily prophetic. She'd known Meg long enough at that point to know that, when hammered, she tended to dart off and disappear, especially if she was extremely excited or if she was feeling upset or angry.

She skates lightly round the subject, not wanting to get to the dark part just yet.

I just didn't want to be chasing her around all night.

She'd been selfish, wanting to enjoy herself before going back to a job where she served the drinks while watching everyone else have fun, instead of babysitting Megan. And she'd regret that decision now for the rest of her life.

Were we in the kitchen when we had that conversation?
she asks.

Yes.

Smudged images float into her brain – leaning against the large oak table while Meg tried to climb into the butler sink to see if she'd fit. She had, of course. At five foot nothing and only six stone, she'd easily folded her slender limbs and slid in. It was getting her out again that had been the problem.

The next thing I remember is talking to Gil in the hallway. We had some deep, in-depth conversation about I don't know what.

She remembers him towering over her slightly, but not in a scary way, just so they could hear each other over the thumping of the music that must have kept half of Fulham awake.

It was about growing up as only children. How you mature faster, how lonely it can be.

She frowns.

It's as if he's reading her mind when another hurried message appears.

He told me afterwards.

Nodding to herself, she replies, **And where were you?**

Megan had flitted off, as she often did, but Simon had been absent for a while too.

She imagines he's scouring his brain, trying to remember. When he replies, three messages come swiftly, one after the other.

I don't know ...

I wish I did.

Seems there are holes in my knowledge of that night too.

Well, she could hardly blame him for that.

What I remember next is the game he adds.

Ah, she thinks, the muscles at her temples tightening. The game. That was the part of the night she would never forget.

CHAPTER THIRTY-FOUR

Present Day

My legs are so tired that I'm sure they have gone completely numb. Even so, I manage to keep moving them, to keep myself afloat, because what else can I do? I stopped looking at the time because it's only making me more panicked, but the last time I checked, we'd been stranded in the water for about an hour. I think it might be closer to two now. We're guessing the boat moved into the bay to the south. I can't tear my eyes from the headland where it must have disappeared, even though I know it makes no difference in terms of whether a craft will appear.

My shoulders are tense, my hair plastered around my face, and I'm sure my cheeks and forehead must be burning. It was at least four hours ago that I put some sunscreen on. If we get out of this alive, I'm going to look like a scorched flamingo.

'Just keep your breathing even,' Gil says. 'Keep moving gently.'

Normally, Gil telling me what to do would get on my last nerve, but I know I need to hear these softly spoken words. Every few minutes, he has something helpful or encouraging to say and it helps me keep on top of my panic.

But when Gil eventually also falls silent, a heaviness descends on both of us. I know this is not good.

Gil is staring at the headland too, and I turn to him. I mean to say something encouraging back to him, but I say, 'I can't die today. I can't do that to my parents, especially my mum. She's already lost one child. I can't be careless enough to let her lose two.' Tears well in my eyes. 'You were right, Gil. I shouldn't have swum away from the group. It's all my fault!'

Gil gives me one of his slow and steady looks. 'Erin, this is not your fault. Yes, you drifted slightly away from the group, but I shouldn't have said what I did when I blamed you. I was just frustrated ... and scared.' He looks thoughtful. 'How do you do that, anyway?'

'Do what?'

'Worry about everyone but yourself when you're probably in the most dangerous situation you've ever experienced in your life?'

I blink the sea water out of my eyes.

'It's what you always do. It's one of the things that always amazes me about you, and frustrates me, if I have to be honest. You always put yourself last ...' A wry, lopsided smile pulls at his cheek. 'Except when it came to calling off our marriage, of course. You dug in and put what you needed first. I'd be quite proud of you if it wasn't such a kick in the gut.'

I swallow and look away. I'm not proud of myself in the least about that. 'I'm not sure that makes me feel any better,' I tell him. 'And I thought you were supposed to be keeping our spirits up.' At least, that's what we promised each other over an hour ago.

Gil stares at me steadily, but he doesn't say anything. When I shiver, he pulls me to him, then turns me around so my back is pressing against his chest, absorbing his body heat. One arm circles around my waist and the other keeps paddling. 'Better?'

'Yes,' I say through chattering teeth. We bob together like that for a moment, legs occasionally clashing, but then we find a rhythm, allowing us to kick and float together. Now I'm facing away from him, I realize there are things that will be easier to ask him if I don't have to look him in the eye. 'Gil?'

'Mm-hmm?'

'Did you really mean what you said earlier?'

'What in particular? We've covered quite a few subjects since we've been floating around out here.'

'What you said about making sure I got out of here?'

I don't feel him move, but somehow he seems to hold me just that little bit tighter. 'Of course.'

'Even if I fly home to Simon?'

Just for a beat, his legs stop moving, but then they start up again in the same easy rhythm. His voice is rough in my ear. 'Yes. Even then.'

It's almost too much. He'd do that for me? Even if it crushed him?

'I'm sorry,' I say. 'I didn't mean to ruin your life.'

I really didn't. And I really am sorry. All the anger and irritation I've been feeling for him in the last few days has melted away, dissolved by the salty water, and I'm not sure if it will ever come back. Because now I've truly seen him for who he is, I can't un-see it.

I want to give something back to Gil, to thank him for being there for me today, even though I've broken his heart. Gil wanted the truth from me, and the truth I gave him was real, but it was also harsh. What he really meant was that he wanted me to open my heart to him. And maybe I can do that, just a little bit.

Even though it terrifies me, I dig deep and find something, a gift I'm not even sure he'll want after all I've done. I tell him something I'd rather not admit to anyone, let alone myself. 'I'm scared.'

The arm around my waist tightens. His chin rests on my shoulder momentarily. 'So am I. But we can't give up, Erin. We have to keep each other going. And I know you can do this. You're strong ... Stronger than just about anyone I've ever known. And if anyone has the determination to get out of this, you do.'

I kick slightly and turn in his arms to face him, looping one arm around his waist as he has mine. We're joined together now, giving each other heat, giving each other rest. I look into his eyes and I want to cry.

It's there again, the expression I saw when I walked down the aisle and he turned to see me. I lift my hand and touch his face. The tiny speck of truth I've given him isn't nearly enough. I need to give him something more.

I press my forehead to his and then holding my breath, I bring our faces closer together until my lips are brushing his, moving in time with the lapping waves around our shoulders. One of his hands paddles while he reaches up with the other and cups my head to hold it steady and then he kisses me properly, slowly at first, making sure he's not doing something I don't want, but then more insistently.

And I join him. I lose myself in the feeling of being held and safe, even amid a vast and unending ocean, where nothing is solid, nothing is certain. There are kisses you relish in the moment because they make your blood fizz and your skin tingle, and then there are kisses that'll mark you for a lifetime. This, I realize, is one of them.

I've lost all time and space, everything but Gil's lips on mine, how his skin feels where our bodies are enmeshed in the water when I hear something.

Erin …

I freeze and pull back. 'Did you hear that?'

'Hear what?' And before I can answer, we're kissing again, clinging on to each other because we need to be close, not just because we need to stay afloat.

Erin …? Are you there?

I break away again. 'What did you say?'

Gil's eyes meet mine. 'Nothing. But I was thinking …' I see sadness in his eyes and it breaks my heart. 'Is it too late, Erin? Is it really too late for us?'

And before I can answer, he kisses me again, this time pouring everything he is thinking and feeling into it. It sweeps me away so I forget where I am, forget that we're in any danger at all.

'I … I don't know …' I stammer but I'm cut off by the same voice, but it's strange — it sounds like a hushed whisper, clear and audible above the sound of the waves and wind.

Erin … Can you hear me? It's time to wake up.

A sensation like lightning passes through my body leaving me breathless, and it's followed swiftly by a dragging, tugging sensation, but it's not Gil's hands on me. It's not anything trying to pull me down into the deep, quite the opposite. It feels as if a black hole has opened up above us and I'm being drawn upward into it.

'No!' I scream as the tugging feeling intensifies, almost swallowing me whole. I close my eyes and clutch at Gil.

I don't want to go. I want to stay here. I want to …

And then it's as if the string that has been tethering me to this place is snipped and I rise upwards, easily. Inevitably. There is a moment where I feel as if I'm one of those bubbles you blow with a wand and washing-up liquid. I'm floating high, my skin so thin I know it's going to pop at any second.

And then it does. My eyelids flutter open, which is odd because I thought they already were.

I see a white ceiling above me. I hear noises – a chair scraping, people moving, words that I can't make sense of at first, but then they start unjumbling themselves and arranging themselves into order.

'Oh, thank God! She's waking up!'

CHAPTER THIRTY-FIVE

Present Day

For a long time, I swim around in a misty soup. I hear voices, see people, but the details are lost to the fog. And then even the memory that those things happened is swallowed up too, until there is nothing but a pearly haze without sense of time or space.

I don't know how long I stay there – it could be days, it could be weeks – but eventually I can tell I'm in a room. I open my eyes and I see Anjali. I close them again. The next time my lids open, my mother is sitting on the edge of my bed, holding my hand.

I try to say something to her, but I don't know what.

'Shh …' she says, stroking my hair, and then back into the fog I go.

It feels as if I open my eyes again almost immediately, but now it's dark outside the long rectangular window. My eyelids feel heavy. In fact, every single part of me feels heavy. I move my hand and I hear a chair scrape. Someone hurries over to the bed I am lying on. It takes an effort to focus, but when I do, I see Gil.

Relief floods me. Did we survive the boating accident? Is that why I'm here? Did we almost drown before someone pulled us from the water?

But I can't ask him any of these things as he covers my hand with his own. The thoughts and questions are inside my head, but I can't seem to find the right words, any words, to express them. In the end, all I can manage is a weak smile. 'Hey you …' I say inside my head, and I move a finger underneath his hand, making contact the only way I can.

I have to concentrate to get my eyelids to stay open, and if I don't pay attention they just slide closed again. Before I return to the mist, I want to see his face, so I put all my willpower behind it. I open my eyes and make them focus.

It takes a couple of seconds, but he gets steadily less blurry. I see him looking down at me with a patchwork of emotions – pain, fear, hope, relief. And something else I can't name. Something warm and safe and …

It's no good. The word eludes me. But it's all I need for now.

I give in to the heaviness and the white blanket of unconsciousness claims me again.

For a long time, there's nothing and then I'm sitting up in bed and a man is on the chair next to it. 'Hey, sweetheart,' he whispers. He leans over and kisses my forehead, then puts his arms around me. The hug feels nice, warm. But it also feels different. Not wrong, but as if I'm trying on an old pair of shoes I haven't worn in a while.

He tells me how scared he's been, how he's so glad I've finally come back to him. That's all he's ever wanted. He loves me. He can't bear the thought of life without me.

Oh, yes, I think, as a thought enters my mind and floats through it effortlessly. *This is Simon. I'm going to marry him.*

But then …?

Who was …?

It doesn't matter.

The memory has gone again. All I can remember is here and now. Exhausted by my mental activity, I slide beneath the surface of consciousness again until my brain is rested enough to have another go at being awake.

CHAPTER THIRTY-SIX

Five years ago

She would rather not think about that night. But she suspects *not* thinking about that night is causing it to burrow into her subconscious and emerge in her dreams. It's as if a loud warning bell is ringing every time she has a nightmare, cautioning her to pay attention to what it's trying to tell her.

And she can't stand the prospect of months more of sleepless nights. She knows it won't get better. Only worse. So, a few days after their last conversation about the night of Megan's accident, she makes herself open up her messages app.

Hey, you …

A few moments later, the reply comes.

Hey yourself.

Do you even remember what the name of that stupid drinking game was? I'm not even sure if I remember the rules.

Unfortunately I do he replies. It was called King Cup.

She frowns. Even though the name has eluded her when she tried to grasp hold of it, that doesn't seem right. But it makes sense – playing cards and bright red plastic cups full of various combinations of alcohol.

I'm not surprised you don't remember much about it. I think you became a bit of a target.

Her eyes widen. **What do you mean?**

She'd thought it was all just honest fun, but his wording makes it seem as if something sinister was going on. Why has he never mentioned this before?

Well, there were a couple of guys in that circle who were showing interest.

Interest? In me?

Of course he replies, as if it should be obvious. **But I don't think they'd have much luck if they tried to chat you up, so my guess is they decided they might have better luck if you were feeling a little more …**

The three dots blink and she knows he's choosing his words carefully.

… relaxed.

She stiffens. **They were trying to get me drunk?**

E, to be fair, you were already quite drunk. But what they did was messed up.

But why? Why didn't they just talk to me?

Don't take this the wrong way, but …

She waits while he works out how to say what he wants to say, sure she probably is going to take it the wrong way. Or maybe it's the right way. All she ever wants is to be one of the crowd, to fit in. And she tries so hard … So why does she always feel as if she's on the outside looking in?

What? she stabs into her phone, irritated.

Sometimes, you can be a little intimidating.

She laughs out loud. That's utterly ridiculous. She's not like Meg, strong and feisty and full of fire … God, how she misses her. Erin Ross is sugar and spice and all things nice. In other words, the boring goody two shoes who sucks the fun out of everything.

I'm not intimidating. Don't be stupid.

You are. A little …

What are you talking about?

Not intimidating in a bad way.

She snorts. There's a good way?

She doesn't know how, but she senses he is chuckling. His reply comes back lightning fast.

> You're very nice to look at, and you've got this air about you.
> Sort of aloof, untouchable.

She makes a face. She didn't realize Simon believed this about her. She thought he understood who she really was. She types furiously.

> In other words, I'm a stuck-up bitch?

> No!

The answer comes back so fast she hasn't even taken her thumbs off her phone keyboard.

> Then what?

> I don't know how to explain it, but there's something about you that's a bit too good to be true, something that makes us lesser mortals feel as if we might not be worthy.

She blushes, and she's glad he can't see the soppy smile on her face. She's pretty sure nobody else thinks that way, but the fact *he* thinks that way … It's everything. But she's not ready to tell him that yet, so she steers the subject back to the matter in hand.

> So what were these guys doing?

> One of them was sitting next to you, and when anyone pulled an ace from the cards … That one was waterfall – everyone has to drink but you can't stop until the person to your left finishes, remember?

> To be honest, I'm a bit fuzzy about the rules.

> Well, one of those guys was sitting next to you and I'm sure
> he was drinking as slowly as he could to make you keep
> drinking, mostly because you hadn't quite got the hang of
> sipping it slowly when that card was pulled.

Great. Now she wasn't just untouchable, she was an idiot.

His words are making the memories sharper, the images more alive in her mind. She can see them all now, sitting in a circle in Posh Guy's living room, the furniture pushed back, red wine stains and crushed crisps on the carpet. She can picture some faces in the circle now: Simon, three places down to her left. Gil right across from her, with Megan separated from him by a loud girl wearing a pink feather boa who had passed out halfway through the game and just lay sprawled on the floor between them.

As she sorts through the images and sounds of that night, one thing strikes her.

> But what about Megan? I don't remember her having that
> much to drink, not at first. And then, of course, he ruined it.
>
> He?
>
> Your friend. Gil.

It goes quiet for a moment or two. Maybe she said the wrong thing. Simon and Gil have been friends since they were at school together. They're an unlikely pairing, and she's never understood how their friendship started and why it's so strong.

> What do you think he did? he asks.
>
> I don't just think it. I saw him. He picked up the last king,

didn't he? Which meant he had to drink the whole cup, and
it was full of all sorts of things by then.

She remembers little about the game, but she remembers that
cup, shuddering each time another drink was added. It had been
a mixture of spirits, wine, cider and even Baileys, which had
curdled and made it look like liquid brains. A real toxic brew.

He gave it to Meg.

Simon, as expected, is doggedly loyal.

I don't think that's exactly how it happened.

I know she swiped the cup from him, but it wouldn't have
been hard to stop her she counters.

You think what happened next was his fault?

Partly. Like you said, I had asked you both to help me keep an
eye on Megan, and there he was, doing exactly the opposite.

She lies on her bunk, the little reading light glowing against
the wall, and remembers the hoots and shouts and laughter that
erupted in the circle when tiny Megan downed that whole cup
in one go. It chills her now to think of it.

At the time she types it didn't seem like enough alcohol to
cause any real problems. Nothing more than a dry throat in
the night, a headache in the morning. I'd seen her drink a lot
more and not black out.

> I thought the same. But that was before we knew she'd taken other things as well.

She sits and absorbs that silently for a moment or two. There were so many things she would have done differently if she'd known everything. But there's something still niggling her. A little detail that won't leave her alone.

> Has that game got another name?

> I think it's got a few.

> Like?

> Ring of Fire. Waterfall.

No. Neither of them is the one she recalls – or more accurately, doesn't recall – from that night. She frowns, trying to think harder, trying to pull the elusive phrase from her alcohol-fogged memory bank.

Her phone buzzes once more just as the words form on her lips.

> Circle of Death.

Ah, yes. That was the one.

CHAPTER THIRTY-SEVEN

Present Day

'Where am I?'

I'm sitting up in bed but it's not the flat I share with Simon. This place is full of cold, hard lines. It smells funny. Outside my room I can hear people rushing back and forth, people talking, the sound of wheels on hard flooring.

My mother is sitting on the side of the bed. She takes my hand. 'You're in hospital. You had an accident.'

'I did?'

She nods.

That feels like a lot of information to take in all at once. I lie back on the pillows propped behind me and close my eyes.

* * *

'Where am I?'

I'm staring at Simon. He's standing by the window. It's early evening, and the sky is a beautiful lavender behind his head. I get stuck looking at it.

'You're in Edge Green Hospital, Erin,' he says. He sounds weary as he says it, as if he doesn't enjoy giving this answer, as if he's feeling as tired as I am.

'Why?'

'You tripped and fell, we think.' He looks away. I can tell he doesn't want to talk about this.

How strange. Usually, someone else being uncomfortable makes me feel uncomfortable too, but I don't feel awkward. I don't feel any sympathy for him. In fact, I don't have any emotions at all. But it doesn't bother me. I feel peaceful. As if I'm a bubble with a thick membrane and everyone and everything else is on the outside. I am a song made up of a single note.

'We think?' I say, echoing him.

He meets my gaze for a split second, then focuses on the end of my bed. 'No one else was around. You hit your head.'

'Am I in hospital?'

His face is turned away from me, but I see his cheek muscles lose tension, as if he's been keeping a smile in place and has now let it go. It occurs to me he doesn't realize I can see he's done that, but then he turns to face me again and the smile is back. 'Yes, but it's okay. You're going to get better.'

I look around the room. This information about this being a hospital seems accurate, but at the same time, I can't make sense of it. 'Will I be better in time for the wedding?' I ask.

Simon lets out a long sigh.

★ ★ ★

I'm sitting in a royal-blue chair with wooden arms. I have shortie pyjamas on and my legs are sticking to the plastic upholstery.

I peel one thigh off and then put it back down, and it slowly adheres itself again.

Anjali is sitting on the edge of the bed. She's smiling.

I open my mouth to speak.

'You're in hospital, Erin.'

I shut my mouth again. That's strange. How did she know I was going to ask that?

I nod, as if I was pretty sure that's what she was going to say all along. 'How's Vincenzo?' I ask.

Her face crumples and then I see her marshal her features back into neutral. It takes her a good couple of seconds, but she doesn't manage to gain complete control over her lower lip, which quivers. 'Is something wrong?' I whisper, and I get up and sit down on the bed beside her, put my arm around her.

She sniffs and then sucks in a breath.

'You can tell me, you know? What's the dickhead done now?'

Oops. I don't usually call Anjali's other half that in her presence, even though he is one. I'm surprised the word popped out of my mouth so easily.

For a few seconds she looks at me, not saying anything, and I wonder if she's cross with me, if she's going to defend him again, but then she launches into a long story about how they broke up.

She seems to think I know this but I don't. But she's so upset I don't stop her and put her right. That would be insensitive, so I put my arm round her and let the words wash over me and when she's finally silent I hand her a box of tissues, although I don't really know why she's crying. Has something bad happened?

CHAPTER THIRTY-EIGHT

Present Day

Just like the haze over the River Dart on a summer's day, the mist burns away. I begin to understand what has happened to me. There is no big moment of revelation. After repeated conversations, most of which I don't remember, the facts sink in and stick. Mostly.

I'm pretty sure they're telling me the bare minimum, but I gather that the night before the wedding, I slipped and hit my head in the hotel garden. Nobody knows exactly how long I was lying there before somebody found me.

I was rushed to hospital in Torquay, where they did various scans and tests. My brain was swelling, so they used medication to sedate me – putting me into a coma, effectively – for a couple of days, and then gradually withdrew the medication as the swelling went down.

Every day since I regained consciousness, one of the hospital psychiatrists has asked me questions. Apparently I got quite irritated with her for bothering me and I refused to answer them sometimes. What I understand now is that these questions were designed to see if I was emerging from post-trauma amnesia.

Yesterday, I answered them all correctly for the first time. I am now officially fully awake.

But it doesn't feel like it sometimes. Over the last week or two I've had numerous tests. People came to visit. I don't remember any of that happening, although I remember Simon and my mum being here. The doctors have reassured me this is completely normal for someone who was as deeply unconscious as I was. It still doesn't make it any easier to grasp.

There is one thing I remember for sure. Something so vivid, so real, that it makes the current impressions of the world around me seem flimsy and transparent in comparison.

I remember getting married.

To a man I hate.

CHAPTER THIRTY-NINE

Five years ago

Do you remember what happened directly after the game?

Her memory is fuzzy, probably because of the sneaky tactics of those guys who'd decided it'd be funny to pick on her when they had to nominate someone to drink, and then everyone else had bundled in and joined the fun. She now remembered lying back on the floor when it had finished, thinking she needed a pink boa to match the other girl, and how the room had spun so hard she'd had to get up again. After that, it was pretty much a blur for an hour or more.

Someone put some music on. People started dancing or passing out.

Her next clear memory was being with Megan in the en-suite bathroom to the master bedroom. It had taken her twenty minutes to convince her friend to unlock the door.

Do you know why Meg ran off? The first time?

Her prediction had come true. Megan plus alcohol equalled 'flight risk'.

No. Not exactly sure. She was dancing, having a great time. Next time I looked, she was gone.

She didn't know if she'd danced or not, or who with, but some time later, when the fuzz had cleared a little, she realized she hadn't seen Megan for a while.

When I found her in the bathroom, she was acting really strange, saying that 'they' were following her, but I never got out of her exactly who.

She now wondered about the guys Simon had mentioned when they were playing the drinking game. Could it have been more sinister after all? Were they looking for *any* drunk girl to take advantage of?

Paranoia? he suggests.

She frowns and types **Megan usually had two stages of drunk: loved-up and sobbing. I never saw her being paranoid.**

But it wasn't just the drink, was it?

No.

And that would explain it.

What happened in that bathroom? he asks.

She cried, rambled on for a bit, but then she seemed to calm down and she ended up hugging me, telling me what a brilliant friend I was. We tried to get to the landing while hugging, but we got as far as the bedroom, ended up bumping into the bed and falling onto it.

They'd stayed there, too knackered to get up, giggling about stupid things. It was as if the hysterics in the bathroom had never happened.

I started to doze. Not properly asleep but also not paying much attention to anything, and then the door slammed open, waking me up. She was already gone.

You don't know how much of a head start she had on you?

She thinks about how to answer his question for a few moments.

I can't have been there on my own for more than twenty minutes. Absolute max. And then your friend came crashing in.

There's a long pause between messages and she gets the weirdest feeling that everything has suddenly got awkward.

Gil?

Yes. And I was fed up because of King Cup, so I told him I wasn't carrying Meg home – he was going to have to do it. And he better go and find her too. It was his fault she'd drunk too much and done a disappearing act.

The fire still burned in her when she thought of his face that night. But now she's thousands of miles and almost nine months away from the tragedy, she wonders if actually she's angrier at herself.

For drinking more than she'd planned to.

For letting Megan do the same.

For falling back to sleep on that super king bed in the upstairs of Posh Guy's house, when she really should have been looking for her friend.

And maybe it was easier to blame all of it on Gil than it was to admit she was a part of the reason Meg never made it past twenty-two.

CHAPTER FORTY

Present Day

I look through the little glass window in my hospital room door. The corridor is busy, but empty of the person I'm waiting for. I sigh and take another circuit around the room. I'm no longer in a hospital gown, or even pyjamas. For the last few days, I've been wearing comfortable, casual clothes. It makes me feel more like a functional human being than an invalid.

'No sign?' my mother says from the armchair. She's scribbling away in a notebook, jotting down everything she wants to ask the consultant when she arrives. I've been here almost four weeks now, and I'm hoping she'll say I can go home today.

Mum has completely astonished me since I've been conscious enough to be aware of it. She spent almost every waking hour in my hospital room at first, only taking breaks to eat and occasionally go home to have a shower, change clothes and come back. Since they've instigated more of a visiting schedule, she's been here every moment she can. She's also been an amazing advocate for me with the medical staff when I haven't been able to do it for myself. I don't know what I would have done without her.

This is what I've always wanted. A parent whose sole focus

is on me, but now that I've got it, I find I just can't summon it within myself to be bothered.

That sounds terrible. But it's how it is. I'm just being honest. With myself, if not with her. But it's not only Mum. It's everyone. Everything. I feel numb. As if all my emotions have left me and taken a holiday. But this too, the doctors tell me, is normal after a head injury. I won't feel like an emotionless robot forever. I hope.

Simon is sitting on the edge of the bed, and I sit back down next to him and shake my head. 'No sign yet.'

He puts his arm around me. 'I'm sure she won't be long,' he says, then kisses me gently on the side of my head. He's also being amazing. The perfect fiancé. I know if it wasn't hospital policy not to have flowers in the rooms, mine would be overflowing. He's been here almost as much as my mum.

'Good news,' he says. 'The office has said I can have two more weeks' compassionate leave, so I won't have to use any annual leave for now – we can still save it for our honeymoon.'

'That is good,' I say, faking a smile. He's been talking about rescheduling for later in the year. And as much as I love Simon, at the moment I just can't bring myself to get excited about it. Part of me wishes I'd had the accident *after* we'd said our vows. It's not getting married I'm feeling lacklustre about but planning another wedding. I just can't face the thought of all that stress again.

An awful thought enters my head. I turn to Simon. 'Have we got enough money to do another wedding? Didn't we lose all our deposits?'

Simon rubs my arm again. 'It's okay, Erin,' he says softly, patiently, and I sense we've had this conversation before. 'Yes, we lost a few deposits, but a lot of the suppliers have been really understanding, even the venue. We can rebook when we're ready. When *you're* ready.'

I lean over and kiss him on the cheek, closing my eyes. I feel something. It's weak, barely detectable, but it's there, a flickering of warmth and gratitude for this man. He's being so patient with me.

I suspect I might seem like a different woman now from the one Simon proposed to. But I also sense the last few weeks have changed him too. He's always been charming and fun to be around. He's always treated me impeccably, but I often wondered if we could be closer. Sometimes, it felt as if we lived our lives together but in separate bubbles. Probably because we're both very independent and neither of us finds it easy to show on the outside what we're feeling on the inside. Simon didn't always share a lot of stuff with me, but that was okay because I knew how much he loved me. Right from the start, he showed me what kind of man he was.

But now … He's doing it all, saying it all. Even though it's bouncing off me, I can appreciate it in a logical kind of way. And as my knocked-around brain heals, those warm, fuzzy feelings will return, won't they?

There's a knock at the door, and I instantly stand up. However, it's not Doctor Sethi who walks through the door, but Gil.

I feel as if a lightning bolt shoots down through the ceiling and straight through my body. I grip on to the side of the mattress with both hands, feeling suddenly breathless. Where there was numbness, there is now life. Emotions. Colour. Memories.

And the very last one I have of him is being wrapped around him in warm tropical water, his mouth on mine, wishing I wasn't a mile offshore and our hotel bedroom was *a lot* closer.

I blush so hard I have to look at my feet. My pulse thuds inside my skull.

When I look up again, Gil is smiling at Simon, but when he turns his attention to me, his expression clouds over. Not with irritation or frustration, as it has in the past, but an expression I saw countless times on his face when I was asleep and dreaming about him.

'Listen,' Mum says. 'She's only really supposed to have two visitors at a time, so why don't I just pop out and—'

Gil looks slightly horrified. 'Oh, no … I don't want to impose.'

Mum packs her pen and notebook into her vast handbag and shakes her head. 'Don't be silly. It's good for Erin to have different visitors. Besides, the food in here is horrendous, processed mush. I've been meaning to pop to the supermarket next door to pick up some fruit and healthy snacks. You'll probably be gone by the time I get back.'

She comes over to me and hugs me like it's the last time she'll ever see me, presses a fierce kiss to my forehead, then disappears out the door. The three of us are left alone in the room. The atmosphere grows decidedly more awkward.

I expect Gil to ask how I'm doing. It's been the first thing out of every other visitor's mouth, but he unhooks the backpack slung over his shoulder and rests it on the armchair. 'I've got you something.'

I watch in fascination as he unzips the bag and pulls out a bundle of wires and a rather ancient-looking bit of technology. He glances up at me, seeming as off-kilter as I feel, and holds the item up. I know the name for it, but I just can't pluck it from my brain.

Simon laughs. 'Oh, my God. Is that a … a Walkman?'

Gil ignores Simon and keeps his eyes on me as he places it on the cabinet next to my hospital bed. 'I know you like books, but Simon said you were struggling to read.'

I nod. 'I can only manage a page before the words all start swimming around.' It's been one of the most disappointing things about being in hospital. Reading would have been a great way to pass the time, but it tires my healing brain out too quickly.

'I thought audiobooks might be a good alternative.'

Simon chuckles. 'For someone who works with technology, you're a bit behind the times. There are apps that do that now.'

Gil doesn't rise to the bait. 'But either Erin would have to download the app, work out how to use it, how to buy the books, or I would need her account details to do that for her. So I thought old-school might be the way to go. A button to start, a button to stop, a button to open the lid.' He presses the corner of the machine to demonstrate. Then he reaches back into his backpack and pulls out a stack of CDs with brightly coloured covers. I recognize them as titles by my favourite authors.

I look up at him in shock. 'Where on earth did you find these? I haven't seen audiobooks on sale like this for ages!'

'Local bookshop had one. The rest are the spoils from a charity shop crawl.'

I read out some of the titles. 'And how did you …?'

He shrugs, answering me even though I haven't finished my sentence. 'Every time I go into a person's house, I check out their bookshelves. Just remembered seeing these names there.'

I'm amazed. But then Gil always was one for details.

A shiver ripples through me as I have a sudden flashback from my dream – one that proved just how mind-blowing all that focus and attention to detail could be, put to the right uses.

I shake my head softly as if to dislodge the memory. Except that it's not a memory, is it? It's nothing. Just something my brain dreamed up while I was unconscious. I have to keep telling myself that, even if all the colour, the sights and sounds, the emotions of that time in dream St Lucia feel more real than the blurry reality I'm currently living in.

It's almost impossible to look Gil in the eyes, so I mumble my thanks and let him show me where the different buttons are. He's right, it's so simple even I shouldn't be able to stuff it up.

When I glance in his direction, he's studying me, and I can tell he thinks I'm behaving oddly, possibly even being ungrateful, but I don't know how to act any differently, and I can't explain why I'm almost hyperventilating, can I? That would be mortifying.

Thankfully, I'm saved from any further embarrassment by a knock on the door and a couple of moments later, Dr Sethi walks into the room. She checks her clipboard and smiles at me. 'Erin … It would be good to have a chat. A little bit of an update. I know you've been anxious to get home.'

Gil puts down the Walkman back on the bedside table and glances at the door. 'I should go—'

Simon cuts him off. 'No, mate. Stay … I mean, you're the one who found her and called an ambulance. You're as much a part of this as any of us are.'

I haven't got time to pick apart how Simon has just skated across any thoughts of privacy for what might be a very personal discussion, because I turn to look sharply at Gil. 'It was you who found me?'

He nods, then looks at his shoes. I want him to tell me exactly what he remembers about that night, but the doctor gives a cough. Gil zips up his rucksack. This might be my only chance to ask those questions, especially as he's feeling charitable towards me at the moment.

'No … you can stay.' And after the doctor has finished, maybe I'll get the answers from him I'm looking for.

Dr Sethi asks if she can take the armchair and I nod, then she motions for us to sit, so we end up lined up on the edge of the bed, me in the middle and Gil and Simon on either side of me.

For the second time in maybe ten minutes, I have proof I'm not completely emotionally numb. Anxiety becomes a low hum in my eardrums, a soft churning in my gut. Instinctively, I reach out and grab the hand beside mine on the edge of the mattress. It's warm and familiar. I breathe out. Just this small piece of contact makes me feel safe.

Gil's head snaps round, and he stares at me. I turn to meet his gaze, but out of the corner of my eye, I spot our fingers interlaced on the bed between us. He blinks, clearly perplexed but not horrified.

'Sorry …' I whisper, quietly enough for just Gil to hear me, and then I ease my hand from his, and reach for Simon with the other. It lands on his thigh and he covers it with his own.

'So, Erin,' Dr Sethi begins, 'test results and blood work are continuing to look good, but I know going through each in detail will probably be draining for you so I'll just give you the bullet points—'

'Will I always be this way?' I blurt out before she even gets going.

She doesn't miss a beat, just answers me patiently. 'Not necessarily. The brain has a marvellous ability to rebuild itself. You'll see more improvements over the coming weeks. Most of the significant healing will take place within the first twelve months, but you may continue to see improvement for some years after that. It's a waiting game to see which things will resolve themselves and I'm not going to lie to you, there may be a few lasting challenges. However, you were luckier than many people I see, Erin. Once the swelling in your brain went down, there wasn't nearly as much damage as I expected, so while I know this is frustrating and sometimes confusing, take heart that the prognosis is looking pretty good for you, much better than for some of my other patients.'

I swallow. 'Thank you.'

She places her clipboard on her knees and smiles at me. 'You may or may not remember that we were considering sending you to the brain injury rehabilitation unit for a few weeks, but you're doing so well we think you'll be fine with outpatient rehab, so the good news is that, yes, you can go home soon.'

'Today?'

She shakes her head. 'In a day or two. We're transferring your care to King's College Hospital when you go home, so we need a bit more time to get everything lined up. The neurology department there will keep an eye on you, but you will also have sessions with the psychologist, a physiotherapist, and occupational health.'

Simon wraps his arms around me, pulling me towards him so he can kiss my hair and whisper in my ear. I've only seen Simon cry three times in my life and from the catch in his voice, I suspect I might be about to witness the fourth. 'I'm so relieved, Erin. I can't wait to have you back home. For while there, I thought I was going to lose you.'

CHAPTER FORTY-ONE

Present Day

I return to the flat I share with Simon two days later. I'm desperate to walk through the front door, but when I do, everything feels strange, the same way it does when you come home after a holiday. I know it won't last long, but I don't like it. I want everything to feel normal again. *I* want to feel normal again. But right at this moment, that feels as possible as if I'd flown home from Devon by flapping my arms.

Simon is amazing. If I thought he adored me before the accident, he's surpassing himself now. I barely have to lift a finger. He doesn't even open his laptop to look at work emails, something I usually chide him for when he's supposed to be off. Instead he spends all his time pandering to my every whim. Not that I have many. Food and naps are pretty much all I require at the moment. Even snuggling up in front of the TV every evening is a bit of an ask. Most nights, I just doze off. By about 8 p.m., I'm good for nothing. When my brain decides it's too tired to do one more thing, it shuts down. I can't think. I can't talk. I can barely move.

Other than that, the thing I need most is time with Simon.

I know we didn't end up having our wedding, but I'd been aching for our honeymoon because it would mean a fortnight alone with nothing to do but rest and relax. At least I've got that now and I'm grateful for it, even if it is in our two-bed flat in Herne Hill rather than under the Caribbean sun. Slowly, I emerge from my bubble of emotional numbness and feel more like my usual self. How could I not with all the love and attention he's lavishing on me?

On Monday morning, about ten days after I come home from the hospital, I hear the door brush on the bedroom carpet and I roll over in bed and blink hazily. When I'm able to focus sufficiently, Simon is standing there beside the bed holding a tray.

I yawn and push myself up to rest against the headboard. 'You don't have to keep doing this, you know.'

He lays the tray down on my lap. This morning it's a bagel with cream cheese and smoked salmon – my absolute favourite – orange juice and a large mug of decaf tea, because I'm not allowed caffeine since the accident. It's too much stimulation for my compromised brain. There's even a small vase full of grape hyacinths and a napkin on the tray.

'Yes, I do have to do this for you.' He leans down to kiss my forehead as I reach for the mug. 'You're everything to me, Erin. I don't always think I've been good at showing you that in the past. Or being the person you deserve.'

I reach out and touch his arm, my eyes misty. 'Yes, you have.' I think back to all the bunches of flowers, the over-the-top birthday presents, the surprise weekends away to Prague and Bruges and Paris. Simon has always known how to make me feel special.

He looks back at me seriously, rare for Simon who always

seems to be on the verge of smiling or bursting into laughter. 'I don't know how to express it, but I know what I'm trying to say.'

I nod, even though I don't understand. Normally, I'm Nancy Drew, digging into the layers of nuance in everyone's conversations, but since the accident, I don't have the capacity. I let moments like these slide, and I have the feeling that one day I'm going to stumble over a pile of discarded half-thoughts I've let tumble to the floor and it'll trip me up. Stupid, really, but I feel my head injury has definitely made me more anxious, possibly even a little paranoid.

'When you've finished that, I'll help you get dressed,' he says. 'You've got that appointment with the psychologist this morning, remember?'

I nod again. It's becoming my default response to almost every question, even if I *don't* remember what I'm being reminded of. I know it's not being entirely honest, but I'm so fed up with feeling so weak and useless. 'I can manage myself,' I tell him.

He starts to argue, but I give him a look and he backs away laughing softly, his hands up in surrender. 'Okay ... okay ... But call me if you need me.'

I nod again. Another lie. When did it become so easy?

I manage to get dressed without Simon's aid, even if I lose my balance trying to put one foot in the leg of my knickers and have to grab the chest of drawers. I've learned my balance is also a bit compromised but that it's good to move around regardless, as it'll help my brain recalibrate in a way that staying still, afraid to move, won't.

I'm just trying to put make-up on when Simon dashes through the bedroom and into the en suite. I put my brush down and peer round the door. He's busy turning off the cold tap, pulling the plug out and then he grabs a bath sheet from the washing hamper and starts mopping up the floor.

My hand flies to my mouth. 'I didn't do it *again*, did I?'

'Yup. Clyde from downstairs called to say his ceiling was dripping.'

I get down on my hands and knees and try to help, but he shoos me away.

'I'm so sorry!'

It's the second time since I've been home that I've forgotten to turn the taps off, and the first instance was bad enough that our downstairs neighbour had to claim on his home insurance. Thankfully, the contractors haven't arrived to patch his ceiling up yet, so today's mishap won't spoil anything further. I hope.

'It's fine,' Simon tells me, even though his face is looking more strained than when he brought me my breakfast. 'You go back to what you were doing.'

I return to my dressing table and pick up my eyeshadow brush. I'm going to go for something simple. Just a bit of colour to make me look a tad more healthy.

'Do you really need to put make-up on?' I can see Simon behind me, holding a sodden towel which I presume he's going to throw in the washing machine.

I meet his gaze in the mirror. 'No, but …' My shoulders sag. 'I just want to feel a bit more like 'me', you know? Put on a brave face. Almost literally.'

Simon nods, but I know he's reflecting my technique back to me. He holds the towel up a little higher. 'I'll just …' and then he heads for the door.

Once the shadow is done, I pick up my mascara, unscrew the

lid, and begin brushing it onto my lashes, but I've only done a couple of sweeps when I jab it into my eyeball, causing me to yelp in pain.

Simon comes skidding back into the room. 'Erin! Are you okay?'

My first reaction isn't gratitude, but irritation. Not at Simon. Not really. At myself. I'm just so fed up with not being able to do *anything* properly, especially if it involves fine motor skills. Forget mascara … my handwriting is a car crash at the moment.

'I'm fine. I just …' I wave my hand to indicate the blackened mess I made of my upper lid when my hand slipped and grab for a make-up wipe.

Simon hovers behind me, watching as I start again with the eyeshadow. 'We need to leave in about ten minutes,' he says softly.

'This won't take long.' I'm already done brushing a nude shade over my lid. I pick the mascara up again and eye it warily.

'Why don't you let me try?' Simon asks, and he leads me to the edge of the bed, makes me sit down and kneels down in front of me.

I hand him the mascara wand. 'Are you sure?'

He lifts it up to my lashes, his lip caught between his teeth in concentration. 'How hard can it—?'

'Ow!' I scream, as Simon pokes my sore eyeball once again in exactly the same spot.

'Oh, my God! Erin … I'm sorry!' Simon grabs the make-up wipes and gets to work, taking off almost everything I've applied so far in his panic.

I reach up and still his hand. He looks at me and then I burst out laughing. Relief floods his features and he begins to laugh too. And then he kisses me on the lips and it feels light and fun, just like it did before all this happened. It's almost as if he's been scared to touch me since we came home from the hospital, scared he'll break me further.

I kiss him again, then take the wipes from him and scrub my face clean. 'The psychologist will just have to meet me *au naturel*,' I say.

But when I've finished, I hold the packet of wipes on my lap and stare down at it, suddenly sombre. I look back up at Simon. I can't ignore the reality of my situation, not after two minor disasters so far, and the day is hardly begun yet. 'We've only got until next weekend and then you're back at work,' I say. 'What are we going to do? I'm scared I'll flood the place again, or worse! What if I put something on the hob and forget about it? I don't feel …' I swallow, not quite able to say the words. Truthfully, I don't feel confident about being on my own, something I thought I'd never think or say. My mother always used to joke that self-sufficiency was my middle name.

Simon makes a rueful face. 'I didn't want to say anything, but I was thinking the same thing. How about we have a chat with your mum, see if you can stay there for a bit?'

I take a few breaths and then meet his gaze. 'Okay,' I reply, even though that one word feels like an admission of defeat.

CHAPTER FORTY-TWO

Five years ago

Hey, you … she types. **Free to chat?**

It's early evening in the Caribbean, so it must be around lunch-time where he is.

An answer pings back within a couple of seconds.

Hey yourself. And always.

She thinks she's falling in love with him, but she also knows it's too soon. Every time he answers her, always caring, always supportive – even if he's always direct, sometime to the point of uncomfortable bluntness – she slips a little further down that slippery slope.

It's stupid, really. Their friendship grew after the accident, and it was only in the couple of weeks before she left it became something more. Both of them knew it wasn't ever going to get serious.

Except it has. For her, at least.

She's still not sure where she stands. It's strange, sometimes he's so vulnerable, so raw, that she can almost feel him there in the room with her as they type back and forth, and at other times he seems oddly opaque, as if there are layers and layers of frosted glass between them and she can only see a fuzzy outline.

She sends another message:

I think I'm ready.

Sure?

She takes a moment to check in with herself before she replies.

Yes.

In their poring through the details of the night of Megan's accident, they've reached the hardest part. She put the brakes on talking about it for a few days, feeling she needed to be ready, but really she was just being a coward. However, the nightmares have stepped up in both intensity and frequency. She knows she can't run forever. She has to face the truth, no matter what it is. There are questions she's wanted to ask for months, but the pact between the three of them never to talk about it kept the answers captive.

The more she thinks about it, the more she wonders why they agreed to it. At the time, she'd felt so guilty, so devastated, that she'd wanted to shut it all out. Is that how the guys felt, too? Simon has shown her in recent weeks that he's happy to open up and talk, but what about Gil? Does he feel guilty about something? Has he got something to hide?

She knows something Simon doesn't know. The best way to find out the truth is to play dumb, to ask the question as if she doesn't already know the answer.

Do you have any idea who gave Megan the ketamine?

She waits for a couple of seconds, and then the reply comes.

No idea. I didn't even know she'd taken it until it came up in the medical reports.

She releases the breath she's been holding in a slow, steady stream. Oh, thank God. It wasn't him. Should she tell him that one of the other partygoers had told her about who they thought was with Megan when she took it? No. Not just yet. She'll tell him later.

Are you sure she didn't bring it with her? he asks.

Definitely not. She'd have told me.

Megan had been very open about those things with her, and it hadn't been the first time she'd had the drug.

Someone at that party gave it to her, which means someone else also knew how much she'd taken she types.

The inquest had shown it hadn't been enough to cause significant harm on its own. However, when you factored in the amount of alcohol Meg had drunk …

She closes her eyes in an effort to squeeze out the memory of Megan downing that huge red King Cup. If she'd known, she'd have knocked it out of Megan's hand, hurled it across the room. So stupid … It had been completely avoidable.

There were so many what-ifs, each a tiny blade stabbing her

conscience. What if she'd known about the ket? What if she'd done what she said and hadn't drunk so much herself? She might have realized Megan had taken something. What if she'd got up and looked for Megan instead of having a nap amid the pile of coats? So many little slips, so many falls from grace she's not sure she can ever climb back out of that pit again.

> Did you see Meg at all around midnight? She must have come downstairs. No other way to get to the garden.

> No. And then the next thing I knew, everybody was looking for her.

That must have been around the time she'd woken up. Someone had barged into the main bedroom, looked around, asked her if she was called Megan, and then disappeared again when she mumbled she wasn't.

And then what they'd said had sunk in. People were looking for Megan. Why? She'd scrambled up off the bed and run downstairs, where she'd found Simon looking white as a sheet.

> You looked really panicked when I found you in the conservatory she taps into her phone. Did you have a sense then that something was really wrong?

It's a minute or two before his reply arrives, and she's expecting something long and detailed, but it's only one line:

> I don't remember that.

> Talking to me or being worried?

Both.

Odd. She expected that his memories, like hers, would be sharper for the parts of the evening when the adrenaline kicked in hard, chasing the effects of the drink from their systems.

I asked you if you'd seen her, and you said no.

I didn't. I do remember ... I think I remember suggesting we looked in the park.

Yes. That's right. I think I remember that too.

Those sober enough had split into groups to look in different places. She, Gil and Simon had searched the garden, then Simon had suggested crossing the road and heading into the small park on the other side. Full of fear, she'd grabbed onto Simon's hand as they walked. They did a circuit of the main path calling out Megan's name, checking nearby bushes in case she'd passed out. And then they'd come across the children's playground.

When did you first spot her? she asks.

The surrounding atmosphere seems to darken as she waits for his answer, even though it's a bright day in the Caribbean and there isn't a cloud in the sky.

When we opened the gate to go into the fenced-off area. I saw something pale slumped on the merry-go-round. I didn't know what it was, but I got weird vibes, like a sense of foreboding.

He had better eyes than she did then. She hadn't realized there was a person lying there, let alone anything else, until they'd been much closer. For some reason, she'd been looking at the swings, hoping she'd find Megan sitting on one, legs dangling, or swinging high, a smile of pure childish joy on her face, but she'd been lying half on, half off the tiny merry-go-round, face down with her hair splayed all around her.

Just thinking about it makes her feel sick. She presses one hand to her stomach and taps at her phone screen with the other.

Was it you who rushed to her? Who turned her over?

The three dots appear and she thinks another message is coming, but then they disappear, then reappear again. Did he just type something and then delete it?

No.

It must have been Gil, then. Funny, she could have sworn it was Simon. But the facts must have been swept away by what she saw next.

I'll never forget her face.

White. Eyes staring up at the hollow moon. Yellow vomit trailing from her mouth. A puddle of it on the flaking painted surface of the merry-go-round. She'd choked on it, apparently. That's what the coroner had said, anyway. She had a bad reaction to the combination of ket and alcohol, and it slowed her heart rate to the point of no return. Another person taking a similar dose might have pulled through, but she hadn't.

Did you know she was dead? she asks.

Not for sure. But I suspected it, even though she was still warm when I touched her.

Simon and Gil had rolled her into the recovery position while she'd dialled 999 and then run to the entrance of the park to direct the ambulance crew when they arrived.

The last time I touched her she types with a tear rolling down her cheeks, **is when we were laughing on the pile of coats. How can she have been so alive in that moment and then not long after …**

She doesn't write the rest of the sentence. Can't. But she doesn't need to, because he replies:

I know.

He understands.

Thank you she types.

What for?

For trusting me enough to break that stupid pact we made. I think it's really helped.

And it has, in more ways than he realizes. Somebody she chatted to at Megan's funeral told her that one of the two guys she and Meg came to the party with gave her the ket. If it wasn't Simon, it must have been Gil. And then he let her drink the King Cup, and he must have known that wasn't a good idea, but he said nothing, saving his own sorry backside.

Yes, Megan's actions had started the chain reaction of events that had led to her death, and they could all have had a part in stopping it, more so if they'd known what they were dealing with. But Gil *had* known. And that meant he was more responsible than any of them, yet he'd never confessed, never showed any remorse. He was a coward. While she knew she couldn't lump the blame on him entirely, she also knew she was never, ever going to forgive him.

CHAPTER FORTY-THREE

Present Day

When I arrive at Mum's the following Sunday, she won't even let me take the smallest of my suitcases into the house. She and Simon move everything while I am made to sit down on the sofa with a cup of tea and a cheesy movie on the TV. I sit back and feel my muscles unknot. I am ready to be fussed over and pampered by my mother, possibly for the first time in my life.

Reality hits hard on Monday morning, however. While I thought I arrived at an ordinary-looking 1930s semi in Bromley, I discover I've actually been enrolled in some kind of head-injury recovery boot camp, with my mother as sergeant major.

She hands me a schedule at breakfast. Mum has my days mapped out for me because routine is what I need, apparently, so while I had a lie-in today, from now on breakfast is at seven-thirty sharp, followed by medical appointments or anything that requires a bit of mental energy in the first part of the day, because that's when I'm definitely at my best.

While part of me bristles at being organized in this way, another part is slavishly grateful that someone else has taken on the mental load of what I'm supposed to be doing when, and after a bit of resistance from me, I give up and give Mum her way and the next couple of weeks pass in a comfortable rhythm.

If there's nothing planned for the mornings, I am expected to dive into a puzzle book. Mum has heard of other brain trauma survivors doing them, so she's convinced I've got to do at least one puzzle a day to stop myself from falling into a vegetative state. I end up messing around with a pencil, doodling over Sudoku grids. I was rubbish at them before the head injury. How does she think I'm going to do them now?

After lunch we take a gentle stroll in the park and then it's nap time. I never argue about that, because I'm normally more than ready for it. It's as if my brain is now worn out by doing the everyday things it always used to do on autopilot. After dinner, we watch TV. It's not very exciting for poor Mum and Emir. I can't seem to manage anything other than comfort watches, so we have the 1995 version of *Pride and Prejudice* on a loop. It doesn't matter if I zone out, because I can still mouth the words along with Darcy and Lizzy from the midst of my stupor.

The only time I really leave the house is for my out-patient appointments. Mum has to drive me around because my licence has been suspended until the DVLA is convinced I'm sufficiently recovered. This is a bitter pill to swallow. I've always prized my independence and now I'm being ferried around by my mum the way I wished I had been when I was a teenager. Back then, if I'd wanted to go to after-school clubs, I had to get the bus.

A couple of weeks after I move in, I have another appointment with Naomi, my psychologist. We arrive at the clinic, a therapy centre housed in a converted Victorian villa in Lewisham. It has beautiful parquet flooring in the waiting room and a view over a well-tended garden out the back. When my name is called, Mum stands up. I walk towards the consulting room and Mum still follows me. Naomi is holding the door open. She sees the look on my face, the look of unbridled determination on my mother's, and moves to the centre of the doorway. 'Erin, would you like your mother to wait outside?'

'Yes,' I say quietly. There's something I'd like to ask Naomi in private.

'But I can take notes in case you forget,' Mum says, looking anxiously through the open door.

'Sorry,' I mutter over my shoulder and scuttle inside.

Naomi closes the door and motions for me to sit down in a comfy green chair. She takes one opposite me on the other side of a low coffee table. 'It can be tough with family and friends,' she tells me. 'Knowing where to draw the line – for both of you. They've been through their own trauma because of this, too.'

'I realize that. And my mum has been absolutely brilliant, but sometimes I just ...' I shake my head, unable to put my thoughts into words. Naomi nods is if she gets it anyway.

We chat about how I'm feeling, of course, but we also look at tools to help me move forward with a more positive mindset. I'm trying hard, I really am. But it often feels as if my own brain is at war against me. I'm used to making a plan and getting things done, not forgetting the plan ever existed or doing the wrong thing. It's most frustrating.

As we round up our session, Naomi asks me if there's anything else I'd like to talk about. On automatic, I shake my head and stand, but then I remember what I deliberated over the whole car journey here and I sit down.

'When I was ...' I shake my head and start again. 'When

people are in medically induced comas, what happens to their brains? Is it just blank, sort of offline, or do they have thoughts or, um, other kind of brain activity?'

Naomi tips her head on one side. 'What was your experience, Erin?'

I knot my fingers together even tighter. 'Well, I might have had a … kind of … It was a bit like a dream.'

She leans forward. 'What happened?'

'Nothing terrible…' If you discount almost drowning at sea, of course, but I don't want to tell her that. 'But it … it seemed so real. And it's not fading like a normal dream would. I can still remember every detail.'

Naomi doesn't look alarmed in the slightest. 'What you're describing isn't uncommon. Quite a lot of coma patients say they experienced extremely vivid dreams while they were unconscious. In fact, you're one of the lucky ones. Some people have horrendous nightmares they can't forget. I hope your dream was a nice one.'

I swallow. 'I suppose it was … I was in St Lucia for most of it.'

She laughs. 'Well, that doesn't sound bad at all.'

I laugh along with her, not wanting to divulge anything else. I'm taking the details of that dream to my deathbed. But I feel better knowing it's just something that brains do sometimes when there's nothing else to occupy them, that I'm not some kind of freak for experiencing this.

I rise out of the chair. 'Thank you.'

'No problem, Erin.'

CHAPTER FORTY-FOUR

Present Day

Mum and I take our daily walk in a small park around the corner from her house. It has neat lawns and well-tended borders and winding tarmac paths. Each day, we choose a slightly different route and today we pass by the fenced-in playground with sustainable wooden structures for the kids to play on and the rubberised flooring.

Parked beside the playground is a pink and yellow ice cream van. My spirits lift. I'm usually pretty disciplined about what I eat, but I get a sudden and intense craving for a soft whip vanilla cone with a chocolate flake sticking out of it.

'Fancy an ice cream, Mum? I'll pay.' It's the least I can do to make up for all she's doing for me.

Mum stops in her tracks, and since my arm is linked with hers, it has the effect of tugging me backwards. 'Not a good idea, Erin. Don't you remember what I've told you about the nutrition research I've been doing? Following a brain injury, sugar is your enemy.'

Mum has been feeding me home-cooked meals full of lean protein and non-starchy veg for almost a month now. I wish

I *could* forget about all the nutritional advice she slips in to conversations at every mealtime. 'Surely one ice cream won't hurt?'

She steers me in the opposite direction. 'You can have a decaf tea or coffee at the kiosk near the pond.'

I look longingly over my shoulder at the van. 'What if they don't have decaf?'

'Every coffee place has decaf these days.'

'Coffee, yes, but not tea. And I fancy a cup of tea.'

My mother's only answer is to unhook her arm from mine and rummage in her handbag for a small resealable bag of what I presume are decaf tea bags.

I laugh. 'How long have those been in there?'

'You know me,' she says. 'I'm always prepared for an emergency.'

It is in that moment I realize I am far more like my mother than I want to admit. However, I know when I'm beaten, so I allow her to lead me to the little wooden hut that looks almost like a garden shed, with a hatch that opens upward.

When I have my cup of hot water to plop my decaf tea bag in and Mum has her cappuccino, we sit down at one of the rickety tables and chairs spaced out in the tarmac area in front of the kiosk. Every single table has a folded napkin under one leg to stop it wobbling.

'Is Simon coming over tonight?' Mum asks.

I shake my head. 'He's really busy at work at the moment. However …' I add this next bit casually, attempting to lull my bulldog mother into a false sense of security, '… I thought I might go home for the weekend. I can't stay here forever, so maybe a staggered return would work?'

Much to my surprise, she nods. 'I suppose that's a good idea. The doctors have said that's okay?'

'Yes. Just the same advice about not overstimulating myself.'

'No,' Mum says, looking serious. 'We don't want you going backwards or, God forbid, having a seizure.'

'It's okay, Mum. Things are going well. And nothing like that has happened yet, has it?'

Along with all the other support, Sudoku puzzles from Mum have been replaced with a proper brain training programme – enough to challenge me but not leave me exhausted. It's designed to help my grey matter grow new neurons and make new connections. My balance is almost back to normal unless I'm exhausted, and my memory is improving. Slowly.

'You know, Simon has really surprised me,' Mum says, taking a sip of her coffee.

'He has? How?'

She looks a little sheepish as she admits, 'Well, he's not always been the most steady of people, but he's really stepped up to the plate since your accident.'

'I thought you liked Simon!'

'I do! He's great company and fun to be with, but you have to admit, he wouldn't win any prizes for seeing things through. But when I'm wrong, I admit I'm wrong. I mean, I never thought he'd get around to walking you down the aisle—'

'Mum! What do you mean?'

She gives me a knowing look. 'Well, it did take him four years to propose, and he always had this air about him as if he had one foot half out the door.'

I put my teacup back down on the saucer and stare at her. 'I was abroad more months of the year than I was at home while we were dating. That makes relationships … different. It takes longer to really get to know each other.'

Mum nods sagely. 'I know … I know. And rushing in would have been worse. But you've always been such a romantic, Erin. I'm concerned that you see things the way you wish they were rather than how they really are sometimes, and I worried that because you wanted Simon to be Mr Perfect, that's who he was to you.'

I'm dumbfounded. 'I never knew you felt that way.'

She shrugs. 'My mum always talked badly about your dad when we were together, and I hated that, so I promised myself I'd keep my nose out whenever you found who you wanted to be with.'

I suppose I should be grateful for that, but I still feel like I'm reeling. I don't do well with adjusting to new information at the moment.

'And nobody's perfect, are they? There's always going to be a learning curve in any relationship, adjustments to make.' She reaches over and pats my hand. 'Anyway, it's a moot point about Simon now, isn't it? Like you said, he's been brilliant.'

I nod. He has. He's stuck by my side like a loyal Labrador for the last two and a bit months.

Mum pushes her chair back and stands up. 'Right. We ought to be getting back. I've got a Zoom meeting in fifteen minutes.'

Had she told me about this earlier? 'A Zoom call? For work?'

She doesn't look at me. 'Sort of.'

'Mum … What are you up to?'

For a second or two, I think she's going to tell me she has no idea what I'm talking about, but then her face breaks into a huge grin. 'It's a surprise for you. You're going to love it!'

My insides wilt. 'Mum, I can tell you're really excited about this … and I don't want to be a party pooper or anything … but I'm not sure I've got the energy for surprises right now.' Or mum's talent for drama. She does love a big reveal. 'Couldn't you just, you know … tell me now? I promise I'll still love it.'

She spends a few moments chewing the idea over and then sits down again. 'Okay … If you're sure?'

'I'm sure.'

'Well … I'm setting up a new charity.'

I smile because that's what I'm expected to do. 'A new charity?' For the life of me, I can't think why this is a) good news or b) has anything to do with me. How is she going to run *two* charities from her dining room office?

'That's what the Zoom is about. After the last couple of months, being in and out of the hospital with you, I've spotted gaps in the system, ways in which other people could really do with support.'

'After the last couple of months?' I echo. I know I should catch on quicker than I am, but I just can't join the dots. 'What sort of charity, Mum?'

'For people like you and me,' she says, looking slightly perplexed why this is not screamingly obvious. 'Survivors of traumatic brain injuries and their families.'

It's just as well she didn't ask me to guess, because this would have been the three-millionth answer I would have come up with. 'Um … I don't know what to say.'

She wraps her arms around my neck and pulls me briefly to her. 'No need to thank me. It's the very least I can do for my baby.'

CHAPTER FORTY-FIVE

Five years ago

Hey, you …

Hey yourself.

She's taking a break while the deck crew supervises their current guests using the water 'toys' – jet skis, wave runners, and various inflatables, including a giant nine-metre-tall slide that can catapult them into the ocean.

She knows they left their fledgling relationship status loose when she left, but since they discussed the party, they've been texting constantly, and she senses it's deepened again, become something more. She's almost certain he feels the same way, but she's also scared that he doesn't. Since they've been an item, he's definitely blown hot and cold. She sends a second message, biting her lip as she presses send, hoping it's not too much:

I wish I could come home for Christmas so I could see you.

She isn't expecting him to answer straight away; it's only 6 a.m. where he is and Simon is a bit of a night owl, but five minutes later, her phone chimes.

> Seeing you again is the thing I want most in the world. It would be the best Christmas present. Such a shame you've got to work.

She sighs. This is what she signed up for when she became a yachtie. She's been doing this for a couple of years now and Christmas is a prime booking for charter yachts in the Caribbean. She's always been quite philosophical about it, but the idea of not going home this year creates an ache in her chest.

There are two female guests who have been hovering near the top of the slide, saying they want to go down it, but also squealing about how high it is. The rest of their group has been taking turns flying down it and splashing into the clear, warm sea. Finally, one girl gets up the nerve and jumps on.

> What are you going to be doing on Christmas Day? Erin types,
> even though she knows it's a bad idea.

If he tells her what he's going to be doing, she'll just end up fantasizing she's going to be there along with him, smiling over the candlelight of a big Christmas dinner, laughing as they pull crackers, maybe even kissing under the mistletoe …

He takes a moment to answer, but then the reply comes:

> The Mears family are going away for Christmas.

Really? Where?

It's the parents' thirtieth anniversary. They're taking the family away to Lapland.

Wow!

We can still message each other. Every day.

There was that.

Can we do a video call maybe? On Christmas Day or Boxing Day? I'll see if I can hop ashore and find somewhere with decent Wi-Fi.

The captain has put an embargo on the crew using FaceTime after one of the other stewardesses was having issues with her boyfriend back in Austria and a) wasn't getting any work done and b) was hogging all the bandwidth that was needed for important stuff.

I have no idea if I'll have decent Wi-Fi either. Better stick to messages.

Here he is, blowing hot and cold again. Sometimes she really can't make him out.

E?

She likes how he calls her that. If anyone else did, she'd think it was an awful way to shorten her name but somehow when he does it, it seems wonderfully familiar, as if he knows her, sees her, in a way that others don't.

Yes? she replies.

I meant what I said. Seeing you, being with you, is all I want.

She smiles sadly. **I know. Me too.**

They exchange a few more messages before he has to go. When she glances at the slide again, the girl who's been chickening out finally gathers up the nerve and launches herself down as her friends cheer her on. She screams in exhilaration, but then flies off the end so fast that she becomes airborne for a few sweet seconds before doing a massive belly flop.

CHAPTER FORTY-SIX

Present Day

The next day, Anjali comes for lunch. She's been on a training course for work, so I haven't seen her in two weeks. It's a nice day out, so we go to sit on the patio at the far end of Mum's long thin garden. Mum insists we sit and chat while she fetches us soft drinks and sandwiches.

'How are things going?' Anjali asks.

'Okay … I'm getting there.'

'Any idea when you'll be able to go back to work?'

I shake my head. 'It turns out household management isn't the best fit for someone trying to recover from a head injury.'

Anjali snaffles a prawn cocktail sandwich from the pile on the plate in front of us. 'Kalinda *fired* you?'

'No. I'm on an extended leave of absence. She's got someone to cover my role for now. You know how the sort of people I work for are … They're used to five-star service all the way, everything perfect all the time. And it can be unpredictable, putting out fires one after the other. I can't even stay on top of my own life at the moment, let alone take care of theirs.'

Anjali gets up and comes over to give me a hug. My eyes well up and I blink the tears away. God, I'm such a crybaby these days. Now my emotions have sprung back to life, it's as if they all come pouring out of me any time I feel the slightest thing.

Anjali sees my face and offers me a tissue from a packet in her handbag. I mop myself up. 'Anyway, I'm sick of talking about myself. What about you? Is …?' I'm about to mention Anjali's evil ex, but it appears I've forgotten his name, so I fudge it. 'Is "you know who" behaving himself?'

Anjali pulls herself up straighter. 'I wouldn't know. I blocked him.'

'You—'

She nods. 'Yep. That's right, blocked him on every messaging app and every social media platform.'

I can hardly believe I'm hearing this. I've been trying to get her to do that for ages. 'What brought that on?'

'He told me he loved me and wanted me back.'

I almost drop my lemonade. 'Did I hear that right? Because, usually, that kind of thing would have you running back into his arms.'

She gives me a helpless smile. 'I found out that Charlene – the girl he left me for, remember? – dumped him and slept with his best friend. Or maybe she slept with his best friend and then dumped him … Either way. He was feeling pretty sorry for himself.'

'But how did you …? What did he …?'

'How did I manage not to get suckered in one more time?'

'Well, yes …'

'I thought about all the advice you'd given me I'd blatantly ignored and realized not only was he an idiot, but I was, too. From that point on, I promised myself I'd only respond to him if I first asked myself "what would Erin do?". Once I'd done that, I told him to delete my number from his phone and never contact me again.'

I start giggling. 'Wh–what would *Erin* do?'

Anjali grins. 'It's going to be my new catchphrase.'

And then we really start laughing. Mum comes back up the garden to see if we need more drinks and finds us almost falling off our chairs. 'Erin!' she says in her best community busybody voice. 'Are you sure you're supposed to be—'

I swallow my laughter and pull my face into a sensible expression. Or at least I try to. 'It's okay, Mum. It's good for me to get endorphins flowing round my system. A little bit of laughter isn't going to kill me.'

Mum looks at me as if she isn't so sure, as if she's afraid if I laugh too much, something will pop inside my head and that will be it. 'Just … try to be sensible,' she says, softening a little. Then she turns to Anjali and adds, 'And don't you tire her out, madam. I always said you were a bad influence.' But she's wearing an indulgent smile, and she pats her on the shoulder as she turns to leave. My mum has always had a soft spot for Anjali.

We both watch her retreat down the garden and disappear into the house. 'She's driving me bonkers,' I say.

'She's trying so hard, though. And at least she's finally present in your relationship. That's what you've always wanted, isn't it?'

I take a sip of my water. 'I know. I suppose this is a case of "be careful what you wish for". I mean, I'm going to spend the weekend at home with Simon, just to have a couple of days off.'

Anjali grins at me. 'Do you think I can come and be your stand-in here? I wouldn't mind getting breakfast in bed and being waited on hand and foot for a weekend.'

I can't help laughing. 'Be my guest.'

'But seriously,' Anjali says. 'She's just worried about you – which is understandable. You had us all in a panic for a while.'

'I suppose you've got a point and yes, you're right – I always wanted Mum to be a bit more interested in my life, but it's also completely exhausting. She's so … invested. The truth is, I have good days and bad days, but on the days I'm not doing so well, I see the fear in her eyes. And that makes me scared too.'

Anjali twirls a strand of hair around her finger. 'It must be quite triggering for her. Do you think something about seeing you not well is reminding her of your brother?'

'That's definitely crossed my mind. But if anything, it means I'm feeling the pressure to not let her down, to make a full and speedy recovery. Some days I even lie and say I'm doing better than I am because I don't want her to worry. It's like she *needs* me to be okay.'

Anjali looks me in the eye. 'But what do *you* need, Erin?'

I shake my head wearily. What I need is to rewind time, go back to that day before the wedding that never was and do something different, so I never end up with a head injury in the first place. But since I don't know why I was in the garden on my own, I don't even have a clue what that might be. Other than that, I'm stumped. Knowing what everyone else needs and serving it up to them is my superpower. I'm not so good at turning it around on myself.

A naughty glint appears in Anjali's eyes, and she leans down to the large tote bag sitting by her chair. 'Well, while you're working it out, maybe these will help…' and she brings out a tub full of salted caramel mini muffins and places them on the table between us.

'Oh my God!' I say, taking a swift look at the kitchen window. 'Don't let my mum see these! She'll confiscate them.'

Anjali salutes me, takes two muffins from the pot, and replaces it in her bag. 'This is why I brought mini muffins,' she says, unpeeling one from its case and pushing the other towards me. She opens her mouth and pops the whole thing inside, then closes it again. 'Eaf … ta hide … effy den,' she says.

I've only just recovered from the last bout of laughter, yet I'm set to go again. 'What?'

She swallows and tries again. 'Easier to hide the evidence! Go on …' She nods at my muffin and waits.

I've just finished unpeeling it when my mum appears from the back door, carrying what looks like a platter of fresh fruit. I shoot a panicked look at Anjali, crumple the paper up and stuff it down my cleavage, then shove the muffin in my mouth because I have literally nowhere else to put it.

'Everything okay?' Mum says brightly as she places the fruit platter on the table. I nod, doing my best version of an angelic smile, muffin threatening to emerge from my closed mouth at any second, and Anjali almost implodes trying to keep the giggles inside. 'Yes, thank you, Julie,' she says sweetly. 'What lovely fruit!' And she picks off a grape and eats it. 'Don't let us keep you …'

'Well, yes … I have got some charity stuff I should get on with,' Mum says, shooting a nervous look in my direction, where I'm close to choking on a salted caramel mini muffin.

'I'll take care of Erin,' Anjali says with a winning smile. 'Don't you worry.'

I hold it together, quickly chewing and swallowing my muffin while Mum walks back down the garden and when she's safely inside and the back door is closed, I explode into a coughing fit, showering crumbs everywhere, and then we both start laughing again.

'Just what I needed,' I say when we've both regained our composure.

'Personally, I think mini muffins could solve most of the world's problems, if we only gave them a chance.'

I stand up, walk around the back of my best friend's chair and give her a big squishy hug from behind. 'Not the muffins, you melon,' I say in her ear. 'It's you. *You* are just what I needed.'

CHAPTER FORTY-SEVEN

Present Day

I curl my legs up underneath me as I hold my phone to my ear. 'I understand that, Rob. But Kalinda is used to having things done a certain way. If she pulls you up on something, you just have to smile and say you'll do better, even if she's being unfair. I know it wasn't your fault the florist cancelled two hours before the dinner party and the replacement wasn't up to par, but I'll give you the number of the one I use. She's very reliable and—'

I freeze as I hear a key in the front door. 'You know what? I'll text you the deets. Bye!' I press end on the call and, just for good measure, tuck my phone down the side of the sofa cushion, then turn and smile brightly at Simon as he walks into our living room. 'How was your day?'

He frowns. 'Busy. Who were you talking to?'

'Um … no one?' I pick up the remote and hold it up, hoping I can make him think it was the TV without actually saying so. The lines on his forehead get deeper. I'm not surprised. I am an absolutely horrible liar.

'You were talking to that guy again, weren't you?'

I blink innocently. 'Which guy would that be?'

'The guy who's covering your job. Erin ...' He gives me a warning look, and then comes over to the sofa, delves down the side of the cushion, and pulls out my phone. I have the grace to blush. 'I thought we talked about this.'

'I know, but ...'

He shakes his head. 'You haven't been given the go-ahead to go back to work yet. That means no answering texts and phone calls from Kalinda or your replacement, and certainly no backseat organizing.'

'But Kalinda just tore strips off Rob for ruining her dinner party! He needed my help.'

Simon slides my phone into his back pocket. He does not look impressed. 'I don't give a flying fart about what Rob needs. It's you I care about.'

I know he's right. I kneel up on the sofa so I can loop my arms around his shoulders. I try to kiss him, but he's just that little bit too tall, so I end up planting my lips on his collarbone. He grudgingly huffs and puts his arms around me.

'I'm just bored,' I tell him. 'I feel as if I've been pacing around this flat for years with nothing to do.'

I feel his chest inflate and deflate as he lets out a deep sigh. 'You haven't even been home from your mum's for a month.'

'It feels longer. And you're so busy at work. I'm spending a lot of time on my own.'

'Can't your mum come round a bit more? I mean, back when you first moved home, I'd find her here every evening. It's as if she didn't trust me to look after you.' He says this in a jokey way, but I don't respond to his comment, knowing there's probably more truth in it than he realizes.

'I've called her a few times, but she's only been able to come round once this week. This new charity is keeping her quite busy.' And I can't begrudge her that. For years, all I wanted was to be on an equal footing with Alex. Not given more attention, just not less. And now she's finally showing her love in the best way she knows how, I can hardly complain, can I?

'What about Anjali?'

'She's at work during the day, and she finally said yes to a date with Lars. It now seems they're the hot new … thing.'

Simon grins. 'I had no idea. Why didn't he tell me?'

I shrug. 'They only had their first date the Saturday before last.'

'Oh, cool …' He eases himself out of my grasp. 'I'm hungry. What are we doing for dinner?'

'Pasta.' I'd like to cook something more complicated, but one step at a time. It's good to feel as if I can do something useful again. However, after a couple of minor mishaps where I walked away from the pan and forgot about it or tried to cook rice with no water, I am not currently allowed to operate the hob unsupervised.

On the whole, though, the doctors say I'm making pretty good progress. Yes, my short-term memory is still patchy. I have problems finding the right word more often than not, but I am learning to adapt. It seems that my love of lists, calendars, colour-coding and colourful sticky notes has been my salvation.

I make a simple supper of pasta and arrabbiata sauce while Simon throws together a salad from a bag and then we sit down to eat at the table.

'Okay,' I say, spearing a piece of pasta, then waving my fork in Simon's direction. 'I promise I won't take any more calls from Rob. He'll just have to work things out on his own. He's got access to my household binder with all my notes and lists.'

'Good,' Simon replies, giving me a stern look.

'But I've got to have *something* to fill my time, and I … Oh! I stay frozen for a couple of seconds while the thought forms fully in my head and then I shout, 'Binders!' surprising Simon so much that he drops his fork and it clatters onto the plate.

'Um … Sorry? What?'

'I think I've got it … The perfect solution! I can start planning our wedding. Again.'

Simon stops eating and frowns. I suddenly get a really weird vibe.

'What? What is it?' I'm aware my tone is shrill and I'm sounding quite confrontational. For the millionth time, I curse the fact that knock on the head has changed me – maybe forever – and that I can't seem to keep a lid on my emotions as easily. I also don't have the ability to rein them back in once they've been let loose. I stare at Simon. 'Don't you *want* to marry me?' Before he can answer, I push away from the table and walk away.

Simon comes up behind me and lays a hand on my shoulder. 'Erin … Of *course* I want to marry you.' When I turn round, he loops his arms around my waist and looks into my eyes. 'I'm just not sure it's the right time to be planning another wedding. You got so stressed last time. And you're not great with large groups still. Even dinner with my family last week wiped you out, and that was only ten people.'

I know he's got a point, but that doesn't stop me feeling completely stir-crazy. I've got to do *something*.

'What if we don't do the whole hoopla a second time over? What if we keep it small, intimate? We can do the ceremony in Lower Hadwell again, and then the wedding breakfast – but only close friends and family. And then we can have a big party back here in London at a later date when I'm feeling much better. Think of it as just postponing the evening reception until I'm ready for it?'

'But that's *two* things to organize! That doesn't sound much like resting to me.'

I smooth my hands across his shoulders in a soothing sweep. 'But not both at the same time. And I promise I'll take it slowly. I won't get all manic about it this time.'

Simon gives me a look that says he thinks I'm talking out of my backside. I probably am, but I'm going to do my best to stick to my word. 'Please?'

He sighs. 'Let me think about it.' He spots the clock on the wall behind me. 'Is that the time?' His grip loosens on me. 'I told Gil I'd go out with him for a quick pint.'

'You didn't mention that to me.' I frown. 'Did you?'

He shakes his head. 'I didn't get the chance. It's a bit of a last-minute thing – he's leaving London for a while, something to do with a change in his job. He explained it to me, but all that cyber threat stuff isn't really my thing.'

I can believe that. If Simon can't get his phone or his laptop to do something, he usually just swears at it until I come and sort it out for him. Or I used to. I have no idea if I can do that kind of stuff now. Concentrating too hard either makes me sleepy or gives me a headache.

'Listen,' he says, pressing a kiss to my forehead and then letting me go completely. 'We'll talk about it when I get back—'

'A "quick" pint? That means I'll probably be in bed by the time you get back.'

'Tomorrow, then?'

This is not the answer I want. Ever since the accident, I seem to have lost most of my patience. When I want to do something, I want to do it right now. And I want to talk about planning our wedding *right now*. But I'm also aware this is something I need to work on. 'Okay,' I say sullenly.

Simon pulls my phone from his pocket and hands it back to me. 'No calling what's-his-face while I'm out.'

I nod. And this time I'm telling the truth. I have no intention of calling Rob back. I'll just send him the text I promised, then switch my phone off.

When Simon leaves and I'm on my own again, it takes all of ten minutes of scrolling through all my available streaming services for something to watch before I give up and head to the bookshelf. I pull out a storage box out and push the lid off. There, in all its tabbed and multicoloured glory, is my wedding binder. Just a little flick through won't hurt.

CHAPTER FORTY-EIGHT

Five years ago

She's sitting in the jacuzzi on *Island Queen*'s sun deck with a glass of wine beside her. They have a day between charters and the crew have some time to relax.

How was the holiday?

They hadn't been able to speak on the phone over Christmas. In fact, the Wi-Fi had been so dire in Lapland, they'd hardly been able to message at all. However, he had managed to on Christmas Day, saying he wished she was with him.

Christmas was fine is his reply.

Thinking of her fantasy of kissing him under a dancing curtain of green at midnight, she asks:

Did you see the Northern Lights?

It was the best time of year to catch them.

So, you did?

Yes.

Is it just her, or is he being oddly short and to the point? A tiny quiver starts up in her belly. Is it happening again? Is he losing interest?

How about you? How was your Christmas?

She sighs. Pretty much the same as it always was on board. The crew did some things to cheer themselves up, even though they were working, and the guests were lovely, but it's hard being away from the people you love.

The usual. Glad it's all over now.

They fall into easy conversation, the same way they did before the holidays, and after they finally say goodbye, she stares up at the cloudless blue sky, imagining herself in Lapland with him, his arm around her as they gaze up at the aurora borealis while snow falls softly around them.

CHAPTER FORTY-NINE

Present Day

A large artist's pad with circles drawn on it sits on the coffee table in front of me, peppered with narrow sticky notes. I've been staring at it for at least ten minutes, my brain feeling like porridge. I thought planning a smaller wedding reception would be easier, but it turns out it is just as much work. More so, maybe.

We've decided to wait for a cancellation at the Royal Marina Hotel, but using their smaller function room that holds only forty people instead of a hundred and twenty. Although we haven't got the date set yet, we've decided we need to work out who's going to get an invitation, so we can get in early and manage expectations. And part of deciding who to invite is working out who won't cause drama.

The seating plan for our first wedding was bad enough, but with fewer seats, it's a lot harder to keep the warring factions of Simon's sprawling family apart from each other. Every time I move someone away from someone they're not talking to, they just end up on a table with someone who's not talking to them. It's an endless merry-go-round of petty family squabbles, half of which I don't even know the details of. I just know not to sit so-and-so with what's-her-face, that sort of thing.

I peel one sticky note off the chart and hold it between my thumb and forefinger. If I could just do away with this one name, it would make everything so much simpler.

We have a large open-plan living space and dining area, with a kitchen next door. I call out to Simon who is making cheese on toast for our lunch. 'Does your cousin Vera really have to come? She seems to have fallen out with just about everyone!'

Simon appears at the doorway. 'I believe my mother's words were, and I'm quoting her exactly, "If you don't invite Vera, we'll inevitably end up with Mears family World War Three".'

I stick the note with "Vera (S cousin)" written on it back down on an empty part of the page. 'Right.'

'And we can't sit her with Rachel?'

Simon shakes his head. 'They haven't got on since Rufus's christening, when Vera told my brother-in-law that the baby looked like his best friend.'

I pull a face. 'Ooh … Ouch.'

'Yeah. And it *might* work if they ice each other out, but you know how Rachel gets when she has a few drinks inside her. They'll just end up in a shouting match.'

I stare at the circle representing table number four. 'How about we move Rachel and Leo to table four? Then they can sit with Maddy and her partner? They get on, don't they?'

Simon nods, but then his expression turns thoughtful. 'But if all my other siblings are on tables one and two and Rachel's at table four, she'll feel like she's been demoted, and then I'll get it in the neck.'

Simon comes to sit beside me, and we eat our lunch. He

puts the TV on and watches somebody cooking something for celebrity guests. I don't know who, because I'm too busy looking at the stupid seating chart. My cheese on toast disappears without me actually remembering eating it. A low pulse of pain begins in my temples, a sign that I'm getting too worked up and that if I don't take a rest, I'll have a pounding headache and will be good for nothing unless I lie down in bed with my eyes closed.

A little worm of resentment burrows deep inside my chest. Why does Simon's bloody family have to be so difficult? My parents are divorced and they still manage to be civil to each other when they're in the same room. A flair for performance and drama must be in the Mears DNA, which makes me slightly worried when I think about the likelihood of passing it down to the next generation.

I growl with frustration and peel all the name labels off but those for the top table. Back to square one, it seems.

Simon stands up, collects the plates, and heads towards the kitchen. 'Right. I'll be off then.'

My head snaps up. 'Off?'

He nods. 'Yeah, I told you I was going to meet up with Marcus and Fred for a kick-about in the park, remember?'

I blink. And then I go into the kitchen and inspect the fridge. There's a mini whiteboard on it for Simon to write dates and details I need to know about. However, the whiteboard is blank. 'There's nothing up here.'

'Didn't I …' He smiles at me sheepishly and lets out a nervous laugh. 'Sorry. Must have forgotten to write it down. But you can't get mad at me for that, can you?'

I glare at the empty board. No, I can't get mad at him for

forgetting stuff. It would be highly hypocritical. But I think I might like to, all the same. 'I was hoping to get this seating chart done this afternoon.'

Simon smiles at me. 'I'm sure you'll get there in the end.' And then he gets ready to go out.

The worm of resentment burrows deeper. I can't believe he's going to leave me here to do this on my own.

But this is what you wanted, remember? You begged him to let you start wedding planning.

Yes, I know that! I tell myself. But it doesn't stop it being annoying that he's about to abandon me to go out and kick a ball around with his friends. I need him here to help me with this!

Then why don't you tell him that?

It's an excellent question. One I don't have an answer for. But somehow I can't seem to make the words leave my lips. Maybe because I don't want to admit he was right, that it's too soon to dive in to replanning our wedding, that actually, I'm finding it all a bit much. Maybe because I don't want to admit I'm struggling, that I'm not still on the trajectory of the perfect recovery I'd set for myself, that I haven't been doing well for a couple of weeks now.

As Simon bustles around the flat looking for his keys and phone, finding the right pair of trainers to wear, I sit with my elbows on my knees, my head in my hands, radiating 'I'm overwhelmed' vibes. When he doesn't seem to notice, I massage my temples, huffing occasionally.

If Simon ever had a radar for this kind of thing, it's definitely faulty.

I eventually give up looking at the stupid seating chart and let my head flop back on the sofa and close my eyes. I can feel that nerve in my temple twanging now, threatening to send the pain round to the back of my eye socket.

'Bye, then,' he says from the other side of the living room.

I slowly open my eyes and look at him. *Say it,* I will him. *Say you can see I'm struggling. Offer to stay and help.*

He walks over to me and kneels down on the sofa beside me, picks my limp torso up and pulls me into a warm and gentle hug. I exhale with relief. Thank God …

And then he kisses me on the forehead. 'I know this is tough,' he says seriously. 'But I believe in you. You've got this, babe.'

He gives me a quick peck on the lips and before I know it, I'm sitting alone in my living room with a TV chef telling me brightly that confit duck isn't so hard to make if you follow these few simple tips …

CHAPTER FIFTY

Present Day

'Oh, God ... Vera's now asking if she can bring a plus one.' I throw my phone down on the bed and dive onto the mattress face first. I try to breathe past my ribs and into my stomach, like my old yoga teacher suggested, but I can't seem to get the oxygen past my bra strap.

'You'll just have to explain to her – again! – that because we've cut the guest numbers by two-thirds, no one who wasn't already with someone when the save the date went out is bringing anyone.'

'Can you do it?' I mumble into the duvet cover. I just can't face it. I want to pretend Vera doesn't exist and I don't have to deal with her.

'Pardon?' Simon says as he moves around the bedroom, getting ready for work.

I lift my head. 'Do you think you can message Vera?'

Simon stops and looks at me. 'I'll try. But you know how full-on it is at the moment at work. I might not have the time until this evening.'

I groan and let my head flop back down, this time with

my cheek meeting the white cotton, and I stare out across the bedroom, my eyes focusing on nothing. I know Vera will 'nudge' well before this evening, so I'm probably going to have to answer her anyway.

But I don't. I know I'm only going to make it worse for myself, but I don't. My batteries are flat. Every time I open up the messaging app on my phone, the letters on the keyboard shimmer and dance and I put it away again.

I spend most of the day sitting on the sofa, the TV on mute, as *Pride and Prejudice* plays in the background. I can't even bear to hear their voices either. I just need … stillness. Quiet. Space. Maybe then I'll be able to breathe all the way down to my belly button, but not now.

When Simon returns home, I'm still in my pyjamas. I haven't even had a shower or pulled my hair out of its messy bun and brushed it, which is most unlike me. What's the point? I've got nowhere to go at the moment, unless it's a medical appointment, and those doctors and nurses see people who look way worse than me.

I'm lonely. Mum and Anjali make sure they visit. Dad has even driven from Wales to see me. But most of my days I'm on my own, and even when Simon's here … I hardly want to admit it, even to myself … even when Simon's here, I feel disconnected from him. As if I'm in a bubble that no one else can see. Another of the lovely surprise gifts my knock on the head gave me.

Halfway through the afternoon, the door buzzer goes. I answer it and let a delivery guy into the building. Did I order something? I don't remember doing that, but these days, that means nothing.

When I open the door, the delivery guy is standing there with an enormous cardboard box. It's so heavy that I struggle to take it from him, but I manage to thank him and totter back down the hallway to the dining area, where I dump it on the table. It's addressed to me, so I set about opening it.

After cutting the tape, I prise open the cardboard flaps and find an envelope sitting on top of organic packing material. Frowning, I open it and read: *Erin, I know you've been bored recently, so I thought this might cheer you up! All my love, Simon x*

I start to cry and I don't even know why. Wiping away the tears, I pull out the straw packing material and find a hamper containing all-butter shortbread, cracked black pepper oatcakes, Tunnock's tea cakes, tablet, the hard crumbly stuff similar to fudge that is my absolute weakness, a bar of heather-scented handmade soap, and a half bottle of champagne.

And then I notice something on the bottom of the note: *P.S. Can you guess the theme? Tonight, when I get home, there'll be a surprise. X*

Scotland? But why? Burns' Night was months ago. I don't get it.

I'm also not sure why Simon has sent me all this. I can't drink the champagne. Not yet. Alcohol is off the menu post brain trauma, along with caffeine and too much sugar and junk. I open the packet of oatcakes and nibble one, but it tastes like hamster bedding on its own and I can't be bothered to cut myself any cheese, so I make do with sniffing the bar of soap. It does smell heavenly.

I'm still confused when Simon bounds back into the flat at six-thirty that evening. 'Did it arrive? Do you like it?' He sweeps me up into a hug and kisses me before I can answer, then adds, 'Are you ready for your surprise?'

To be honest, I've been ignoring messages from Vera for

the last two hours, so there's a tight band of tension around my forehead. 'Yes,' I say, more because I want to get it all over and done with. I'm too tired for dramatics today.

'We're going to Scotland!' he says, practically bouncing up and down.

'What? When?'

'Next month. For the Edinburgh Festival. You always said you wanted to go, and you've been complaining about how bored you are sitting at home with nothing to do. I thought this would be the perfect thing!'

I sink down into one of the dining chairs. 'I wish you'd talked to me about it first,' I reply wearily.

Simon stops bouncing. 'Why? Don't you like the idea?'

'I do … It's just …' Suddenly, I'm finding it hard to line words up in a sensible order.

Simon sits down next to me and takes my hands, looks into my eyes, his features a picture of compassionate concern. 'What? You can tell me, Erin.'

I know, I reply silently. *But I hardly ever do. Why is that?*

But maybe I need to. I think back to that weird and elaborate dream I had while I was in a coma, how I was brave enough to tell Gil the truth, and how free and light I felt afterwards. I know that wasn't real, but I want to feel that way again, I really do.

'I … I …' I take Simon's face between my hands and kiss him on the lips. 'I *really* appreciate you doing this, for thinking of me this way. It's very, very sweet.'

'But …?'

I swallow. 'I don't know if I'm up to it.'

Simon's brow wrinkles. 'But you don't have to do anything. I'll drive up there. I've booked a hotel. We can get cabs to and from the venues. All you have to do is sit there and enjoy yourself. Fill the well … You've been saying you needed to do that, right?'

I nod sadly. He's tried so hard. I'm tempted to take back what I've said, to endure the noise, the lights, the people, but I can't. I have a feeling overloading myself that way will put me back months.

I kiss him again. 'I'm so sorry … But I have to listen to my brain and my body. I don't think I can do this so soon. Maybe next year?'

'Of course.' He nods. 'Whatever you need. It's fine.'

I can tell he's upset as he stands up and sees the contents of the hamper splayed all over the dining table. I pick up a packet and tear it open, paste on a bright smile. 'Shortbread?'

He takes one and attempts an answering smile. 'Listen … I'm going to change out of these work clothes. After that, I'll heat up some of that casserole we made at the weekend, okay?'

'Okay.'

I wait for a minute or two, but the atmosphere between us is bothering me. It's like an itch I need to scratch. I need to sort this out now, smooth things over. I stand up and walk down the hallway. The bedroom door is ajar and I'm about to push it open when I hear Simon's voice.

'What am I going to do? I don't suppose you want tickets to the Edinburgh Festival, do you?'

There's a few seconds of silence and I realize he's on the phone.

'Yeah. No … Right. It was worth a shot. But seriously, what do I do?'

Is he talking to my mum? I know they've been in cahoots

with each other since my accident. I know I should back away and leave him to it, but I need to know if my hunch is right. However, I haven't got much to go on, as Simon is mostly silent. The person on the other end of the line is obviously dominating the conversation.

'Yeah … Yeah … I'll think it over. Thanks for that. I'll let you know, okay?'

I get the feeling farewells are imminent and I skulk away like a guilty child.

When Simon comes back into the living area, he finds me putting the contents of my hamper away in the kitchen cupboards. Maybe I'll save the champers until I've got the all-clear from the doctors to have a drink now and then – if I ever do.

Simon rubs his hands together. 'How about that casserole, then? And what do you want with it? Rice or mash?'

CHAPTER FIFTY-ONE

Five years ago

Are you awake?

The message lights up the phone on the windowsill beside his bed. He blearily rubs his eyes and picks it up. It's just gone five. He's a bit of an early bird, so he'll be getting up soon, anyway. Can't seem to stay asleep past six, even if someone offered to pay him.

Yeah he taps in. **What's up?**

Had a nightmare.

She doesn't say any more than that. Doesn't need to. She's told him all about her nightmares, how they crawl into her brain in the early hours of the morning, their bony fingers swirling dark mists inside her head. It has to be … what? Midnight or thereabouts on her side of the Atlantic?

He doesn't ask about the subject matter. It's always the same.

That night. Megan. He had dreams like that for weeks afterwards, but they seem to have left him alone now.

What do you want to talk about? he asks.

Not about the dream. It's too soon, although she might tell him later, or in a few days. Right afterwards, she likes to chat about something light, something happy that'll take her mind off it. He racks his sleep-blurred brain for the right topic, but before he can come up with anything, another message arrives.

Tell me about Lapland. About the Northern Lights.

He feels as if a bowling ball has landed right in his gut. She keeps going back to this. And it's the last thing he wants to talk about. He hated lying to her about Christmas. But he couldn't tell her the truth. Not yet. And maybe not ever. Because he's got himself in far too deep and he doesn't know how to get out again.

But how could he have done anything else? She needed someone to talk to. Even if she didn't realize it fully, she'd needed *him*. No one else. He'd already been more than half in love with her when she went away. And now …?

Well, now he was in big, big trouble. Neck deep. Only just able to keep his head above water, and that might not last long, because he was falling hard and deep for Erin Ross, and that would be a wonderful way to drown.

He's never been to Lapland. He's never seen the Northern Lights outside of the TV or a YouTube video. But he's watched countless reels of them now, drawn to them because she's fascinated by them. So he pulls the images from his memory banks and starts to weave words about inky night skies, stars like shards of ice and dancing unearthly lights in shades of green and pink and blue.

She interjects now and then, asking him questions, and he answers every one. When the questions finally stop, he knows he has lulled her back to sleep. His job is done. It doesn't matter if he's lost what he's given her. He'd give her anything.

If only she'd let him.

He places his phone back down on the windowsill and opens his mouth wide with an enormous yawn. He punches his pillow to get it how he likes and rolls over, but then his bedroom door crashes open.

'Mate! You won't believe the night we've had!'

He rolls back over to face the door. His housemate is standing there, coat hanging off one shoulder and a half-drunk bottle of something gripped loosely in one hand.

'I bet I can fill in some of the blanks.'

The guy laughs. 'Well, you know me!'

Another yawn, but he can't help smiling. Yes, he does know his friend.

'Come and join us! Hopper is going to make us bacon butties.'

He considers it. He loves a good bacon butty, but he's still enjoying the gentle afterglow of the conversation with Erin. His housemates are too loud, too full-on. They'll scrub it away and then he'll have to wait for the next time the soft tinkling of chimes he reserves just for her light up his phone. Besides, Hopper always burns the bacon.

'Nah. I think I'll catch some more Zs.'

'Sure? We can cook extra, just in case you change your mind.'

'Sure.' He yawns again as the door closes. 'Thanks, Simon.'

'Sweet dreams, Gil.'

CHAPTER FIFTY-TWO

Present Day

I'm running through the flat, tights on, no shoes. My dress is only zipped halfway up my back because I can't contort myself enough to pull it all the way to the top without Simon's help. 'Si!' I yell. He's in the bedroom, doing up his tie. 'You haven't seen my handbag anywhere, have you?'

'No!' he yells back. 'What about the basket thingy by the door?'

My blood pressure climbs another couple of notches. 'If it was in the basket, I would have found it by now, wouldn't I?'

I can't seem to remember where I put anything down these days, so the strategy has become to have a place for everything and everything in its place. I have a pot for my keys in the hallway and a nice little rattan basket that I put my handbag in when I walk in the door, along with a variety of other receptacles for further essentials all around the flat.

I run from the living room into the kitchen, scouring the counters. It's only two-bedroomed flat, for goodness' sake! It's got to be somewhere.

It wouldn't be so bad, but Simon and I are supposed to be

going out to dinner with his sister Rachel and her husband to celebrate their tenth anniversary. We're already late, partly because I was on hold to the Royal Marina hotel to see if they'd got any cancellation dates for later this year. And at the same time, Replacement Rob kept texting me because he's having some kind of existential household management crisis that only I can solve.

I know, I know … But I kinda got suckered in a few days ago when Kalinda and her family were preparing to move to their villa in Majorca for a couple of months and everything went pear-shaped.

Anyway, the upshot is I was late getting ready and now I have an absolutely thumping headache and I can't find my painkillers because they're in my bloody handbag.

I turn a circle in the kitchen and make myself slow down. *Breathe, Erin …*

I keep finding things in the strangest places, so I've learned not to look in just the obvious places, but all the really weird places too. I've already been through the living room, the bathroom, our bedroom and the spare bedroom/study, so this is the only room left.

I walk to the kitchen cabinet right beside the door, open it up and look inside. Nope, just plates and cups and glasses. I close it again. And then I go onto the next one. I repeat this procedure, working round the room. I check the cupboard under the sink last, and then, just because it's sitting right next to it, I open the door to the washing machine.

And there it is, my lovely leather handbag. I instantly burst into tears.

Simon finds me sobbing, cross-legged on the kitchen floor, my face in my hands. Sometimes I feel as if I am going crazy.

I know I'm not. I know it's just the results of the head injury, but it still feels as if I haven't fully got a grip on reality, and that's both scary and frustrating.

'Erin … What are you doing … Oh!' He crouches down beside me.

'I found my handbag in the washing machine!' I'm shouting, even though he's right next to me. I want him to get it, to understand how maddening this is, but he just looks on, clearly bemused but also very calm. That just makes me angrier.

'And it doesn't help that I was late because I was doing wedding stuff,' I tell him. 'I mean, you're getting married, too. Why can't you help with some of this? Why is it all left to me?'

Simon pulls away. 'But I thought you *enjoyed* doing all of this. You begged me to let you do it.'

'That's not the point! You should know … You should have …' I swallow the rest of the sentence, not wanting to say it out loud.

'That's a bit unfair, Erin. Until now, it seemed as if you were perfectly happy to take it all on board.'

I make a noise that is somewhere halfway between a snort and a gurgling sob. Whatever it is, my nose runs. I stand up, grab for a piece of kitchen roll, and blow my nose loudly. 'Well, I'm not coping, okay? Is that what you want to hear?'

I'm right up in Simon's grill now. He backs away, looking pretty pissed off.

I don't care. I'm on a roll.

He's going to make me say it, is he, instead of working it out himself? Well, he might as well have it, both barrels. 'You know what people tell me? You know what they say all the time if I tell them what happened to me?'

Simon shakes his head.

'That on the outside, no one would ever be able to tell I'd suffered a traumatic brain injury almost six months ago. On the outside, apparently, I seem to be pretty much who I used to be – confident, together, on top of things. The doctors told me I've been a star patient, working hard at my physiotherapy and neurological programmes. I'm gearing up to go back to work. I'm getting married … But you know what the problem is, Simon? The outside is a lie. One I can't stop myself from telling.'

He looks at me, more confused than angry. 'I didn't … Why didn't you tell me?'

Because I wanted you to know! I scream inside my head. But he doesn't.

'I say nothing because I see the relief in my mother's eyes when she knows that her remaining baby is going to be okay. Because I see how tired you are of all of it.'

Simon's eyes widen, and even though I hoped I was getting it wrong, I know I've hit the nail on the head.

'I don't blame you. I probably have no idea how bad it was while I was unconscious or still in my post-traumatic amnesia stage, or even how taxing I've been since then. But I can see that it's wearing you down just as much as it's wearing me down. And I don't want to be that person. I just want to go back!'

'Back to what?'

'Back to my life! Back to who I am.' And then I just start to cry harder, like a big fat, whiny baby.

'I don't want to say I told you so, Erin—'

'Then don't!' I flip from soggy to fiery with frightening speed. 'And I know I'm being unfair. I know I'm being a nightmare. But I can't help it, Simon. And I hate it …' Uh-oh. We're back

254

to the waterworks again. Even I can't keep up with my own emotions this evening.

Simon advances warily again, and since I don't lash out at him, he puts an arm round me loosely. 'I've been mulling something over, something …' He shakes his head, as if he realizes he's about to go into too much detail and needs to keep it simple. 'I think you need to take a break.'

The thought of that just makes me want to cry harder. 'I don't want to go backwards … I want to go forwards. I want to make progress.' My gaze is snagged by the oversized clock on the chimney breast, 'Oh, God … We're so late. I haven't got time to have a breakdown now. Will you zip me up?' I say, trying to hold back the sniffles and not doing a very good job.

'No,' Simon says.

I spin around to look at him. A wave of tiredness crashes over me, except it's more like an avalanche than a wave, weighing me down. I sway on my feet.

'It doesn't matter that we're late,' Simon says. 'Rachel and Tim will have another anniversary.'

I'm filled with relief. He's going to say we don't have to go, and while I feel horribly guilty for letting his sister down, I'm just so happy that Simon knows this is exactly what I need.

He takes the handbag out of the washing machine and puts it on the counter. 'Listen, get yourself changed into your pyjamas.' I nod, filled with relief we can just collapse on the sofa and do nothing, but then he adds, 'I'll go to dinner and explain.'

I go still. 'You're not staying with me?'

'I'll feel bad if one of us doesn't go,' he says, very reasonably. 'And you probably should get some sleep.'

He's right. I should sleep. The doctors have said it's an

important part of my healing process. So ten minutes later, I'm lying in bed, propped up on a couple of pillows. A single lamp is on on the other side of the room, but even that is verging on being too bright for my overstimulated optic nerves. Simon gives me a kiss on the cheek, then moves towards the door. I want to grab his hand, to pull him back, but I don't.

'I'll see you later,' he says, even though we both know I'll be out for the count by the time he returns. The bedroom door closes softly, and a few moments later I hear the front door close too.

I don't know what time it is when he comes back in, although I rouse from sleep long enough to feel the mattress dip as he gets into bed.

Once upon a time, he would have snuggled up tight behind me, maybe even run a cheeky hand up my thigh or stroked my bottom, but tonight he keeps his distance. I know it's probably because he's being considerate, that he doesn't want to wake me, but I can't help being weighed down by this tiny rejection.

I feel completely unsexy. Broken. Who would want to marry this anyway?

CHAPTER FIFTY-THREE

Present Day

The following morning, Simon brings me breakfast in bed. Once the tray is on my lap and I'm tucking into yoghurt and berries, he sits down on the edge of the mattress, facing me. 'I know how you can get away from this flat and still find some peace and quiet, you know, proper rest,' he says.

'Mm-hmm?'

I'm not sure how I feel about that. My body is screaming at me that he's right, that it's something I desperately need, but my stubborn will is digging its heels in. I want to be able to cope.

However, words like 'relaxation' and 'peace' bring to mind luxurious country house spas and fluffy white robes, so I have half an ear open to what he's about to say.

'I think the problem is that here, you're always going to get sucked into doing too much, taking too much on. And I can understand why you're frustrated just being in the flat all day, every day, with nothing of real purpose to do.'

I feel a rush of warmth in my chest. The fact Simon has not only listened to me but came up with a plan to help shows I really can count on him when it matters.

'I know a place in the countryside where you won't be disturbed, and you can stay there as long as you like.'

Okay, maybe not a spa, but a gorgeous little thatched cottage with views over rolling hills, maybe a trickling stream running through a cottage garden? I could handle some of that. 'Thank you … This is really sweet of you.' I take a spoonful of yoghurt, making sure I also catch a couple of blueberries, and ask, 'So where is this perfect haven?'

Simon just smiles. 'You'll see.'

★ ★ ★

Exactly one week later, Simon and I leave our flat at the crack of dawn, get in his car, and head west. He won't tell me where we're going, wanting it to be a surprise. Since I rained on his parade about Edinburgh, I play along, even though it's making me stressed not knowing our destination. By the time the sun is high in the sky, we've travelled through a handful of counties, passed Stonehenge and crossed the border into Devon. I recognize this route. We take it every time we visit Simon's parents.

'Are we going to Lower Hadwell?'

Simon keeps his eyes on the road and his lips firmly pressed together. It's infuriating.

'We're not going to your parents' house, are we?'

As much as I love Michael and Grace, I really don't want to move in with them. That won't be restful at all. Even if they tell me to relax, I'll still feel as if I've got to be on my best behaviour, especially as I'm responsible for wasting a ton of money they generously put into the kitty for the wedding that never was.

Simon just flashes me a smile and gives a one-sided shrug.

I give up, facing the front again as my stomach begins to churn gently.

We continue our journey through the Devon countryside. It's the beginning of August and the fields are lush green or a warm glowing yellow. Now and then, we dip down into a valley and cross a bubbling river on an old stone bridge before cresting yet another hill. I recognize each landmark, and so I'm not surprised when we pass through Stoke Moreton, then turn off the at a sign that says 'Lower Hadwell 3'.

Oh crap. We are going to his parents' after all. So much for Simon understanding what I needed.

The centre of the village is up on the hill, with amazing views over the water and surrounding countryside, but buildings also spread down towards the riverbank, where there is a pub, some cafes, and a small quay. Grace and Michael live just beyond that, past the village green, the only true piece of flat land in the village.

We begin our descent down the hill, past ice-cream-coloured cottages, some with window boxes, some with thatched roofs. I get ready to put my game face on, my I-had-a-nasty-bump-on-the-head-but-now-I'm-doing-fine face, but just before we reach where the road swings left in front of the Ferryboat Inn, Simon takes a right, down a lane I'd never really noticed was there before.

I sit up taller and glance at Simon. He's staring straight ahead, looking pretty pleased with himself. We travel for maybe half a mile, past a couple of other dwellings. We're practically on top of our destination before I see it because the drive is almost level with the flat roof of a of a two-storey building that sits on the edge of the hill, almost on the very shoreline itself.

It's only when I get out of the car and draw closer that I realize I've seen this building before. If you take a boat up to Lower Hadwell or stand at Whitehaven Quay, you can see a boathouse with a small concrete jetty tucked into the woodland on the opposite bank.

I've always wondered who it belonged to, what it looked like inside. It's not old like many other structures around. Well, not centuries old. From its square shape and flat roof, I'd guess it was built in the 1950s. The exterior looks older, though, because it's covered in blocks of local stone that echo the colours of the river. The bottom floor lies level with the shore, where large arched doors open onto the water, and possibly is only half the size of the upper floor, thanks to the steep hill it nestles into. Above that is a floor with wide horizontal windows and a balcony that wraps around both water-facing sides of the building. Instead of being a concrete monstrosity out of place with its surroundings, it somehow manages to stand apart yet blend in at the same time.

This is where I'm going to stay? It wasn't what I was expecting, but it's breathtaking all the same.

Simon gets the smaller of my two cases from the boot and I follow him to the front door, which is on the upper of the two floors, and he knocks loudly. I've only ever seen this place from the river before, so I didn't realize there was another wing joined to the main house by a flagstone hallway, topped with a glazed roof.

When no one answers, Simon tries the handle. The door swings open and we step into the narrow atrium, which has only an old church bench and a rubber plant for decoration. The walls are an achingly bright white, which makes me think it's just been decorated.

'Hey!' Simon calls out. I hover behind him. It's not easy meeting new people these days. It never used to bother me making a first impression, because I always knew when I walked out the front door I'd tried my hardest in how I presented myself. But that Erin feels like my prettier, more successful cousin.

Simon walks the length of the hallway and opens the door at the far end. We emerge into a vast space that serves as a living room, dining area and kitchen. It's been renovated to look modern while paying homage to the mid-century architecture. Perhaps the most unusual feature of the room is that the centre of the ceiling is raised, leaving only a metre or so of a border to meet the walls. Narrow horizontal windows at the top allow light to flood in from above. Back near floor level, two wide windows run down the adjoining side of the large square room, revealing a stunning view of the bend in the river as it widens. The water is dotted with small boats that are moored to bright buoys, and beyond that I can make out the village. 'Wow …' I can see why the architect chose not to stick to a traditional house layout and placed the main living space upstairs.

Simon comes to stand behind me and drapes his arms over my shoulders, joining them in front of my chest, holding me tight. 'You like it?'

I turn in his arms and give him a kiss. 'I love it.'

There are footsteps in the hallway. Simon grins. 'Here the owner is now.'

I wait, desperately trying to quell the quiver in my stomach, but when the owner steps through the doorway, I can't make sense of what I'm seeing.

Simon releases me, walks over, pulls the man into a bear hug, and claps him on the back. 'Good to see you, mate!'

The guy hugs him back, and then he glances over Simon's shoulder to me. 'Hi, Erin.'

'Hi, um … Hi, Gil,' I croak.

I'm still in shock as Simon explains Gil just inherited this place, and he's doing it up for the next few months. 'You've always said how much you love this part of the world, how much you'd like to live here,' Simon says, coming back to loop an arm around my shoulder. 'And now you can! For a while, at least. Didn't I tell you it was the perfect solution?'

Gil is watching me carefully, as if he's not sure how I'm going to react to him.

'Are you okay with this?' I ask.

He gives a curt nod. 'Sure. Welcome to Heron's Quay.'

CHAPTER FIFTY-FOUR

Five years ago

Do you miss her?

He shifts uncomfortably as he looks at the message that's just arrived on his phone screen. He knows talking about the night Megan died is the whole reason these messages are pinging back and forth between them, but he always feels a bit queasy when she brings it up.

Yes.

It's true. He hadn't known Megan for very long, but she'd been a big-hearted ball of energy that you couldn't help feeling drawn to.

That helps she types back. **Knowing I'm not the only one who feels this way. Thank you for taking the time to talk to me about it. I know you didn't want to at first, but it's meant the world to me. I'll never forget what you've done for me.**

How can you be three thousand miles away from someone but still feel as if you've given them a hug? His thumbs hover above his keypad. **There's something I need to tell you …**

He deletes it, types it again and deletes it a second time before running a hand through his hair and throwing his phone down on his desk. He's supposed to be working, but all he can think about is Erin.

He hates lying to her, has been on the verge of coming clean for more than a week, but …

It's clear as they've picked over their memories of that night that she's not Gil Sampson's biggest fan. He could live with that if he thought she'd still talk to him, but he doesn't think she will. And although he wants that for himself, he'd be ready to give that up if it wasn't for the fact she needs to talk to someone, and Simon is not prepared or able to be that person at the moment.

She said it herself, didn't she? *Not* talking has caused her real psychological trauma. Back then, when Simon gathered the three of them together, suggested they should never mention that night again, even among themselves, Gil thought it was a good idea.

They'd talked enough, been grilled by the police over and over until it was all they could think about. But now he realizes maybe that was the wrong move, too. One extreme or the other hasn't worked. It's balance they need – dealing with what happened but not letting it consume them.

And he was helping her do this. How can he stop?

He loves Simon like a brother, but it's all his fault Gil got sucked into this in the first place.

Simon's phone ran out of battery on a night out and he'd asked to borrow Gil's and then had promptly dropped it in the street, where it was run over by a taxi. The apologies had been over the top – Simon even lay down in the street saying he'd be happy if the taxi ran him over too. And then he'd thrust his newer, fancier phone at Gil, saying it was his now, and had refused to take it back.

In the end, Gil had shoved it in his pocket. Simon was all about the grand gestures, especially when he'd had a few beers. He reckoned he'd just give it back to him in the morning, no harm done. But the next day, his best friend had rocked up with an even newer, even fancier phone and insisted he keep the old one.

The problem was that he'd hadn't just inherited Simon's phone, but his number.

That's when the messages from Erin had begun to arrive, asking why he wasn't answering back.

He'd sighed as he'd scrolled through the one-sided text conversation. Simon had been so into Erin over the summer and even when she first went back to the Caribbean. He'd noticed that Simon had been mentioning Erin less, hungry for any bit of news about her, but he'd assumed Simon just wasn't sharing, not that he'd been ghosting her.

He'd called Simon out on it, of course he had. Told him he owed it to Erin to be honest with her if he'd lost interest. And Simon had promised he would do just that. Soon. But that was Simon all over – great with the promises, but follow-through could be patchy. If he didn't know Simon had it in him to be the most loyal friend ever, he'd have ditched him a long time ago.

It was hard to watch Erin's messages day after day while he was waiting for Simon to fulfil his promise, and finally he'd cracked, picked up his phone and answered. At the time, his reasoning was that it was cruel not to, and that after that very short exchange, he intended to drag Simon over the coals for not doing what he'd said he would and call things off with her.

Simon, as always, was truly contrite, promising he was still intending to contact Erin, but that he was 'building up' to it. Seriously, procrastination was the man's middle name.

More texts came while all this 'building up' was going on, so Gil answered the occasional one, usually just with a one or two words. Hopefully, not so much that they got into a fully-fledged conversation, but just enough to stop her getting frantic and jumping on a plane to come home and rescue Simon if she thought he wasn't doing well. That was exactly the sort of thing generous and kind-hearted Erin would do.

What was the harm in it? he'd reasoned. Was it so wrong to send a little kindness her way, let her down gently on Simon's behalf?

But he hadn't counted on his best friend's ability to stick his head in the sand and avoid tough conversations, especially when it was a case of out of sight, out of mind. He also hadn't counted on Erin's talent for burrowing under his skin, for teasing him out and making him talk. She was the first person who'd truly been able to do that. And now he'd found it, he was reluctant to let it go, even though he knew it was wrong.

Be honest with yourself, man. You make it sound so noble, but you know why you're being a shitty best friend, texting your best friend's girl behind his back. It's because you like her. Way more than he ever did. Right from the first moment you laid eyes on her. Don't kid yourself that this is all for the greater good.

He stares down at his phone, knowing it would be easy to keep chatting back and forth for hours. The little voice in his ear is right. If this is all just some selfless exercise, he'd stick to letting her talk about the night Megan died, but they've mostly left that subject behind now and have begun talking about other things. About everything, really. How is that all part of his grand plan?

I'd better go, he taps into his phone. **Catch you later.**

He goes to find Simon, who's watching the footy in the living room. He picks the remote up off the coffee table and presses the power button.

'Mate …!' Simon says, looking both perplexed and pissed off. 'I was watching that!'

He rarely loses his temper with Simon, but he's getting close to doing it now. 'When are you going to tell Erin it's over?'

Simon frowns. 'I'm not being funny, but … what's that got to do with you?'

He holds up the evidence – Simon's old phone – and Simon's eyes widen as the penny drops.

'She's still messaging? Wow. To be honest, it's so long since I texted her, I thought she'd have worked it out. She's probably dating some American deckhand by now, called Brad or Tyler or something …'

The thought of some tall, blond, wholesome-looking meathead taking Erin out on a date sends Gil's blood pressure through the roof. 'You've got two weeks!' he says, brandishing the phone towards his best friend. 'Or I'm going to do it for you.'

Simon just laughs. 'All right, I'll do it. Christ. Calm down, Gil.'

CHAPTER FIFTY-FIVE

Present Day

Gil leads us to my room, well, mine and Simon's room for tonight, which is across the hall in the annexe. It feels quite private, which instantly puts me at ease. He says I have use of the whole space – a bedroom, a bathroom and an extra room which is still part-office, with a desk and office chair, but it's also a living space with a sofa, coffee table, and a flat-screen television above a stone fireplace. Both this room and the bedroom have French doors that lead onto a small, shady garden full of mature plants that overlooks the riverbank.

Unlike the main part of the house, which has obviously just had a makeover, these rooms are in good order but populated with hand-me-down furniture that is clearly a few decades older than the house. There's lots of dark-stained wood and floral patterns, but it makes it feel homely rather than tired.

Simon doesn't bother unpacking his overnight bag, and he doesn't notice that I don't unpack my case either, just pull something comfy from a pocket and shove it on. Once we've settled in, Simon insists on taking us all out to the open-air cafe opposite the pub in the village. It is famed for its seafood, especially crab, and he only manages to grab a table because he's a local and the owner is his cousin's best friend's dad. But the fresh air, along with the journey and getting used to a new place, exhausts me. I collapse into bed when we return to the boathouse, leaving the boys to catch up.

It's a wrench to say goodbye to Simon the next morning. Not just because I'm going to miss him, but because I feel off-kilter. I can't get my head round how this set-up – me and Gil living together – is ever going to work. I know Simon always makes light of it if I mention that Gil and I don't get on, but I thought he was always just encouraging me to give his best friend the benefit of the doubt. Now I'm wondering if he's ever truly realized how much friction there is between us.

And since I'm not allowed to drive, I can't steal a car and follow Simon back up the motorway. For now, I'm stuck.

After Simon leaves, I head back to my annexe. I throw the French doors open to let the balmy summer breeze in. Yesterday was overcast, threatening rain but never coming good on its promise, but today is a perfect English summer's day.

I stand at the open doors and fill my lungs. The air is fresh with a tang of salt and seaweed from the scrubby beach revealed below the garden when the tide is out. As I exhale, I'm sure I can feel the small muscles at the base of my skull unknotting.

When I venture into the kitchen to get myself a cup of tea, Gil is nowhere to be seen, although I can hear banging coming from the floor below. It sounds like someone is hammering or drilling, which confuses me. I thought Gil worked as a consultant in cybersecurity. Is my faulty memory doing me wrong again? But what do I know? He might be building a desk or putting up a bookshelf for a home office.

I find a folded-up piece of paper with my name on it propped up against the kettle when I go to turn it on: *Help yourself to anything in the cupboards or in the fridge if you want anything to eat or drink. But don't worry about dinner. I'll cook us something. Gil.*

It's not wordy, but it says all I need to know. I sense Gil is making himself scarce, which is fine by me. I've never been on my own with him before, not for any significant length of time.

Unless you count that other *time …*

Which I don't. Because it didn't happen, and I'm doing my best to forget all those images were in my head.

However, it's been months now since I woke up, and that dream or whatever it was still feels as if it actually happened. It's as crystal-clear in my memory as the days leading up to the wedding, maybe even more so. While, logically, I know I can't have been in St Lucia, when people talk about me lying in a hospital bed, hooked up to machines with tubes coming out of me, I struggle. That just doesn't seem possible. It wasn't fuzzy and nonsensical like dreams are. It really did feel as if I'd slipped into another reality for a while.

I remember Gil's face as we were bobbing in the water together, full of earnest intensity, his eyes telling me what he was saying was true: that he would die to save me if he had to. My heart does a strange little hiccup, and then I flush with heat as I remember just how close we got afterwards. Another good reason to keep my distance from him.

I make myself a sandwich with gorgeous fluffy white bread and thick-cut ham, glad to see that Gil has strong English mustard to add to it, and then I grab an apple, put some shoes on and go outside to explore.

It's low tide, so I walk along the muddy beach for a bit,

then circle the house and head up the stairs that take me to the driveway. From there, I walk down the lane until I feel my energy levels start to dip and then I retrace my steps. Back inside, I try to listen to an audiobook on the Walkman, but end up falling asleep on the sofa in my little living room, chapters and chapters rolling past unheard.

The sun is lower in the sky when I wake up, casting golden streams of light through the doors to dance on the wall. I yawn and stretch. When I open the door to the hallway, delicious smells waft towards me. I follow them without thinking.

Gil's back is to me as he stands at the hob, stirring something fragrant and spicy. He goes still as he hears me approach, then carries on as if nothing happened. A moment later he rests the spoon on the counter and turns around. 'I'm cooking Thai – is that okay for you?'

I have to swallow the saliva in my mouth before I can reply. 'Yes. That's … amazing. Thanks.'

He nods and goes back to doing whatever he's doing with the dinner. I slide onto a stool at the breakfast bar and watch him. I'm intending to just let him get on with it, but it turns out I have questions, and more often than not these days, they pop out of my mouth before I have time to stop them.

'So what's up with the house? When Simon said you were going away and it was something to do with changing jobs, I don't know … I suppose I imagined you were off overseas again, jetting away to somewhere exotic. I didn't think you'd end up going back home. Am I right in thinking you're from around here, too?'

He continues cooking, but looks over his shoulder now and then when he doesn't have to pay 100 per cent attention to what he's doing. 'I didn't grow up here, but this house belonged to my mother – she inherited it from an uncle about twenty years ago – and now I have inherited it from her.'

I have a sudden stabbing flashback to the top table at the *other* wedding that never happened. I see Gil's face as he looked at the seat where his mother should have been sitting. Did I know she'd died before I'd had my accident? I must have done. Even so, I wrack my brains and find no memory of a conversation about it. Mind you, in my current condition, that's hardly smoking-gun evidence, is it?

'I'm sorry about your mum,' I say.

He shrugs. 'We had – how shall I say it? – a complicated relationship. I have mixed feelings about owning this place.'

'But you're living here anyway.'

'For now.' He leaves what looks like a red curry bubbling on the stove and starts chopping some coriander. 'But I'm going to rent it out as a holiday let once I've finished working on it.'

Ah … That makes sense of the ultra-modern living space and the slightly dated bedrooms and bathrooms. 'It's a shame,' I say. 'I mean, those views …'

We both turn and look out at the river beyond the windows that run down two sides of the open-plan space. The water is blue and grey, tipped with glints of peach and yellow as it reflects the setting sun.

He doesn't respond to my comment, but answers a question I asked earlier. 'And Simon's right – I have changed jobs recently. I've decided it's time to move on from security testing. It was fun while it lasted, shooting off at a moment's notice to sort out someone's system after a cyberattack, but I'm tired of the travelling, so I've been doing some cyber forensics consulting on the side, and now it's got to a point where I'm going to bite the bullet and do it full-time, start my own firm. I can work from anywhere, so I thought, why not here? Then I can do the rest of the house up at the same time to get it ready for rental.'

'That seems like a good idea.'

'Listen, I'm about ready to dish up—'

I jump up. 'Shall I set the table?'

One corner of his mouth twists upwards. 'Already have.'

I turn to look at the long wooden dining table, but it's empty. He hands me a bowl full of steaming curry and a fork and nods towards a doorway leading onto the wraparound balcony. I follow him outside and then up a flight of metal stairs where we emerge onto the roof, which also has a railing around it. A wooden table and chairs are already set up.

My mouth falls open. If I thought the views from the living room were good, up here knocks those out of the park. I catch a familiar flash of white high on the steep banks on the other side of the river. 'That's Whitehaven …' I almost whisper.

'Yes,' he says, pulling out a chair for me. 'Possibly my favourite place in the world.'

CHAPTER FIFTY-SIX

Present Day

There's a reason hundreds of thousands of holidaymakers flock to South Devon every year, clog up the roads, and fill every available dwelling that could conceivably be listed as a holiday let, and I'm lucky to be in one of the prettiest spots of all.

Every morning I wake up, open the French doors and walk barefoot onto soft green grass and breathe in the slightly salty air that snakes its way up the curves and bends in the river. The light is different here, I swear. Everything seems to be brighter, the colours more vivid, especially when the sun shines. But even when it doesn't, the dusky blues, greens and greys of the river are soothing.

I fall into an easy daily routine, waking when I want to, eating breakfast, then going for a walk. Sometimes I get the ferry across the river to Whitehaven Quay and I walk up the winding hill and stare at the drive through the wrought-iron gates before turning round and retracing my steps back to Heron's Quay.

Gil has made good on his word; he leaves me to my devices during the day, and I often don't see him until the evening. The only evidence I'm sharing a house with him is the noise coming from the downstairs rooms: occasional banging, sometimes scraping, the sound of furniture being moved. I don't venture down to see what he's up to. I'm happy to keep my distance for now.

Each night, he appears from downstairs and cooks dinner, and it's always really good. Nothing fancy, but he seems to prefer fresh local ingredients over speed and convenience, flavour over presentation. We eat on the roof if the weather is fine. I don't start any conversations and even though I feel him watching me occasionally, he doesn't either, which is a relief. I know he's letting me stay here as a favour to Simon, but my wonky brain hasn't forgotten all I know about him. I'm not going to let myself get lulled into a false sense of security.

I've been at Heron's Quay for almost two weeks when I walk into my little suite of rooms after lunch and head for the bedroom. I'm just kicking my shoes off, ready to take a nap, when I realize the cotton wool feeling inside my head that drives me to my bed in the afternoons is missing. I stand there staring at the pattern on the duvet cover, realizing I don't actually feel tired enough to sleep.

I feel a strange sense of hunger deep in my being. Not for food, but for something to do. For the last few weeks I've been happy drifting where the current of the day takes me, but now I feel as if I want to take the rudder and point myself in a direction I choose. The only problem is, I don't know where to head for. Not work. I'm clued up enough now to know I'm still not ready for that. But something …

I turn away from the bed and open the doors of the art deco wardrobe. A few of my clothes hang at one end of the rail, but I push them aside and pull out the smaller of the two bags

I brought with me. It's still heavy, even though I've unpacked all my shoes and toiletries.

After placing it on the bed, I unzip it and pull out my wedding binder. When I packed for this trip, I smuggled it in there while Simon wasn't looking, but it's been in here since I arrived.

I hug it to my chest and head out of my rooms, across the hallway into the main living area. The light is better at the long dining table and I might need space to spread things out so I can look at them properly.

I make myself a cup of tea and then sit down in front of the binder and flip it open. There are colourful tabbed sections for different items like 'Dress' and 'Flowers' and 'Cake', and within those sections dozens of colourful page markers.

I stare at the binder for a good two minutes, paralyzed by indecision. *Just start anywhere, Erin.* But I don't. And the longer I look at the contents page in the front, the more uneasy I feel. I keep thinking about my epic meltdown, as I now refer to it, how I felt so out of control of my own emotions, so helpless. It scared me. This book was part of what prompted that.

The dregs of my tea are cold in my cup when I admit defeat, close my binder and deliver it back to its hiding place at the bottom of my wardrobe.

CHAPTER FIFTY-SEVEN

Five years ago

Something has been bothering her, something they didn't address when they talked through the night Megan died. She picks up her phone and taps out a message:

Why do you think we all agreed not to talk about it again?

She remembers the days following the 'accident' as the three of them had come to refer to it. It was awful. Not just the shock of seeing her like that, finding her and realizing it was too late, but everything that followed.

The police interview made her feel guilty, as if she were responsible, and she's never quite managed to shake that feeling off even though, logically, she knows she might not have changed the outcome. Even if she found Megan earlier, it might still have been too late. And it was Megan's choice to drink and take drugs, knowing there was a risk in mixing the two.

Seeing Megan's parents had been the lowest point. They cried on her, hugged her, thanked her for being such an amazing friend. She felt like a complete fake. So when Simon suggested not rehashing the details of that night with each other, it felt like a relief.

Do you think we made the right decision?

She senses he's mulling her question over, but he eventually replies.

No, I'm not sure we did. But we're putting it right now, aren't we?

She smiles, glad of his no-nonsense, direct approach. He's never harsh or blunt, but he never hedges around an issue. He's always so honest. It's one of the things she likes best about him.

How are you doing with it all now? she asks, because she remembers that he's still having to deal with all the gossip and speculation in their wider friendship group.

I don't let it get to me.

Yes, she believes that. He's dependable, solid, but not in a boring way. She finds him anything but boring. He's a safe pair of hands. Someone who can take care of the person they're with, if how he's been by her side for the last couple of months is anything to go by. She hopes things won't change when she finally goes home.

Home …

She flops back on her bunk and stares at the ceiling. Her return flight is booked for May. How can she last another four, almost five, months without seeing him face to face?

She raises the phone above her face and types **I miss you.**

Likewise.

She sighs, and happiness seeps through her body like warm caramel. And as her eyes drift over the different bubbles that make up their most recent conversation, an idea forms in her mind. A solution.

CHAPTER FIFTY-EIGHT

Present Day

I'm just hiding my wedding binder back in the wardrobe when I hear a crash from downstairs and a shout.

I run out of the annexe, across the hall, and down the stairs to the lower level. 'Gil? Is everything okay?'

There are only three doors down here. The first one is old and sturdy and locked when I try it. The second room is empty, bar some truly ugly carpet in an aggressive shade of orange. I find Gil in the third room, staring at a pile of wood on the floor.

He stares at the pile of wood, then up at me. 'Bugger.'

'What is it?' I ask.

'A bookcase,' Gil replies.

'Not any more,' I say, and then I can't help myself – I start laughing. I know it's horrible, that he might have hurt himself and I'm being incredibly insensitive, but then Gil laughs too. I don't think I've ever heard him laugh like this before – not a short huff of agreement, but a full-bellied rumble. When I accidentally let out a snort, it only makes us both laugh harder.

I'm still getting it all out of my system when Gil sobers and starts picking up pieces of wood and stacking them against a side wall. I can now see that there are holes in the wall above a row of cabinet doors that stretch down one whole side of the room, probably about fifteen feet. I also spot some ugly gouges in the wall, some still containing Rawlplugs, and realize this was probably on its way to being a stunning built-in storage cabinet. If half of it wasn't on the floor, of course.

'I think I underestimated how heavy it was going to be,' Gil says.

I look at the wall. 'You might need a different-sized Rawlplug,' I say.

Gil raises his eyebrows.

'You've seen the shelves in our living room. Do you really think Simon put those up?'

He nods, as if this new information makes complete sense.

'What are you doing down here?' I look around the room and it's clear that there is fresh flooring, and the otherwise smooth walls are the telltale soft putty pink of new plaster.

'I'm turning this one into another bedroom. Possibly for kids. I was thinking about built-in bunk beds over there.' He points to the alcove on the opposite wall to the shelving.

My mouth twitches. 'I'd make sure you've got those shelves nice and strong before you try anything that is supposed to hold a human body.'

'Ouch,' Gil says, totally deadpan.

I take a proper look at the room. It must be underneath the kitchen, next to the jetty. 'What was this before you decided to turn it into a bedroom?'

'All of the space down here was functional space for the maintenance of small boats. This one used to be a sail store.'

'What are you going to do with the other rooms?'

Gil looks mildly surprised that I'm interested. 'Do you want to see?'

'Yeah, sure.' This wasn't what I was thinking of when I was searching for something to fill my afternoon, but it beats staring at the pattern on my duvet cover.

He takes me back to the other room, which he says is going to be another bedroom. The locked door turns out to lead out to the wet dock next to the jetty. He then leads me upstairs to show me another of the rooms in the main block, which will also be a bedroom. This one is just about finished, even if it looks a little spartan. There is oak flooring, and one wall is covered in blocks of natural stone, similar to the exterior of the house, and the others are painted white.

I'm so used to opening doors and looking inside rooms by that point that I just move to the next one along the corridor, only hearing Gil say something as I turn the handle and push the door open. Inside, there is yet more of the ugly orange carpet, along with an old-fashioned camp bed, the kind that's basically a canvas stretcher with metal feet, a sleeping bag, a few suitcases, a dining chair and an old kitchen table housing a fancy computer set-up. Apart from the high tech, it looks like someone is camping out there.

Gil reaches past me to close the door again. 'That's, um …'

The penny drops. 'This is *your* room?'

He's heading away from me, back into the main living space. 'Yes. For now.'

I trot behind him. 'But why are you …? Oh!' He walks over to the kettle and fills it from the tap. I put my hand on his arm and he freezes for a couple of seconds, then turns his head to look at me. 'You gave me your room,' I say. 'And you moved into …' I put my hand over my mouth. 'Oh, Gil … I had no idea!' And what's even worse than my obliviousness is that it hadn't even occurred to me to ask that question.

'No need to apologize. It was my choice.'

I open my mouth to offer to switch rooms and the look on his face stops me.

'Don't,' he warns me. 'You're staying put.'

'But I … I …'

'It's non-negotiable, Erin. Besides, I've got a king-size bed and some furniture arriving for the other room up here in a couple of days. I'm going to move my stuff in there when it's all set up.'

'But—'

'No.'

We stare at each other, and I realize maybe one of the reasons we have clashed so much in the past is because we're both stubborn old goats. 'Well, maybe I can help in some other way.'

'You're supposed to be resting.'

'I know, but I feel like I'm getting some of my energy back. I think it would be good for me to have something to do.' I flash him a winning smile. 'I'm a whizz with a drill …'

His expression doesn't change; he's not buying it. 'Simon warned me you might try to do too much. And I'm declaring DIY as officially "too much".'

Gil gets two mugs out of the cupboard, makes the tea and hands one to me.

'How about painting?' I say, thinking of the stark white walls of the just-about-finished room. 'I've always found that kind of soothing.'

His eyes narrow slightly. I can tell he's chewing it over. 'I'll let you choose the paint,' he says. 'You've always been good with colours and shapes.'

I ignore the compliment and choose offence instead. 'You'll "let" me?'

'It's my house. What I say goes.' His jaw is set, but I see a glimmer of humour in his eyes. The bastard is enjoying this. I should choose a shade of orange to match the ugly carpet he's trying to get rid of. Then he'd regret giving me that job.

But then I realize choosing paint colours might mean a trip to a DIY store, and although I've been happy not to stray too far from the boathouse in the last few weeks, I'm suddenly excited at the thought of going somewhere new.

Even though I'm irritated with him for being his usual condescending self, I eventually sigh and then say, 'Okay. You've got a deal.'

CHAPTER FIFTY-NINE

Present Day

A couple of days later, Gil and I head into Dartmouth to check out paint colours for the back bedroom. I've always loved this town, with its narrow cobbled streets and ancient buildings, some dating back as far as Tudor times. Around every corner is a fascinating piece of history.

'Are you sure this isn't going to be too much?' Gil asks me as he pulls into a parking space next to the Boatfloat, the enclosed harbour for small craft in the centre of town.

I ponder his question. It's high summer, the busy season, but we've chosen to come into town early, hoping the holidaymakers are still enjoying their lazy lie-ins and bacon sandwiches before heading out for a day sightseeing. I'm aware that too much information to process all at once – colours, noise, movement, light, even people – can tire my brain out quickly. However, I'm feeling energized, almost excited. This will be a snippet of 'getting back to normal'.

'I'll let you know if I start to flag.'

Gil nods, his expression saying, *Let's do this then,* and we both get out of the car.

After perusing the paint colours in the store, I choose a dusky greyish-blue. It should add some interest to the bedroom without making it too bright, and the shade echoes the surface of the river on an overcast day perfectly.

We deposit the heavy cans in the boot of Gil's car, then head towards the small supermarket in the centre of town. Gil needs a few bits for dinner tonight. I just stroll along enjoying the familiar buildings and narrow streets, silently greeting them like old friends. Dartmouth is definitely more bougie than a lot of seaside resorts I've been to. A few shops do plastic buckets and spades and assorted inflatables, but the town lends itself more to boutiques, art galleries and stylish homeware shops.

I look in the window of one of the upmarket gift shops. 'If you're going to rent the boathouse out,' I say, 'it would be good to have some finishing touches, something that will make any photos you put on letting sites appealing.'

Gil stops beside me, frowning slightly. 'Is that really necessary? Isn't the building itself and some decent furniture enough?'

I stifle a smile. Gil certainly is a no-frills kind of guy, isn't he? 'Yes, Heron's Quay is stunning, but also yes, it's necessary to dress it up a bit if you want it to be a successful business. How much are you planning to charge per week?'

He mentions a figure that prompts me to let out a low whistle.

'At least, that's what the letting agent said I could get if it's done with high-end finish.'

I nod. 'The sort of people who might end up at the boathouse won't be short of a penny or two. Take it from me: they'll expect a certain ambience. There's minimalist, Gil, and then there's spartan. You want to aim for the former, not the latter.'

He looks back at me with a granite expression and then, when

I stand there with my arms folded, he actually rolls his eyes. 'Go on then. Lead the way …'

I make a little 'Well, how about that?' face to myself as I walk into the shop ahead of Gil.

The shop is filled with ornaments made from shells and driftwood, silk screen prints of beach huts and golden sand. There are gadgets made from brass and/or rope that look as if they should have some nautical use, but probably don't.

Gil picks up a framed print of the river from a local artist. 'I won't have to fill the boathouse with lots of pictures of boats, will I? It seems a bit too … on the nose.'

I take the print from him and put it back on the shelf. 'Of course not. You don't even have to have a boating or seaside theme at all, or you can do it really subtly, by using textures and colours that suggest those things, like maybe the odd shell or bit of driftwood here or there. Your guests might expect at least a nod to the house's riverside location.'

Gil wanders around the shop some more and then returns a few minutes later. 'How about this?' He holds up a creamy pink conch shell and I have a sudden and intense flashback to the honeymoon that never was: the argument we had in the sea while the boat was leaving, clinging together when we thought we might die, and then … the kissing. In fact, the flashback is mostly about the kissing.

My face heats and I have to look away. Gil is too good at reading me. 'I think I've changed my mind about shells,' I say and hurry out of the shop.

What is wrong with me? I wonder as Gil follows me, looking confused and concerned, and I mumble some excuse about finding the shop hot and claustrophobic.

CHAPTER SIXTY

Five years ago

Hey, you …

The message arrives and his heart contracts. He waits to see if it continues to be light and breezy or whether she's going to tell him she has news. Big news. Heartbreaking news.

He's dreading it.

He also can't wait for it all to be over, for the decks to be cleared and then maybe he'll have a chance.

Hey yourself he replies. It's become their thing.

You'll never guess what happened today!

Oh, wow. This is it. This is the moment she's going to say Simon has finally talked to her, and he realizes that amid all his issuing of ultimatums and threats, he hasn't fully worked out what he's going to do next.

He shoots a casual, **No, what?** back to her, hoping his nerves cannot be read in those two simple words.

I got promoted! Sort of ... Shelley had to go home for a family emergency, so I'm acting chief stew until she comes back. Sad for her, but it gives me the opportunity to show what I'm made of.

All the breath leaves his body in one long stream. He doesn't know whether to be irritated or relieved. It's been over a week since he gave Simon his ultimatum. Bugging him about it would only make him dig his heels in, so Gil hasn't brought it up since. He should've known that Si would leave it until the eleventh hour.

That's amazing! he types back.

Later, when his phone is silent and he's lying in bed staring at the ugly, textured ceiling his landlord must've plastered up there in the Seventies, he tries to work out a scenario in his head where he and Erin end up together. The more he thinks about it, the less likely it seems. How had he made such a stupid mistake, not telling her who he was right from the start? It had seemed like a tiny white lie the first time. But now it's snowballed into a fecking blizzard.

In the end, he decides to focus on the near future rather than his long-term goals. When should he tell her he's the one who she's been messaging all this time, not Simon?

As far as he can see it, he has two choices: he can tell her now, before Simon breaks up with her. But she'll probably freak out, call him all the names under the sun for impersonating his best friend – as he's starting to think she rightly should – and then she'll probably never speak to him again.

289

Yeah, so maybe let's *not* do that.

The other option is to wait until after Simon has told her. There's mileage in this. Possibly. If Simon is honest and tells her he lost interest a long while ago, then at least Erin might understand why he stepped in and took over communication, especially when he breaks it down for her, bit by bit. He's just got to get her to listen to him long enough to do that.

Yeah, maybe it's best to let Simon and Erin's relationship run its course. Simon will break up with Erin soon.

Of course, when it happens, she won't answer his messages, or even pick up if he tries calling, because she'll still think this number is Simon's number. But maybe it's time he got himself a new SIM card rather than having to pay Simon every month for the bill.

But what will he say when he can contact her as himself? *Hi, it's Gil. I'm really the one you've been talking to for the last couple of months, you know, the one you've been baring your soul to. Sorry I didn't get around to telling you. Whoops!*

He composes a thousand different messages in a thousand different ways and all of them make him sound like an A-grade jerk. Which he is starting to believe he might be. Accidentally.

But what's done is done. He can't change it now. He can only move forward and try to do the right thing from here on. What if, instead of messaging, he calls her? Hopefully, she'll be able to hear in his voice how genuine he is, how this isn't some cruel trick.

But then again, people always tell him how buttoned-up he is, how when the big emotions are going on inside him, he's all calm seas and clear skies on the surface. And Erin already seems predisposed to be suspicious of him for reasons he just can't fathom.

If only he could talk to her face to face …

He sits up in bed staring blankly into the darkness, his mind whirring.

Could he? It's madness, but the whole situation has been pretty bizarre. Maybe this is the perfect left-field solution.

He picks up his phone and logs into his banking app. He's been saving up for some hardware for a top spec computer he wants to build, but it should cover an air fare to the Bahamas, maybe even a couple of nights in a hostel. His heart starts to thud against his ribcage.

What will she do if he just turns up there? Will she even talk to him?

Yes. She will. Because Erin isn't rude. Even if he's not her favourite person, she wouldn't blank him. And if he can get just five minutes of her time, if he can stand in front of her and let her see a tiny spark of what's been fizzing between them over the last couple of months, it might be worth it.

He pulls up a travel app and checks out flights. Oh, wow. He's really going to do this, isn't he? When should he book for …?

He checks today's date. How many days ago did he have that conversation with Simon? Counting back mentally, he settles on the twenty-fifth of January. That means it should all be over with Erin by the eighth of Feb. Of course, he can't go dashing over there straight away. He's going to have to be patient.

But how long does he leave before he flies over four thousand miles and tries to mend her broken heart? Or maybe even just a slightly disappointed heart, when she finds out the truth of the situation? He doesn't want somebody else to swoop in and get there before he does.

His itchy trigger finger wants to book a flight for the next morning, but with supreme self-control, he chooses one for exactly one month after the break-up, and hopes the dust will have settled by then.

Now, all he has to do is wait.

CHAPTER SIXTY-ONE

Present Day

Even though I know I don't need one, I pretend I need a nap when we get back to the boathouse. It's close to four when I emerge from my room again. I find Gil in the back bedroom, hands on hips, staring at a tester patch of paint on the wall. 'What do you think?'

'It's more important what *you* think.'

He turns and smiles at me, and my stomach flips like a pancake. 'I think I like it. Thanks, Erin.'

'No problem,' I say hoarsely. We both stare at the wall for a moment and then I feel the need to fill the silence. 'Did I tell you I'm handy with a roller?'

'You did. And the answer is still no. I'm not letting you paint my house for me.'

I huff in mock outrage. It has absolutely no effect on him.

'You and I both know that painting can be quite physical, especially in this heat.'

'I don't mind,' I bleat, aware this really isn't the point, and pick up a clean brush that's sitting in an empty paint tray on the floor.

Gil gives me a long, hard look, then eases the brush from

my fingers. 'You're not very good at taking care of yourself, are you?'

I don't say anything, just try to make my eyes large and appealing. I hate myself for resorting to my puppy-dog look, but I'm desperate for something to do beyond picking paint colours. I like to be busy. Useful.

Gil lets out good-natured snort. 'I've seen you pull that on Simon. It's not going to work on me. But I do have another bit of painting you might be interested in,' he says over his shoulder as he turns and walks from the room.

I trot after him. 'Really?'

'Really.'

He heads into the living room and opens a drawer in a long sideboard that graces the only wall that doesn't have a window in it, pulls out a wooden box and hands it to me. 'These were my mother's,' he says as he opens a door, bends down and rummages inside for something else. 'I thought you might like to use them?'

I open the box to find a set of artist's materials. Watercolour and acrylic paints, gouache and pencils, brushes in different sizes. 'Oh! I … I don't know what to say.'

He stands up and I see he's holding an artist's sketchpad. 'Didn't you say once that you enjoyed painting when you were at school?'

'I … I did.' I don't remember saying that to Gil, but I must have at some point. 'But Mum wasn't so keen on it as a hobby. I think she thought it was indulgent. She encouraged me to develop what she called "physical skills", you know, things that had a practical application.'

He gives me a bemused smile. 'Paintings aren't physical?'

I close the lid of the box and hold it close to my chest. It's lovely. Made at a time when things weren't automatically shaped out of plastic because they were cheaper to produce that way. I feel honoured he's letting me borrow it. 'Well, of course they are … But Mum meant doing something to help other people.'

Gil walks over to the long dining table and lays the pad down on it. 'If there was a time in your life to indulge yourself, Erin, this is probably it. But I won't press you if it's not something you want to do.'

I clutch the box a little tighter to stop him taking it from me. 'I'll give it a go, if that's okay?'

'And maybe it will end up helping *someone*,' he adds, giving me a knowing look.

'Maybe,' I reply quietly. 'But the results might not be very good – I haven't messed around with paints since I was eighteen.'

'Maybe that's not the point.'

CHAPTER SIXTY-TWO

Present Day

That night we eat dinner on the roof again, but this time the silence feels a little less heavy. I feel something in our relationship has shifted, but I'm not exactly sure what. It feels rude to be sitting here eating beside him saying nothing after he's been uncharacteristically kind to me.

'I know you've never exactly warmed to me …' I begin, unsure exactly where I'm going with this.

'It's not that,' he says quickly.

I'm staring straight ahead, still just able to make Whitehaven out as a smudge of white amid the dark trees on the opposite bank, but I turn to look at him. 'Then what is it?' I really want to know. As much as I've always told myself it isn't important, that *he* isn't important, it's always bugged me.

He lets out a heavy breath. 'I can't say.'

'Can't or won't?' I ask, my tone harder than I intend. He has to make everything a battle, doesn't he?

He turns to meet my gaze. 'Both. But I won't apologize for it. Just trust me that no good will come from that conversation, for any of us.' After a few silent moments, he adds, 'But I want to apologize for arguing with you the night before the wedding. You're right. It was a shitty thing to do.'

'I did say that, didn't I?'

'You remember?'

I nod. 'It's the last thing I recall about that night.'

Gil frowns. 'Well, then I'm doubly sorry. That's a crappy last memory to have before what happened next.'

He looks so solemn that I want to say something to lighten the mood, but unfortunately, my mind is full of serious thoughts too. Questions. Always more questions. I fiddle with a button on my dress, breaking eye contact. 'No one has told me much about that night. At the beginning, I think they didn't want to upset me, and it feels wrong to ask now, as if I'm harking back to something I should have left behind.'

'Have you left it behind?'

I sigh. 'No. Not really.'

'I don't know everything, but I can probably fill in some of the gaps.'

There's a hint of warning in his tone and a shiver rolls through me. I suddenly realize he was the last person I saw that night in the hotel garden. I've pushed these thoughts away before, but now they all come rushing back. Am I foolish to be sitting here with this man? Alone. In the middle of nowhere? It doesn't feel that way. But I can't really trust myself at the moment. My damaged brain could be giving me a false sense of security.

'Yes. Tell me. What happened after we argued?'

'You went back inside, and I hung around in the garden for a bit. There was no point in causing a scene.'

I let out a snort of laughter.

'What?' he says, genuinely perplexed.

I sigh. As much as Gil Sampson has driven me to distraction over the years, I can't accuse him of that. 'You are the least likely person I know to make a scene.'

He blinks and I swear I see a hint of a smile on his lips, in his eyes. But maybe it's the twilight gloom making me see things that aren't there. 'Later, I went back inside,' he continues.

'Did you see me there?'

'Yes. From a distance. I think you left before I did, but I didn't notice you go.'

I chew over that information. It gives me a little more detail than I had before, but not much. 'Simon said you found me, though, in the garden?'

His expression becomes grim, and I realize this isn't a memory he enjoys revisiting. I've been a bit blind, too caught up in my own frustrations about the trauma of that night to fully appreciate how it affected others, and not just Simon and my family.

'Yes.'

'What brought you back out there? Getting some air from the party?'

He shakes his head. 'It was way after that. I couldn't sleep. Insomnia …'

'… is a bitch,' I blurt out, finishing his sentence for him. When he looks at me quizzically, I tap my head. 'It's been an issue, you know, since that night. Never had a problem with it before.'

He doesn't move, doesn't even blink, but the weight of his understanding is like a comforting blanket.

'So it was late when you went back out?'

'Past one.'

'Wow. I hadn't realized.' On the one hand, that's reassuring,

298

because I know it happened hours after my argument with Gil and couldn't have had anything to do with him, but on the other, it's troubling. 'I wonder what I was doing out there. Surely I should have been getting my bridal beauty sleep?'

'You didn't look like you were ready for bed. You were still wearing the same dress you'd had on at the party – that red one,' he says.

I frown. 'That means I didn't even make it into bed.'

'That's all I know. I'm sorry I can't give you more.'

I yawn. Fatigue finally is catching up with me. 'No ... Thank you, Gil. For both the information and the apology. I don't know if it means anything, but I'm sorry I was salty with you too that night – it wasn't really about you, you know. I was feeling a bit overwhelmed.'

'I knew that.'

I give him a disbelieving but good-natured look.

'At least I did when I calmed down.'

A moment of silence hangs between us, one where neither of us looks away.

'Well, thank you for finding me, for taking care of me until the ambulance arrived.'

Gil gives a gruff nod. 'Always.'

CHAPTER SIXTY-THREE

Five years ago

'Here ...' He pushes a pint of beer across the bar towards his best friend. Simon isn't paying attention, having turned round to watch two girls in tight dresses walk to the back of the pub. They're giggling and one turns and smiles at Simon.

He turns back to Gil with a triumphant grin on his face. 'I think I'm in there.'

The idea of bringing Simon out for this drink was so they could have some time away from their housemates to talk undistracted. Maybe this wasn't such a good idea after all? Even so, he allows Simon to chatter on about the rugby match they watched that afternoon, letting the beer do its work before he brings up the issue that's burning the tip of his tongue. The issue he can't stop thinking about, day and night.

His phone buzzes in his pocket and his instinct is to reach for it, but he stops himself. He's been trying to wean himself off her. It felt wrong to keep messaging so frequently with Simon on the verge of dumping her. His thinking is that now he's pulled back on contact with her, the break-up won't come as such a shock, that it'll help let her down gently. So instead of long, in-depth conversations, he's stopped initiating chats and has been sending shorter and shorter replies. It's killing him.

Even worse, it's now the thirteenth of February, five days past the date when Simon was supposed to break things off with Erin, and Gil is pretty sure he's done nothing of the sort.

When Simon's beer is half gone, Gil puts his elbows on the bar and takes a long gulp of his own pint. 'You still haven't done it, have you?'

Simon looks innocent. 'Done what?'

'You know.'

'I've been thinking about it. But I just haven't had the chance.'

He stares at Simon, not amused. 'You've had plenty of chances. You and I know the reason you haven't contacted her is because you would do anything to avoid an uncomfortable conversation.'

Simon doesn't miss a beat. 'Then why don't we avoid this one and have some shots instead?' He turns and raises his hand to catch the bartender's attention and manages to order two shots via sign language. The girl also gives him a smile and flips her hair.

Gil folds his arms. Free tequila isn't going to work on him. Not this time, anyway. 'You've got twenty-four hours, Si. If you haven't talked to her by then, I'm going to do the talking for you. It's been months now. You can't keep her hanging on like this.'

'All right, all right. But I can't do it today or tomorrow, can I?'

Gil starts to feel as if he'd like to punch something. 'Why not?'

'Because it's Valentine's Day tomorrow,' Simon says, laying down his trump card. 'That would be cruel.'

He has to admit Simon's got him there. It would be horrible for someone to break up with you – via text – on Valentine's Day. Although he's pretty sure Simon's motives aren't as altruistic as he's making out.

The shots arrive. Simon claps him on the arm and pushes one in his direction. 'Look … give me to the end of the week. If I haven't broken up with her by Friday, you can do whatever it is you need to do.'

Gil feels as if he's had this conversation a hundred times before, but what other option does he have? He has to give his friend this one last chance to do the right thing.

He's sitting there on the bar stool, body turned half towards the bar, half towards Simon, when the heavy door of the pub opens and a gust of icy February air slices in. This tends to happen every time someone enters or leaves the pub, but usually it's just a quick blast. This time, the arctic wind just keeps on coming. Goosebumps pucker his skin, and he's about to turn and yell at whoever it is to shut the flippin' door when he sees who's standing there. His mouth drops open.

It's Erin.

She's wearing a coat the colour of ripe berries, with a cream-coloured knitted hat and matching gloves. He doesn't think he's ever seen her look so adorable.

The last time he saw her in person was probably last September. There was a heaviness about her then. Today, she's holding herself differently, as if she feels lighter, almost buoyant. If he had to pick a word, he would say she was glowing. And it makes him feel warm inside to think that their text conversations might have brought her some relief, that he might have had a part in that.

His muscles tense, readying himself to move, to push himself off his barstool and stride across the pub to where she is standing, but he doesn't get any further than that. He's completely arrested by her, by the quick intelligence in her eyes, the nervous, hopeful smile on her face. She scans the crowded pub and when her eyes rest on him, the smile blooms and grows into something even more glorious.

She walks towards him and his pulse slows to half speed, each beat pounding in his ears. She doesn't take her eyes off him. This is everything he dared hope for. More.

But when she's ten steps away, he realizes she isn't looking at him. She's looking at the man sitting beside him.

Simon looks just as frozen as he is, possibly more so. On the surface, his friend's face is a mask of smiling surprise, but Gil knows him well enough to see the shock – and horror – that lies behind it. If it wasn't such a horrendous situation, he might laugh. If what goes around, comes around, Simon really is getting his comeuppance now.

She stops right in front of them, smiles sweetly at Simon. 'Hey, you …'

Gil's heart contracts. She's speaking their secret code, but Simon doesn't know it.

'Hey …' Simon mutters back. His face is blank. He doesn't kiss her cheek, doesn't hug her. The beautiful, full-wattage smile she's wearing dims.

Gil jumps off his barstool. 'Erin! This is a surprise!'

Her gaze flicks across to him, rests on him for a split second. 'Hi, Gil,' she says in an absent-minded way, as if it's a politeness, an automatic response she's put no thought into, and then the beam of her attention returns to Simon, leaving him cold and shivering.

He wants to jump in between them and wave his arms, tell them not to have the conversation they're about to have. Not because he wishes it was him she was looking at with such devotion – although he does – but because it's just hit him she's flown across the Atlantic to surprise Simon and this joyful reunion will not go the way she's expecting. It strikes him that Simon might well be about to break her heart.

'Listen, Erin …' Simon begins.

She nods, smile returning slightly.

He looks around. 'Why don't I take you out for a bite to eat? Somewhere more … private. And we can talk. Properly.' He shoots a look at Gil, one that both says *Help me!* and *Wish me luck!* And then he takes Erin by the hand and leads her back out into the frosty evening.

CHAPTER SIXTY-FOUR

Present Day

Gil is busy doing whatever he's doing on the lower floor, so I gather up my nerve and make myself a watercolour station at the long dining table overlooking the river. It's soothing preparing the space, setting out the artist's pad and brushes, getting a couple of tumblers of clean water. I tape a piece of watercolour paper to an old board Gil found in a storeroom.

The day is bright but slightly overcast and I check the exact colour of the sky and try to replicate it on the saucer I'm using for mixing colours. When I've got it just right, I take a clean brush and wet the paper, then add the paint at the top and work downwards, creating a gradient. When I've finished, I look at the landscape I'm trying to replicate again. I decide not to paint the village – too many houses and fiddly bits for a first attempt – but the rolling hills behind them, divided by dark green hedgerows into patchwork fields and dotted here and there with either trees or sheep, are the perfect subject.

Only painting is harder than I remember. Possibly because it's been around a decade since I've held a brush, and almost certainly because it's exposing the deterioration of my fine motor skills since the accident. I struggle to draw even a vaguely straight line with my brush to start off with.

After twenty minutes, I declare the paint-streaked piece of paper in front of me as my tester page and throw it away. The only problem is that the next three attempts go exactly the same way. Instead of the elegant little sketch of the Devon countryside I'd pictured before I sat down, all I have is a colourful soggy mess worthy of a preschooler.

Prickly warmth surges through me and I rip the wet paper off the board and squash it into a ball, then throw it across the room. And then I feel cross at myself for being such a baby.

As I stand to fetch it, I hear footsteps on the stairs. I almost knock a chair over as I dive for the evidence of my temper tantrum. Gil appears in the doorway as I'm attempting to hide it in the kitchen bin.

'How's it going?' he says, following my hand as I lift my foot off the pedal and the bin lid clunks closed.

'I suck,' I say sulkily, even though I had intended to pretend everything was going wonderfully.

He blinks. 'That well, huh?'

'And I'm being a brat about it,' I add, unable to quell the urge to explain myself. I don't want anyone to see me struggling, let alone this man, but he's kind of caught me red-handed, so what else can I do?

'It must be frustrating to find things that used to be easy more challenging.'

'It is …' I stare at him, wondering how he knew that.

'I read a book,' he adds, clearly having read my telltale features.

I used to pride myself on my 'stew face', as I once heard someone call the calm, polite expression used by yacht interior crew the world over when a charter is going to hell in a handbasket. *Nothing* could make me break my mask of professionalism. But I seem to have lost that ability too.

'On traumatic brain injuries,' he adds. 'When I knew you were coming to stay. I thought I should be … prepared.'

Once again, Gil has surprised me. This isn't the Gil I knew from five years ago, who was cavalier and uncaring. Did Megan's accident have more of an impact on him than I realized?

I'm so used to bickering with him I'm not sure how to respond, so I press my lips into a wry smile. 'Did this book of yours tell you what to do when your painting sucks?'

'Nope.'

I sigh. 'Pity.'

Gil looks at the closed bin. 'Are you going to show it to me?'

It's my turn to laugh. 'No.'

He shrugs. 'Moping around isn't going to solve anything.'

'Ouch,' I say, but I can't argue with him.

He regards me carefully for a short while, then heads towards the atrium. 'Come on …'

'What?' I call after him. 'Where are we going?'

He's disappeared out of sight, but I can hear him picking up keys from a hook in the hallway. 'Fresh air always helps,' he calls back.

'Now you're sounding like my mother,' I grumble under my breath, but I stop guarding the bin and follow him.

★ ★ ★

When we reach the end of the lane and turn into the village, the weather has shifted. The clouds have melted away, revealing a glorious August day. Gil turns towards the river and heads across the road to the Ferryboat Inn. 'What do you you want?' he asks, standing in the doorway.

I peer into the gloomy interior of the centuries-old pub, with its thick walls and beams on the ceiling. It's the last week of the summer holidays and even on a Friday lunchtime, it's packed, and the noise level is far from comfortable. 'Um … I'm okay.'

He gives me a look. 'Sit on the wall over there and I'll bring it out to you.'

I turn and spot a low wall at the edge of the road that leads past the jetty. The thought of sitting there in the sunshine watching the boats bob up and down on their moorings, a cold glass in my hand, fills me with relief. 'A sparkling water, please.'

He nods and disappears inside. I find a pleasant spot on the wall and support myself on my arms while stretching my legs out. Gil appears a couple of minutes later. 'Thanks,' I say as I take my drink from him. He's holding what looks like orange juice mixed with something fizzy. 'I thought you'd go for a craft beer or something.'

He shrugs and looks out across the water. 'Simon said a while ago that he'd given up the drink while you couldn't have any. Thought I'd take the same approach.'

I'm strangely touched by this. I don't remember being that appreciative when Simon made the same gesture, but I suppose I was still numb inside my post-coma ball of emotional cotton wool. Looking back, it's as if my feelings were there but greyed out and insipid when I first woke up, and they've slowly been regaining colour and vibrancy as the weeks have gone by.

I squint against the sun. 'Well, he did … but only for about a month after I got out of hospital. You know Simon and his red wine.'

Gil's lips curve into a smile. 'Oh, yes. I do.'

For the next ten minutes, we sit in silence and sip our drinks. When we've finished, Gil takes the glasses back inside and then leads the way down the jetty. The tide is right in, covering the strip of shingly, muddy beach and all four of the long pontoons are floating on the water. We walk to the end one, feeling the breeze from the river ruffling our hair, a wonderful counterpart to the midday sun.

There are two boys on the pontoon next to us, almost identical in looks, but one is slightly taller than the other. I'd put them at about fourteen and sixteen. Each has a bright plastic bucket at his feet and is holding a fishing line wrapped around a plastic contraption.

'How many have you got?' the taller boy asks, peering at his brother's bucket.

'Three,' the younger one replies, and then adds, 'More than you!'

'Are you crabbing?' I ask them, trying to peer inside their buckets.

The older one looks at me suspiciously, but the younger one nods. 'Dad's challenged us to catch ten each.'

I look around, but I can't see anyone who looks like their father. 'Where is he?'

'In the pub.'

'What's the prize?'

'A portion of chips instead of just another packet of ready salted crisps,' the younger one says. He looks hungry in a way that only teenage boys can get hungry.

'Crabbing's lame …' the older one says. He looks as if he wants to throw his line in the water and walk away.

I'm hit by a sudden surge of nostalgia for family holidays before my parents split up. Dad taught me how to crab on a trip to Cornwall when I was five, and I begged to do it every holiday we went on after that, whether we were by the sea or not. 'Can I have a go?'

The boys look unsure.

'I'm quite good,' I tell them. 'My record in one session was twenty-eight. I'll get you those chips in no time.'

That does it. The older one hands me his crab line before his brother has a chance. The younger one scowls at him. 'I'll have a go with yours if you want, mate?' Gil says. The boy grins and hands Gil his line.

I pull the weight and hook to the surface and check the bait – bacon rind. Nice. Crabs love that – and then I drop it back into the dark green water and wait. The brothers sit down on the opposite site of the pontoon and dangle their legs in the water.

Gil checks his line and nonchalantly says as he throws it back into the water, 'In the summer, Simon and I used to do this for hours. On this very pontoon.' He shoots a look across at me. 'My top number was thirty-two.'

There's a moment where we hold each other's gazes and a flash of something familiar passes between us, like our old sense of one-upmanship, only lighter and more playful. 'You're on,' I say, accepting his unspoken challenge. 'First one to ten.'

We each catch a crab almost straight away, and I call out the number of crabs in my bucket each time I add more. Gil does the same.

'Six!' I yell as I pull my line up and discover two tiny greenish-brown crabs with beady black eyes clinging on for dear life. I shake them both into my bucket of river water to join the others. But then I catch nothing more for a good five minutes, while Gil hauls in another three, overtaking me.

I am not about to let him win, not when it was my idea to do crabbing in the first place, so I pull up my line and move it to a fresh spot. It works. I add crabs number seven, eight and nine to the bucket in quick succession, but Gil is hot on my heels. The boys end up turning round to watch us, and the older one cheers me on while the younger hypes Gil up.

Only one more to go and I've won! I keep glancing over my shoulder to see how Gil's doing, scared I'll lose my lead, but I'm not paying proper attention when I try to shake crab number ten off my line into the bucket. Instead of plopping into the water, it lands on the pontoon and scuttles towards me, angry claws snapping. I drop my line and run away screaming. The boys roar with laughter and so, much to my surprise, does Gil. The crab thinks better of getting its revenge, shoots sideways off the pontoon and back into the water.

I laugh too until I see Gil has snagged his final crab. I rush back to my line and pick it up. 'That's cheating!'

Gil laughs even harder. 'Is not. It's not my fault if you abandoned your line!'

He holds the crab above his bucket, a challenging glint in his eye.

I sigh as I pull my line up again and find it empty. 'Go on, then,' I say wearily. 'Gloat all you want.'

But before he can rub his victory in my face, the older of the brother's shouts, 'There's Dad!' They both rush over and gesture for us to give us the lines. 'He might not get us the chips if he thinks we didn't do it ourselves,' the younger one says with pleading eyes.

Gil reaches over to hold his line above my bucket. The valiant little crab loses its grip and splashes into the water below. I frown gently, sending him a silent question with my eyes. He looks pleased with himself. And something else … but I haven't the slightest idea what he's thinking.

We thank the boys quickly so we don't give the game away and march back down the pontoon, then walk back to Heron's Quay in comfortable silence.

When we get back inside, Gil notices my painting station and looks thoughtful.

'I'm struggling to make the finer, smaller strokes,' I tell him, feeling it would be petty to hold an explanation back. 'My handwriting's also a bit off at the moment. But it's been improving slowly. I'm sure this will too.'

One of my discarded attempts is poking out of the closed bin lid. Gil walks over and presses the pedal with his foot. 'May I?' I nod and he picks up the ball of crumpled paper and opens it out. After studying it for a moment, he looks up at me. 'My mum went to classes for a while. They encouraged her to be less … careful. Her teacher always said she ought not just to try to copy perfectly what she saw in front of her but to bring something of herself to the painting, even if it was wilder, less … I was going to say "accurate" but I suppose it's a different kind of authenticity. Maybe acrylics might be better to start with?'

'Maybe …'

'You can paint up on the roof when it's fine,' he adds. 'I promise I won't sneak up on you and try to look.'

I see the earnestness in his eyes before he turns and walks away and something inside me shifts. 'Gil …?'

He stops and turns. 'Yes?'

I swallow. 'Thank you for all of this – for letting me stay and finding me the paints and, well, everything. I feel I ought to do something for you, to make it up to you.'

'You don't have to,' he replies. 'I didn't do it because I was expecting anything from you when I suggested to Simon you stay here.'

I stare at him. 'It was *your* idea?'

He nods. 'Simon said you needed to get away ... It seemed like the obvious solution.'

I'm struck by both his generosity and the fact that I know he wasn't expecting anything back from me because I'm usually such a bitch to him. And there was me thinking he had me here under sufferance because Simon had begged him. I realize simple thanks is not enough.

'I also ... I want to say I'm sorry.'

He frowns. 'For what?'

Here goes. 'For judging you too harshly in the past. I think ... I think I might have been wrong about you.'

He stares back at me, dumbfounded. 'Then you don't need to do anything in return. That's all the thanks I need.'

CHAPTER SIXTY-FIVE

Present Day

I turn my pillow over, enjoying the momentary coolness beneath my cheek, but the rest of me is still sticky and hot, even though the French doors to my bedroom are wide open. There doesn't even seem to be a breeze blowing in from the river.

I tap my fitness tracker to check the time and discover it's the wrong side of two. I puff out a breath and roll onto my back. It's no good. I've been tossing and turning for hours, dozing occasionally, but now I'm wide awake. And I'm thirsty.

I swing my legs over the edge of the bed, shove them into a pair of flip-flops, then grab my robe from the back of the bedroom door. I don't bother turning on any lights. The night is clear and the moon is almost full. I cross the hallway into the main living space, pull a glass from one of the kitchen cupboards and fill it with water.

Sipping as I go, I wander over to the windows and stare out across the river. My gaze sweeps upwards. Wow. I'm not sure I've ever seen stars like this. I can hardly count them. It's breathtaking. I get close to the glass, trying to look upwards to see if I can find Sirius, but the roof is in the way.

However, since it's the middle of the night and I have nothing else to do, I decide to go up there to get a better view. The balcony door is unlocked, so I step outside, then climb the nearby stairs to the roof, keeping a firm grip on the railing as my eyes accustom themselves to the darkness.

When I reach the top step, I let out a scream. Someone is sitting on one of the chairs near the table. Although it was only a tiny screech, the sound seems to echo across the water. 'Sorry …' I whisper to Gil. 'You scared me.'

'No … I should have said something when I saw you coming up the stairs, but I didn't want to make you jump and cause you to trip.'

'Well, one head injury in a year is unfortunate. Two would be careless,' I quip, and then, because I'm feeling as if I've intruded on him, I add, 'I don't want to disturb you, so I'll just—'

'No. It's okay. Stay if you want to.'

My hand is on the railing, my foot hovering above the first step. 'If you're sure?'

'I'm sure.'

I'm secretly relieved I don't have to go back downstairs to my sweltering bedroom. Up here, it seems a couple of degrees cooler and I can even detect the faintest movement of air. I sit down in the other chair. 'Couldn't sleep either?'

Gil sighs. 'Nope.'

'It's a beautiful night.' I pull my robe across my knees, aware that the silky material keeps sliding off them and exposing more leg than I mean to. Gil is staring resolutely ahead, but I still feel a little awkward.

I spot something in the water, a lump with something long and straight pointing upwards from it. It looks like a boat, but I can't be sure. 'What's that out there in the river?'

'That's the Anchor Stone. You can only see the pole sticking out the top when the tide's at its highest, but when it's almost out, like now, you can see the rock beneath it.'

I squint into the darkness. Now I know what I'm looking for, I realize I've noticed it before. 'Do people actually anchor their boats there?'

'Maybe once upon a time, given its name, but I've never seen it.'

The water breaks softly around it, the white frills of the waves barely visible in the gloom. 'That's a nice idea, isn't it, to have somewhere that's safe and steady in the middle of all that change – tides and currents and stuff?'

'It is …'

I've run out of inane things to say, so we sit there in silence, our heads tipped back, staring at the sky. Now and then Gil points out a shooting star, or the slow steady track of a satellite. I name a few constellations, and then so does he, but we can't find any of them in the blanket of blinking stars, and then we spend ten minutes trying to work out where Orion is buried and if it can even be seen at this time of year.

After a while, I realize the subject that's keeping me up will also interest Gil. 'Just as I was getting ready for bed, I got a text from Simon.'

'Oh?'

'He doesn't think he's going to come down for a visit this weekend, after all.' I try to keep the disappointment out of my voice, but I don't quite succeed. Simon visited the first two weekends I was here, but this is now the second time he's cancelled. 'Some big project they've got on at work. He says he is putting out fires on an hourly basis and he probably needs to go into the office on Saturday morning. It's a long drive to come just for a few hours, possibly stay overnight and then have to go straight back again.'

'That's a shame,' Gil says.

'He says he might come next weekend.' I pause for a moment, then add, 'I hope he'll be okay on his own. He must be getting lonely.'

Gil tips his head slightly and studies me. 'How are you able to worry about everyone else when you're going through what's probably the most difficult time of your life?'

I feel something akin to a flash of lightning sear through me. He's asked me something very similar to that before. When we were in the water. When we almost drowned.

Only he didn't. Did he?

Then why does it feel so real, as solid as any other memory I have in my head? Sometimes, I really do wonder if I got a glimpse at another version of my life.

'I don't know,' I reply softly. 'It's just how I am.'

Gil doesn't push me further. If he did, I'd probably push back, banish this subject just because I'm so used to being stubborn with him, but the fact he leaves the silence untroubled means I don't shoo the topic away as I normally would. It's an interesting question. Why *do* I do that?

After a few minutes, I say, 'Maybe it's to do with my brother. Maybe I'm always trying to make up for the child that's missing, ensuring I'm doubly good so I'm not letting them down.'

'It's tough enough being an only child without all of that.'

'I remember now … You're an only child, too.'

'Yes.'

I nod, recalling another night, a shouted conversation in

a hallway, back in a time when I didn't hate Gil. Back in a time when I liked him more than I've ever wanted to admit since. I don't know how to react to that admission, so I just gloss right over it in true Erin style and keep talking. 'The weird thing is I never felt as if I was an only child, because if that's the case, you should get all the attention, right?'

'You never really talk much about your family. Well, about Alex. But I've seen how … single-minded your mum is.'

I huff out a laugh. 'That's one way of putting it.'

He looks at me as if he's trying to work out a puzzle. 'Alex got all the attention, didn't he, even though he wasn't there?'

'Yes.' His words bring a lump to my throat and I swallow it down. 'The spectre of Alex was everywhere when I was growing up. My mum kept the box room decorated as a nursery, something that caused a lot of conflict between her and my dad. And there were photos of him everywhere.' I wince at the memory of a line of large pictures of my brother on the mantelpiece in the living room, along with one tiny one of me. 'My mum insisted we make a big fuss of his birthday every year – a cake with candles and everything – but when I turned eight, I didn't even get a party because Mum was doing a charity run that weekend and she had too much on her plate. I spent my birthday in a freezing park in the rain, cheering Mum on.'

I didn't think anyone ever noticed how I would feel about being the one left behind after my brother's death. It wasn't my feelings that were important, were they? But it shocks me that Gil, of all people, is the first one to make all the pieces fit. Maybe that's why I keep talking, spilling out secrets I've never told anyone.

'It got worse once my parents' marriage fell apart about five years after he died. My mum was really depressed for a while. Another gaping hole in her life. I think she set the charity up to fill it, and I don't know what she would have done if she hadn't, so I can't be mad at her for that. It gave her something to get out of bed for in the morning. It gave her a purpose.'

' Erin …' I can hear the censure in his tone, and I know he's thinking that there should have been something, *somebody,* else to give her that sense of hope and purpose.

I shake my head. 'I couldn't stop her, even if I'd known how to express that feeling when I was a child, because even then I knew how selfish it would be. She was helping other parents. Other *babies.*'

Gil's expression tells me he doesn't agree with me. 'Maybe there could have been a better balance. Have you ever talked to your mum about this?'

I laugh at the absurdity of the idea. 'I couldn't.'

'Why?'

'The thing that fuels her is that she feels she let Alex down. How could I add to that? How could I tell her she's an even worse mother than she thought she was? Besides … It's changing now. I think my accident really shook her up.'

'I'm glad things are changing.'

'Me too.'

We fall silent again, but this time we don't stare at the stars. I have the feeling that neither of us is ready to go back to bed so I root around for something else to talk about. I land on what I presume is a fairly safe subject. 'How did you and Simon become such good friends? I know you met at school, but I'm not sure I've ever heard the full story. If I did, I've forgotten it. I forget a lot of things these days.'

319

'My mum was from around here and when I was twelve, she decided to move back to this area. I was enrolled in the local high school in Dartmouth. But you know what it's like … I joined part way through Year 8. Everybody else already had their friendship groups and I wasn't from around here. I got bullied.'

'Really?' I wouldn't imagine Gil to be someone who got bullied. He seems so sure of himself, so together.

'And then Simon broke his arm playing rugby and our form tutor assigned me to help him at lunchtimes, carrying his tray and things like that. The bullying stopped after that.'

'Because you carried his tray? I know Simon likes to be made a fuss of, but even so …'

I hear the smile in his voice as he continues. 'Yeah. But he was popular. You know Simon … cheeky, good with the banter. Everybody liked him. After that, if anyone tried to pick on me, he called them out. And even when his arm healed, we kept hanging out together, bonding over things like cars and motorbikes and sports, the way teenage boys do. He's always had my back. I appreciated it because it was a tough time. My dad had just died. From a stroke – his second one. My mum was devastated and she just kind of checked out.'

'I'm so sorry. I didn't know that about your dad.'

He stares into the darkness, at the shadowy hills on the other side of the river. 'It's okay.' He smiles and then sighs. 'My mum loved Simon. Sometimes I think she wished he'd been her son instead of me.'

I don't know if it's true, but I can't leave that comment hanging in the silence. 'I'm sure that's not the case.'

'Simon reminded her of my dad, I think. He was one of

those people who charmed everybody he met. I'm not like that. I'm probably more like her if anything, but I don't know if she ever saw that.'

I feel sorry that he's lost the opportunity to connect with her. At least Mum and I have a chance for a different future. 'Why do we always feel we need to be something other than what we are?'

He turns to look at me and his eyes lock on mine. 'You don't need to be anything other than what you are, E.'

E …

That must be something he got from Simon, because Simon always used to call me that when we were first going out. I realize that this one little letter of the alphabet might signify a seismic shift in my relationship with Gil. Against all odds, I think we are becoming friends.

I get up and walk to the railing, place my hands on the cold bars and stare out across the water. After a few moments, Gil comes to join me. My voice drops to a whisper. 'Since the accident, I've been … struggling. You say I don't need to be anything other than who I am, but what if I don't even know who that is?'

I turn and look for his reaction. His gaze is steady, but he just waits for me to say more.

'I feel as if there are two Erins, the person I used to be before the accident: competent, confident, had all her shit together, and who I am now: haphazard, insecure, shit all over the place …' I stop to chuckle softly, even though it's not particularly funny.

Gil is still looking at me with that intensity that is pure him, but it's not scathing as it used to be. 'I don't see much difference. I just think the real you is poking through the veneer.'

'That's what I'm afraid of,' I say quietly and then I look away because the backs of my eyes are stinging.

We stand in silence for a minute and then Gil says, 'You're worried Simon won't love this new Erin the way he loved the old one?'

My head whips round. 'Y-yes!' But then I shut my mouth firmly. I don't want to be disloyal.

'I know Simon just about as well as anybody on this planet,' Gil says. 'Anything you say won't put a wedge in my friendship with him, so if you need to get something off your chest, say it.'

'I don't know …'

'It won't leave this rooftop. I promise.'

Maybe it's being here in the dark. It makes the conversation feel slightly anonymous. Maybe that's why I open my mouth again instead of hurrying back down the stairs to lie in my stifling bedroom, all my secrets left intact. 'I'm worried it's not just work keeping him away. What if he's drifting away from me?'

Gil turns fully to face me, resting his right hip against the railing. 'What makes you think that?'

'When I first got here, he called every night, but then it became every other night. Now, sometimes he just sends a message. And he's just said he's not coming to visit. And it's not the first time he's cancelled.' I look down at the concrete floor. 'There's a name for it, you know … when someone has to care for someone who's very ill or is facing a long recovery like I am. It's called compassion fatigue. And I know I've been a lot to handle. I know that maybe it's too much to ask, especially as I'm not even the woman he proposed to any more.'

Gil steps towards me and his hands come to rest on my

shoulders, warm, comforting. And there's also a tingle of something else … For me, at least. A tingle of something that definitely shouldn't be there.

It's just that stupid dream, I tell myself. *Pay no attention to your poor scrambled brain.* I'm superimposing dream Gil on real Gil. I have to separate the two. But it's hard when he's determined to act more like the fantasy than the reality I thought I knew.

'Erin …'

I lift my head and look at him. Time seems to slow, suspend … I feel a familiar prickle of electricity in the air around us. Gil swallows.

Stop it. Stop feeling like this. Stop thinking like this. It's Simon you want to hold you and tell you that you're okay. Not this man.

I'm about to take a step backwards when Gil's hands drop away from my arms and he moves first. 'It's late …'

I nod and swallow. Oh, God. He sensed it too … He could tell that I was having weird mixed-up feelings for him. How absolutely mortifying. I look down at my feet. 'Yes. I'd better go.'

I hurry down the stairs, only realizing when I get to the bottom that I've left my glass of water up there. I'll have to get myself another.

I do it as fast as I can before Gil follows me down from the roof, and then scurry away to the safety of my bedroom, where I bake and sweat for the rest of the night with not much more success of sleep.

CHAPTER SIXTY-SIX

Five years ago

He stayed at the pub until closing time, choosing to give Erin and Simon plenty of space, but it's killing him not knowing what they're talking about, or how she is. She's probably upset. And why wouldn't she be, after flying thousands of miles to get dumped a few hours before Valentine's Day? He'd want to punch his best friend if he wasn't so relieved the deception is finally over. How he digs himself out of the hole he made for himself is another matter. But even if there is no hope for him and Erin, she deserves better than what Simon has been dishing up. She deserves to know the truth and be free.

He finally returns to the house he shares with Simon and another guy just after midnight. He walked the long way home, almost enjoying the way the chilly night air pinched at his face and hands.

There are no lights on when he opens the front door. He walks through the ground floor in darkness. They share a tiny Victorian two-up, two-down in Telegraph Hill. Simon and Mizhir have the upstairs rooms, one either side of the flight of stairs that goes up the middle of the house, and he can see no hint that anyone is awake or even that either of them is home. He could knock on their doors, but he's guessing Simon's best tactic for dealing with the uncomfortable emotions produced by dumping Erin is to wipe his short-term memory of the evening with a shedload of alcohol, and he probably won't be home for another couple of hours.

He checks out the kitchen-diner at the back of the house – also empty – and then heads to his bedroom.

Once in bed, he pulls out his phone. He wants to message her so badly, to find out how she is, but there's no point. He's still got Simon's old number. It makes him feel sick when he realizes he's already had his last message from her. That she might never contact him again.

Is she awake too? Is she crying? He hopes not. He'd go and find her if it wasn't so late and, of course, if he knew where she was staying.

Patience, Gil. You can't rush in. You've got to give her time.

And so he puts his phone away and sleeps in fits and starts, but at 4 a.m., when he's been awake for more than an hour, he gives up. He pulls on a pair of tracksuit bottoms and shoves a hoodie on his top half, leaving the zip undone, then heads into the kitchen to make himself a cup of tea. He'd have something stronger, but someone nicked the bottle of bourbon he had stashed in his allotted kitchen cupboard.

Perhaps after he's had his tea he'll go for a run. That ought to eat up an hour or so. Knowing Simon, it'll be past noon before he's a) conscious and b) hungry enough to force him to leave his bedroom. Gil knows he probably won't get a sensible conversation out of his best friend until mid-afternoon. It's going to be the longest day of his life.

Not wanting to wake himself up any further, he leaves the lights off. The glow from next door's security light through the kitchen window is enough to pick out the table and chairs, the layout of the units.

He's just rinsing his mug out when he hears a creak on the stairs. Quickly, he places it on the drainer and turns around. Someone's coming this way. It has to be Simon, because he's suddenly remembered Mizhir is back at home for his sister's engagement party.

A dark figure draws closer along the hallway and as it reaches the threshold, Gil opens his mouth and prepares to ask, in the most nonchalant way he can manage, how it all went. But then the figure steps further into the kitchen and the neighbours' security light illuminates them more fully.

The first thing he sees is one of Simon's T-shirts, but those aren't Simon's hairy legs underneath. They are smooth and nicely toned, ending with toes tipped with dark nail polish.

Definitely *not* Simon.

Definitely his worst nightmare.

CHAPTER SIXTY-SEVEN

Present Day

Simon arrives, as promised, for a visit the following weekend. By that time, the walls of the back bedroom are painted a lovely bluish-grey, and Gil has moved in there. I have been painting every afternoon instead of having a nap. I find the swish of the brush over the paper soothing, even though my passion far outstrips my talent. If it's fine, I paint on the roof, and if it's cold or rainy, I set up the easel Gil found me in the corner of the living room, where I get light from both of the long, horizontal windows.

Simon arrives as he usually does, with a fanfare of movement and noise. Ever since I've known him, he's always seemed to bring more light, more colour, into any room he enters. He presents me with a huge bunch of flowers, and hauls me into his arms and spins me round.

Simon is keen on going out to the Ferryboat Inn, where he might bump into old friends, but I can't face it on a Saturday evening, so Gil cooks and we choose a film to watch. I fall asleep before the end and crawl off to bed while the guys pick another one full of car chases and explosions. When Simon eventually comes to bed, I don't even stir.

I get up around seven, hoping he might join me for a cup of tea and we can have a chance to reconnect after only seeing each other face to face a handful of times in the last month or so. But Simon snores on until almost ten, and then insists we all go out for brunch at the open-air café near the jetty. I won't lie: sausage sandwiches taste amazing with a side order of salty river air, but I feel restless, knowing the minutes are ticking away until he leaves again.

Just as Simon is paying the bill, a call comes through on my mobile. I get up to take it, wandering through the café and stopping on the narrow road outside.

'Hello, is that Erin?'

'Yes.'

'This is Sandra from the Royal Marina Hotel. Sorry to call at the weekend, but I had a feeling you wouldn't want to wait until Monday to hear this news ... We've had a cancellation.'

'You have?'

'Yes. The call came through just half an hour ago. We have an opening on the sixteenth of November and it's yours if you want it.'

I blink. 'I ... I don't know what to say.'

Sandra laughs, clearly delighted to be delivering this news. 'We need to know if you want to book it fairly quickly, of course, otherwise we'll offer it to someone else.'

'How long have we got?' I say, my pulse trotting a little. It's not just the venue, is it? There are other things to organize too, and we need to make sure we can get all our ducks in a row for the same day.

'Normally, we'd say forty-eight hours, but you can have until Saturday morning.'

'Thank you,' I say, and I genuinely mean it. The hotel has been so understanding and I think they may have bumped us up the queue a little bit because they've felt so sorry for us.

'No problem! Have a nice Sunday,' and Sandra rings off, leaving me to break the news to my fiancé.

I wait until we get back to Heron's Quay, needing the familiarity of the surroundings to ground me. When Simon heads towards my little suite of rooms, I hurry after him.

'That call …'

He picks up his overnight bag from the armchair and pops it on the bed. 'Uh-huh?'

'It was the Royal Marina. We've got our cancellation.'

Simon unzips his bag, then raises his head to look at me.

'We can be married by the end of the year if we want.' I feel a quiver of butterflies in my stomach as I say this. Why am I nervous? We should be laughing and hugging and jumping around the room together.

'That's great,' he says.

'Yes.'

Still, neither of us moves. Neither of us smiles.

'I'm worried, though …' I begin as Simon opens the wardrobe, takes a shirt out, and folds it haphazardly before stuffing it in his bag. Suddenly I'm gripped by all the fears he voiced a few months ago: that I'm not ready, that'll it'll be too much. I'm only planning on getting married once in my life and I really don't want to limp through the day, too wiped out to enjoy it. 'Can we take some time to go through it all? I really need to process it out loud.'

Simon comes around the bed and kisses the wrinkled skin

between my brows. 'Of course.' And then he gathers his toiletries and stuffs them into his bag.

I glance towards the little living room. 'I can make us a cup of tea—'

'You mean now?'

'Well, when else?'

Simon walks over to me and plants a kiss on my forehead. 'I was hoping to get away in the next thirty minutes. Try to beat the traffic, you know? If I don't hit the M25 before three, it's going to be manic.'

'Oh.'

'I'll call you … we can thrash it out over the phone. Video call if you like, as long as the Wi-Fi's good enough?'

I nod. I don't think anyone has to worry about the Wi-Fi signal in a house that Gil owns. 'Should be. What time shall I call? Will seven give you enough time to get settled after the journey?'

Simon jams his underwear in the front pocket on the bag. 'I'm probably gonna be wiped out this evening,' he says. 'And you're not yet your sharpest at that time of day, either.'

'But they need to know quickly. Tomorrow?'

I'm due round at Rachel's tomorrow for dinner. She's decided to take care of me since I'm home alone a lot of the time.'

'That's nice,' I say. 'Tuesday?'

Simon thinks for a minute. 'I can do Tuesday.'

My shoulders unclench a little. 'Okay, good …'

'If not, Wednesday is the only other day I can do. I've got that training course on Thursday and this weekend is Felipe's stag thing. We're leaving for Amsterdam at the crack of dawn on Saturday.'

'Oh yes.' One of his work colleagues. I don't remember him telling me that, but he probably did. And I didn't know he and Felipe were that close. 'So you won't be coming down next Saturday either?'

He shakes his head. 'Sorry.'

I sigh, disappointed, but I can hardly stop him living his life, showing up for his friends, just because I'm feeling needy, can I? I let the subject drop and return to something more important. 'We've got to let the hotel know by first thing Saturday, so as long as we chat before you go off with the boys, it should be fine .'

Simon pulls me into his arms and holds me tight. 'Anything for you.' We stay like that for a few moments, and then he pulls away. 'Gotta grab a few last bits.'

I nod. 'Of course …' And before I know it, his bag is full, and he zips it up and heads across the hallway to say his farewell to our host.

'Good to see you, mate,' he says to Gil and gives him one of those laddish hugs with lots of backslapping, and then he turns to me, pulls me into his arms and kisses me properly for the first time all weekend before disappearing out the door.

Something occurs to me and I turn to Gil. 'Have you been invited to Felipe's stag weekend?' As much as I want more independence, I feel suddenly panicked at spending time here at Heron's Quay on my own.

He shakes his head. 'I don't really know him that well. Besides, from the handful of times I have met him, I got the impression he doesn't like me very much.'

'Oh, dear,' I say, wincing. 'Sorry.'

Gil shrugs and smiles at me. 'No problem. I don't like him much, either.'

CHAPTER SIXTY-EIGHT

Present Day

After Simon leaves, I feel heavy and listless. I try to finish my painting of Lower Hadwell, but in my efforts at perfection, I add too many things and end up ruining it.

I steadfastly ignore my easel, but when Gil has to go into Exeter for a meeting on Tuesday, I get so bored I pull it out again. I stretch the paper ready for painting and draw a quick outline of the village with a pencil, intending to have another go at the scene I destroyed a few days earlier by too much tinkering. But when it's time to add paint, I think of all the careful strokes I'm going to have to make for the painting to work and I just can't bring myself to start. Instead, I dip my brush in a blob of bright crimson paint and swipe it across the canvas. And then I add emerald green, then fuchsia.

I'm not thinking about what I want to create; I'm thinking about how Simon's visit gave me a strange vibe, as if he was here in my arms and in my bed, but not really here. He seemed distracted, eager to get back home. But is that just my paranoia talking?

I've been much more anxious since my accident, much more

prone to getting an idea in my head and running with it, no matter how ridiculous it might be. Trying to work out what's real and what isn't is making my brain spin in three different directions at once.

I add this into my painting, picking up a narrow brush and loading it with an egg-yolk yellow. It feels good to stab my brush onto the paper, adding sharp lines and dots to the swirls of deep colour. But then I stop thinking about Simon and think about myself, how I feel so different from the person I was before the accident, but also feel essentially 'me' at the same time. It's so confusing. I pick a deep, sad midnight blue and a wide brush and I cover huge swathes of the bright colour with its heaviness, hardly paying any attention to shape or design, just to the motion of the brush, what feels right in that moment.

I stop not when I feel I'm finished, but when I'm too mentally exhausted to go on. When I stand back and survey my work, I don't see beauty. I don't see skill. I just see a mess. I see myself.

I turn away, unable to look at it, and retreat from the living room to my bedroom, where I bury myself under the covers, then fall into a restless sleep.

★ ★ ★

I dream of white sandy beaches and brilliant blue skies, of palm trees and seashells, and a white-painted cottage with a veranda that leads out onto a deserted beach. The morning sun is golden, peeking through the slats in the shutters, highlighting the creases on the rumpled snowy-white sheets.

I feel the warmth of a body spooned tightly around me, and my mind doesn't just wake from its dozy state but my body does

333

too. His breathing is even, his muscles lax, and I enjoy the feel of him wrapped possessively around me, but after a few minutes I'm hungry for a different kind of touch.

I wriggle out from under his arm and push myself up onto one elbow so I can see him properly. He's so beautiful asleep. I reach out and trace the curve of his cheekbones, then draw the tip of my finger over each eyebrow in turn. I lean closer and press a kiss to the tip of his nose.

He's all I ever wanted. My Gil.

My hair tickles his face and he brushes it away. I'm about to lie back down, leave him to sleep, when he reaches out, pulls me down on top of him. We're pressed together now, torso to torso, and his other hand comes up behind my neck and draws me down towards his lips.

The first kiss is so soft, so deliciously slow and gentle, that I forget to breathe. He might have been dozing just a few seconds ago, but from the way his lips brush and tease mine, I know he is now fully in control of all his faculties. And maybe some of mine. When his tongue explores my parted lips, I let out a deep sigh and slide my hand up his bare back. I'm fascinated by the planes and dips of the muscles and I map out each and every one.

Gil makes a noise deep in his throat and flips me so I'm lying beneath him. His lips never leave mine for a millisecond, but his hands begin to move over me, touching me with both confidence and familiarity – he knows my body so well – but also with tenderness and awe. I feel … treasured.

And then his hands move lower, skimming my knees, drawing a lazy path up my inner thigh, one finger hooked around the hem of my nightdress. The slip of the silk over my skin only adds to the torrent of sensations. My breathing becomes ragged and uneven.

I bring my hands around to his chest and give him a shove so he falls onto his back and we reverse our positions. A low chuckle rumbles through his chest and he lets his arms fall flat out on the crumpled sheet, spreadeagled in surrender. I push myself up, swing one leg over him and come to sit low on his belly and then, as his eyes grow dark, I cross my arms, reach for my nightdress and pull it slowly up over my head.

For a few seconds he lies there, then he blinks softly and reaches up for me, his fingertips making contact with my ribcage, where they drift and tease. 'I can't believe you're all mine,' he says. There's desire in his tone, but wonder too.

We make love, slowly, tenderly at first, but then any gentleness is swept away by a building need to consume and be consumed. But even amid the building pleasure I never lose sight of him, and he never loses sight of me. We lock eyes. I don't need him to tell me he loves me. It's there in every touch, every look.

Just as everything is rising to a crescendo, I hear a noise off in the background. I try to ignore it, concentrate on letting the waves of sensation take me to their peak, when it happens again, louder this time. It sounds like … it sounds like someone knocking on the door.

'Erin?'

In a whoosh of sensation, suddenly I'm ripped from one world into another. The air is chilly around me, the light beyond my eyelids dimmer. I snap them open as the bedroom door brushes against the carpet.

And there is Gil, fully clothed, looking concerned. It takes a moment to make sense of how he managed to teleport from one place to the other, but then reality crashes through my brain. I roll over and bury my face in the pillow, cheeks flaming.

Oh, God …

It was like I was revisiting *that* dream. Writing the ending that surely would have happened if I hadn't woken sooner.

'Are you okay?' His voice is soft with concern, which only makes *other* parts of me burn along with my face.

I nod, still hiding in the pillow, and let out a muffled 'uh-huh'.

'When I came back and it seemed as if the house was empty, I got worried.'

I lift my head but avoid making eye contact. 'I, um … just needed a nap.'

'Okay.' He hovers at the door, not indecisively, but as if he knows exactly what he wants to do, where he wants to be. I sense he'd stand there like a sentry if he could, only leaving his post if he was convinced I was all right.

'I'm fine,' I say, flicking a glance towards him and adding a weak smile.

'Do you need anything?'

My body is screaming an answer I don't want to hear.

'I'd love a cup of tea,' I say, checking the clock and realizing it's almost evening. 'I should probably get up if I don't want to be awake all night. I'll be … I'll be out in just a second.'

I can tell I'm not giving the most convincing performance of my life but he reluctantly nods, then the door closes softly behind him. I lift my head and stay frozen in that position until I hear his footsteps retreating towards the main part of the house, and then I collapse back down onto the mattress and let out a silent scream.

Gil is silhouetted against the windows when I eventually pluck up the courage to enter the living room. He's staring at the easel. I want to rush over, to pull my painting from it and turn it face down on the table, but it's already too late. Embarrassment is a corkscrew within my gut, its sharp tip tearing through me, turning, churning everything as it goes.

'E … This is …'

'A mess?' I ask with a laugh, feigning nonchalance.

'It's …' He turns and looks at me, his brows pinched as he searches for a reply. 'It's beautiful.'

No need to fake the next laugh. 'If you say so.'

He turns and walks over to me, takes me by the hand and leads me back towards the easel. Electricity jolts through me at his touch, and I get a full and X-rated flashback to the dream I've been valiantly trying to shove into one of my memory's many trapdoors.

'I do say so,' he responds, staring at the painting. 'It's not pretty, but look at all that colour, all that life. It's … honest.'

He turns to me to see how I'm weighing up what he just said. I want to look away, but I can't. Even if he's unable to fully put it into words, just as I couldn't when I was creating it, he sees everything that's there, everything I spilled onto the canvas. And I can tell he really believes it's beautiful.

'You said I should decorate the house more, introduce some texture and colour … Wouldn't this be perfect? Would you … would you let me have it?'

I break eye contact and look beyond him to the river, where the sky is a warm heather-grey streaked with yellow. I don't want the picture, but I'm not sure I want Gil to have it either. It's too raw. Too personal.

'Let me think about it,' I say as I head to the kitchen to collect the cup of tea waiting for me on the counter.

CHAPTER SIXTY-NINE

Five years ago

She hasn't seen him sitting in the darkened kitchen. As she crosses the threshold, he says 'Hi …' as softly as he can. She jumps back, pressing her hand to her chest. He stands and reaches for the light on the cooker hood and when he presses the button, a gentle glow fills his side of the room.

'You scared the life out of me!' she says, laughing nervously. Her face shows she's considering sprinting back upstairs. It's so easy to read her now, even though it's the first time he's seen her since she's been away. He feels as if he knows her inside and out.

'Sorry. Couldn't sleep. Didn't mean to scare you.' Her expression doesn't change at all as he issues his apology, and he adds, 'I thought you were Simon.'

At the mention of his best friend's name, she begins to glow again, even while she glances awkwardly at the floor. Gil tries not to notice her bare legs under Si's shirt.

'I just came to get some water.'

He nods, reaches into a cupboard, pulls out a glass and fills it from the tap for her.

'Thanks,' she says as she takes it from him. Her gaze shoots to the ceiling, where Simon must be snoozing above them and then back to the tiled floor.

He's torn. On one hand, he can't stand being so close while she's treating him like he's a stranger, but on the other, he's waited so long to be in the same room with her, it feels like a wrench to get up and leave. He does it anyway. She's feeling awkward, and he doesn't want to do anything to cause her even the slightest discomfort.

As he passes her, he can smell her perfume – something floral with an edge of sandalwood, a fitting mix for a woman of so many facets, so many contradictions. 'Night, E.'

'Night,' she replies softly as he walks down the hallway and closes his bedroom door behind him.

CHAPTER SEVENTY

Present Day

Simon doesn't call. Not on Tuesday or Wednesday, not even on Thursday. I get a hurried text from him the next morning:

> **Sorry! Training course ran on and then we all went out to the pub.**

> **They need to know TOMORROW!** I message back.

Has he forgotten this?

I wait a few minutes for his response. What's so hard? Is he going to call me or not?

> **Yeah, let's do it** he replies.

I frown and tap back a reply. **The call?**

> **The wedding!**

Oh. I wasn't expecting that, but I suppose a decision is what I've been waiting for. I stare at the screen.

Why not? he types while I'm still trying to work out how to reply.

Why not? He's making it sound as if I've suggested going out for a quick pint, not making life-altering vows that will bind us together for the rest of our days.

He's acting as if it's no big deal. But it is. It's a really big deal. For all sorts of reasons, including the one I've been asking myself over and over since the hotel phoned: am I ready? I thought the news we could go ahead and plan the rest of our lives would make me feel more settled, but I just feel nervous.

Maybe we should wait until I'm twelve months post brain injury, when things will have settled down more and we'll have a realistic idea of my limitations, if any, going forward. Maybe we should keep it super, super small and just elope. Do it in a town hall with just our parents as witnesses. Everyone would understand. I know they would.

All the different options swirl around my head until they become a soup of confusion, so it's no wonder I can't seem to doze for more than fifteen minutes at a time when I go to bed that night. At 3 a.m. I give up and I make my way upstairs to the roof.

I reach the middle steps of the staircase and I wonder if I'll find a familiar figure up there in one of the chairs, head back, staring at the night sky, but when I reach the roof, there's no one there. The chairs round the wooden table seem too empty, so I walk to the railing and lean on it.

The night air has a slight chill, but I refuse to retreat downstairs. *Never let them see you sweat,* I think, realizing it's probably not the best metaphor when the goosebumps are out in full force, but it's practically my motto. I'm a survivor, I remind myself. The kind of person who sees things through to the bitter end. I need to keep pushing forwards until I reach the finishing line. It's what I do.

But do you want to? a little voice inside my head calls out.

Of course I want to get better, to reclaim as much of my former life as possible. But I also know I have to be realistic. It might never be *exactly* the same.

Does that include Simon?

The thought pops into my head out of nowhere, and I bat it away on instinct. Of course it does! Of course we should get …

But then my gut catches up with my stubborn logic. *Should we …?*

My future with Simon will not be the same as the one I was planning last year. And that's because I feel something has changed between us, and I don't know what and I don't know why. Even though Simon was physically close to me last weekend, I still feel as if he's drifting away, like a boat on the river that has snapped its mooring.

And what do I do about Gil?

Ever since that stupid dream the other day, I can't quite put my feelings into reverse and go back to where we were … friends, I suppose, as unlikely as that sounds. I keep feeling those feelings I had when I dreamed we were in the water, when he looked at me and said he'd give up his life to save me.

Maybe it's time to go home to my flat in Herne Hill, because I think I enjoy being here with him a little too much. No, that's a lie. I know I do. My heart does a little skip every time I think he might be about to walk into the room, and I find it hard to take my eyes off him when he does. And when he does things like bringing me a new watercolour pad before I've even realized myself that I'm about to run out of pages, something warm and permanent lodges itself deep in my soul.

At least, that's the way it feels.

I lean my elbows on the railing at the edge of the parapet and rest my head in my hands and massage my scalp gently. I need to be honest with myself, don't I? And if I'm being really honest, I know I will be relieved if the deadline to call the hotel tomorrow passes. I don't want to marry Simon in November. I don't want to marry him maybe ever.

And that's because … because …

I close my eyes, shying away from saying it to myself, even in the silent confines of my skull. But I need to.

Because I think I'm starting to have feelings for Gil instead.

There. I've admitted it. My heart lurches as the words ring in my ears.

I know it's quite possibly a mirage, something that my bumped-around brain has cooked up from a combination of feeling slightly abandoned by Simon, my new friend's kindness, and a stupid dream. I've tried hard to untangle it all, pull the different parts from each other and compartmentalize them, but it's impossible. Naomi, the psychologist, warned me my brain might do some unexpected things because of the trauma, that I might develop obsessions or be tempted to make huge life-changing decisions on a whim. Is this one of those times? Could I be about to make the biggest mistake of my life?

What do I do? I can't decide my future on nebulous emotions, on something that might merely be an illusion. So do I marry Simon, or don't I? Do I stick to the plan, because it seemed a good one to me when all was right and orderly inside my head, or do I go with my gut, which is screaming all sorts of conflicting information at me? No wonder I can't sleep …

I walk away from the railing and sit on the small section of raised roof that makes up part of the living room ceiling. My legs dangle down past the narrow windows underneath the square concrete slab. I'm just so tired, both physically and mentally. I want to rewind time a year, to go back to when I was certain about the path I was heading down, when I was completely in charge of my life.

I want that Erin back. I don't like this new, needy, unpredictable person I've become. I rifle through memories of that version of myself, starting with the bride-to-be and flicking back through time until I rest on the optimistic, capable young woman who travelled the world, living and working on the waves. Where is *that* version of myself? What would she tell me to do if she were in my shoes now?

I'm just pondering this when I hear footsteps on the stairs, and my pathetic heart leaps to attention. Gil's head appears, and he scans the roof.

'Hey, you …' I call out gently, letting him know I'm here because I have the feeling he's looking for me.

'Hey yourself,' he replies, his tone low and warm, and my pulse skips even faster. 'Everything okay?'

'Yes,' I say on automatic.

Gil walks over to sit beside me on the concrete ledge. 'Then why do I get the feeling that it's not? You've been a bit checked-out since Simon visited.'

Gil doesn't cajole a response out of me; he just sits, lets me be. After about five minutes, I crack. 'Do you think he seemed okay at the weekend?'

Gil stares back at me, and I sense his hesitation at answering my question. Why is that?

'Simon seemed like Simon to me. The pertinent question is: what do you think?'

I grip the ledge to anchor myself. 'I think ... I think something's up with him, but I'm not sure what.'

'Why do you think that?'

I sigh in exasperation. He's turning it back on me again. Why can't he just sympathize, agree?

I try to gather an answer for him. I'm still haunted by that memory of the younger, five-years-ago version of me, who knew what she wanted from life and wasn't afraid to go and get it. Maybe that's why I take the subject down its next path. 'I'm getting a vibe,' I say, swinging my legs and looking down at my knees, 'similar to when I returned to yachting after Megan's death and Simon slowly went quiet on me. It feels like he's behind a glass wall and I can't quite reach him any more.'

Gil shifts uncomfortably. 'I can't give you advice regarding your relationship with Simon.'

'I know ...' It's not fair to him to put him in the middle, not now that we both have a friendship with him. And his loyalty will always remain with Simon, won't it?

'Are you still worried his feelings have changed for you since the accident?'

'I don't know ...'

'I meant what I said, E. I don't see that much change in you, only that you're letting out what you keep packed away

346

so carefully on the inside a little more often. And I don't think that's such a bad thing.'

My eyes fill with tears. I had no idea how much I needed to hear that until the words left his mouth. I reach out and touch his hand, resting my fingertips lightly on his skin as if it's the most natural thing in the world to do. Without breaking eye contact, he interlaces his fingers with mine and curls them round my hand. I feel as if I have found my anchor stone, my safe place, and I exhale, tension leaching out of me.

I swipe at my eyes, then meet Gil's again. 'I think what frustrates me most is that for years, I lied to everyone, telling everyone I was fine when I wasn't, soldiering on when I really should've asked for help. And now I really need Simon to step up and I feel he's just … AWOL. And the most frustrating thing is that I know he has it in him to do this for me, to be by my side and help me through a difficult time in my life, because he's done it before. So why won't he now? Don't I matter to him as much as I did back then? And I'm angry with him for not being who I need him to be right now. That's selfish, isn't it?'

Gil's fingers squeeze mine gently. 'You're the least selfish person I know.'

That's when the floodgates open. I sniff loudly and tears stream down both cheeks.

Gil turns to face me. He reaches up and brushes the moisture away with his thumbs. 'Don't cry. It breaks my heart to see you like this.'

I stare into his eyes, and he stares back at me. My heart thuds and the air around us pulses in time with the beat. He's looking at me exactly the way he did in St Lucia when we were stuck in the water and he said he'd die for me. Only that Gil wasn't real. And this one …

Oh.

This Gil feels it too. It's not just a kooky, one-sided crush whipped up by my confused brain. He really cares about me. Not only that, he desires me. On a pure whim of instinct, I lean towards him and my eyelids drift closed. I can feel the heat of his lips millimetres from mine when he whispers, 'This isn't a good idea, E …'

E … He calls me E all the time now.

And Simon hasn't, not for years. I scrolled back through my messages to check.

This is a puzzle piece, an important one, and I start trying to work out what to do with it. I feel that the intuitive, instinctive part of my consciousness has stumbled upon something significant, but that my logical brain is struggling to join the dots.

In my mind's eye, I see Gil walking up the steps to the roof.

Hey, you …

Hey yourself …

My eyes spring open and I pull back. It almost feels as if I've had another smack on the head, because what is dropping into place inside my skull is world-changing, paradigm shifting. 'It was you!' I say, as my heart slows and comes to a stop. 'You were the one messaging me when I was in the Caribbean!'

CHAPTER SEVENTY-ONE

Present Day

If it was Simon I'd just caught out in a lie, he'd laugh, bluff and bluster a little.

Erin, sweetheart, why would you think that?

It wasn't quite *like that. Let me explain …*

But Gil does none of this. He meets my gaze. 'Yes. It was me.'

I back away from him, reach for the railing for support. A few short months ago, it felt as if everything I knew about myself, about my world, was shaken up like a snow globe, and the pieces haven't even all come back down to land yet. Now it feels as if it's happened all over again.

'It was *you*?' I whisper hoarsely. I heard the words coming out of his mouth, but it doesn't seem possible for it to be the truth.

Gil's expression is closed, serious. He nods, just once.

'Why? Why would you do that?' Suddenly, I need to move. I turn and run down the stairs, aware that I'm moving faster than is safe, but I don't care. I have to get away.

'Erin!' I hear his feet banging on the metal stairs behind me, but I don't stop. I yank the door to the living room open and run inside. Gil is only half a second behind me.

I spin around to face him. 'Give me your car keys. Now!'

'Will you just let me expl—'

'No! Just give me the car keys!'

'No!'

We're staring at each other, fire in our eyes, and it feels as if we've rewound seven months, as if we're back in the hotel garden.

'I can't let you drive my car. You know I can't.'

I put my hands on my hips and glare at him, breath coming fast. I hate that I have absolutely no comeback because he is 100 per cent right. 'I'm leaving.'

This news doesn't shock Gil, but he doesn't look happy. Good. I don't care.

'I'm calling an Uber.'

He shakes his head.

'You can't stop me!'

'No, I can't. But I think you'll find they don't cover the wilds of Devon.'

All the swear words I want to yell at him jumble together in the front of my brain, making it impossible to pick one, so I just end up letting out a frustrated grunt and stride off towards my bedroom. I lock the door before he can follow me inside, secure the French windows, and then I pull my suitcase out of the wardrobe and begin throwing things inside.

CHAPTER SEVENTY-TWO

Five years ago

He goes out for a run, and afterwards he doesn't go back to the house. How can he? How can he stand seeing them, especially after what might have been their first night together? And what the feck is Simon playing at? This was not the plan. This was not the plan at all.

But then he can hardly blame anyone but himself. It was his own stupid fault for not being honest from the get-go. As they say … the road to hell is paved with good intentions, and he's created his own private purgatory. He has no idea how long it will last, how long they will stay an item, especially when Erin returns to yachting. When it comes to romantic entanglements, Simon prefers variety rather than longevity.

After his run he sits in a café for a couple of hours, and then he goes to the library, even though he hasn't got a pen or a notebook. He spends longer than he could have thought possible browsing the section on computers and technology, especially as many of the books are hopelessly out of date.

When he can put it off no longer, he returns home, sliding

his key gently into the lock and opening it slowly, hoping no one will hear him. He hides in his bedroom but eventually he has to use the bathroom, which is on the ground floor beyond the kitchen. As he passes through, he finds Simon whistling, one hand on the open fridge door as he stares inside.

When Si hears him, he turns and grins at him. 'Morning.'

He and Simon have had their share of disagreements, but they've never actually fought about anything, not properly. However, at this very moment, Gil wants to punch his friend so hard he'll be feeling it until Christmas. 'So I take last night didn't exactly go as planned,' he says, and he's surprised how even his tone is, how normal.

Simon raises his eyebrows.

'I bumped into Erin when she came downstairs to get a glass of water.'

Si gives a sheepish chuckle and looks away.

'I thought you weren't interested.' There's an edge to his voice now, but Simon doesn't seem to notice.

'I wasn't. At least, I wasn't until last night.' Simon closes the fridge and turns to lean against the kitchen counter. 'But I didn't want to dump her in a public place over dinner, so we started talking and I remembered what a great girl she is. I have no idea why I let myself forget that!'

As he laughs at himself, Gil frowns.

'And she is *really* into me. Like, completely besotted. It's hard for a guy not to get swept up by that, if you know what I mean?'

Gil nods tersely. He knows exactly how easy it is to get swept up in Erin Ross. 'So what happens next?' He holds his breath. As much as he hates himself for it, he hopes Simon is going to say this is a one-night stand, that now he's satisfied his curiosity he'll move on to pastures new when Erin goes back to her superyacht.

Simon shrugs. 'Maybe it's time I got serious with someone, and if I'm going to get serious, it might as well be with someone like Erin.'

It feels as if all the blood rushes from Gil's body in a downward motion, leaving him chilled to the bone.

Simon walks over and gives him a one-armed hug. 'And it seems I might have you to thank for this chance. Erin was talking about messages …'

Oh, God.

'And I know you said you answered her a couple of times when I first gave you my phone. I don't know what you said, mate, but it has earned me serious brownie points!'

Gil thinks he might be about to vomit as Simon claps him on the back.

'Thanks for keeping her warm for me. You're the best friend a guy could have.'

CHAPTER SEVENTY-THREE

Present Day

By the time I pack all my belongings, it's past four. I don't sleep. Instead I check the time of the first train out of Totnes back to Paddington. I'm going home. To Simon – where I should have been all along.

It wasn't safe to send me here with my brain in the state it is. I've allowed it to blur the lines between dream and reality, and all that ever brings is pain. I knew better than to count on Gil. And I'm disappointed in Simon, too. The only person I can really trust at the moment is myself, which is why I am going to put myself on a train, even if the thought of all those crowds on the Underground when I get off at the other end terrify me, and I'm going to get myself back home to south-east London.

I contact three cab firms in the South Hams area. One is a one-man band who is already on his way to Exeter with another fare, and the other two firms, both about twenty miles away, can only get here at six and 6.30, respectively. I book the earlier one.

When it gets to 5.45, I slowly and quietly turn the key in my bedroom door. Gil didn't pound on it or shout through it after

I locked myself inside. He made a couple of polite, contained requests for me to open it and talk to him, but when I refused to answer, it went quiet. I presume he walked away.

Once the door is unlocked, I turn the handle slowly. When it opens, I'm surprised to see Gil, long legs folded up underneath him on the cold tiled floor, back against the wall. His head is lolling on his chest, but it snaps up when he hears the bottom of the door dragging over the thick carpet. In an instant, he's on his feet, towering over me.

My heart begins to pound. But not because I'm scared. Because some small, pathetic part of me is thrilled to see him there, wants to put my palms on his chest and feel if his heart is beating this fast too. How messed up is that?

He takes in the suitcase sitting just inside the door. 'You're really leaving?'

'Of course I'm leaving! I told you I was.'

I've never seen Gil at a complete loss for words, but he seems to be now. 'But …'

I take advantage of his bewilderment to grab my suitcases and my handbag and roll them past him into the hallway and up to the front door.

'E …'

'Don't call me that!'

He flinches as if I've slapped him. I don't care if I sound shrill and angry. I am angry. Absolutely furious. With him and with myself.

'I can explain. Let me explain. Just let me know what's going on in your head and I can put things right.'

My back straightens. 'What's going on in my head is that you've been lying to me. For five years, Gil! Why did you do it?

Have you finally got the victory over me you've always wanted? You took advantage of me while I was really vulnerable and made me trust you with all my soul? Well, ha ha, Gil. I fell for it. You've won.'

I see the shutters come down behind his eyes the way I've seen them come down so many times in the past, usually when I've said something that I haven't been proud of later.

'You always think the worst of me, don't you? Why is that?'

'I judge you by your actions, Gil. So stop doing awful things and I'll stop thinking you're a cockroach.'

'If you'd let me explain, you'd understand why I did what I did. It isn't what you're assuming. Let's sit down, talk properly.' He glances towards the open door of the living room.

'You'd better hurry, because ...' I make a show of checking my phone for the time. 'I've got a cab coming in three minutes. So don't give me any of your excuses, Gil. I don't care. Just tell me why you thought it was okay to impersonate my boyfriend when I was grieving and lonely. Tell me how that, in any shape or form, is an okay thing to do!'

I see Gil's jaw clench and I know he's losing his cool. It feels like victory, which is childish.

'You really want to know why, Erin?'

I fold my arms and smile sweetly at him. 'Yes, Gil. I really do.'

He shakes his head. 'I don't think you do. I don't think you want to listen to anything I've got to say. Because you want to be right about me. You want to think I'm a monster.'

I let out a short dry laugh. 'Why would I want the last five years of my life to be a constant lie? Why wouldn't I want to think things were better between us, that maybe we could co-exist comfortably after Simon and I are married?'

I see a flash of something in his eyes as I say the last few words and a little muscle spasms in his cheek. 'Because it's safer for you that way. Deep down, you've always known why I make you uncomfortable, why you've never liked being around me.'

'And why is that, oh wise one? Tell me what I don't understand.'

I expect Gil to launch into his argument straight away, but he stares back at me. I get the feeling he's weighing up what to say and then gearing himself up to say it.

He takes a step closer and my silly heart goes into overdrive. 'Because there's always been this hum between us, this tug. I can see inside you sometimes, past all the polish to the unvarnished truth, and I know you've never liked it. It made you uncomfortable.'

'Well, that's ... I don't think ...' I trail off, unable to come up with a logical or honest retort.

'And I think you could do the same with me, if you only chose to look. But I think you stopped yourself. I think you *chose* not to look, although I never understood why. I'm not afraid for you to see, Erin. I don't need you to see me as perfect. I only need you what's real ...'

I step back. He's right. That idea makes me nervous, and I don't know why. We need our layers of protection, don't we? Like that conch I found in my dream. Without its shell, that little soft, vulnerable creature wouldn't be able to survive.

'I can't ...' I mutter.

'Can't or won't?' he asks, echoing what I once asked him.

'Both,' I whisper.

I see the frustration wash through him, but he doesn't push. Instead, he returns to my earlier question. 'You want to know why I messaged you while you were away, why I spent hours talking to you, being there for you when you needed someone?'

My insides are quivering like jelly. I'm not sure I do, but I don't want to admit that, so I set my shoulders. 'Tell me.'

Gil waits a couple of heartbeats before he answers. He closes the distance between us until I can feel his warmth radiating towards me. But he doesn't reach out. He doesn't touch. Those steel shutters he often puts up come down. I see it in his eyes, even though his focus doesn't waver.

'I did it because I fell in love with you more than five years ago, Erin.'

My mouth falls open. I don't even try to find any words.

'And I am still in love with you. Possibly more than ever. As much as I've tried to move on, find someone else … I haven't. It was always and only you.'

CHAPTER SEVENTY-FOUR

Present Day

I feel as if I've been smacked in the face. I also feel as if I'm flying. But he's right once again. I don't want this. I want to run away from it. Because it doesn't feel safe. It doesn't feel safe at all.

The only way I can come up with to protect myself is to attack. 'You love me? And you think that's an okay thing to say to me? I'm Simon's fiancée! That's a great way to show your loyalty to your best friend!'

'I can't help what I feel. What I've always felt. I tried so hard not to. You have no idea.'

He looks pained, but I can't let myself be fooled again. I can't give in to him. 'Even if what you say is true, that it's not just some "ha, I got you good!" scheme and you really have feelings for me, that makes it worse. It's so manipulative! You made me think you were Simon so I'd open up to you in a way you knew I wouldn't if I were talking to you. You lured me in and you made me trust you with things I'd never told anyone else. And I still don't understand why. I was with Simon! What were you ever going to get out of it?'

He's stopped from answering by a ding from my phone. I hold

up a hand and check the text message that's just arrived. It's the cab company. There's an accident on the road from Kingsbridge and they're going to be delayed.

That can't happen. I know I'm teetering on the edge of believing Gil, even though I want to hate him, I want to believe he's the waste of space I always thought he was. 'I can't listen to this any more,' I say.

Leaving my cases in the hallway, I stride past him into the living room and head for the kitchen drawer where he keeps all his odds and ends.

'What are you looking for?' Gil asks, his voice tense and heavy as I scrabble through the drawer looking for a small white business card I'm sure I saw there a week or two ago.

'The number for the taxi driver who lives in the next village.'

'If you really want to go back to London, I'll drive you.'

'No way. I'm booked on the 7.20 out of Totnes.'

'You're going to go all that way on your own?'

I've been through the mostly empty drawer three times now and the card is nowhere to be found. I spin round and take my frustration out on Gil. 'Yes, on my own. I won't die. I was a capable woman once upon a time, and I still have a few working brain cells, you know.'

'I wasn't doubting your ability. That's not what I was saying. It's just that some situations still make you nervous—'

'There you go, telling me about myself again. But you know nothing about me, Gil Sampson.'

His gaze is steady. The fact he's relatively calm while I feel as if I'm climbing the walls only makes me feel more out of control. 'Then at least let me drive you to the station. I can explain on the drive there.'

'No,' I say quietly.

'You've got to give me a chance!'

'I don't have to do anything you tell me to do. I'm my own person. I'm not going to stay here to please you. I'm going to please myself, and what I want to do is call a cab to take me to the station.'

He steps closer, runs a hand through his hair and then meets my gaze. It feels as if he's letting me look into his very soul, but I know I can't trust that feeling.

'I'm not telling you to do anything. I'm begging you, Erin. Please let me explain. I'm not the person you think I am, I'm really not.'

I shake my head. I feel as if I'm in an earthquake, that his revelation he was the one I was talking to all those years ago has split the ground, making it shift beneath my feet, and now it's all I can do to stay upright as the aftershocks roll through. I have to grab on to the one thing I believe to be true. 'All you can do in this life is judge people by their actions, and you have betrayed me twice, Gil.'

Gil looks as blindsided as I feel. 'Twice?'

'First by pretending to be Simon, by manipulating me and lying to me and then … Because you did it all over again. Here. At Heron's Quay. Over these last few weeks you made me trust you again. You made me—' My next word was about to be 'feel' but I stop myself. I clear my throat and regroup. 'What matters is you've just proved to me I was right all along. You are not worth my time or attention. You're nothing to me.'

Gil stares back at me for a few seconds and I see the desolation in his eyes. If he isn't lying to me, if he really has feelings for me, then I know I have just ripped his heart out with my bare hands and shredded it before him. I have to look away.

I hear noises and turn to see Gil rummaging in the open drawer. He pulls out a notepad and pen, scribbles something down on it and hands it to me: *Jeff's Taxis*, with a number beneath. And then he turns and walks away.

CHAPTER SEVENTY-FIVE

Present Day

I'm not expecting the journey to be a doddle, given my head injury and my current mental state, but it's worse than I expect it to be. The train gets increasingly more crowded as we near London. There is a party of four on the table seats opposite me talking loudly, and behind me is a new mum with a tiny baby. My heart goes out to her, but that doesn't mean that the constant screaming isn't drilling into my brain, making me feel as if I want to join in.

I spend most of the journey failing to hold back the tears. Naomi had explained to me that emotional regulation might be tricky after an injury like mine, and I just can't seem to get a grip of myself. I don't know what to do. It feels as if there is a great gaping hole inside my chest, one that is raw and jagged, and I don't know why. Gil isn't anything to me. I thought he was, but he's not. I shouldn't care.

I curse my new, slightly more impulsive nature. I did what I would normally never do – I let my guard down. I learned early not to get my hopes up when it comes to other people. They always disappoint you. I should have known better.

When I get to Paddington, I wait until everybody in my carriage has disembarked before I move out of my seat. The long platform is a blessed relief after the noise and heat of the train carriage, but the concourse is packed. People everywhere. Noise, colour, light. I want to crouch down on the floor, cover my eyes and ears, and pretend I'm not there.

I glance at the entrance to the Underground station and almost have a panic attack. No. Not doing that. Not today.

Instead I grab my bags and limp to the taxi rank, where I grab the first available one and tell him my address. The fare will probably be equivalent to one month's salary, but it'll be worth every penny.

I cry all the way home in the back of the taxi, too. I feel so tired, so overstimulated. So betrayed.

When we turn into our road and I see the row of red brick Victorian terraced houses with their white-painted masonry, my tears of overwhelm turn to tears of joy. I'm disappointed Simon won't be there, that he'll be with Felipe and the guys, but I also know the flat will be quiet, cool and familiar. I can pull the blinds, climb into bed, and forget about the world, my own sheets around me, my own pillow under my head. At this moment I want nothing more. I almost wish I could climb back into that coma, except I'm scared of what my muddled brain would dream up for me next. I just want it all to go away. I want to switch my head off and let it do nothing for a bit.

I'm not sure how I manage to haul myself up the stairs. When I slide my key into the lock, my legs are shaking. All I can think about is dropping my cases and crawling into the bedroom.

But when I open the front door, I hear voices, not the silence I'm expecting. I freeze. My heart begins to pound.

Adrenaline surges through me, powering me down the hallway towards the living room. I stand in the doorway, frozen. *'Simon?'*

He's lying on the couch in a T-shirt and boxers, a can in his hand. Hearing my voice, he jumps up, sloshing beer everywhere. 'My God! Erin? What are you doing here?'

'I could ask the same of you!'

CHAPTER SEVENTY-SIX

Present Day

Simon and I stand at opposite sides of the room, staring at each other.

'You're supposed to be in Amsterdam,' I say.

'You're supposed to be in Devon,' Simon says at the same time.

He has that same look on his face he gets when his mum scolds him for something. Keeping a careful eye on his reaction, I add, 'I decided to come home early.'

Simon puts down his can of beer. For a moment he seems unsure of what to do, but then he gathers himself. 'This is such a wonderful surprise!'

When he tries to hug me, I fold my arms and duck out of his way. He starts to gabble on about flights and timetables, that he thought he had a stomach bug yesterday but it just turned out to be gas. In the end I hold up a hand, palm facing him, and stare him down until the stream of bullshit dies away. 'Enough!' I sound stronger than I feel.

As I look at my fiancé, I can't help despising him a little. 'Just tell me the truth, Simon. Why aren't you on Felipe's stag weekend?'

Simon looks at the carpet. 'I … um … wasn't invited.'

'You weren't … Why lie? Why tell me you were?'

He says nothing, just shifts his weight from one foot to the other.

'It's because you were supposed to be coming down for the weekend, isn't it?'

He keeps his head bowed but looks up at me. 'Sort of … but, you know, it's got nothing to do with you, Erin. I just needed my space.'

'Space?' I step forward and plonk myself down on the edge of the smaller of the two sofas. 'From what? From *me* …?'

Simon retreats to the safety of the larger sofa. He picks up his can of beer, holding it to his chest but not drinking. 'I know you've had a horrendous time this year, that it's been really difficult for you, but that doesn't mean it hasn't been difficult for me too.'

I rub my forehead with my hand. The adrenaline is draining away, leaving me even more exhausted than when I first walked through the door. 'I do understand that. Or at least, I'm trying to.'

I'm so confused. I don't know what to do. I'm aware I've been horrendously focused on myself – I had to be – but that doesn't mean I shouldn't have compassion for Simon for all he's been through because of my accident. His wedding was cancelled. He had to look after me, worry about me … Is it really so horrible if he just wanted a bit of time and space for himself, too? That's the very reason I was at Heron's Quay. Am I overreacting?

Maybe I am, but something still niggles at me. I thought we had finally worked out how to emerge from our own bubbles and be a good team together, but it feels as if we are slipping back into old patterns, him behind his glass wall and me behind mine. Or maybe I'm not behind mine. I think my bump on the head smashed it to smithereens. It feels as if Simon has retreated from me and I'm out on my own, stranded.

'You could have talked to me about it instead of lying,' I say quietly.

Simon nods. 'Maybe I should have. I'm sorry.'

'So that's all this is … You just needed some 'me' time?'

Simon nods.

'And there's nothing else?'

'No.'

He takes a sip of his beer and his gaze wanders to the flatscreen TV where a team he doesn't particularly support is playing against one he hates.

This is usually the moment in our discussions when I let him off the hook, where I quietly tuck my misgivings and questions away and go back to being good old dependable Erin. Sensible. Measured. But I don't feel I'm any of those things today.

'So, this time you need …? You think you'll have had enough of it by November?'

Simon turns to me, his eyebrows raised. 'November?'

It's not even on his radar, is it? That says something. Something big. I stare steadily at him. 'When we're supposed to be getting married? The hotel gave us the cancellation date, remember? You said to go ahead and book.'

If I hadn't been studying him so carefully, I might've missed it, but I see a flash of panic in his eyes. It feels as if a trapdoor opens underneath me and I fall through it. 'You're not ready, are you? You're not ready to get married to me?'

Simon opens his mouth. He looks as if he's trying to work

368

out what to say, which answer will put this awkward discussion to bed the fastest.

'I want the truth, Simon. You owe me that.'

Simon stands up. 'Before we do that, I just need to ...' He hurries from the room and comes back a minute later, wearing trousers. I slump further into my sofa. Oh God. If he has to get fully dressed for what he's about to say, this does not bode well. He sits back down, resting his elbows on his knees, and looks at me seriously.

My stomach wobbles. 'Is there someone else?' I blurt out before he can say anything.

'No! Of course not! Why would you think that?'

Tension has been gathering around my temples all day and now it starts to squeeze hard. 'Then what is it? Simon ... just spit it out, will you?' In half an hour's time, my brain will turn to rubber and everything he tells me will bounce off of it. If he's going to get it off his chest, he's got to do it now.

Simon swallows. 'There's something I need to tell you ... About the night of your accident.'

My fingers fly to my skull, feeling the area that was bumped and bruised the most. 'My accident?' Suddenly, I'm scared. In my worst predictions of this scenario, Simon had got cold feet, maybe wanted to postpone the wedding, but now I wonder if he had something to do with what happened to me.

He nods. 'We had a fight ... That's why you ran outside. That's why you were in the garden.'

'We ... We ...' I can't seem to process the information. 'We had a fight? About what?'

Simon stands up and starts pacing. 'I told you something I should have brought up a long time before. But I could never

369

find a way to introduce it into the conversation and so I just kept putting it off and putting it off until ...' He shakes his head. 'I don't know, it just felt like the right thing to do to tell you before we got married. It wouldn't be right to keep a secret that big. It would have eaten away at our relationship.'

Deep inside, I start to shake. 'Simon, you're scaring me. Please tell me what it is!'

He exhales heavily and looks down at his feet. 'It's about Megan ...'

'Megan?'

'About that night ...'

I cross my arms over my stomach, hugging myself tight. All my instincts are telling me to get up, to run.

'I was with her ... when she took the ket.' He swallows uncomfortably. 'I gave it to her.'

'You ...' And now I'm the one who's pacing around the living room, hardly knowing what to do with myself.

Now Simon has opened the floodgates, it seems he can't stop. 'I lied to the police. I told them I didn't know who had given it to her or who was with her. I was scared. You have to understand that, Erin. Yes, I gave it to her. But I took the same amount, and I was fine. How was I to know she'd been drinking with you before she even got to the party, or how much she'd have once we got there? It wasn't my fault! I shouldn't have to pay with my future because she made a mistake.'

I walk right up to Simon, wait until he looks me in the eye. 'Yes, you're right – there were a lot of things that you weren't responsible for that night, but there are things you could have done ...' I have to pause for a moment to hold myself together, to prevent myself from lashing out at him physically. A ball of rage is burning inside my chest and I'm barely keeping control of it. 'You knew she'd taken it when we played King Cup! You could have stopped her having that drink. At the very least, you could have told someone. We might have been able to get her help, you know, medical help!'

Simon runs his hand through his hair, looking distraught. 'Don't you think I know that? But I was drunk – we all were. You too! You've always said you wished you'd done things differently that night. And I'll always regret that I didn't say I'd seen her leave the house and go in the direction of the park!'

'You … you saw her leave, and you didn't tell anyone?' I scream at him.

'See!' He throws his hands in the air, walks away from me. 'This is why I didn't want to tell you any of this, because I knew you'd get upset. I knew you'd be angry with me! And you got angry that night too … the night before our wedding. You wouldn't listen! You said you didn't even know who I was any more, that there was no way you were marrying me the following morning, and then you ran off and I didn't see you again until …'

I think about what he's said. 'Until someone else found me.' I meet his gaze. 'Why is that, Simon? Why did someone else … Gil … find me in the garden and not you? Did you even come and look for me?'

Guilt washes over his face and I know I've hit the nail on the head.

'If he hadn't stumbled upon me, I could have died out there in that garden! So why didn't you come after me? You know I don't do that sort of thing for attention. You know if I run off like that, something has to be seriously wrong.'

Simon just stares at me, saying nothing.

And then the penny drops. 'You *wanted* me to be all upset.' My brain races through a series of memories, like cards being shuffled before a game of poker. Image after image comes at me. How Simon ghosted me for weeks after I left for the Bahamas. How he's been withdrawing a bit more from me every day since I've been staying at Heron's Quay. How we were feeling disconnected before the wedding, yet I couldn't put my finger on why …

'You were *relieved*,' I finally say, eyes wide, and I see the confirmation in Simon's expression. 'You were glad I said I didn't want to marry you. Because you wanted to call the whole thing off, but you didn't have the guts. Telling me about Megan had *nothing* to do with coming clean and everything to do with dropping a grenade in my lap and hoping I'd pull the pin for you!'

'No, that's not true. I really wanted to tell you about Meg.'

His blue eyes stare into mine and my gut tells me he's being truthful, but that doesn't mean I'm not right about the rest of it. I drop back down onto the sofa. 'Why didn't you want to marry me any more? What did I do?'

'Nothing …' Simon comes to sit at the other end of the sofa, just out of touching – or hitting – distance. Coward. 'You're amazing … perfect. I told myself that a thousand times over. And when we'd been together a few years, it seemed as if everyone expected it of us. It seemed that *you* expected it.'

I shake my head. 'Only because you led me to believe you were on the same page! Why didn't you say anything? Even after you proposed?' But as the words leave my mouth, I realize I already know the answer. Simon would beat Usain Bolt at the hundred metres if it meant he could avoid an ugly confrontation.

'If it helps, I don't think I'm ready to marry anyone. But it wasn't until the big day was almost on top of us I knew that for sure. And if I did ever want to tie the knot, it would probably be with you … You're the only one who's ever come close.'

'What? To winning such a prize as you?' I get up and walk towards the door. I can't stand to be in the same room as him any more. 'And you *probably* think it'd be me? Geez, don't do me any favours, Simon!'

He blinks, shocked. 'It's not like you to be sarcastic. You're starting to sound like Gil.'

I want to open my mouth and scream, scream until there is no breath left in my lungs. 'And I didn't think it was like you to lie to me through the *whole five years of our relationship*! And what was the deal at the hospital, anyway? The whole devoted groom-to-be, the I-can't-bear-to-live-life-without-you act?'

'It wasn't an act!' Simon says, jumping up and looking offended. 'Just because I got a case of cold feet, it doesn't mean I don't love you, Erin.'

'Just not enough to marry me. Or tell me the truth.'

'I felt terrible about what happened to you that night. It was a wake-up call, I thought. My chance to be the person you deserved me to be. I really wasn't lying when I said I wanted to go through with the wedding a second time. At least, not then …'

I hang my head wearily for a second. 'So you were basically going through with the wedding after that point out of guilt?'

He looks away. Oh God. I'm right. He was marrying me out of pity, not because I was the love of his life.

Something snaps inside me then. 'Well, no need to worry, Simon. That date in November that the hotel gave us? Some other couple is going to start their happy-ever-after that day. I let the deadline pass. Because, as it turns out, I'm not sure I want to marry you either.'

CHAPTER SEVENTY-SEVEN

Present Day

'Oh my God, Erin. What's the matter?'

I fall into Anjali's arms almost before she finishes opening the door. I am a sobbing, blubbering mess, and she practically has to carry me down the hallway and into the living room of her shared house.

'I ... I ...' I have no idea how to start, mainly because I have no idea which man I'm crying hardest about, or whether it's just extreme frustration that I'm crying about either of them in the first place. 'All ... m–men are ... b–bastards,' I finally manage.

'Ain't that the truth? Apart from Lars, of course,' she adds hurriedly, but I can't be cross about that. I picked him for her.

She leads me to the sofa, makes me sit down, hands me a box of tissues, then waits patiently while I mop myself up. 'What's going on? Last I heard, you were in Cornwall with Gil.'

'Devon,' I snuffle. 'And I came home early, because—' I break off, not even knowing how I can explain it.

'In that case, why aren't you at the flat with Simon?'

I have to control my breathing to stop myself from crying. 'It's off ... The wedding is off.'

She instantly pulls me into a fierce hug. 'No! Oh, my God, Erin … What happened?'

I clamp everything down – lips, eyelids, jaw – in an effort to stop the Vesuvius inside from exploding. I have *got* to get a grip of myself. It takes me close to a minute, but eventually I pull back and wipe my eyes, try to smile.

'No …' Anjali says, narrowing her eyes at me. 'Don't do that.'

'Do what?'

'Stuff it all down and paste a sparkly 'Erin' grin on top so everyone thinks you're okay when you're not.'

She knows I do that, too? Crap. 'But I *want* to be okay.'

She shakes her head and smiles at me as if I'm a naughty but adorable schoolchild. I'm about to bristle when I realize it must be like looking in a mirror. How many times have I given Anjali that look? Suddenly, I'm ashamed of myself. Not only am I a total mess, but I'm a patronizing bitch, too.

'And don't do that either,' she adds. 'Sometimes, in fact, most times, I needed to hear what you had to tell me.'

I sit very still, aware I must be giving my thoughts away just by breathing. I feel raw, as if my skin has been peeled back and all I am is a bundle of exposed nerve endings. I have no idea what to do next. My usual options – pretence, self-loathing – have been snatched away from me.

'You don't have to deal with everything on your own, Erin. I'm here. I've always been here.'

I sniff loudly. 'I know that.' At least I do now.

'So I am going to run you a bath, and then I'm going to make you a giant cup of hot chocolate while we watch *Pride and Prejudice*, and then, when you are ready, you are going to tell me what this is all about.'

I nod, giving her a wobbly smile. It feels nice to be told what to do. 'How did you get to be so wise and wonderful?' I ask as she gets up to head for the bathroom.

She grins at me as she reaches the door. 'Learned from the best, didn't I?'

* * *

After we've watched the whole of the Netherfield Ball, I mute the TV and turn to Anjali. 'Okay. I think I'm ready'

She nods encouragingly.

'But it might be easier if you ask me questions, because seriously, I have no idea where to start.'

She stares at the ceiling for a second or two. 'Okay, let's start with the big one ... Why is the wedding off?'

'Because he's been lying to me for the last five years.' And then I recount, as precisely as I can, the conversation I had with Simon earlier today about his part in Megan's death.

'Do you think there's any way back from this?' she asks when I've finished. 'Would you even want there to be?'

I study the paused image of Lizzy Bennet looking a bit peeved on the TV screen. 'No. I don't think there's any coming back from it. I don't remember saying this to Simon on the night I had my accident, but I told him I didn't even know him, and I feel that way now. Our entire relationship has been based on lies.'

Anjali nods. 'Let me play devil's advocate here ... He lied to you about something that happened before you were properly together. It doesn't change who he is, does it? He's still the same man you've loved for years.'

I shake my head. 'I'm not sure about that either. Because that wasn't the only thing he was lying about.' And I tell her what I found out about it not being Simon who was messaging me while I was away in the Bahamas that first season, and something strikes me, something I'd been too upset to figure out earlier. 'Simon must have known. He knew Gil had his old phone. He knew *he* wasn't messaging me, so when I came back and talked about all the things I thought I'd discussed with him in those messages, he had to have worked out at some point things weren't adding up. And I've even told him, multiple times, that those messages made me fall in love with him. I mean, I came home and we slept together for the first time on the back of the romantic high I was on. He took advantage of that.'

Anjali pulls a face. 'Putting it like that, it does sound pretty sleazy.'

'The weird thing is, I don't think Simon is evil. I just think he's lazy. He didn't put the work in to woo me. Gil did, but Simon wanted to reap the benefits.'

Anjali's expression becomes pained.

'What?' I say.

She blows out a breath. 'Well, Lars said a couple of things recently I found quite surprising.'

'Like what?'

'Like you and Simon had fizzled out a couple of months after you got together. He thought you'd broken up. But then you came back to surprise Simon for Valentine's Day, and Lars thought you both decided to give things another go.'

I take a moment to absorb this information. It kind of makes sense … It would explain why Simon wasn't messaging me the same time Gil was, why he was practically ghosting me for a while and then everything seemed to get back on track.

'That's not all,' Anjali says, biting her lip. 'Lars also said there may have been other girls during that time. Nothing serious, but other girls, all the same.'

I must be numb now, overloaded with too much information, because I receive this calmly. 'It was a mirage, wasn't it, my relationship with Simon? I thought it was one thing, and really, it was something completely different. The sad thing is, it was an illusion I created myself.'

'I think you're being a little hard on yourself there, babe.'

I shake my head. 'Of course, I had Simon's help. But the signs were there now I think about it. I just chose to ignore them, too invested in finding my Prince Charming to give them air. Oh God … my mother was right!' I shoot a fierce look at my best friend. 'But don't you dare tell her!'

Anjali shakes her head vehemently.

I stare at the blank wall as more of the puzzle pieces fall into place. 'On some level I knew it all, didn't I? My subconscious was trying to warn me, sending me those dreams where my groom had no face, where he was a man I didn't know or recognize … And I ignored every one of them.'

'Even *I* would have said you were being overdramatic if you'd called off your wedding because of a dream,' Anjali says.

'I know. I still wish I'd taken it all on board. I suppose I just badly wanted to believe that someone loved me that much.'

'The person who wrote the messages?'

I nod.

'That person still exists, you know.'

'Only in my head, Anj. Yes, there's a thread of truth in that story, but I cooked up the rest of it myself too. I can't be trusted when it comes to men at the moment. I really can't.'

I close my eyes, suddenly feeling very tired. It's an effort to open them again. 'Did you see it? Did you think Simon was the same person I did?'

Anjali takes a sip of her hot chocolate and repositions herself on the sofa. 'I suppose I always saw Simon as a bit too cocky for his own good but like you say, it doesn't mean he was bad.'

'But it also doesn't mean he didn't do bad things … He let me believe it was Gil who'd given Megan the ket, who'd let her wander off into the park without stopping her. It's the whole reason I didn't like Gil after that summer.' I sigh. 'It seems Simon's not the only man I thought I knew but didn't and, oh boy, how I didn't …'

'Which leads us to why you came shooting back up to London early, I guess?'

I nod. But if I was confused about Gil before, I'm doubly so now. How much do I tell Anjali? I can't really explain everything that went on with Gil without sharing what happened inside my head when I was in a coma, and she's going to think I'm unhinged.

But I feel so much lighter for having shared what I have already. She's right. I carry too much on my own, too scared of what other people will think of me if I say everything I'm thinking and feeling. However, if there's one thing I know after tonight, it's that Anjali has my back.

'Okay,' I say, looking her in the eye. 'Stay with me for this next bit … It's going to get a bit weird, but I promise it'll all make sense in the end.' And then I take a deep breath and tell her about what happened, starting with standing outside the church doors on the afternoon of the wedding that never actually took place.

CHAPTER SEVENTY-EIGHT

Present Day

The following morning, I breathe deep and call my mum. She listens patiently while I tell her that Simon and I have called the wedding off and I don't want to go back and live in the flat with him. Forty minutes later, my stepfather is outside Anjali's house to pick me up. Emir really is the kindest man and the most soothing presence. He doesn't ask me any questions as we drive back to Bromley, but exudes serenity and comfort. I feel better just from being in the car with him for the brief journey.

I spend the first day home in bed, binge watching any period drama I can get my hands on. I feel heavy and listless, too exhausted even to cry. But the tears come on day three, and then I can't stop. I was so arrogant, wasn't I? So full of myself and my perfect life? And now I'm facing the fact that I may never return to a job I excelled at and I've wasted five years of my life on a man who didn't even respect me enough to be honest with me. The worst thing of all is that I miss a man who also betrayed my trust more than I thought possible.

Gil messaged a few times. Short, polite requests to talk, but when I didn't reply after the third one, he stopped. Unlike

Simon, who's blowing up my phone with texts and voicemails begging me to come back. I end up blocking him, which is a stupid, childish move, because I will have to talk to him at some point, even if I have no intent to reconcile. There are practical things we need to untangle.

After two weeks of moping around feeling sorry for myself, Mum has had enough. She makes me get out of my pyjamas and takes me to the park for a hot drink. September has turned cold, so the playground is almost empty. I choose a hot chocolate when we get to the kiosk and we find ourselves a table.

'Erin …'

I brace myself for what's coming. 'Let me have it, Mum.'

'I need your help.'

I blink. This was not what I was expecting. 'My help?'

'Yes. I need some admin help with the Head Start Trust, and I was wondering if you'd consider it. Just temporarily, of course. I don't expect you to make this your career. And I'll pay you the going rate.'

As much as I've always resisted getting sucked in to mum's charity whirlpool, this sounds amazing. I'm sick of focusing on myself, and it would be good to feel productive, useful.

'But what about those days when my brain feels like rubber and all I want to do is lie down and close my eyes?'

'They've been coming less and less frequently, but if you have one of those days, you have one. Part-time would be good, with flexible hours, and if it's too much, we'll do something else.'

It feels like a chink of light has opened up in my dark world. 'I'd like to try it, but what exactly will you want me to do?'

Mum takes a sip of her coffee and leans back in her chair. 'A little office admin – answering emails, taking calls, managing the calendar – but I've also been thinking about setting up a support group for brain injury survivors, online at first, and I wondered if you'd be able to help with that?'

'Maybe.' It's strange. I've been so focused on my recovery that I forget other people struggle with exactly the same things, and I'm worried about hearing heart-wrenching stories of lives never regained, of permanent damage. 'I'll need to think about that.'

Mum smiles. And then she leans across and kisses me on the cheek. 'Thank you, Erin. I really appreciate it.'

It's taken her a lot to do this. Not to offer me a job, but to ask for help. I shake my head and smile.

'What?' Mum asks.

'The apple doesn't fall far from the tree, does it?' I reply.

'Nope,' Mum says, looking pretty pleased with herself. 'I've always known you were going to be okay, Erin.'

It warms me to hear her say that, but I also realize this maybe is why she seemed so hands-off to me for most of my life. She always assumed I was going to be fine, and I felt shoehorned into playing that role for her. If I want things to change properly going forward, there are a few things I need to say.

I put my hot chocolate down and give her my full attention. 'I'm pleased you've got faith in me, but sometimes I wished you were around more, especially when I was a kid.'

Mum sighs. 'Emir is always telling me I'm a workaholic, that I need to slow down.'

'Emir is a very wise man. You ought to listen to him once in a while.'

'I'm sorry if I was busier than I should have been when you were little,' she says to me. 'It was the only way I knew how to cope.'

383

I lean across and give her a one-armed hug. 'I understand that, but it doesn't mean I didn't miss you.'

Mum looks at the table. 'I don't think I've ever told you this, but I felt so ashamed after Alex died. Everybody told me it wasn't my fault, that there was nothing different I could have done, but inside, I felt I had to make amends. I had to do better. I kind of got lost in that, didn't I? I forgot I had another child who needed me.'

Another piece slides into place in understanding my mother, and possibly even understanding myself. 'You know you don't have to do anything for us all to love you, don't you?' I say. 'We just want you.'

Mum pulls me into a proper hug. 'Look at my wonderful, wise daughter,' she says with a catch in her voice, then she releases me. 'I promise you, I will try not to get sucked into this new project. I will try to be there for you.'

'You already have been, you daft woman. Who put their life on hold to be there with me in the hospital? Who's let me move back home – twice! – and hasn't complained about all the money she lost that she put into my wedding? You don't have to prove anything to me, Mum. I know.'

Mum dabs her eyes with a tissue and then hands me one from a packet she pulls from her bag. We both laugh as we mop up.

'Anyway, back to the matter in hand … Let's say you work for me until you reach the one-year anniversary of your accident, and then we'll think again. By then, we should have a better idea of what you're going to be dealing with going forward.'

'That sounds like a plan.' It will give me enough to do to keep me from getting bored and will give me challenges to help increase my brainpower.

'Have you got any idea what you might like to do after that? Do you see yourself going to work for Kalinda again?'

I sigh. 'I don't know … I spent so much of my working life making sure everybody else's life was perfect. Maybe it's time to do something for myself?'

'Any ideas?'

I play with a knot on the top of the wooden table. 'I kind of like the idea of being my own boss, setting up a business of some kind.'

Mum smiles. 'Just don't rush into things, okay?'

I laugh. 'If that isn't the pot calling the kettle black!'

She purses her lips, but her eyes glitter. 'Cheeky! Anyway … I think it's time to get back, and when we get home, you're going to do two things.'

I roll my eyes. 'Oh, am I?'

'You're going to get out of that tracksuit and put some proper clothes on, and you're going to call Simon. He's been leaving me messages and I've had just about enough of him.'

He's been calling Mum too? I don't suppose I can put this off any longer.

CHAPTER SEVENTY-NINE

Present Day

I meet Simon outside a café near the station, overlooking Brockwell Park in Herne Hill. It's a brisk September morning, and there's an autumnal chill to the wind. He looks unsure of himself and aborts an attempt at a hug or a kiss on the cheek when he sees my face.

'Thanks for coming,' I say.

'Do you want to go inside?'

I shake my head. All of the other tables outside are empty, and I'd prefer privacy for this conversation.

'How are you?' he asks when we've both sat down.

'Doing okay,' I reply, which is the truth. It's been almost a month since Simon and I last saw each other, and I am feeling stronger every day. 'We have a few things we need to discuss.'

He looks nervous as he pulls a piece of paper out of his pocket. 'I think we need to go over what we're going to do about the flat first, which will have an impact on what you want to do with your stuff. Then other financial stuff, and lastly, I suppose, us.'

I'm flabbergasted. Simon has actually made a list instead of waiting for me to do it? Wonders will never cease. 'Okay. Fire away …'

After the waitress takes our coffee orders, we get down to business, agreeing that Simon will take over the lease for the remaining three months. I only have the money from Mum's part-time job at the moment, and it definitely doesn't pay as well as my old job, so I can't take it on. But thank goodness for the substantial savings I built up while working on yachts. I was going to use them as a deposit for a house, but at the moment, it's allowing me to heal at my own pace and take stock of my life.

'Will you move out?' I ask him.

He shrugs. 'Haven't decided yet. I might get a room-mate. Gil said he might need somewhere to stay for a bit.'

At the mention of Gil's name, cold lightning shoots through me. He's moving? Does that mean Heron's Quay is finished? I'd so love to see how it turned out. Where's he going next?

No, Erin. You do not need to know these things. Leave it well alone.

I turn my attention back to Simon. 'So, how about my stuff? I'd rather come and collect it when you're at work.'

Simon looks slightly disappointed, but he agrees. And then we discuss our aborted wedding plans, which deposits we will lose if we never reschedule, what other associated costs we might have to bear.

Simon sighs. 'It seems a shame to let all that money go to waste.'

'What else can we do?'

After taking a few warming sips of his coffee, Simon says, 'I'm sorry, Erin. Really, I am. I didn't mean for it all to end up like this.'

I look into Simon's eyes, and I believe he means this.

'Do you think …? Do you think there's any chance for us? I miss you.'

I sigh. 'I miss you, too. It would be strange not to after spending so many years together and then suddenly not seeing each other every day.' I push the foam on top of my latte around with a spoon. 'There's a part of me that still loves you …' Simon sits straighter as I say these words, then slumps again as I add, 'but I don't think I will ever feel the same way about you again. I don't think there's any going back.'

He presses his lips together, looking defeated. 'I understand why you feel that way. Of course, I'm disappointed. And so, so sorry. But if there's anything I can do for you, Erin, anything at all …'

'The one thing I need from you is answers, Simon. True, complete and honest answers. Do you think you're capable of that?'

'Ooh, ouch,' he says, with a glint of one of his naughty grins, but it disappears again quickly. 'But yes. I will do my best.'

I watch his face carefully. Whether this is something Simon can manage remains to be seen. I dive in with one of the most difficult questions first, just in case he decides to bail early before I've finished getting everything off my chest. 'Why did you lie and say it wasn't you who gave Megan the ket?'

Simon looks confused. 'Hang on, now … I didn't ever actually lie to you, did I? I never said that.'

'Yes, you did. When I asked you about it afterwards, you said you knew nothing about it.'

'When did I say that? Before you left for the Caribbean?'

'No … after that. When we were messaging … Oh! That wasn't you? That was Gil?'

Simon shrugs. 'Must have been.'

It takes me a few moments for me to fully process the irony of this revelation. I convicted Gil of the crime, using his own declaration of innocence as my evidence. 'But even if you didn't lie to me at the start, you certainly knew that's what I believed later on. Why did you never put me right?'

'I was afraid.'

'Afraid I'd tell the police?'

He shakes his head. 'No. Afraid of what it would do to us. It was such early days.'

'I don't understand.'

'You've asked me to be honest, and I'm going to be honest with you, Erin. But I warn you, you're not going to like what I'm about to tell you.'

'That's okay,' I say. 'It's still better than being in the dark.'

'I saw the chemistry between you and Gil right from the very first night Megan introduced us to you. He liked you, you know …'

I look away, scared he'll think the flush in my cheeks is caused by something other than the cool breeze. 'Yeah, I know.' An image of Gil's face as he told me he loved me, that he'd always loved me, fills my mind, and it takes my breath away.

It was always and only you …

Simon's voice drags me back to the present.

'It all started with a girl I met about six months before I first met you. I liked her. I mean, really liked her. But the moment she set eyes on Gil, it was clear I'd been instantly friend-zoned. They hit it off, had a bit of a fling, and I was salty about it.'

'Gil knew you liked her?'

He shakes his head. 'But I held it against him anyway. Gil has

389

always been better than me at everything – better at academic stuff, more successful in his career.' He looks across at me, his eyes filled with regret. 'Better at being a human being … I suppose I was jealous.'

'But he's always been such a good friend to you.'

Simon looks sheepish. 'I know. I said you weren't going to like this, and I'm not proud of myself either. But when I saw he liked you, I decided it was time for a bit of payback, so I swooped in and chatted you up first.'

I blink. Wasn't this almost *exactly* what Dream Simon said in his speech at my fake wedding? How did I do that? How did I know? 'So you didn't even like me for me right from the start. It was just childish tit for tat? Thanks a bunch!'

'But I did like you! As soon as we spent some time together, I could see why Gil had a crush on you. So when you told me why you didn't like him, that you thought he was partly responsible for Meg's death, I didn't want to put you straight. And you have to remember that you didn't tell me this until after you came home for Valentine's Day and were back together. I didn't want to lose you.'

'Back together? Why were you the only one who knew we'd broken up? And if you were that into me, how come Gil ended up messaging me in the first place?'

He gives me a helpless look. 'All I can say is that I was young. Stupid. That I didn't realize what I had until you'd practically slipped through my fingers. When you came back and surprised me, it changed everything.'

'You didn't answer my question.'

'How Gil ended up messaging you?'

I nod.

'I broke his phone, so I gave him mine, and then I ended up buying another one.'

'You could have bought him the new one instead of giving him one of your cast-offs,' I say.

Simon's eyebrows lift in surprise and he laughs nervously. 'I suppose I could have done. You know, I really didn't think of that?'

Why am I not surprised? 'When did this happen?'

'Oh, God … It was so long ago. Um … Let me think … I dunno … around November time?'

'But why didn't he tell me he had your phone? Why didn't you? There wasn't any need for the charade at all!'

Simon coughs. 'Yeah, well … I kinda thought you'd get the message that things were fizzling out between us, but Gil said I should tell you, because you kept messaging him thinking he was me. To be honest, I thought he was just finding it annoying, and it wasn't such a big deal. Anyway, yes, I suppose I knew I needed to be honest with you, but I kept putting it off.' He drains his coffee cup and puts it back down on his saucer. 'He got quite angry with me about it. Said he'd had to send a few short replies because you were so upset or worried, but I didn't know you two had been talking at length.'

'You must have worked out it was more than a couple of quick messages eventually. I told you I fell in love with you while I was away that first year! Did you think that was just going to happen from a few "Hey, babe … can't talk now. I'm off to the pub" messages?

He shifts uncomfortably in his seat. 'Yeah, but I didn't work out just how deep those messages had gone until months later, and by then we were already in a pretty solid relationship. Stupidly, I hoped you might like me for me by that point.'

391

'Don't turn this on me,' I snap back at him. He'd been doing so well until now. I'd been quite proud of the fact he was actually laying it all out there rather than trying to minimize or deflect. 'And maybe I would have liked you for you if you'd ever opened up and let me see the real you instead of hiding behind Gil.'

'Yeah, okay … Sorry.'

I stare out across the park at the sky, tracking the fluffy trails from planes that have long since passed while I work out how to frame what I want to say. 'You always do that, don't you?'

'What?'

'You use Gil. You bask in his reflected glory.' I stop and laugh at my blindness. 'I always thought it was the other way around.'

'I know you hate me at the moment, but I'm not that cynical. Gil's my friend because he's the sort of person I'd like to be.'

'I don't hate you,' I tell him.

Simon looks relieved, but confused. 'You don't? I pretty much hate myself at the moment. I've ruined your life!'

'I'm disappointed. And I'm very sad, but you haven't ruined my life. Marrying me under false pretences would have done that. No one deserves to not know the person they're going to spend the rest of their lives with.'

Simon studies me. 'No, I suppose I never really let you see me. I was too afraid you wouldn't like what was underneath. But I don't think you really ever let me see you either.'

I dip my head, aware he's called it right, too.

'You might not have missed out, but I did,' he says. 'I always knew you were smart, capable, generous. And I knew I liked the way you looked after me, but now I can see how strong you are. You amaze me, Erin …' He trails off, and I can tell where his brain is going. I hope he's not stupid enough to ask again if

I'll go back to him. I'm relieved when he merely adds, 'I really messed it up, didn't I?'

'Yes. But I don't know if you truly want me, even now. It only seems to be something that happens when you think you can't have me.'

He lets out a low chuckle. 'Ah … Maybe that's true. I'm a fickle bastard.' He leans forward to catch my eye. 'But even though there's no road ahead for us, I want you to know I've learned a lot from this whole situation, about how I want to live my life going forward.'

'That's good.' I can see the seeds of change, but I don't fully trust Simon will allow them to grow into anything more. He's always full of unrealistic optimism at this part of the mess up/ redemption cycle.

I take the last sip of my coffee and push my chair back. 'I hope you find happiness in your future, Simon. In whatever shape it comes in.' And I mean this. I might not want this man in my life any more, but I don't wish him ill.

He comes round to my side of the table and we share an awkward hug. 'I hope that for you too, Erin. I hope you can find a guy who'll look after you the way you'll look after him. You deserve that.'

CHAPTER EIGHTY

Present Day

Autumn disappears in a blur, and it isn't long before Christmas is looming. I continue to live with my mother and Emir, although I start looking for somewhere of my own. I work part-time doing basic admin tasks for my mum that I could have done in my sleep in my previous life as a house manager for very wealthy clients, but that's actually a positive rather than negative. It gives my brain something to do without taxing it too hard.

I still try to get my head around how my life imploded so spectacularly, but I can't quite bring myself to regret falling and hitting my head in the hotel garden. Yes, I lost my relationship, the future I'd planned out in colour-coded, tabbed and highlighted detail, but that future was an illusion. I have a feeling it would have all gone sideways within a decade if I'd married Simon. No, as much as it hurts, it's better this way. To be honest, I'm not even sure if it's Simon I miss, but the idea of love and belonging I projected into my future with him.

It's been almost three months since I left Heron's Quay. Gil hasn't messaged me other than those first few times. He's respecting my silence by giving me his. So why do I feel disappointed?

Why do I check my notifications for something that never arrives?

I think about him all the time, especially late at night when sleep is hard to find. I wish I could walk up those metal stairs and see the stars from his roof, feel his reassuring presence as I pour out my heart.

Sometimes, I even want to pick up my phone and message him.

I miss him.

I think I may be falling in love with him.

But that's just the problem, isn't it? I *think* I'm falling.

But how do I know if it's real? And if it is, what do I do about it?

It's been more than nine months since my accident and most of my rehabilitation appointments have either ended or will soon move into regular check-up mode. I'm doing well. But I worry these big emotions I'm feeling are just another side-effect from my brain having bounced around inside my skull. I worry that neurons have created wonky connections as they've tried to heal themselves, tricking me into thinking and feeling things I shouldn't.

I could contact Gil, I know that. But I'm afraid to do that, too. I have a feeling if I see him in the flesh, I'll just get even more confused, and that won't help me make a rational, sensible decision.

What I need is something solid I can build a foundation on. Facts and figures, dates and times … Words on the page. Those are what I need. If only …

I hold my breath.

How about words on a screen? I have those. Our messages.

What I really want to do is start right back at the beginning and read everything through in order. I've changed phones since then, so I've no idea if older messages will still be visible if I scroll all the way back, but when I try it, they're there. However, they only go back as far as the February five years ago.

Oh. Of course they do. He told me when I came back on Valentine's Day that he'd got a new number. I tap my way out of that message thread into the list of chats and scroll further down. Near the bottom, I find another thread entitled 'Simon', one attached to his old number. The number Gil must have messaged me from. I click on it.

Oh my goodness. There are hundreds of messages. Thousands.

I take a moment to steady myself, grab a lungful of soothing air, and then I scroll back to the autumn of five years ago, find where I mention landing in the Bahamas, and begin to read.

CHAPTER EIGHTY-ONE

Present Day

The messages start off chatty, silly, sometimes a little cheesy. I can tell it's Simon who wrote these. They have his tone and vocabulary, the same sense of humour. There are multiple messages every day for the first few weeks and then they slowly peter out.

I see the pattern now. This is exactly how communication went with Simon when I was at Heron's Quay. The first few weeks were full of enthusiastic, chatty messages but by the time I left, I had that same feeling he was pulling away.

Now I come to think of it, he was the same running up to the wedding. I'd noticed he wasn't always messaging me back or that his answers were short and to the point, but I just put it down to us both being busy and stressed. The clues were there. I just didn't give them enough attention.

I turn back to the thread of messages and check the dates. As October turned into November, he ghosted me completely. But good old Erin didn't give up. Reading it all back now, I'm asking twenty-three-year-old me why she bothered. It's clear he's lost interest. I would judge Past Erin for being pathetic if

I couldn't see how worried she was about him. She might be an idiot, but she's got a good heart, that girl.

I sigh as I scroll through the one-sided conversation. When Anjali was cross with me once, she told me I treated people as my personal projects. Maybe that's why Simon seemed so appealing back then. I could swoop in and fix him. Of course, now I know it wasn't just grief eating him up, but guilt. There's no way I would have been so persistent if I'd known the truth. I probably wouldn't have messaged him at all.

I scroll down to reveal more messages. There it is ... finally, he answers again.

Is this the moment when the identity switches? I double check the date. November. From what Simon said when we met for coffee, that seems about right. This could be it.

I'd forgotten that he didn't dive straight in to fully fledged conversations. The messages are brief, as if every word was given reluctantly. He certainly doesn't seem to be eager to reel me in and fool me. So why did he start?

The next chunk of messages reveals the answer. I come across a series of rambling messages from me to him.

Can we talk? It's important.

I close my eyes, remembering how I felt when I typed these messages. The emotion was all-consuming. I felt trapped, stuck.

Please, Simon. I'm lonely and homesick and I'm grieving in a strange country ...

Please help me ...

Oh, my God … I *begged* him to talk to me. My desperation leaps off the screen. No wonder he finally gave in. Far from it being a heartless, calculating act, I realize it would have been heartless *not* to do what I'd asked.

Does this marry up with what I know about Gil in real life? I need to separate that Gil from dream Gil, go only on the facts. I look away from the computer screen and lean back in the chair.

He let me come and stay with him when I needed to get away, when I needed rest, even though I'd made my dislike for him obvious. And then he took care of me, fed me, listened to me, bossed me around when I was being stupid and didn't know how to pace myself. Real Gil had my back, just like dream Gil promised he would.

Not knowing quite what to do with that, I return my attention to the messages. We talked through the night Megan died in fits and starts. It's still painful to read now. And once we were done opening that can of worms, we just … talked. About everything. Stupid moments in our days. Big fears. Big dreams. I didn't just bare my soul to him, but he also bared his to me. And all the emotions I felt at the time, the sense of connection, the longing to be in the same room as him, roll over me like breakers on a stormy seashore. It's as if I'm back in that moment, giving tiny pieces of my heart away to him with every short message, until finally he holds them all.

Reading the messages back now, I can practically hear Gil's voice. How did I never realize? How was I so blind?

But then, in January, those messages trail off too. Did he lose interest as well?

No.

My gut answers for me. Firmly. Definitively. I don't know

whether to trust it. The only other way to know for sure is to ask Gil himself, and I'm definitely not ready to do that at the moment.

I see plenty of messages from me, telling him I can't wait to see him, telling him while also not telling him I am completely and utterly in love with him. But I can also read the silences, the secret I was keeping about my surprise visit home for Valentine's Day. It's almost as if I can feel the effervescent hopefulness resting between the message bubbles, knowing I was going to see him soon.

And then I came home.

I remember that evening in the pub clear as day. I pushed the doors open and looked around. I saw Gil first, and I knew wherever he was, his best friend couldn't be far behind. And then I laid eyes on Simon, and everything else was forgotten.

Thinking back now, I realize they both looked surprised, but Simon also looked uncomfortable, as if he'd been caught out doing something he shouldn't. And Gil …

He wore that locked-down expression he often wears. I always thought it was because he didn't like me, but I've seen it on his face countless times since I arrived at Heron's Quay, even after we became friends. The last time was my last day, when I pushed and pushed when he didn't want to tell me something, but I made him. And then he told me he loved me. Finally, I fully understand what that expression means. It's the one he wears when he's trying to hide something, when he has a secret. I just didn't realize that, for years, *I* was his secret.

I put my phone down and place my head in my hands. He was telling the truth. He loves me. He's always loved me. A great pit of regret and fear opens up inside me, but I also feel like I'm soaring. If only I'd known at the time. Instead, I came back home to a man I didn't know I'd broken up with, and Simon had a change of heart.

It's all I can do to stop myself picking up the phone and ringing him, or getting on the first train out of Paddington. It's only the fact that I don't know if he'll be at the boathouse that stops me clicking onto a travel website and booking a ticket. Didn't Simon say that Gil needed somewhere to live for a while?

I open up a new browser window and search for Heron's Quay to find some more answers. The search results come in quickly and I click on the first link, hardly bothering to read it, but when the website loads I discover it's not a holiday let website but an estate agent's. There's a thumbnail with a picture of the boathouse with 'Coming Soon!' splashed across it.

Gil is putting Heron's Quay up for sale.

CHAPTER EIGHTY-TWO

Present Day

The letter arrives on the second Saturday in February. I open it and a huge grin spreads across my face. It's my new licence. Twelve months and six days since I had my head injury, I've been given the all-clear to drive again.

Mum insists on sitting next to me in the car while I take my first trip, but she's such a nervous passenger I drop her back home and Emir takes over. I drive around the familiar roads where I grew up for over an hour and when I return home, I feel as if I've reached an important milestone. One more small freedom has been reclaimed, and hopefully, there will be more to come.

I've found out Simon's seeing someone. But I suppose I shouldn't be surprised at that. It's been five months since I walked out on him now. I'm not proud of myself, but I checked out his Instagram feed, mostly because I was being pathetic and hoped Gil might have been tagged or there might be a photo of him. There, at the top of Simon's grid, was a selfie with a girl I didn't know. She's younger than me, and a lot more glamorous. They seem to be having fun. I got the impression from the lack of other images of her on his timeline that it must be relatively new and relatively casual. I want to say good for him but I'm still feeling a little bitter, it turns out. I'll get there in the end.

But there are no images of Gil on Simon's page. And no activity on any of Gil's social media accounts either, not that he was one for posting much anyway. Even so, it's like he's disappeared from the face of the earth.

I pick up my phone, head through the living room, and drop onto the sofa. I've been putting this off, but I think it's time to see if Heron's Quay had been sold. It's the only link I have to Gil at the moment, and I'm desperate.

Once on the estate agent's website, I search for Lower Hadwell and I'm relieved to see a picture of the boathouse near the top of the list, sporting a banner alerting prospective buyers that it's newly on the market. When the page loads, the first thing I do is scroll hungrily through the photographs.

It looks amazing, and I'm warmed to see he's put some of my suggestions into place – a doorstop made of a ball of white waxy rope that looks like it belongs on a yacht, a driftwood carving on a windowsill. That bloody conch shell in the bathroom.

I scroll further down the page to remove it from view, and that's when I spot some large type in bold letters: *Open House, 10 – 4 p.m.* … And it's today's date! I check the clock. It must have only just started.

I close my eyes. I want to go so badly. I've forbidden myself from reading those messages again in case it muddies the waters, but I still have all these big feelings towards Gil. It's almost more than I can bear.

I talked to Naomi about it when I saw her for the last time just before Christmas, even though I felt like a complete idiot. She says it's unlikely my feelings for Gil are down to the head injury. I'd probably have other random fixations too if that was the case. She said to step back, give myself breathing space rather than responding in the moment when I'm up in my emotions and ready to jump in and follow a whim. So that's what I've done.

I've waited, and I've waited.

And I can't stop thinking about the way Gil looked at me the last time I saw him.

Always and only you.

Stuff it.

I head back to the hallway and pick up my car keys.

CHAPTER EIGHTY-THREE

Present Day

Devon looks different in February compared to high summer. All the bright blues, fresh greens and warm yellows have been stripped away, leaving browns and greys, with the odd sprinkling of snowdrops and crocuses to add dots of colour. I drive down familiar roads that twist through fields and hedgerows, across bubbling rivers and ancient bridges, and begin the descent down the steep hill into Lower Hadwell.

When I spot the turning for Heron's Quay, I take a deep breath and flip my indicator on. The lane is muddy and I have to crawl along certain stretches to avoid the potholes, but finally I pull into the drive. Four cars are parked there. None of them are Gil's.

I tuck my little Fiat into a gap and take a moment to breathe the sharp river air and then hurry towards the front door. According to the clock in my car, I only just made it. The open house ends in just over fifteen minutes.

I knock on the open door rather than marching straight through it and when I hear footsteps, my pulse goes into overdrive. However, it's not a familiar long, lean frame that turns the corner into the atrium, but a shorter, stockier man in a suit. 'Good afternoon,' he says.

'I'm here for the open house,' I say breathlessly.

He walks towards me and extends his hand for me to shake. 'There are a couple of other people looking around at the moment. How about I show you the key features and then you can take a bit of time to look around yourself?'

'That sounds perfect.' I peer past his shoulder. 'Is … is the owner here?'

'He's not in the house at present.' He clasps his hands in front of himself, making him look more like a bouncer than an estate agent. I sense he's been trained to keep nosy people in their place.

I knew when I got in the car it was a long shot that Gil might be here, but my spirits sink into my comfy boots. I don't want to explain to the agent I already know this house, so I just play along and allow him to give me a tour, tuning out his spiel about mid-century architecture and the benefits of riverside living.

I don't have to speculate why Gil changed his mind. Being here is bittersweet. Heron's Quay is full of memories I didn't even realize I was making, but now I've come to cherish them.

As I walk through the kitchen pretending to admire the cabinets, I see the empty space where Gil used to put a mug for me in front of the kettle each morning so I could make myself a cup of tea when I was ready. It was always the same mug because somehow, he'd worked out which one was my favourite.

When we go up to the roof, all I can hear is the sound of his voice drifting through the darkness towards me. The entire universe had been sparkling and twinkling above our heads, but yet it had felt so intimate.

When we look at the rooms downstairs, both complete now,

I can't help laughing out loud at the memory of those stupid shelves collapsed on the floor in a heap. The estate agent gives me a funny look and I have to hide my smile. They're attached to the wall now, painted a beautiful soft grey and the matching built-in bunk beds look wonderful, the perfect den for a couple of children.

When he shows me the primary suite, the set of rooms that once were mine, I'm stopped in my tracks. Gone is most of the pre-loved furniture, save a few pieces, and in its place is a stylish and inviting private space with off-white walls and soft furnishings in muted greys and greens. And there, as a pop of colour above the bed, is a painting. My painting. The one I didn't know I wanted Gil to keep, but then left with him anyway. It makes me sad and hopeful all at the same time.

When we come full circle and return to the living room, I'm not listening to the sales patter. All I can see is the look on Gil's face when he stood on the corner of that rug. All I can hear are the distant whispering echoes of the moment he told me he loved me, that he'd always loved me.

What an idiot I was not to have realized it was him I loved back all along.

Or maybe I did realize … My subconscious had certainly been aware of it, hadn't it? Just as my pre-wedding nightmares had been warnings that I didn't really know the man I was about to marry, my strangely long and complicated dream in hospital had been an accurate depiction of Gil. I *had* known. I just hadn't known I'd known.

'Is there any last thing you'd like to see, madam?' the agent says, moving to the doorway. The new oversized sunburst clock on the wall tells me it's five past four. I really should be going.

I smile weakly back at him. 'Maybe another look at that view,' I say as I walk to the large horizontal windows and take it all in for one last time. Mist hides the tops of the hills beyond the village and dilutes the pastel colours of the cottages. The colourful flags on the ferry flap in the breeze, and tiny people hurry into the pub, pulling their waterproof jackets around their necks. I let my gaze wander over the dark hills on the opposite side of the river, the trees almost black, Whitehaven glowing pink from between the bare branches, basking in the rays of the low winter sun.

I'm just about to turn away when I see a dark figure standing at the end of the stone jetty, looking out across the rippling water to the anchor stone. My heart goes still and I press my palms against the glass in front of me. I'd know the back of that head anywhere.

CHAPTER EIGHTY-FOUR

Present Day

To the estate agent's astonishment, instead of crossing the living room and heading towards the atrium, I run in the other direction and exit through the door leading to the balcony. 'Madam …?' I hear him calling after me, but I'm down the stairs leading to the jetty before I can hear anything else.

I'm afraid Gil will disappear before I get to him, so I keep my eyes fixed on him, and when I reach the top of the jetty, I take a moment, make myself catch some oxygen.

He's still looking out across the river and I start a slow walk towards him, feeling my pulse drumming harder with every step. When I get halfway, he turns, registers surprise that someone else is close, and I see the moment he realizes who it is, because, even at this distance, his eyes grow dark and seem to bore into me.

'What are you doing here?' he calls out as I get close enough.

'I came …' I'm about to say I came for the open house, but that's not really true, is it? 'I came to find you.'

He nods. Waits. Oh, he's not going to make this easy for me, is he?

'I broke up with Simon, but I expect you know that.'

He grimaces in acknowledgement. 'Yes. And so did I … sort of.'

'You did?'

'He called me very soon after you moved out. It seems he was on a roll when it came to confessing things.'

My eyes widen. 'He told you about Megan?'

Gil nods again. 'Yes.'

'I thought it was you who gave her the drugs, not him,' I say. 'I thought it was you who let her run off into the night without chasing her.'

His eyes darken even further, cloud over, and become stormy. 'You thought I could … that I was capable of …'

'No.' I quickly step in and explain the misunderstanding. How when I thought he was Simon, his own denial had helped form my opinion of him.

'So that's why … Oh my God! All these years …' He shakes his head. 'I never understood why you used to look at me as if I was something you wanted to scrape off the bottom of your shoe!'

I step forward. 'I'm so sorry, Gil. No wonder you always seemed in a bad mood when I was around, silently judging you. It was all my fault.'

'No …' he stuffs his hands in his pockets. 'If anyone should take responsibility, it's me and Simon. I begged him to tell you the truth for so long. I would have said something myself, but I didn't think it was my place to tell you he'd moved on, but then …'

'But then I begged you to talk to me,' I finish for him. 'I read back through the messages. It's all there, as clear as day.'

He looks so relieved, but then he frowns. 'You came all this way to tell me this?'

My pulse becomes uncomfortably loud in my ears. 'Yes, and …'

I don't know how to say this. It feels as if I'm walking on a tightrope, doomed to slip and fall at any second, but I also can't back away. I'll regret it for the rest of my life if I don't, whatever happens next.

I swallow the lump in my throat. 'The last time I was here, you said something to me …'

He looks down and I can see he's as uncomfortable with the memory of that conversation as I am. But then he looks back up at me, giving me space to continue.

'You said … you said you were in love with me. Not just back then, but now.'

Gil's eyes are steady on me. If this had been Simon, he would have blustered around, tried to play it down, but Gil simply says, 'Yes.'

The churning in my stomach has become a ferocious whirl-pool, but if he's brave enough to answer my question so honestly, I need to dig down and find my courage, too. 'You said I was your 'always and only'. Am I still?'

He turns back towards the river. I can see his shutters coming down. He's getting that look on his face, that tension in his frame that always takes hold when I've said something spiky or judgemental about him.

'Because I …'

Gil stops. His eyes lock on mine.

'Because I'd very much like to be.' Deep breath, here goes. 'Because I think I love you too, Gil. I fell in love with the man who was kind and generous and supportive during one of the worst times of my life, who gave me space to be myself but was always there when I needed him. I should have known that man wasn't Simon. I should have known it was you all alon—'

I don't get any further because he sweeps me into his arms and kisses me like he's been starved of oxygen and I am his air supply. His hands slide between my open coat and my pullover. It's as if he can't believe I'm here and he's having to run his hands over every bit of me to check if I'm real. I throw my arms around his neck, lift myself onto my tiptoes, and join him. Is this real? Is this finally, finally real?

If it is, I have to say the kissing isn't how I imagined it at all. It is much, *much* better.

When we finally come up for air, he places his hands on either side of my face and laughs out loud, and then he just kisses me all over my face. I feel like I'm flying. I never believed I could be this happy.

CHAPTER EIGHTY-FIVE

Present Day

We arrive back in the living room. The estate agent is looking peeved that work is eating too far into his Saturday afternoon. From the look on Gil's face, the man's day is about to get worse. 'I've decided to take it off the market,' Gil tells him. 'For now, at least.'

The estate agent shoots a look at me as if I am to blame for this unpromising turn of events – which I am – so I grip Gil's hand and stare back at the man. In days gone past, I would have been fussing around him, apologizing profusely, but now I remain silent. I'm sorry we wasted his time, I really am, but I will never be sorry I made the trip here today and took my future in my hands.

When the estate agent has collected his papers and stuffed them in his briefcase, he makes a hasty, and much less polite, retreat, and then Gil and I are left alone in Heron's Quay once again.

There's lots more kissing and touching. The sky dims outside the enormous windows. Eventually, we get hungry and Gil gets up and turns a light on in the kitchen, then pulls a few ingredients from the cupboards and fridge and whips us up a simple spaghetti carbonara.

It's too cold to eat it on the roof so we sit at the long dining table. The darkness is so complete now that we can only see our own reflections. We talk about everything, filling in the gaps in each other's knowledge.

'Simon told me he knew you thought I was to blame for Megan's death,' Gil says. 'Yet he never put you right.'

'I couldn't get over that. The real problem wasn't that he made a stupid mistake that had tragic consequences. It was the cover-up, the lies, the secrets. The cowardice. And then letting you take the fall, the one person who'd had his back over and over again.' I shake my head, still unable to get my head around the extent of Simon's selfishness. 'I knew I couldn't marry a man like that.'

'I'm glad. That you're not marrying him – purely for selfish reasons, you understand – but also because I always hated the fact I knew he hid things from you.' He sighs. 'I should have said something.'

I reach out and touch his arm. 'No, you shouldn't have. You wouldn't be you if you had. Of course you wouldn't do anything to break up your best friend's relationship. You're too loyal, too straight down the line.'

'I wanted to,' Gil says. 'You don't know how many times I wanted to.'

'But you never did.' I push my bowl of pasta away and go to sit in his lap, placing my hands on his cheeks, making him look at me. 'That's the difference between you and Simon; he gave in and did what was best for him but you never did, not even when it cost you.'

He looks at me seriously. 'I shouldn't have messaged you while you were still with Simon. That was wrong.'

'But I wasn't really with Simon, was I? He was seeing other girls …'

Gil's eyebrows shoot up. 'You know about that?'

'Only since we broke up. Lars told Anjali and Anjali told me. For a long time I wondered why you messaged me, but when I realized I was still mooning over Simon while he'd moved on, it changed everything. I couldn't betray Simon, and neither could you, if he'd betrayed me first.' I sigh. 'I was so blind.'

Gil kisses me on the nose. 'So was I. I saw the boy who'd stood up for and protected me, not the man who threw me under the bus to make himself look good. Maybe we'll stay in touch, maybe we won't. Either way, we'll never have the same friendship again.' He sighs. 'Or maybe we never did.'

I sense his sadness and I press my forehead against his, put my arms around his shoulders. It's time to change the subject. Simon is in our past and I would much rather talk about our future. I stand up, take him by the hand, and lead him into what used to be my old bedroom. 'You kept my painting. I didn't say you could, you know.'

He tips his head and smiles softly. 'Do you want it back?'

I pretend to consider his question, but I already knew the answer before he asked. 'I think you should have it. That painting wouldn't exist without you. You helped bring all that out of me with your patience, your integrity. You believed in me even when I didn't believe in myself.' I blush a little. 'Besides, you said it was beautiful.'

'It is. But not as beautiful as you.'

He begins to kiss me again, but this time it is slower, more deliberate. It feels as if he is unpeeling me, layer by layer. We fall onto the bed and a few items of clothing end up on the bedroom floor. I go to peel Gil's T-shirt over his head, but he puts his hand on top of mine.

'You don't want to?' I ask, slightly surprised. I know I've been fantasizing about this moment since I slid into that other life for a while.

He kisses me again, then props himself up on one elbow so he can look at me. 'More than anything. But I've been waiting for you for so long … I know this might sound stupid, but I don't want to skip over anything. I want to start at the beginning, and I want to do it all.'

I nuzzle into his neck and bite it gently. 'Oh, don't you worry. We are going to do it *all*.'

He laughs and pulls away to look at me again. For a while he just stares at me, smiling softly as if he can't believe I'm real, that he actually gets to touch me, and then his expression grows more serious. I'm starting to realize I love it when Gil gets serious.

'I mean, I want to message you for real, me as me, you as you. That I want to take you out on a first date and walk you home and kiss you at the end of the night. I want to … I don't know … *court* you.'

'Court me?' I just about keep a straight face, even as my silly heart melts inside my chest.

Gil gives me a playful nudge. 'Forgive me … I'm still in shock and it's the only word I can think of, but you know what I mean.'

I smile at him. I love his earnestness, his integrity. 'Yes, I know what you mean. I don't want to miss any of it, either.'

'And I want to be sure this is really what you want. I don't want you to jump into anything after all you've been through and regret it later.'

'Gil Sampson,' I say, looking into his eyes. 'I will never regret you. Not in a million lifetimes.' And I kiss him again, then sneakily slide my hands up under his T-shirt, feeling bare skin. I swear I hear the moment his resolve snaps. He kisses me the way he kissed me in my dream, as if he is a drowning man and I am the only thing that can save him.

'Why now?' he mumbles into my neck as I roll him over and take charge. 'How did you work out how you finally felt about me? I convinced myself it was never going to happen.'

'Funny you should say that,' I whisper into his ear. 'I'll tell you all about it later, but I had this really strange dream …'

CHAPTER EIGHTY-SIX

The following year

Today, there is no quaint country church, no bouquet of white roses. There are no uncles sitting on a pew, secretly wishing they were watching the football instead, no aunties with hankies at the ready to dab their eyes, or naughty little cousins to shriek through the wedding ceremony, then be hauled outside by frazzled parents. It's just me and Gil, and less than a dozen close friends and family, inside the grand drawing room of a gleaming white Georgian mansion that stands overlooking a bend in the River Dart. A small marquee stands on the lawn behind the house, bustling with caterers and waiting staff getting ready for the reception.

I stand at the top of a flower-lined aisle, a bunch of wildflowers and roses in my hands, with Anjali beside me. I'm wearing a simple empire-line dress with a chiffon skirt. My hair is down and my make-up is soft and natural. Gil is waiting for me near the great bay windows, dressed in a charcoal suit.

I can't believe how much has changed in the last two years since I had my accident. It's almost as if I slipped into a parallel universe once again. New man, new job, new home ...

Gil and I spend most of our time at Heron's Quay. He can do the majority of his job from anywhere, but we bought a small flat as a bolthole near Mum for when we need to be in London – he sometimes has to meet corporate giants in towering office buildings, and I have to meet new clients in their luxurious homes or interview hopeful candidates for their household positions. I started off informally, finding my full-time replacement for Kalinda, and then some of her friends wanted to use me to vet their staff, too. I've also had a steady stream of yachties wanting a job that keeps them on dry land and, as I know from experience, their skills are brilliantly transferable as household staff or even estate managers. So far, I've been acting as a bit of a consultant, but next year I'm planning to set up my own agency. Small at first, but I have big plans for the future. I like the idea of helping other people find their perfect fit.

I'm still seeing changes in my capabilities since my accident, although progress has slowed. Headaches are something to watch out for if I get too stressed and tired, and my memory can still play a few tricks on me, but I've got systems in place to help me along and, most of the time, they prevent disaster. On the occasions they don't, I've learned to go with the flow.

A lone violinist stands and begins to play, and I take a deep breath. This is it. My wedding day. I'm going to marry Gil for real this time.

My mother and father walk down the aisle first, followed by Anjali and Lars. They moved in together last month and seem gloriously happy.

And then I am alone, and all I have to do is walk down the soft carpet towards my waiting groom.

I don't have to wait for him to turn round and look at me,

because he does it as soon as he knows I'm standing there. He's smiling so broadly I'm sure his cheeks will be hurting before I even reach him.

And there's that look … the one I've always wanted. But I haven't been waiting for it. I don't need to. I see it every day. It doesn't have to be just one perfect moment when I know I am seen … loved. I know there are going to be an entire lifetime of them.

I arrive at the end of the aisle to meet my groom. He doesn't wait for the minister to give him permission to kiss me, which causes a few chuckles from our assembled guests.

'Hey, you …' I say when we pull away to look at each other.

'Hey yourself,' he says back.

Acknowledgements

Many people have a vision of writing a novel being a lonely process, and it is – at least for some of the journey. However, the reality is that there is a huge team of people that go into taking this story from a whispering idea in my head to a beautiful book sitting on the shelf in a bookshop.

I would like to thank the editors who worked on this book – Emily Kitchin, who loved the potential of the original idea and helped me in the early days of the journey and also Clare Gordon, who has helped me shape it into the book it is today. I value the energy and your insight you both devoted to this book. Thank you too, to the wider team at HQ – the copy editors, publicists, marketing team and wider editorial team who are always so positive and energising to work with.

Huge thanks also to my agent, Amanda Preston, who is the best champion and a truly cool chick.

Lastly, I want to thank my family. Your patience, love and understanding definitely helped me complete this book in the midst of a trying and stressful time. I don't know if I could have done it without you.

ONE PLACE. MANY STORIES

Bold, innovative and
empowering publishing.

FOLLOW US ON:

@HQStories